SHOCKWAVE RIDER

He was only a mile or two from home when it came: first the quiver of the air crowding together ahead of it, then a flat black shadow across the stars, then the scream it made as it stooped and swooped high again, like an eagle striking; and after that came the fire.

Suddenly there was a heavy stillness around him. He heard a small, irregular noise and recognized it as his own breath. And that was how he knew he was still alive. But when he sought for his people, there was nothing, not even a death cry.

DEATHGIFT

Ann Tonsor Zeddies

A Del Rey Book
BALLANTINE BOOKS • NEW YORK

A Del Rey Book
 Published in the United States of America by Ballantine Books, a division of Random House, Inc., New York, and simultaneously in Canada by Random House of Canada Limited, Toronto.

Library of Congress Catalog Card Number: 88-92149

ISBN 0-345-35092-8

Manufactured in the United States of America

First Edition: January 1989

Cover Art by Chuck Gillis

For Timothy, who was Singer's friend from the beginning.

1

They rode with the boy. They had tied his hands and feet and slung him belly-down across the high-backed war saddle; he jolted breathlessly to the mount's hard paces. Evening stooped quickly over the city, and no one seemed to see them as they rode past. He felt as if he had become a ghost already, but the fear in his belly told him that he was still alive.

They galloped when they came out onto the broad streets. The gate was opened for them. He had never been through the gate before. Then they were outside the walls. They traveled a broad road that curved steeply upward. He could hear the horses' laboring breath, and sweat darkened the flexing shoulder beneath him. Soon everything was dark, and the horses' dancing legs were shadows against the lighter gray of the stone blocks that made up the road. Then they left the road and climbed upward among the tumbled rocks of the mountainside.

"How much farther?" one of the soldiers grumbled. "The horses will break their legs on this path, and we'll all break our necks."

"To the place of the Eater north of the road," another said. "You heard the order."

"All right, you don't have to say his name in this dark," the other replied.

"Be silent," the one who held the boy said, and they all obeyed him.

The boy was sure he would die. He wondered how it felt; he knew only that it hurt, that one fell down.

The horses stopped. They lifted him down and set him on a great stone, still bound. They waited for a few minutes. The sound of the horses shifting their hooves and blowing out clouds of warm breath was very clear in the cold air.

"Must we wait here till we freeze?" the soldier who had first spoken asked. "I have no stomach for the blackrobes. They could put a curse on us or feed us to the Eater ourselves, to shut our mouths. It would be like them."

"Your stomach's as weak as a girl's," the leader said. "But it's true our orders don't say we have to wait. We were to deliver him to the Eater, and we've done that. Let the Eater take care of his own."

They turned their horses and rode away. They had never dismounted. The light patches that were their backs got smaller and smaller, and he knew they would not come back. He struggled not to plead, not to call out to them, but finally he could not be still.

"A curse on you," he screamed. "A curse on you!"

When the echoes died, he heard their hoofbeats going away for a long time. A few tears came, but not many. What was the use of crying? It was very silent, very cold; the white rocks glittered in the cold moonlight, and the shadows were very dark. The rocks were darkened where they were piled together, and he did not like to look at that place. It looked like a dark door that something might come through.

The moon journeyed slowly up the sky as he watched. He remembered what old Makarenha had told him once, that the moon was the white lamp of the lady of the fountains. In her journeying she poured out rain for the earth and dreams for the earthborn. The sun was her great hearth by day, and all the bright stars were the journey fires lit on the great plain by night. When he had asked the old woman to tell him more, her face had shut up, and she had told him that it was all a fairy tale and that he had better remember that the Destroyer of Flesh heard everything that was said and worship Him alone like everyone else.

But later, on the street, he had heard a song about a lady who journeyed in a shining boat, and he began to sing it now. The song trembled a little because of the cold, but it made him feel warmer to sing.

Then he faltered and stopped. Surely he had heard something, like hoofbeats on the hillside—not below, where the road was, but off in the direction where the shadows fell.

Sitting absolutely still, he clearly heard the ring of hoofbeats on stone. The horse was picking its way one step at a time toward him.

"Ayei, singer!" a voice called softly. "Where are you?"

The boy did not care anymore who it was; anything was better than staying there alone. "I'm here," he called back.

The horse was white; the rider was a dark shape on its back. The rider dismounted and came over to the boy, eyes level with the top of the rock. The boy was confused for a minute; the hair was long and curling, and ear stones glittered—a woman? But the arms that lifted him down were hard and sinewy.

"Hé hé, little brother, how came you here?"

Suddenly, tears choked him. "They left me here, they left me," was all he could stammer out.

"Who? Your people? Your mother and father?"

"The soldiers! They came to the door, and Makarenha let them take me away, and they left me."

He knew he must not cry, that it was bad to cry, but he could not stop. The stranger put him away, but only for long enough to cut the ties. Then he lifted him and held him tightly for a minute.

"I have no reason to love those soldiers myself," the stranger said. "Suppose we go together, quickly, before they come back."

The boy twisted his fingers into the curly sheepskin of the stranger's cloak and nodded.

"Good, then, we'll be traveling companions. They call me Deronh where I come from—and I come from the Riders, from the Free People. Will you tell me your name?"

The boy took a long breath and found that the tears had stopped. He was ashamed, though. "I can't," he admitted. "They call me Ti'daron, but Makarenha says that's not a true name."

"Child of the darkness, is it? That's not a good name for you, little singer. When we travel together, I'll call you Rellai. That's 'Singer,' as the People say it. When we get there, you can take a name for yourself, and it will be as true as you could wish.

"Do you know what Deronh means? It's Thanha for 'Young Horse.' The other name they have for me is Rommane, 'Friend of Horses.' And Shiya here is my friend. He's a beauty, isn't he? His name means 'Snow'—because he's a mountain horse and will carry us above the snow and down again before morning comes.

"There—now let's go."

While he was speaking he had opened a saddlebag and taken out a woolen shirt for the boy. The sleeves had to be turned up several times, and the hem hung down to his knees, but it was warm.

Deronh set the boy in front of him, and the horse started up the mountainside again. The saddle was hardly more than a pad, and there was no horn, but Deronh showed him how to hang on to the neck strap and kept a protective arm around him most of the time. The Rider pulled his sheepskin cloak forward to cover both of them. The warmth was delicious, and the boy fell half-asleep in spite of Shiya's uneven climb over the rough ground.

He woke up once and looked out from the shelter of the cloak into a mist that was bitterly cold. The horse's hooves plunged deep into whiteness that glowed dimly in spite of the mist that kept out the moon's light.

"We are passing through the snows now," Deronh told him. "Our heads are among the clouds. This is the Mountain Spirit's country, where sky touches earth, where he walks on the mountain with the wind in his hair." He began to sing softly to himself.

The boy huddled closer in the sheepskin and dozed again. He woke up suddenly and completely and found that the gray light of dawn was spreading over a wide and desolate land like nothing he had ever seen before. The mountains were gone. He twisted in the saddle and saw that they towered up behind him. Before him, a gray-green plain stretched on forever. It was rocky and riven by gullies; it rolled away in ridge after ridge, each one hiding the flanks of the next. Long grass hissed against Shiya's knees, and little stunted trees clung to the hillsides. It was a country swept by the wind and open to the sky. He had never been more than a few yards from walls in his life: tenement walls, castle walls, alley barriers, the great walls of the city itself. For the first time he was in a place where there were no walls at all.

"Now we are home, little brother," Deronh said. "Here is food, water, shelter—all that we need is given to us by Mother-of-Horses, this great plain endless and mighty."

"If we are home, where are the people?" the boy asked. He was overwhelmed by these wide, empty spaces.

"Oh, when we come to the Rock, you'll see many of them," Deronh said. "That's where we keep our winter hearth, where we stay. But never forget that your true home is this great plain and the hearts of your brothers—not in any roof or wall."

When they had crossed several ridges and the sky had turned from gray to gold, Shiya stopped in the lee of a thorn thicket, and Deronh helped the boy down. Too stiff to stand, the boy landed on the cold ground.

Deronh laughed gently and did not pick him up. Instead he showed him how to stretch and loosen his stiff joints. In a few minutes the Rider got up and began to search for fire makings among the scrub, and the boy found that he could follow. Deronh paused briefly and cocked his head, inviting the boy to listen: A horn was blowing, very faint and far away.

"They've seen us and they're sending a welcome ahead," he said.

Their fire burned quickly to coals while they warmed themselves and the white horse grazed untethered. Deronh poured water into a little skin bag of flour, twirled his fingers in it, patted the resulting dough flat on a stone to bake, and passed the bag to the boy.

Ti'daron sucked his fingers as he waited for the cakes to bake; he had somehow become quite sticky imitating Deronh's deft movements. Deronh hooked the cakes neatly out of the fire without burning his fingers. He broke the bread in shares and crumbled a bit of it into the fire. Ti'daron copied him again.

"You honor the Mountain Spirit?" Deronh asked. He used the Thanha word: *Taurhalisos*. The boy thought he had heard it before, but he could not tell when. He nodded shyly.

"You came from that way," he said. His fingers went to his face, where the long scar ran from just below his eye to cut the edge of his lip. "When the priest did this, he said I was for the Eater. And when the soldiers came, they took me to his place. But you took me out of it. Can the Eater cross the mountains?"

Deronh pulled a knife from behind his neck so fast that Ti'daron could barely see it; then he cast it to land, quivering, in the earth before the fire.

"By this edge and the blood on it, if the Destroyer crosses the mountains, he shall himself be destroyed. When you come to the Rock, you will hear *Relle Tyrelha*, Tyrel's Song—the tale of the thousand slain. There was a city killed children of ours. In that city, the wild horses graze and the foxes build dens.

"Now eat. Get strong."

When they had finished, Shiya came to Deronh's call, and they rode on over the high plains. The sun shone brightly, but the wind had the chill of altitude in it. Ti'daron occasionally caught sight of sheep or horses on a hillside, and once Deronh pointed out to him the tiny shape of a man showing against the sky.

"One of the herd guards greets us," he said.

They went at an easy pace, and night was falling as they came to a well-marked path going up into the hills. At last there were signs of human habitation: many trails worn through the grass, the smell of wood smoke, and faint sounds of voices ahead of them.

"The Rock," Deronh said. "Our home."

It loomed over them, a thing like the black stone stub of a broken-off mountain. A rock, yes, but Ti'daron could not think why anyone would call it home.

As they came closer, he saw that the sides of the rock were pierced. Some of the openings were window-sized and window-high; others seemed to be doors, with people going and coming about. Suddenly, high-pitched war screams broke out, and a band of long-haired children, riding bareback and at breakneck speed, came tearing down from the hills and circled them.

Ti'daron heard them crying Deronh's name, but the rest was shrill jabber that he supposed must be Thanha. Then they galloped away again, disappearing into the twilight ahead. Shiya pricked his ears and neighed after them, breaking into a trot.

When they reached the foot of the great rock, the children appeared again and led the white horse away, while Ti'daron followed Deronh up the steep winding stairs cut into the face of the rock. There were people everywhere, and all of them were greeting Deronh, but Ti'daron kept his eyes on his feet to keep from stumbling with tiredness.

As they passed through the doorway, the guards embraced Deronh warmly, saying "Deronh, *paliao*!" Then they said something, gesturing to Ti'daron, at which Deronh laughed.

"They aren't laughing at you, *barasheli*," Deronh assured the boy. "They say I've been gone long, but they didn't know it was long enough to get a son. So I tell them in love the spirit always leaps ahead of the body. And they say with me they are not so sure. It's good to make happiness for the People—so let them laugh."

Through the doorway, they entered a cavern that was surely bigger than a king's hall. The roof went up out of sight, except where flaring torches high above occasionally cast a flicker on it. The walls on both sides were a maze of corners, lofts, and alcoves. Fires burned on many hearths, and there were people everywhere. Heads turned toward Deronh, but no one made a move to interrupt his walk to the far end of that marvelous hall. The boy followed him through half a dozen curtains of richly embroidered wool and finally came into a room where weavers worked at great looms. At the far end, someone sat on piled furs and pillows; Deronh went straight to that person without stopping to greet anyone else. He sat down cross-legged without speaking and motioned to the boy to do the same.

After a few minutes the seated person spoke. "We have a guest."

To the boy's surprise, he could understand the words. He looked up into the face of someone very old.

"Yes, Grandmother," Deronh answered, and the boy knew that it be must a woman. She was muffled in long robes and wore a three-cornered cap worked all over with silver and many-colored embroidery. Her face beneath the cap was embroidered with age, a mass of wrinkles, but in that weathered face her eyes were as bright as jewels in velvet.

She sighed. "Well, come closer to me. Let me feel your breath. Tell me this story. It sits ill to hear Giristiyah words from your mouth after so long an absence. But I can see you would honor this little one and hide no thought from him."

"Thoughts cannot be hidden, Grandmother—not among us. See for yourself, and then I think you can tell me the story."

The boy changed his mind. Maybe the words were not Thanha, but the thought behind them was, and he could not understand what was being said.

The old woman leaned toward him and put her hand on his head, looking into his eyes. He wanted to shift his gaze, but he could not. Strange, troubling things stirred in his mind, like clouds taking shape on the shoulders of the mountains. In just a moment longer, they would become solid and real, and he knew that he did not want that to happen. She let him go.

"Who is this child?" she breathed.

"You can answer that as well as I, Grandmother. Think what we have heard from Erech Tolanh. I found him in the place of the Destroyer, north of the road. Soldiers brought him there, he said. And as we rode, I saw three blackrobes coming down from the Holy City. It is in my thought that they were looking for something—something I have brought away with me."

"Deronh, is this wise?" she asked.

He put his hand on the boy's shoulder, and Ti'daron felt his grip tighten. "Grandmother, I know you have to look ahead for all of us. But you know yourself wisdom is not everything. The little brother was singing, all alone—a song to the Lady. Should I have passed by?

"He is my spoil from this battle without weapons. This is my right. Look at him, Grandmother! He will stand tall."

"Yes, he will stand very tall,' she said, and Ti'daron felt the sorrow in her voice. "But the price will be high."

She sat up straighter and spoke briskly. "But I see it is done already. Who can keep fire in a basket, or separate hearts that are joined? What is your name, child?"

"Deronh calls me Rellai," he said.

"And does that please you?"

He nodded shyly.

"Good, then. And you shall call me Grandmother, as everyone does. Rellai, I want you to answer the questions that I will ask, and then I will answer for you some questions that you have not asked."

Deronh shifted uneasily as if he would have liked to protest, but she gave him a quelling glance.

"Do you remember anything the soldiers said when they came to take you away?"

Rellai shook his head; then, fearing to be rude, he added, "No—Grandmother."

She placed a hand on his shoulder and held his gaze again.

He swallowed hard. He felt as if her eyes could lay bare everything that had ever happened to him.

"They spoke of the Master of the City," he recalled. The words came back to him. "They said that the witch's bastard was going back where he belonged. And—that the master should 'do away with me'—they meant kill, I know—not give me back to the blackrobes, and wondered what would happen if they did him that favor. And then the other one said it was not for them to question their orders.

"I know I belong to the Eater," he said desperately. "The priest who cut me told me so."

"And do you believe his lies?" the old woman asked disdainfully.

"He must be real. They all fear him so. I can feel it."

"Learn to believe otherwise. No one fears him here. Now listen to me. The blackrobes and the master are enemies at heart, but sometimes they must work together. Can you understand that?"

The boy nodded. He had seen the older boys beat and cheat

each other but stand shoulder to shoulder when a stranger came into their alley.

"Both the master and the blackrobes wanted you. The master found you first, but the blackrobes bought you from him, at a price he had to accept. You were not truly left for the Eater. His priests were coming for you even when Deronh found you."

"They cut the ones who are for the Eater," Rellai whispered. "I've seen them. He has black teeth." He shuddered uncontrollably.

"Listen to me! They would not have killed you. They wanted to make you like themselves."

Rellai shuddered again. Nothing was more terrible than the blackrobed priests with their cropped hair who called themselves Somostai, the Wise. Everyone ran from them when they walked through the city, for they could choose anyone as a victim for their god, who had to be fed with blood. He repaid them with gifts of secret knowledge. In return for that knowledge, even the Master of the City gave them what they wanted.

"Grandmother, we're frightening him," Deronh said.

She sighed. "One day you will have to know this. If it is too hard for you tonight, put it out of your mind." She stroked his cheek, and he felt the terrifying knowledge receding from him again till it was only a shadow.

"So, what he has said confirms that you are right, Deronh. We have troubled the counsels of the master and the Somostai; they will quarrel again over this matter, and that is good. We have a new brother, and that is also good.

"Deronh, take the little brother to his *beshani*, and go to yours and be happy. There are some who have missed you, if I still have eyes and ears. We will talk again tomorrow, when you have rested. And we will make a rejoicing for you. We owe you honor and love."

She patted Deronh's cheek as if he had been a child himself. Then he swept the boy up on his shoulders and danced out into the main cavern with him. As he walked, people called to him from every direction or ran out to embrace or pat him.

He took the boy to one of the many hearth fires burning around the cave and set him down in front of a slender girl who seemed to be directing a group of other children.

She beamed with obvious pride as she reached up to kiss Deronh's cheek and issued quick orders to the children who were tending the pot and the baking stones next to the fire. They came running with a dish of stew and cakes of hot, flat bread.

Deronh took a bite or two but then waved them gently away.

"Rellai, you call Teyala here *barasha* because she is your older sister. I've told them all to show love for you and treat you like a brother."

"But I want to stay with you," Rellai whispered. "Please don't leave me."

Deronh sat down and took the boy on his lap. "Little brother, I will stay here if you need me. But I have many friends to greet tonight and much to do. You are tired. It will be better for you to eat and sleep. Tomorrow I will see you. Remember, I live here and so do you. I will certainly not leave this place after traveling so far to find it!"

The girl Teyala leaned down to him. "Everyone in here I know," she said. Her accent was much heavier than Deronh's, but he could understand her. "If you need our brother of the horses in the night, I find him for you. Promise. Now you stay with us—you do us much honor. How sad we'll be if you don't like us!" She pulled a mournful face as if she would cry in a moment, then winked at him. She had round, merry eyes and a smiling face.

He stood up and nodded to Deronh. "All right, I'll stay here. But you come for me in the morning."

Deronh grabbed him and waltzed him around. "Good! Good! I knew you were truly Thanha! Stay with Teyala. She loves to talk, and soon she'll have you talking Thanha so we can all share hearts. Sleep well now, *damas paliao*."

He waved and walked away. The boy watched after him until he was hidden among the strangers. Then he turned to the other children, a little apprehensively. So often he had been beaten and kicked by similar groups. They might smile at first, but it was only to lure him close enough.

But nothing of the sort happened. One boy handed him a bowl of stew from the pot and hot bread to dip in it. Another ran to fetch a piece of honeycomb, and a little girl hardly big enough to walk put her blanket across his shoulders. After the soup Teyala gave him sweet tea and sat down to drink a bowl of it with him.

"Everyone will love you," she remarked, "because you make Deronh happy. His friend—his promise-friend—is dead, and it is dark in his heart. She would surely have been chosen to be one of the mothers, and he would have been a father for sure. So if he takes you for his son, it will be right again."

The boy nodded. He was trying hard to pay attention, but he felt too sleepy to understand.

"Come, I'll show you where to sleep," she said. "There is time to understand later. Plenty of time."

She took him up into one of the lofts along the wall. The floor was strewn with furs and blankets, and children were already sleeping there. A low partition screened the loft from the cave, but the murmur of voices, firelight and shadow, and the smell of cooking still rose soothingly. At one end of the sleeping place, a lamp burned and several women sat with their babies.

"You lie here next to Hira. He'll keep you warm till I come back. I'm just going to sit up awhile with the mothers. Call me if you need anything. This is your *besha*, your sleeping place, and all these are your *beshani*—young ones your age, of your hearth. Tonight they'll keep you warm. Tomorrow they'll be your friends."

At first he could not sleep for the strangeness. It was so different from his pallet on Makarenha's floor, with the dogs barking and the drunken voices in the street outside. The blankets smelled of smoke, of strange spices, and faintly of horses and sweet grass. But the odors were soft and warm, and Hira's even breathing lulled him. An easy, comfortable feeling spread through him. He could not put a name to it, because he had never felt it before. He felt safe; he felt at home.

2

When he woke up in the morning, there was no one nearby. Pale daylight filtered in from somewhere; the torches were out. He sat up and realized that he was naked, and he did not see his clothes anywhere. He remembered a long dream of riding on horseback, but he was not sure which parts had been true. For a minute he could not even remember his name, and when it came back to him, it seemed irrelevant and vaguely distasteful, like a dirty garment he had thrown aside. He heard someone down below singing in little snatches. The song came closer.

"Singer," he said to himself. "Rellai. That's my name."

"Rellai?" As if in echo, Teyala called his name and came into his sight, smiling. *"I te-na zhanna, barasheli*? And now you should say '*Ame zhanne-au*,' or, if you wanted to be especially fine and Thanha to me, '*Teha zhanne*,' or something like that."

"Te-ha zhanne?" Rellai asked cautiously. "What does that mean?"

Teyala hugged him and tugged on his hair affectionately. "I just want to kiss you when I hear you talking Thanha. I ask you, 'Is it shining on you, little brother?' And you say, 'It's fine and shining,' or like you just did, 'Your face is shining.' But it's just what you say in the morning. Sounds different, funny, in Giristiyah words. Everything good comes out wrong in that language. Learn Thanha in your heart, and it will come out your mouth." She smiled. "Come, now, we'll go and see the river. We are clean here, not like city people."

"But I don't have any clothes on," Rellai mumbled.

Teyala looked astonished and laughed. "Barasheli, your

beauty is not so great that you have to be afraid we'll go blind by looking at it.''

''Only animals go naked,'' he said, quoting Makarenha.

''Why do you say that?'' Teyala asked. ''Only animals have to wear their clothes all the time.'' But she saw that he was turning red and uncomfortable, and she relented. ''I'm sorry. I forgot. Deronh said not to make you feel like a stranger. Here, you carry the towel. You can carry it any way you like!''

The strip of cloth was big enough for Rellai to wrap around his middle. He still felt badly clothed and was mortified to find that they were going to walk right through the hall. But no one stared at him. It seemed to be good manners not to.

''Where is Deronh?''

''A great *pallantai* like Deronh runs ahead of the sun. He has been out since dawn.''

When she saw how disappointed the boy looked, she laughed again. ''Truth—Deronh's face was seen not long before yours. The song is sung that a great welcome was made for him, and this morning he was found laid out like a saddle blanket after the race. Of course, he has gone out to the horses first thing. Maybe we'll see him coming back.''

She took him out by a different way, and after a short, steep path, they came down into rolling meadows. She ran across them, talking steadily as if running were as easy as walking. He had a hard time keeping up. After a while he took off the towel; it kept tripping him.

The river astonished him; he had never seen so much water. The music of it enchanted him. It rumbled with a deep sound of power, like muttering drums, and over that constant chord the countless tongues of water near the shore sang to him with changing voices. They walked along the bank till they found a gravelly shore not muddied by horses.

''Jump in,'' Teyala said.

He leapt, and the voices vanished in a blinding flash of cold. He came up shouting and went under again. He could not seem to find earth with his feet. Something solid came around his shoulders, and he grabbed it. He stood up gasping, wiping the water out of his eyes, while Teyala supported him.

''Your beshani can teach you to swim,'' she said cheerfully.

She scrubbed his hair and his whole body with something that foamed and then took a brush made of grass stalks to him as if he had been a horse. When she had rubbed him down with the towel, he was not cold anymore. His skin tingled as if the top layer had been peeled off.

"We found clothes for you," Teyala said.

She handed him a linen shirt and a pair of short drawers that tied with a string, and he put them on, thinking that they were beautifully white and soft even if they would not be as warm as his old shirt.

"Wait, that isn't all," Teyala said. She giggled. "You're so anxious not to be naked, and now you want to eat breakfast in your underwear?"

She gave him a second shirt with longer sleeves, made of wool like Deronh's, and a pair of woolen trousers—something he had never worn before. An embroidered green vine ran around the neck of the shirt. She looked him over.

"You look very nice," she said. "Except your hair. Why did you cut it all off? Are you in mourning?"

"Boys always wear their hair short in the city," he told her.

"Well, it doesn't matter; it'll grow out soon. Now listen, don't think we're poor in love just because of these clothes. We took them out of the common store so you'd have something to put on, but of course you'll have proper ones soon, and riding boots and a warm cloak, and all the rest if it. Don't think we haven't thought of that."

He was already wearing more clothing than he had ever seen in one room before.

"Look! Yonder comes Deronh!" she exclaimed. She raced off down the riverbank, still naked, with her clothes trailing from one hand. She came back trotting beside Shiya, tugging him along by a handful of mane. Deronh sat the white horse bareback and halterless, as if it were more natural to ride than to walk. Shiya put a grass-flecked pink nose up to Rellai and snorted a puff of warm breath into his face.

"He remembers you," Deronh said. "So, Teyala *isé*, what do you think of the new brother?"

"Well, he hasn't got much in the way of legs, and he can't swim," she reported. "There's a lot of work to be done if he's to be an honor to his besha. You'd better send him down to throwing practice in a bit so we can test his eye and have some of the little ones see if he's a fighter. But he's a good catch, barasha. You haven't lost your eye for a colt. Let us work with him awhile, and you'll be surprised." She smiled. "I have to go now."

She threw a back flip, realized that she was still naked, tugged on her clothes, and ran off down the riverbank.

"Teyala does you great honor to serve you," Deronh said. "One year into weapon training, and already she is the best with the throwing spear and knife of all those born to the Mane."

Rellai nodded. He did not understand a word of that, but he was already in awe of the round-faced, nimble girl.

As they approached the Rock, Deronh slipped off the white horse and let him go back to cropping the grass. Inside, they found their way to a hearth where a few belated Riders were breakfasting. Two of them looked up and smiled as Deronh came near. One was a woman, dark and slight like Deronh and with long curling hair like his. Rellai stared; he had never seen a woman in pants before. The other had long hair like a woman, too, but yellow and bound up with a great gold pin. When the latter got up to greet them, his broad shoulders and deep voice told Rellai that he was a man.

"Taurekke, Lindhal, I bring my spoils back to the People. This is Rellai, newest of our beshani, if not youngest in years."

The woman held out her hand, and Deronh covered it with his, palm to palm. Then she waited for Rellai to greet her. Her palm was warm but tough and work-hardened; the skin of her wrist was delicate and soft to his fingers. As their hands touched, a picture sprang into his mind: the gray fox, with its long delicate legs and sooty paws, drifting silent as a feather along the mountainside. The bright, lively eyes met his. Suddenly he was looking at the woman again.

"The fox," he said involuntarily. "I saw a fox—the mountain kind, it must be; I've never seen one like it."

He felt that he was babbling and turned to greet the big man. Lindhal grinned at him. "Don't ask me to believe this boy is yours," he teased Deronh. "Look at those sky-colored eyes and his hair—he's as fair as I am."

Rellai's hand was nearly swallowed by Lindhal's; the blond stranger was the biggest person he had ever seen. But the thought that came to his mind was a field of grain waving on narrow stalks. The milky gold kernels swelled in the sun; he could taste their rough, sustaining sweetness.

Lindhal said something to Deronh wordlessly, with the tilt of his eyebrows, and Deronh extended a hand to the boy. Rellai felt confused. He touched Deronh's hand, and the three saw him smile. The little black horse that sprang to life was so much like Deronh. He saw the tough gaiety, the endurance, the joyful zest for living as the little horse pranced.

But there was something beyond that: a wanting, a hurting

that Deronh could not ride away from. The black horse faded from his mind as he tried to understand. It almost seemed that there was another person there with them, or a place that expected her and was empty.

"There should be another," he murmured. He almost saw her face—and then he knew that if he saw her, he would see something else, too, something terrible and hard to bear. But suddenly he was standing on his feet next to the hearth again. He felt as if he had walked into Deronh's room and the Rider had picked him up and gently but firmly placed him outside again. He found that his hand was pressed against Deronh's chest. The Rider's face was calm, but tears streamed from his eyes. He turned his face away from his friends.

"It's hard," he said apologetically. "I come home, but still she isn't here."

"Barasheli-de," Taurekke said gently. "Look—the little brother."

She touched Rellai's face; he had not realized till then that he was crying, too.

"I'm sorry," he said. "I didn't mean to." He was terribly confused. He thought he had hurt Deronh.

"No, no, no. You haven't done anything wrong," Deronh said, hugging him tightly. "Only something very surprising. You startled me. Tell me, you saw pictures, yes? For Taurekke, the mountain fox; and Lindhal, corn growing. I told you my name already, so that was too easy. Now you see that names truly mean something to us."

"But the other," Rellai said.

Deronh sighed. "Little one, I meant only to show you our names, but you see past the name and straight into the heart. You are too young to understand everything that you can see. Like a greedy hunter, you can bring down more game than you can carry home."

"Names have meanings, yes," Lindhal said. "You brought us home a singer."

"Leave that trail," Deronh said. "He is too young."

The big man shrugged. "Your word is gold, little brother. Just remember, in two years or three, that for once I looked ahead."

Suddenly he grabbed Deronh in mock horror. "What's this? His face is wet on the day he comes home! Woman, how can you be so careless? This man is supposed to be too limp to cry."

He got Deronh in a neck hold and tried to wipe his face with the hem of his shirt while Deronh kicked violently to keep Taurekke from getting hold of his feet. They let him go only when he finally began to laugh.

"You have no respect for anything you can't eat," Deronh complained, pulling his clothes back together.

"Speaking of things to eat, this stomach is empty," Lindhal replied. "Is it allowed, father of herds, to send your colt on an errand more suitable to his age? Find some hay for this mane wearer, little one, and some cake and beer for me."

Rellai had gone halfway to the hearth to see if there was anything left in the pot before he realized that Lindhal had been speaking Thanha.

At first he could understand only Deronh, Taurekke, Lindhal, and Teyala, and only if they were speaking directly to him. When he thought about it, he could not understand most of the individual words, just the general sense. He could hardly speak at all. After a month or two, though, he could speak to and understand everyone. When Deronh occasionally spoke what they called Giristiyah to him, so that he would not forget it, it gave him a bad feeling. He sometimes had dreams, bad ones, in which he heard the language of his childhood spoken. He dreamed about being beaten again or left alone in dark places. Often he had that sense of almost seeing a woman's face—a sad face, turning away. He came to feel that his lost mother and Deronh's dead partner were the same, though he knew that was not so.

Most of the time when he woke up frightened, he moved closer to his beshani and was comforted by their warmth. Sometimes even that did not help, and he would wrap himself in a blanket and go hunting for Deronh in all the Rider's favorite sleeping places. Usually he was there, with Lindhal or Taurekke or both, sometimes with another of the pallantai—warriors—from the Mane. The good, familiar smell of horses and horsemint that hung around Deronh made Rellai feel safer, even in his sleep.

Once or twice he found Deronh crying while Dhali and Rekki held him and spoke to him without many words that anyone else could hear. He wished that Deronh would take them for his *kamari* in place of the one who had died, but he understood that Deronh could not, at least not yet. Still, as Rellai's dreams gradually faded, the grief faded from Deronh, too. His solitary ways and the sadness that sometimes shaded his face were no longer painful but just a part of him, like the faint bitterness of horsemint. Dhali and Rekki stayed as close to him as if they were kamari and treated Rellai as if he had been born to them. In fact, Deronh often teased Lindhal, telling him that Rellai must have sprouted from his seed, thrown away on some lowlander woman.

Rellai entered joyfully into the games on the practice ground. The bumps and bruises he got were nothing compared to what he was used to in Makarenha's alley. And since they were given without malice, they did not hurt him half as much. Still, he wondered why they were necessary.

He asked Teyala about it one day. "In the city, I had to fight. Though I'd much rather have run away. But here, where everyone's so friendly, I don't understand why we try to hurt each other."

Teyala laughed. "We are the Riders! Fighting is our life! Besides, we don't try to hurt—we learn not to get hurt. Don't you listen to the weapon master? It will be years before you're old enough to learn the killing skills."

She noticed Rellai's frightened look. "We don't kill each other, little brother! Don't be afraid. We fight against the cityfolk, and they pay us to do it."

"That seems foolish."

"No, it's really very clever. They know that we're the best, we are the swift and fearless. We can fight much better than they can. They're slow and lazy, so we do the fighting for them. They offer pay for our service, and Grandmother decides each year who it is best for us to serve. She doesn't think only of money—sometimes we play one city against another to make sure they don't get too strong.

"We have cousins living in other places, and they sometimes serve the cities, too, but the Asharyas like Grandmother get together to avoid sending Rider against Rider. That would be truly dangerous. Going against the cityfolk is nothing."

Rellai recalled scarred and crippled men he had seen in the city. When they could find the money to get drunk, they would sit in the tavern and curse the renegades who had done that to them. He went to find Deronh, who was sitting cross-legged with an enormous heap of bridles and straps that needed oiling and mending.

"Deronh, are we renegades?"

Deronh looked up at him. "Yes," he said calmly. "That's what they call us. It's because they say we're bandits who have run away from their masters. It's not true. Haven't you been listening to the songs? We came down from the north in a time long ago, a time of great thirst, seeking grass and water for our horses. At first we warred with the cityfolk, but we could not live within walls like them, nor could they live here on Mother-of-Horses. So we have our place, and they have theirs. It's true, though, that we accept anyone who asks shelter from us. If they are brave and willing to fight, they can make a place among us. The first Riders were small, dark-haired people like me. As you can see, there are many different kinds of faces here now—all of them Riders."

"But why do they hate us so much?"

Deronh laughed quietly. "Men do commonly hate those who defeat them in battle."

"They say we are evil witches. They say we work accursed magic."

Deronh shrugged. "It's easier for them to say we are evil than to admit we can do things they can't. We have a feeling for each other that they don't understand. Those who are greatly gifted in this way often become healers, and they don't understand that, either—how we can lend each other strength to live. When we fight, we move together like the fingers of one hand, without masters to beat us into line. And often we can see the blow prepared before it is given, so they can't strike us. You'll learn that art when you're old enough. It seems like magic to them."

"They call us bastards, as well as witches. Bastards and other foul names. They say we do foul things." Rellai was not sure how to be specific. Makarenha had told him that the street words were dirty, but they were the only ones he knew.

"Lovemaking, you mean?" Deronh said. "I've never understood what they think is right and wrong."

"I don't, either, because they did every one of those foul things in our alley. When I asked Makarenha about it, she said to hold my tongue or she'd get out the stick. I used to wrap my shirt around my head to try to keep them out, but it didn't help much. Some of the things didn't seem so bad." He shot a guilty look at Deronh to see what he was thinking, but the Rider did not seem to be angry. "Most of it hurt, though. I was glad not to be a girl, but it doesn't really make much difference. There was a man we had to hide from whenever he came by the tavern. He sold boys to the guards. But what they do here doesn't hurt people. I can sleep at night. So I don't see how it's worse than it was in the city."

"Fucking children—that's foul," Deronh said. He used the Giristiyah word that Rellai knew. His voice was angry, but he pulled Rellai close, so the boy knew that it was not anger against him. "Listen, barasheli, no one will be angry if you play children's games with your beshani. And when you're old enough, you'll find out what the game of delights is really about. But grown people will not bother you. That's not our way. No one will use you against your will."

Rellai stayed for a while, enjoying the comforting warmth that was Deronh.

"Even though they are cityfolk and liars," he said finally, "it was sad to see the men without legs who used to beg money outside the tavern. I wish we didn't have to fight with them."

"We are the Riders. Fighting is our life," Deronh said. "I have wished the same thing often, barasheli. I don't know who made the world as it is. It wasn't me."

Rellai went to the practice ground with renewed determination. He wanted to make a place for himself among the Riders and wanted to learn all the skill they could teach. Never again would he be helpless.

Taurekke, the Mane's best archer, taught him the art of the bow. The beshani instructed him in most other things; they taught him to swim and to dance, to wrestle and to fight with a knife. Deronh passed on to him as much as he could of his gift with horses. As Rellai's legs continued to grow longer and longer and his shoulders broadened, Deronh admitted that he would never make a real horseman. Lindhal, who had the same handicap, or advantage, began teaching him how to handle the long sword and the moves of fighting on the ground.

No one had to teach him to sing. Their songs beat a way into his memory like geese flying north to their homes. Through the long winter nights, when the drums thundered through the hours like the flying hooves of the Mountain Spirit's immortal horses, his voice was woven into their music. He forgot that he had ever been different. He forgot the Asharya's words on that first night. He forgot the past and the future, living fiercely in the present. He feasted when there was food and fasted when it ran short. He danced when his brothers rejoiced and wept with them when they grieved. Many fingers, one heart; many tongues, one song." So ran the saying. And he plunged into that oneness like a bird into the air or like a fish into the falls of Thunder River.

3

Another spring came to the great plain; new green was showing among the dry grasses, and the sun had strength in it, though the wind was cold. Deronh had taken the herd far south in search of better grazing; a band of Riders had gone with him, for the winter had been bitter and the wolves were hungry. On the seventh day without snow, Rellai heard the old ones testing the air and agreeing that it seemed the hard weather was over. He found Shin, one of the pallantai who kept an eye on the young ones.

"It's too bad for the brothers on wolf watch to be hungry," he observed, "when it would be such a simple thing for someone to ride out with more food for them."

"Where is the person who wants to do this simple thing?" Shin asked.

"Even a boy like me could manage to load a packhorse with food and follow the trail of the herd."

"Even a boy like you could make a good meal for wolves," Shin said.

"It's sunny and warm. The wolves don't hunt human meat unless they're starving," Rellai argued. "And you know yourself I'm good with the bow. I'll sleep out one night and find them in the morning."

Shin rubbed his mustache, a sign that he was thinking it over. Riding out alone at the tail end of wolf season was not really smart. On the other hand, it was the kind of thing a young would-be pallantai should do to show his spirit. Shin's denial would be like saying that Rellai was still a child. Finally he smiled.

"You're right, barasheli, it's not for our honor to let their bellies go empty. Tell Shorne to help you pick out a load of supplies. And take a jar of honey; I know Deronh's liking for sweetness."

Rellai chose two horses: the bay gelding that had been captured from the lowlanders and was bigger than most of the mountain horses and a steady mare to carry the supplies. He loaded the pack bags with meal, honey, dried meat and fruit, and dried *resh*-beans. Since the hunters were living with the herds, they would have mare's milk in abundance, but a diet of milk and curds palled quickly.

Shin came out to see him off. Rellai knew that the pallantai had come to make sure that his gear was in order. It would not be for Shin's honor if the wolves ate Rellai and it was said later that the boy had gone off without arrows enough or poorly mounted. So he was proud that Shin said nothing and merely nodded and waved to him as he rode away.

Rellai had never been out of sight of the Rock and alone since he could remember. He sang for company as he rode, guiding the horse with his legs and patting out the drum rhythm with his fingers. When he was tired of riding, he ran beside the horses for an hour. He saw nothing all day but birds flying and an occasional rabbit startled from its afternoon rest by the horses' hooves.

He found a good place to camp before dark, built a small, nearly smokeless fire, and set some bean stew with fruit in it to cook. The horses eagerly hunted out the small new blades of grass while Rellai chewed on a strip of dried mutton and thought how good it would be to eat his fill again one day soon, now that spring had come.

The sky faded to gray, and the stars began to show for the first time in many days of cloudy weather. To get a better view of the sky, Rellai climbed to the top of the ridge that sheltered his fire. The horses moved around restlessly below him. They were too well trained to neigh out loud, but he heard them stamp and snort. He congratulated himself on being weapon-wise enough not to have climbed up there without his bow. Placing an arrow on the string, he crouched and searched the shadows for wolves. Instead he saw something coming on two legs. The bay horse reared as a stranger seized the picket rope. Rellai loosed his arrow without a thought of hitting the horse. At that range, even in the twilight, he could not miss. The stranger crumpled to the ground, and Rellai felt a quick surge of triumph. Almost in the same instant, he knew that he had been very stupid. The cooling breeze brought him a scent of sweat and onions, unmistakably human. Before he could turn around, someone landed on him hard enough to knock the wind out of him.

Before his head cleared, they had bound him hand and foot and laid him out next to his fire. They threw more wood on it to make a light while they searched his saddlebags.

"Good, we can use this stuff," one of them said.

The words were strange, but he understood them. He struggled with that idea as he tried to catch his breath. At last he realized that they were Giristiyah. Terror struck him as hard as their blows.

They took most of the food, stuffing some dried fruit into their mouths, but the beans they dumped out on the ground.

"Ugh, can't eat this trash. It's fit for animals only."

I piss on your altars, Rellai thought fiercely, trying to fight down his fear. May the Lady withdraw her favor from you for that word, and may you starve hearthless.

Heavy boots came closer and stood by his head.

"You killed Surya, dirty little renegade," the stranger said. His Thanha was very bad, and Rellai noticed with some pleasure that he had used the word that meant the slaughter of an animal, not the polite one for the death of a human.

"My friends there think you should pay for that. I think you should start by telling us some things. Where were you going with all that stuff? Where are your friends?"

"They're here, on this great plain. Go look for them. They'll make wolfmeat of you."

The boots kicked him, hard. He caught his breath carefully. There were new pains in his ribs.

"It's too early for the Riders to be going off to war," the man said reasonably. "We know that. But maybe you can tell us who they will ride for when they do go, yes? That's not a big question."

"How would I know?" Rellai mumbled with his face in the dirt. "I'm only a boy."

He curled up under another volley of kicks. His heart was jumping painfully because he realized suddenly that he did know. He always tried to ignore it when the elders he was close to had worries. Deronh had told him that children should not concern themselves with those things, so he would run off and play and distract himself from their thoughts as best he could. But when they all thought together about the same thing, it was impossible to distract himself entirely. It was too easy to hear what was not meant for his ears and to guess at the unspoken. No one had told him where the pallantai were going that year, but he knew. The man barked an order. One of his friends came and hauled Rellai to his feet so that the man with the boots could stare into his face.

"Renegade rat," the man said slowly, "I don't believe you're as stupid as you look. Let's try to loosen your tongue for you. Maybe you will at least speak politely to us in a little while."

Rellai stared at the man's chest to avoid meeting his eyes. The man was very hard and muscular for a traveling merchant. His boots were very fine. They reminded Rellai of something. As the man turned, his sword swung forward, and Rellai saw that the plain iron hilt had a design stamped on it. The pattern made him feel cold and sick, as if he had seen something evil. Then he remembered. That was the city master's insignia, the sign worn by the soldiers who had carried him up into the rocks on that cold night. The strangers were soldiers, not traders. And if it was so important to Erech Tolanh that they would send spies across the mountains in wolf season to find out who the Riders were fighting for that year, Rellai knew that he must not tell them.

They looked around for somewhere to string him up. Finally they tied his wrists to a thornbranch that grew from a steep place in the hillside.

"Tell us now—where were you going, you little *bastard*?" The word they used was Giristiyah. He remembered it very well. There was no word for it in Thanha.

"Where were you going in my country, slave?" he replied.

They hit him again, slamming his face against the rocks.

"We in the south know how to break horses, too," their leader said. "We teach them manners with this."

His whip whistled through the air as he spoke and smacked into the rock next to Rellai's head. They all laughed.

"Look at the brave little renegade, afraid of the sound of a whip!"

The next stroke landed on his back.

They went on whipping him for a long time. Sometimes they waited between strokes long enough to give him hope that they would stop and make the next blow a surprise. At first he tried not to cry out, but he could not help it. So he yelled as loudly as he could, hoping that someone would hear him. In the end, all conscious reason deserted him, and he screamed and struggled like a wild animal, knowing only that he would die if he could not get away.

He came back to himself again with cold water dripping down his face. The men were speaking their own language again, as if he were not there.

"He's too stubborn for the whip," one of them said. "Too bad we don't have a priest here. They could make him talk, all right. That's one thing they're good for."

"We have plenty of ways to make him talk," said the decisive voice he recognized as the leader's. "Not tonight, though. We've made more than enough noise already. Tomorrow we'll find a more secure spot and work him over thoroughly."

"Maybe he doesn't know anything," the third voice said.

"He knows, all right. He wouldn't be so stubborn, else. Take him down and give him a drink. We don't want him to go out on us."

Someone reached for his bonds and then chuckled. "Why tire myself out with the knife? Here—this is a little taste of tomorrow for you."

The man dropped a glowing ember between Rellai's bound wrists and watched him struggle while it burned through the thongs and skin. Rellai fell in a heap when the thongs parted. They dragged him closer to the fire and tied him up again.

Two of them rolled up in their blankets and slept, while the third kept watch. Rellai tried to stay alert, but he kept drifting off into a stupor of pain.

The man on watch showed no sign of falling asleep, anyway. He moved about restlessly. When the others had been quiet for some time, he came over to Rellai. He was breathing heavily.

"I hear you horsefuckers like to do it with each other," he said.

Rellai pretended that he was unconscious. When the man tugged at his clothes, though, tearing them loose from bloodied welts and bruises, he gasped.

"That's right, stay awake," the man said. "Make the most of it—it's the last night your ass will be in one piece."

Rellai understood what the man was going to do and tried to scream, but the man clamped a hand over his mouth so tightly that the boy could hardly breathe. He could not struggle under the soldier's weight. Stars burst behind his eyelids as he fought for air. He could not make a sound, but he cried for Deronh with all his might. And bright and clear and far away, he saw Deronh cock his head as he always did when he was startled.

"Help me," he pleaded, but it was already too late.

By the time the soldier finished, he had made enough noise to wake up the second on watch.

"Gods, you're a pig," he said in disgust when he saw what his fellow was doing.

"What are you talking about? I did the little bugger a favor. If you had any sense, you'd grab yourself a morsel before it gets scorched."

He stretched himself out to sleep with ostentatious satisfaction. The second man looked down at Rellai for a moment, then got a horse blanket and dropped it over him. The rough fibers stung his raw back, but he felt warmer. He was shivering uncontrollably. He thought it must be his last night on earth. He prayed to the Mountain Spirit that he would die quickly, before he disgraced himself and lost his right to be welcomed on the Road to the North, the Heroes' Road. He tried to stay awake, as if he could stave off the dawn, but he was too exhausted.

When he woke up, it was dark, but the night was passing. He could tell by the smell of the air that morning was coming. The small crescent of sky he could see from where he lay was very faintly paling.

And as he watched it, without hope, something stirred on the hillside. The sound was no louder than a leaf touched by a breath of wind, but his heart leapt within him. Again came a sound, too irregular to be the footfall even of an animal yet, to him, louder than a cry. Then gentle hands touched his face, searched for his bonds, and slashed them.

He staggered to his feet as a great shout rang out. "Open your eyes and look at death!" Only two of the soldiers got up. The one who had been on watch lay still.

Someone threw a handful of sticks on the fire. It blazed up brightly. Rellai saw Deronh and at least two others circling the two remaining soldiers, who stood back to back with their swords out.

"Give me a knife," Rellai said fiercely. But his legs were unsteady, and before he could reach his enemies, Deronh and the others had cut them down.

"You shouldn't have done that," he said. "I wanted to kill them myself."

He took one more step, and Deronh caught him.

There came a day when he awoke to an absence of pain. In his mind there was the memory of a long darkness that left an aftertaste as bitter as the taste of medicine lingering in his mouth. He was in some unfamiliar sleeping place behind curtains, where it was very quiet. But he was in the Rock.

"So, how does the morning look to you, little brother?" The voice was gentle and half-joking. He recognized Shernhalla, the oldest and most skilled of the healers.

"Fine and shining," he replied politely. "But what morning is this? How long have I been here?" He tried to sit up and found that he was ridiculously weak.

"You've been asleep for the best part of six days," the healer said, helping him up. "There was a fever on you. We gave you a sleeping medicine so you would lie quiet."

Rellai investigated his back and found scabbed, puffy ridges.

"It feels worse than it is now," Shernhalla told him. "You'll have a fine set of scars. Your weapon teacher will be proud—though I am a healer, and I say you come to us too soon. The smith does not decorate the blade before he has finished the tempering."

Rellai touched the healer's hand in gratitude. "Thank you, barasha," he said. "I never thought I would see the sun again."

"You have yourself to thank," the healer said kindly. "When Deronh brought you in, we were afraid for you. We thought you might have set out already on the Road to the North. You had lost more blood than a boy can spare. But you fought to live. You have courage.

"If the dark dreams come back, remember I have walked down those roads beside you. You know my hearth—come to me.

"And now there are others who have waited a long time to hear your voice."

Shernhalla slipped away, and Deronh came in. He hugged Rellai so tightly that the boy experienced a moment of panic. The Rider felt him pull away and eased up.

"You saved my life again," Rellai said. "They would have killed me."

Deronh's normally gentle face turned stony.

"I know the tale," he said. "Grandmother had the healers question you in your sleep. She needed to know. When I heard it, I wished they still lived so I could kill them again."

"Never mind," Rellai said. "Their names are cut off. Why talk about them?"

He leaned his head on Deronh's shoulder, and they sat in silence for a while, gently touching. Listening-for-the-heart, it was called. Their breathing fell slowly into harmony, and they were at peace again.

Deronh sat up, smiling. "Come," he said. "Shernhalla told me to get your legs moving again. Those-cut-off had money and good weapons, also horses. Come and see."

"The horses!" Rellai exclaimed, suddenly remembering. "Are they all right? That's how it started. They tried to steal the horses, and I shot one of them."

"Yes, the horses are fine. We saw the man you killed—those pigs had not bothered even to honor his body. So you have first-blood honors in this fight."

As they walked out into the hall, some of the other children caught sight of Rellai and began to sing out the praise-cry and drum on walls or chests or whatever was handy. Deronh saw him hunching up his shoulders in embarrassment and rebuked him gently.

"You raise their hearts. They honor you, and you make them feel taller. This is not something to be ashamed of. And you'd better get used to it. One day you'll come back from the summer with twenty horses behind you and every youth of the People singing your name. Are you going to hide your head then?"

Rellai could not find words to explain that he did not feel like a hero. The soldiers' possessions were laid out on the long table in the storeroom, where he had often seen the spoils piled high at the autumn gathering. It seemed strange to him to be going there in the spring.

The lowlanders had been carrying a surprising amount of money as well as some finger rings and a belt worked with snakes done in gold and lacquer. There were also three plain mail shirts and a good one with silver studs, four short swords, and assorted odds and ends. Deronh picked up one of the swords and looked it over. They were all of good plain workmanship, and all bore the stamped seal on their hilts.

"This mark was put on in the Iron City," Deronh said. "A reckoning is coming."

Rellai turned away from the table. "All of my share is for the People," he said. "Tell the store master to sell it, if he can. I don't want to see it again." He knew that he was distressing Deronh by his lack of enthusiasm, but even looking at the heap of goods made his skin crawl.

"We'll go look at the horses," Deronh said, as if that were balm for every wound.

And it did feel good to be out in the sun again and to breathe

the clean wind. Spring had conquered the land while he had been in bed, and the horses were feeding eagerly on fresh new grass.

"This little bay is a very ordinary horse," Deronh said, patting it apologetically. "The gray there is fast and fine—I'd keep him for myself, but unfortunately they are both cut horses. We'll take them south and sell them later in the year. The brown mare can run in with the herd. She's nothing special, but we can have her bred in a month, and we'll see what quality she gives in a foal. And this one—this one is worth the rest put together. His manners are too rough, and his mouth has been hardened—he'll never make a good mount. But he's big and fast together. We'll keep him for breeding.

"I'll tell you what, barasheli. We'll ask this one to beget you a colt, and you can begin training it next spring. It will be tall and swift, yet able to bear up under the size you'll be in a year or so. If you think you can handle two, we'll raise one of its brothers along with it, and you can make a gift of it to Lindhal. That would please him more than anything." He grinned and ruffled Rellai's hair. "He'll probably give it some grand name like 'Spoils of War' or 'Gift of the Spy Killer' so he'll have an excuse to brag about you to everyone who asks after his horse."

Rellai smiled in spite of everything. "You shine on my heart, Deronh. Where is Dhali? I want to see him."

"And he wants to see you. There's a big feast preparing at our hearth, and he's out hunting. But there's one other who must see you before then. Grandmother wants to talk to you personally."

"What for?" Rellai asked faintly.

"Only she can say. But listen, barasheli, I know there is a shadow on your heart. Everyone can see it, but you don't want to speak of it. Talk to her. I think she has a plan which will be good for you and also good for the Rock. Trust her."

Rellai found his way again to the Asharya's sleeping place at the end of the cavern. He felt as if he were dreaming; he remembered the way so vividly, but as if someone else had walked it for him. He parted the last curtain and dropped down cross-legged, with his eyes on the floor.

"Come closer to me; let me feel your breath," she said, just as she had years ago. "Aren't you the boy Deronh brought here on his saddle from the Iron City?"

"Yes, Grandmother."

She took hold of his wrist gently. "Already you have started to grow tall. Tell me, how was it that you survived with so many enemies against you?"

"Deronh saved me. He rescued me at night." Rellai knew that she must have heard the story already, but for some reason she wanted him to answer.

"Ah. How remarkable that Deronh, brave and wise as he is, was able to find one little boy in the midst of this great plain and bring him back behind his saddle like a bag of beans, saving his beautiful face and sweet voice for us all to enjoy."

Rellai felt that she was making fun of Deronh and remained stubbornly silent.

"How did Deronh know where to find you?"

"Deronh is brave and wise, as you say. Why not ask him? I'm only a little boy, as you say."

"I have asked him—as you say, little brother. He says you called to him from far away, that he saw your face."

Rellai shook his head. He could not think of that time without a fear that almost stopped his breath.

She smoothed the bright hair from his forehead.

"You know, don't you, what a rare gift this is? Even among one's own *barhedonh*, those who live and fight together, this touching from far away is rare. And it is rare, also, to see so clearly what others think or feel. Sometimes kamari who are partners in everything learn to sense without words what the other is doing or feeling. But you made Deronh hear your very words." She paused. "Tell me, can you see my thoughts at this moment?"

"Oh, no, Grandmother. You see, I don't really know you very well. Most of the time it's not like seeing. It's just a feeling, like finding the path in the dark. It comes from living with people. I know them so well that suddenly I just see things. I don't make it happen. That would be disrespectful, like trying to force a brother to talk to you if he didn't want to."

"Have you ever tried?"

The thought made Rellai uncomfortable. "I wouldn't want to. Most of the time I spend trying not to know things."

"How do you manage that?"

"I think about songs, and how the music goes together. That helps. Or I go with my friends. When I'm with them, I can feel them around me, and it helps me ignore the other people. When it gets too bad, I run away to the grazing ground and stay with the horses.

"I didn't find out who we were riding for on purpose, Grandmother. I truly didn't mean to. I don't try to know what the elders are thinking. Most of the time I couldn't if I wanted to, because I'm not close to their hearts the way I am with Deronh. But you were all thinking about the Iron City, even Deronh. It was on your minds, like *chah* on the pallantai's breath when they've been drinking, and—I just smelled it!"

That made her laugh, but she was not yet ready to let him go. "You made Deronh hear you, and you are safe with us now. What, then, is troubling you? I may be old, but my nose is still sharp, too!"

He kept his head bowed, but she could feel his fear. She relived in his mind the terror and shame he had known. She felt each wound, but far worse than the pain, she felt their hatred, their mindless cruelty, their will to destroy him, choking him like bitter, filthy water. He was drowning and had no way to escape.

She almost flung her arms around him to protect him. Then she realized that it would be a long time before he could endure to be held tightly.

"I'm ashamed," he whispered. "I want to be a pallantai like Taurekke, like Shin, like Lindhal. But none of them are afraid as I am. They're brave."

"How do you know this?" she asked.

"I know," he insisted.

Probably he does, she thought with some exasperation. Will there be anything he doesn't know? It isn't easy to raise a child from whom nothing can be hidden.

"Listen to me," she said. "Who is wiser—me or that bear Lindhal?"

"You are," he said—reluctantly, for he loved Lindhal dearly.

"I am, indeed. Lindhal and Deronh are brave and beautiful, and they are the life of the People. It is theirs to fight without counting the cost, to take the Heroes' Road and never look back. But it is my job to remember the past and look into the future, and set a price on the blood of my children. And I tell you, little brother, I am afraid more often than I care to say.

"I apologize to you on behalf of all of us. This has been troubling you for some time, and we have done nothing to help you. That is not right, and must not continue.

"Now listen: I'm telling you what is to be done. The kind of knowing you have is a weapon like any other, and you must learn to use it, to drive away this fear. I am taking you from your weapon training. You will still practice with the others of your beshani. But you are for the Hard Way, as well as the Heroes' Way. From now on you will go barefoot, and Shernhalla will be your teacher. One thing Shernhalla can show you is how to keep your knowing at a distance when you need to. Healers must know the pain of others, but they must be the rider and not the horse, or they would not be able to heal."

"But I don't want to be a healer," he protested in confusion.

She snorted. "I think it unlikely you will be a healer. There are other uses for this training, believe me. Now look into my heart. I want you to be satisfied."

She held out her palm. Reluctantly, he slid his hand over hers. He did not quite catch the name she had once borne, but he had a glimpse of blue steel. He felt the weight of old hurts long endured, the bitterness of a river of sorrows, and under it all the fire of a heart still burning. He knew he was only one thread in her weaving, but he understood why they all let her choose the pattern.

"I will trust you, barasha," he said quietly.

She waved to one of her weavers, who came swiftly, carrying a little package wrapped in silk.

Rellai unrolled it and found a throw knife, sharp as a razor, with a gilded hilt.

"I was so sure of you, little brother, that I had this made for you. Remember me when you use it, and remember, too, that you will be the weapon closest to my hand if you learn well what is set before you."

He went back to his beshani and was mobbed with excited questions by his friends. He showed them the knife and gave away his boots. After a while they realized that he wanted to be quiet and left him alone. Teyala came in and rubbed his sore back with soothing ointment.

"You know they are all completely in awe of you now, little brother. You'd better dance and joke with them and stuff your face at this feast if you don't want to be a stranger for life. What do you think I did when it appeared that I would be a pallantai before I grew hair under my arms? I made sure my beshani stayed friends, that's what. You don't want to be the world's greatest solo fighter, believe me. Brother's arm is the best shield, as they say. Now, go on out there and sing for them. Do the one about Shorne being dragged by her horse. They like that one."

4

Ten days later the pallantai left for the summer. They rode out in a blaze of color and glory, all wearing their finest clothes and every jewel and piece of gold they owned. The horses' manes were braided with ribbons and bells, and each rider's long hair was pinned in the war knot and wound with silk head cloths. Those left behind drummed for them until the sound of their going faded and even the earth beneath their feet was still.

Rellai had painted lucky marks on Deronh's face himself: a circle around one eye, that he go and return still beholding the light of the sun; a crescent for the other, that the Lady be with him and give him sight in the dark. His voice shook as he said the parting words. But Deronh smiled. The paint made him look like a spotted pony.

"I've had good dreams, little brother," he said. "Don't chew your tether over me. I'll be back."

He rode away as joyfully as a boy going out to play shoot-the-hoop.

Rellai knew that they would wear their ornaments all day. But when they stopped at the first campfire, they would stow them soberly away, not to be worn until battle was joined at the end of the journey. Then they would ride into the fight decked out as if they were going to a party. The jewels always came back, even when their owners did not. There was no lowlander alive who could boast that he had spoiled the Riders.

When they were gone, the Rock seemed very quiet. Grandmother and her weavers were left with the older captains chosen by lot to safeguard them through the summer. Children, mothers in the last months of bearing, and those too old or crippled to ride stayed, too. The young pallantai in their third year of war training were the entire force Grandmother was left to command, and they swaggered nervously about, always armed. They had looked forward to the summer for a long time, but now that it had come they were afraid. Once, just once in all remembered time, a lowlander force had surprised and killed a group of the People in the summer season. The young ones had driven a hard bargain for their lives, but in the end they had all gone down. When the Riders had come home and found them dead, they had made the first winter war in history, and the last. Tyrel had been the last of the young pallantai to die, and Tyrel's Song honored forever her death and the accounting made for it. No one sang Tyrel's Song in the summer.

For the younger children nothing much changed. They spent more time swimming and holding secret dances and games in their private meeting places. Goats had to be milked and beans had to be picked, herbs had to be dried, berries hunted, and the cities of the bees bravely besieged and looted. There were colts to catch and tame. Their training went on, and with the weather fair, there were all-day runs and hunting trips far out into the northern plains beyond the Rock.

For Rellai, everything had changed. He still joined in some of the things he had always done. He ran to the practice ground every morning with the others. But he did not have much time for gathering honey or teasing goats. He spent his days with the old ones, practicing over and over again things that he saw no use for. It was completely unlike weapon training. On the practice ground, he saw immediately the point of what was done. And if he did not see, the demonstration was painfully quick and clear. In his new training, one flicker of Shernhalla's eyebrow was the equivalent of being dumped ignominiously in the dirt. But Rellai seldom got even that much reaction. He was often hungry, often cold, and often aching all over from exercises that seemed easy but left him trembling and wet with sweat before he was allowed to stop.

He was also lonely. There were a few others who were going barefoot, but none he had known well. They were older. He still slept and ate with his beshani, when he was allowed to sleep and eat, and he joined in the games of love that they were beginning to play. As long as it was a game, it pleased him. He loved his mastery over their senses. It was like riding one of Deronh's horses, he thought. He could guess what handling each one needed and give the deft cues that turned all that power in the direction he wanted it to go. But once he had learned to do that, he was shocked to discover how much more they wanted from him. In a glance or a caress, they showed him their most secret fears and wishes. If he slept too many nights with his beshani, he woke up sweating from dreams of being pinned down and smothered.

Teyala scolded him kindly from time to time. "You're always in such a lather," she said. "Shying at every twig and stone. Go easy."

He slid his fingers along her smooth brown arm and tried to slip his hand under her vest, but she elbowed him out of the way.

"No thanks, little brother," she said. "You're a big boy now. Some things you have to take care of yourself."

So he went back to Shernhalla and threw himself into his work again. The old one did not want love or understanding from him—only maximum effort. To be with Shernhalla was safe and reassuring, like stepping up onto smooth rock after struggling through thickets of flowering thorns.

He found comfort also in the great plain itself. He could run for hours over hills where there were no trails, leaving all the confusing voices of his brothers behind. The wind's large voice was restful to his ears, though it spoke to him in no words he could understand. The dun sameness of the hillsides held endless variety for attentive eyes.

But in a far valley where he was sure he was alone, he began to notice signs of some other presence. At first the signs were small: a broken twig or an almost invisible parting of the grass, as if some creature man-high had passed through not long before. He searched the hillsides. He spent hours lying motionless among the rocks, waiting for the presence to become careless and show itself. But he never saw anything. The signs became more obvious, as if someone were mocking him. He found tufts of grass tied in knots; he found riverside pebbles dropped on crests of hills where no river had ever flowed.

Finally he decided to take a water skin and some bread and keep watch until he found out who was interfering with his solitude. He spent most of a long hot day listening to flies buzz and watching ants crawl up and down grass stems. Nothing else moved. When the sun descended from the peak of the sky and the shadows began to change, a small breeze stirred. It brought him a scent he did not recognize. It was not the familiar Rider smell, but there was wool in it and some kind of herb that did not grow among the grasses he had been smelling all day. To be surprised from behind had become his worst fear. He scanned the area around him, but he could not see anything.

Something brushed his shoulder very gently, and he nearly jumped out of his skin. It was thistledown. Another puff of it floated by him. He knew there were no thistles there. He watched and saw another bit of down begin its lazy journey down the wind from a certain place not too far from him. It took him a long time to work his way carefully to the spot without revealing himself. He had his knife ready when he broke through the final screen of grasses.

"Greetings, brother," a voice said. "I've been watching you scurry around on your belly. You're hunting mice, maybe? But that's an awfully big knife for mice."

She was curled up comfortably in the grass. She seemed to be weaponless, and he recognized her as one of the others of his age—not from his own group, the Mane, but from the one called the Lightning.

"They call you Risse, the Arrow," he said. "Is that because you're so long and thin, or because you have such a sharp point to your tongue?" He was angry that she had been teasing him for so many days, and so successfully.

He remembered her as shy, but his jab did not seem to embarrass her. She stood up, grinning.

"Maybe because I'm so fast," she said. "Maybe because I fly unseen. I hear you think you can run."

He looked her over. She was a thin, bony girl, as tall as he was. She was barefoot, too, wearing nothing but a loose tunic that had never been fancy and had become the color of the earth.

"I think I can run as far as that tree over there without falling down," he said.

"Good, I'll come along and see," she said.

He put another knot in the strap to his water skin so that it would not bob around and began to run. He started off easily. She stayed with him, just behind his shoulder. He gradually increased his speed, but she did not fall back. Then he realized that she was forcing his pace, coming on behind him faster and faster. Suddenly she pulled even with him. She seemed to be all flying legs and arms. He strained to keep up with her, feeling his legs grow heavy and his heart laboring. Their hands slapped the tree trunk almost together, but hers was first.

"Well, you didn't fall down," she said when she caught her breath.

"Why didn't you challenge me on the practice ground, if you can run like that?" he asked. "Did you follow me around for a moon of days just for a race?"

"I didn't follow you. I was here first. I saw you jogging around as if you were the only colt in the valley, and I thought I'd let you know there was someone else. It's not my doing that it took so long for you to catch on."

"What do you do out here?" he asked.

She shrugged. "I learn from Mother-of-Horses. She has many lessons to teach."

Her fingers brushed his wrist as they walked, as if she would like to taste his thoughts before she said anything more.

"Sometimes I grow weary learning lessons of war. It is the life of the People, I know, and when the time comes I will try to honor my beshani. But out here in the grass I learn how many beings there are who live woven in one pattern. None of us would scatter a nest full of eggs or tear up a stalk of horsemint without reason. It's hard for me to believe that those out there are more different from us than a tame horse from a wild one. But I will uproot them from the earth like dry vines, I will gut them like fish.

"Well, I know it has to be done. But so many of the brothers think that's all there is in life. I like to be out here, where I can have these thoughts without offending, and where I can see beyond my horse's nose. Do you know how many different kinds of herbs and grasses there are? Even the healers don't know them all. This one, for instance."

She stooped and parted the grasses and came up with a small white flower. He recognized the sweet, dusty smell that he had first noticed on her.

"What does it do?" he asked.

"I don't know. Maybe nothing. It lives. It doesn't even have a name. But then again, maybe it is good for something. I've made tea from it. It tastes all right, but it's nothing special. I have seen goats hunting for it under the grass. Maybe it makes better milk.

"These are the things I would like to know, not how to split a man's heart with one blow or drive an arrow through his eye. But if I don't learn the language of arrows and edges, I'll never live to give this flower a name. So I practice. But when I can, I come out here by myself."

"Have you ever thought of becoming a healer?" Rellai asked her.

"You know how it is," she said wryly. "Grandmother catches your thoughts before you have them yourself. She called me to her one day and spoke about the healer way. But in the end, she let me go. She said, 'Little sapling, you are new wood to me. You need a few more seasons to show which way you will grow and what gifts you will bear us. I will tell them to let you run free, as long as you do well in your weapon training.'

"Now I've told you a long story. What tale will you give me in return?"

Rellai shook his head. He did not know what to say.

"You know they are calling you 'Little Knife.' They think Grandmother has seen a great warrior's destiny for you. Is that why you run out here day after day, head down, as if wolves were after you?"

"I think, like you, I am looking for things with no name," he said finally.

The wind was rising, sweetly cooling his sweaty face, and he heard the beginnings of a tune. Risse waited patiently for him to speak, and in a few minutes he sang it for her.

> I follow wild trails through the long grass.
> Where, you ask me?
> And I say
> Where the wind brings me thistledown
> And the smell of flowers.
> I go hunting weaponless in the long grass.
> What do you hunt? you ask me.
> And I say
> I am hunting the game no weapon can bring down
> And my snares are made of flowers.
> My heart is restless as the wind in the long grass.
> Why? you ask me.
> And I say
> I have lost my treasure in the long grass—
> My best arrow, never missing—
> It brings down only flowers.

Risse stared at him, but she did not look as pleased as he had hoped. She seemed troubled.

"Now I see what Grandmother has in mind for you," she said. "She gambles high when she sends that throat out among the sharp edges. But there is no need to prove it by making fun of me."

"Making fun?"

"It's well known that my sleeping place is not overcrowded," she said dryly. "Whereas our beautiful little singer is welcome under every cloak."

He reached for her hand and made her look at him.

"It would make me happy if you came to my sleeping place tonight," he said. It was surprising how much harder it was to speak than to sing.

At last she smiled at him, and he felt his heart expanding like the red glow of the sun on the horizon.

"Why not share my place instead?"

"Tell me where," he said.

"This great plain," she answered. "Nights are hot in the Rock, this time of the year. Mother-of-Horses will shelter us. I'll show you."

They turned away from the Rock, and he followed her through the grass.

Rellai woke from a light sleep; the moon was high in the sky. He stretched and laughed.

"What's the joke?" Risse asked sleepily.

"Me," he said. "I am. This boy who is so sure he knows everything and worries so hard about all those things he knows."

"And what are all these things you know so much about?"

"Love. I was sure I understood the game of delights, and I worried because it didn't make me happy."

"Well, you seem to have a certain grasp of the basics," she said judiciously. "You could learn something more without fear of excess." She imitated the weapon master's tone so exactly that he laughed again.

"I will come more often to the practice ground," he said.

5

Rellai had gone up to the hill above the grazing ground. From there he could look down on the People coming and going around the Rock as he imagined the Mountain Spirit might look down on them. There was joy because the Riders were home, but it was a subdued kind of joy. Until the autumn singing, until the dead had been praised and mourned and sung on their way, all the people walked lightly and kept their hearts quiet.

Rellai was grateful for those quiet days. He felt that the summer had gone by too fast. The wind had turned cold; it breathed down from Stormfather, where the snow was already falling. Rellai could feel it, though it no longer troubled him to be cold. He felt uneasy, as if time were moving him out of the warm shallows and into the full force of a cold current. He still had the winter to prepare; not until summer would he be called a pallantai. But looking down at his long legs, feeling the strength that had grown into his shoulders and his hands, he knew that his boyhood had passed with the summer.

An inquisitive colt came up behind him and pushed its nose against his neck.

"Run along, little brother," he said to it affectionately. "One of these days you'll stick that nose out and they'll put a halter on you." He put an arm over its withers, and they walked down together.

He found Risse busy checking the last brew of chah. Bread was baking on every hearth.

"The Singer is coming," she told him. "He'll be here before the night. We've started the fast."

Rellai wished momentarily that he had come down for lunch

but shrugged off the thought. A day's fast was no longer anything more than an inconvenience to him.

He wandered over to his own hearth. Deronh had washed his long hair and was brushing it with oil of horsemint and braiding it tightly. Rellai sat down next to him and started to braid at the back. He knew that Deronh's shoulder was stiff where he had broken it once and that he could never get his hair parted straight without help.

"Thanks, paliao," Deronh said. "But you'd better go take a currycomb to yourself. Shernhalla was looking for you—they want you to drum tonight. Your turn comes at twilight."

Rellai retired to his favorite sleeping place. He combed his hair, rubbed himself with sage leaves, and put on his best pants, but there was not much more he could do. He had the right to paint his scars, but he was the only young one to wear such honors, and it still made him uncomfortable to call attention to them.

Then he wandered around looking for something to do until sunset. All the pallantai were ostensibly preparing for the feast, but he could feel how they had withdrawn into themselves. Things would be happening that night that he did not understand. When he had been a child, he had enjoyed the excitement and endured the fasting without needing to understand. But he was not a child anymore.

He finally found work hauling and stacking wood for the bonfires. It was a hot and dirty job. By the time the fires were laid ready, the sun was getting low, and Rellai was covered with dust again. He walked the horses he had been using down to the river and washed them off, then plunged in himself. The sound of drumming already throbbed in the air as he hurried back to the Rock.

Three huge bonfires burned on the dancing ground. Behind them, the Rock loomed like a shadow against the bonfire glowing in the sky. All the people of the Rock ranged themselves in ranks around the fires, with the Asharya at their head in a high seat built for her by the first fire. At the high end of the circle, firelight gleamed on gold and picked out the flash of ear jewels and arm rings. At the far end, the young ones of Rellai's year took their places more humbly. They were unscarred and unadorned, but they were ready to dance. And high above them, on the seamed flanks of the Rock, the children huddled together in aeries. They watched everything, unseen except when the flames flared up and were reflected for a moment from their lively eyes.

Rellai remembered how it had been to perch up there. At first the children would be giddy with excitement, pushing and shoving their beshani for the best places, cheering in hoarse whispers for their favorite heroes. The boldest among them would climb down at times to dance at the edge of the circle in imitation of their elders. But toward midnight the pallantai would slip away by twos and threes to their own hearths, taking with them the young ones who would enter into their fellowship that night. The drumming and the singing would continue, but hoarse and low, like the heart and breath of a sleeper who dreamed and was ill at ease. The red coals burned low, and the dancers moved like shadows in and out of the dying flame. That was the time for small ones to huddle close to each other's warmth and to close their eyes against the sharp stars and the fires of sorrow. In the early dawn they would wake and creep stiffly down off the Rock to stretch out in the grass and wait for the sun to warm them.

As Rellai stepped into the circle of firelight, he imagined the children up there whispering his name to each other, and the thought gave him courage. He walked between the fires and sat down next to the drummer he was to relieve. She slipped the padded stick into his hand, and he took up the rhythm without missing a beat.

The *toman*, the great drums, faced each other in the center of the circle. They kept up a steady, deep-voiced rumble that seemed to shake the earth. Rellai felt as if he were sitting in the clouds, listening to the thunder roll. He was not lead drum but second, and the leader across from him let him know with hand signals when the beat would change so that they were always in unison. Around them, skillful players improvised on the lighter descant drums.

The beat quickened, and the pallantai raised a shout as the Singer came forward and struck the first chord on his *thamla*. Rellai stared at him. In times past, he had been outside the circle with the children and had never seen the Singer so close. He was an old man, and lean, but still well muscled and straight under the black ashes he was painted with. His face, too, was marked with black. His gray eyes and white hair gleamed strangely in contrast; to Rellai he looked like a burnt-out brand with white ash still glowing at its tip. His name was Hilurin. He came to them every winter and went away in the spring. He was not really one of them, but it had not occurred to Rellai before to wonder why.

The Singer looked right at him; with a graceful and deliberate gesture, he raised his hand and traced the red death mark painted across his face. Rellai's left hand went on drumming, but his right moved as if by itself to the scar that marked his own face.

He knew what Hilurin was saying to him with that compelling look. "You and I are alike. I know you."

That frightened him very much, but he kept drumming.

And Hilurin's voice was like a strong silver thread that wove in and out among them and tied them all together. The chorus sang fast and deep like the sound of horses running all together, like Thunder River in spring, like wind on the mountain. Above the chorus, solo voices sounded in turn, high and clear as hawks calling above the bloody field or moonlight silvering the torn grass. They sorrowed for strength that had failed and grieved that what was most precious passed most swiftly. Sparks showered up as the fires collapsed inward, consumed in their own fierce burning, and the people danced as if that fire had taken hold in their hearts.

Rellai's eyes were open, but he did not see anything; his soul was running with the music. He forgot to look for the leader's signs. He knew with his own body when Hilurin would pause for breath and when the dancers would turn in their circle and go back. He was not aware that he had demanded another stick and was drumming two handed. He drummed till the sticks were slick in his hands and he had to shake his head impatiently to clear the drops away from his eyes. His relief came, but she left him alone until it was clear that he was tiring. Even then she had to touch his shoulder and speak his name before he came back to himself and relinquished the drums.

He could not rest or stand still. He let the ranks of the dancers close around him and began to dance, beating the earth with his feet as if it were a great drum that he could force to answer him.

He found himself next to Risse. The circle had grown much smaller, and the song had faded to a low, steady chant. He looked up at the stars. They seemed to have jumped halfway across the sky. While he stared up at them in surprise, she drew him aside, off the dancing ground.

"I thought you said you would dance only a few rounds tonight," she said.

"I lost track of the time," he stammered. "How did it get so late?"

"Well, you drummed through most of the second watch," she said. "Then you danced like spit on a griddle."

He was slick with sweat, and now that he had stopped moving, he felt the chill in the air.

"Come, it's late," she urged him. "The pallantai have all gone away. Let's climb up the Rock a little way and watch the fires die."

He followed her, but the recklessness was still on him. "I want to go all the way to the top tonight," he said.

Every child of the Rock climbed to the top once, just to see if it could be done. It was not impossible, but it was dangerous; in the dark, it was foolhardy. Risse followed him without argument.

"I hope you've outrun your shadow now," she said to him when they rolled onto the top, "because we have nowhere else to go unless you plan to grow wings and fly."

It was even colder up at the top. Rellai looked over the edge and saw the coals below twinkling like hosts of fireflies. Then he drew Risse down into the shelter of the rocks, out of the wind.

"You're soaking wet," she said. "Here, take my blanket."

"Hold me," he said. "My heart is cold, not my skin."

She pulled the blanket tight around both of them and waited for him to go on.

"The Singer looked at me in a way that frightened me," he said. His hand went to his face again, fingers along the scar, palm hiding his mouth. The gesture felt familiar, as if long ago he used to do it often.

"He made me remember that there was a time before I came here, that Deronh is not my father. And I felt that he caught me in a loop and bound me—binding so fine and light, it weighs nothing at all, but I'd cut myself to pieces if I tried to get loose. I entered into the song, and I was caught.

"It's fearful to be the Singer, Risse. His power is fearful. He can't help it, I suppose. Like the light—it only shows whatever is there, but there's no escaping it."

"You are not so unlike," Risse said gently. "Look how you have drawn me to you, how I follow you around fires and up walls. But it's not all bad, surely."

Rellai groaned. "Why do I have to be different, and why will no one tell me what I am? I look to Shernhalla for wisdom, and I get riddles."

"Maybe no one can tell you because no one knows," Risse

said. "Maybe this is why I love you more than all our beshani—because you are something growing wild that they have no name for. So for a little while I will be the only one who knows how to gather this flower."

He moved closer to her warmth, skin to skin. He felt all raw ends. Whatever was happening that night to the new pallantai stung him, drove him. It curled and whispered around him like fire around dry wood.

He stood up and took off the rest of his clothes, pulled Risse to her feet, and yanked the ties of her shirt loose.

"What are you doing?" she protested. "You know this isn't done tonight."

"I don't know what is done tonight, and I don't care," he said. "Look—now there's nothing between us and the stars. The Lady has left her lamp burning for us. If we do wrong, let her tell us."

They measured themselves against each other as they had often done in play—lip to lip, breast to breast, palm to palm. And he breathed the scent of her breath and felt her long fingers twine with his till he was not sure which was which. As had happened once when he stood palm to palm with Deronh, a door opened and he stepped through, and this time there was no one to set him outside again. He felt her catch her breath as she realized what was happening—or was that half protest his? He did not know. Bright images and memories fluttered around him too swiftly to be grasped. In the midst of them they clung together like eagles coupling in midair, beating their wings together. There was terror in that fierce delight; he could not tell if they were plunging or soaring, but they were heading straight into the sun.

After some time, he knew that he was back in his own skin; he looked down at himself and flexed his muscles curiously to be sure of it.

"Are you all right?" he asked her shyly. "I didn't know that would happen."

She gave him a bold and reckless grin. "I am as you are, my *kamarh*. As you should know. For my life and your life run on the same rein now."

"Yes," he said. "Well, I hope they won't be too unhappy with us."

There was enough light to see by as they stiffly descended from the heights. Rellai looked down on her and felt perfectly happy. He expected a difficult talk with Shernhalla, but he did not really care. They could not undo what he had done.

He saluted the Asharya respectfully, though she appeared to have fallen asleep in her chair, but inside himself he was grinning.

She said herself that you can't carry fire in a basket, he thought. The Singer was the last one awake, as he was supposed to be. Playing the last chords of his dawn song, he looked up and smiled at them. And Rellai remembered that he was not really sure just what he had done.

He and Risse found a sunny place and lay down for a second sleep. Most of the Rock had gone to sleep. They were weary and sore; they were hungry and thirsty. They slept until the shadows grew long again. Then they wandered down to the river and refreshed themselves and gathered again around the fires. Again the Singer came to them between the fires, but his song was a solo, clear and sweet as the first starlight. *"Elassyon, elenyon,"* he sang. "Be at peace, be free." Tears flowed as they sang it back to him, but they were tears of release. They put their grief behind them. They could once again speak the names of the dead, for the dead had passed into memory.

The time had come to celebrate: time to eat and drink and get drunk, time to dance and make love and be glad they had come home alive. The party went on long into the next day. Around midafternoon, when the last of the drink was gone, those who could still move cleaned up the remnants of the feast and swept the dancing ground. The children, in a state of high excitement, ran wild over the prostrate bodies of their elders, making rude jokes and giggling. Finally they all retired, glad to be back in their own blankets for one night at least.

The scolding Rellai expected never came. Several hands of days after the feast, Deronh met him by the river.

"I hear you've found your kamarh," he said. "You should tell your friends so we could give you our good wishes."

"I didn't know," Rellai stammered.

"Surely," Deronh said, "when two people find themselves so matched that they want to share all their mind, what else can it be?"

"I thought Grandmother had to approve; I thought you had to make promises. That's why I didn't tell you, barasha. I thought you'd be angry because we're not pallantai yet; we're too young."

Deronh shrugged. "We call it 'making promises,' but the

promises are already made in your heart. The rest is just words. But it's like this: Your lives run on one rein, as long as you go on living. And there's much pain in that, not just joy. That's why it's better to have your barhedonh around you before you find your partner. You'll need them when the hard times come. Like Lindhal and Rekke. I have needed them."

"Deronh, why didn't you make them your partners? After you lost the first one, I mean."

Deronh fumbled for words. "No one can tell you what it is to lose your kamarh. When they are hurt, you feel it. When they die . . . next year you will understand it better. Maybe it would have been better to choose again, but I could not do it."

He looked modestly at the ground. "I never really expected to live so long afterward, or maybe I would have chosen otherwise. Ah, this is all foolishness, this talk of mine about the future. I came here to talk about happiness and good wishes."

He reached inside his shirt and handed Rellai an ornament on a gold chain. The pendant was carved ivory in the form of a white horse.

"It's Shiya," Rellai said.

"She gave this to me," Deronh said. "It is yours now. You will give it to Risse. You will tell her that Deronh wishes to honor the friend of the son he loves."

He went away quietly, and Rellai knew that he did not want to be followed.

He did see Shernhalla later.

"The Singer wants you," the old one said abruptly. "He wants to teach you music."

Rellai felt the healer's sharp eye on him and kept his face quiet.

"I told him no," Shernhalla continued. Rellai gathered from the tone that the Singer had been insistent but had been definitely refused. "I have no wish to make a healer of you. I am not a fool. You are too young. You have no quietness in you. You must go out and test yourself with war. But I have no wish to throw you away, either. You must spend this winter with weapons, so that you will come back to us. Blades before music. So I told him."

"I understand," Rellai murmured.

He was very happy to spend his winter in weapon training. Risse, who had never shone on the practice ground, worked with him and became skillful. She also spent much time with Rekke, practicing with the bow.

Rellai found that she seemed to be always with him, even when she was not by his side. He began to know her thoughts and memories as he knew his own. And though he was not fully aware of it, her presence supported him, bracing him against the confusing babble of others' minds. She gave him peace, as if she held her cloak between him and the wind.

But he also tasted in some small measure the truth of Deronh's words. As winter waned and the pallantai began to talk about the coming season, he saw that she was unhappy. She never showed it, but he felt it aching like a bruise. Finally he asked her about it, gently stroking her arm, and the answer leapt clearly into his mind even before she had spoken.

He saw her just as she had been: a small child screaming by the door of a burning house. The frightening blood-spattered objects around her had been her parents and brothers. Strange, monster shapes galloped through the smoke and carried her away from everything she had known.

"So when I think of war, I see only those things," she confessed. "I see the children dying in their mothers' arms. I could never set fire to a farm. I would die first. I am afraid I will disgrace us with my poor-spiritedness, but I can't change this."

"Do we make war on children?" Rellai protested in outrage. "There is a place for us: Like wolves, we destroy those who are unfit to live. The People rescued you; they never set that fire. It is soldiers we will kill—like those who hurt you."

He could feel her bracing herself.

"Yes," she said. "I would like to kill soldiers—many of them. Ten for my father, ten for my mother. And for my brothers. And I will kill several of them in memory of my dog. He was a good dog, and they rode him down just for fun. I saw."

"I will be honored to help you make them a deathgift," Rellai said. "Are you happier now?"

She laughed, half-ruefully. "I must be, if only because you want it so much. Yes, we will become great together, and that will make me happy."

6

On the morning when the pallantai finally set out, Rellai's heart was bursting with happiness. It was hard for him to believe that he was not just imagining what he had wanted for so long. He had a new shirt on, and new boots that felt very strange after three years of going barefoot. Every few minutes he checked his knives. They were all in place. The great sword and his bow waited with his saddle and bridle.

At last they were loaded and mounted, and the time for parting came. But to Rellai, it was no parting. Everyone he loved was with him. He and Risse and Belian had been asked to ride with the Lightning. But he could see Deronh and the rest of his old barhedonh, the Mane, not far away. Teyala was with Crimsonvine, just ahead of him. All the other beshani of his year were scattered through the host. When he came back, it would be as part of the barhedonh. He would be with his family always then, and only death would take him from his brothers. He was not leaving home. He *was* home.

As they rode, it became apparent that they were bearing south, toward Wolf Pass, and the Riders began to guess that they might be taking service with one of the southern cities that year. That caused much comment and discussion. Even after the outrage committed against Rellai, the people of the Rock had ridden most often for Erech Tolanh, the Iron City, which was the closest to them as the crow flies. They had never fought directly against it.

They stopped for the evening meal an hour's ride from the pass, in a spot where they would see anyone crossing from the other side as soon as they began to descend. It was early enough in the year that there was still plenty of snow on the slopes, and the air was cold after the sun went down.

When they had eaten and put away their finery in favor of warm, plain-colored clothing, Verenya—Grandmother's summer captain—stood up to tell them their destination.

They were riding to the City of Gulls, to lift the siege laid against it by its southern neighbor, the City on the Rivermouth. They would be paid partly by the City of Gulls, if they succeeded in lifting the siege, and partly by Hadhla, master of the Iron City, who had maintained the City of Gulls as his ally. They would depend on Hadhla's soldiers to engage the main force of the besiegers while the People descended on them in the slashing attack for which they were famous. Their first assignment, before they reached the city, was to scout southward for supply trains destined for the besiegers and to eliminate them.

The Rivermouth forces would be expecting an attack from the north. The best trail from Wolf Pass led east and south, directly to the City of Gulls. The only other trail hugged the steep wall of the White Curtain, running directly south. If they took that way, they would come down off the mountain wall some distance south of the besieged city, at a point where they could overlook and ambush any traffic going toward it from that direction. It sounded simple.

Shin, one of the Lightning's oldest fighters, laughed softly without opening his mouth. "Ever been down the Curtain, yearlings?" he asked the three of them.

"As it happens, no," Belian replied politely, ignoring the fact that Shin knew perfectly well that he had never been east of the mountains.

"Well, I have," Shin said. "Twice. They don't call old Verenya 'Iron Belly' for nothing. You'd better pray your horses have eyes in their feet."

They started out the next morning while it was still dark. They would cross the pass before dawn and descend the highest section of the trail, where they were most vulnerable to discovery, with the earliest light. They rode slowly through the shadowy dusk, reaching the crest of the pass just as the east flushed with a rosy glow. Verenya had timed the ride well. Looking back, Rellai could see the broad dark swath their hooves had cut through the frosty dew on the grass. It would vanish as soon as the sun rose over the shoulder of the mountain. Ahead of them, the trail seemed to drop over the edge of a sheer cliff.

They all dismounted, watered their horses, checked their

girths, and made sure the packhorses' loads were tightly strapped down. Then they lined up in order, each barhedonh with a seasoned rider at its head and its captain last to keep an eye on the whole group. With Verenya leading, the riders disappeared over the cliff edge one by one.

When Rellai's turn came, he saw that the trail was not quite as steep as it seemed. It zigzagged back and forth across the wall. The ledge was wide enough to be safe in most places, provided the rider kept his horse to the outer edge and avoided bumping into the wall. His bay paused for a moment on the edge, tested its footing, and snorted, then climbed over and down.

Rellai experienced a dizzying exaltation as the pale rock wall rose higher and higher beside him. The dawn light cast a wash of color over the wall and sharply picked out the form of every rock in the trail. He could see nothing but sky on his left. He heard the riders below him on the trail, but he could not see them. He looked down on hawks lazily circling, seeking their morning meal.

The excitement faded after several hours on the trail. The sun rose up above them and beat down fiercely; its heat radiated from the rock as if from the wall of an oven. Rellai heard the bay mumbling its bit, dry-mouthed, and saw the flakes of foam drying around its mouth. The riders' legs ached from leaning back against the slope. The horses slipped on loose stones and had to check themselves continually to keep their balance. Their shoulders quivered with the strain. But Verenya would not allow any pause. He knew they were pinned against the cliff like ants on a wall. They had to get down before they were seen.

The only rest came when they found parts of the trail that were partially blocked by rockfalls or washed out by the spring rains. None of those points was impassable, but none could be ridden over. They had to dismount and lead the horses carefully across them, hoping their mounts were trailwise enough to pick their way across and not try to jump the gap. They lost a pack mare at one such washout. She felt the rocks slip as she tried to cross, panicked, and leapt for the higher ground. There was no firm footing for her on the other side, and she slid down the wall. The boy who had been leading her climbed as far down the cliff as he could and leaned out precariously, looking for her. She seemed to be badly hurt; she could not get to her feet, and if she had, she would only have fallen farther. The captain signed for the boy to get his bow and shoot her. The boy rode on silently, with tears streaking his dusty face.

Unexpectedly, in the late morning, they came to the foot of the wall. There was a half hour's difficulty descending the scree slope where all the debris from the cliff had piled up. Then they were among rocky hills that seemed good, even ground by comparison. Rellai looked up and saw the wall they had come down rearing up to heaven, with their trail clinging to it frail as a thread. They rode till they came to a secure place, a hanging valley that overlooked most of the hills southward while providing plenty of cover for them. Verenya ordered guards posted, and the rest of them rolled off their horses for a rest. There was nothing moving that they could see; the chances were good that they had not been observed.

"Lucky for us none of those rockfalls were bad enough to block the trail," Belian remarked. "I don't think we could have turned around."

Shin looked at him as if he were crazy. "They call him Iron Belly, not Iron Head," he said. "You don't think he'd take that kind of a chance, do you? He sent three riders to check out this trail before the snow had melted. Fortunately, they all came back and reported that once the blizzards stopped, the trail should be passable. Otherwise Grandmother would have told the city master to go ride a stick."

"It wasn't you who made that report by any chance, was it, barasha?" Risse asked. But Shin just shrugged, straight-faced, and would not say anything.

They spent the rest of the day working their way slowly east through the hills. By dusk, they were close enough to the South Road that they could not light any fires. They rubbed the horses down thoroughly and gave them a little grain; they had not brought much with them, but they expected to get more once they encountered the supply train. Then they ate some bread and dried meat and curled up in their blankets. Rellai still could not shake the feeling that they were on another practice trip.

In the morning, Verenya sent out several groups of light riders mounted on fast horses. All were good archers, but they had instructions to avoid being seen at all costs and, if seen, to flee any contact. They were to search for any sign of Rivermouth forces while the main body of the host continued more slowly southward. Rellai watched the scouts enviously. He wished that he had been chosen.

"There's no need to envy them," Shin told him somewhat

grimly. "Your turn is coming. With that big horse and your strong arms, you're the kind that gets saved for dessert—the best for last, eh? The long sword's your weapon, isn't it? Yes, after we've tickled them up with hit-and-runs and flights of arrows, you'll be sent to bull your way through the line."

He pulled up his sleeves and showed Rellai his arms, crossed and recrossed with old cuts.

"You'll have the Lady's own plenty of scars, surely. Now, what are you looking so worried about? You're a good little fighter—you'll survive. Barring bad luck, of course."

By nightfall, scouts rode back in with news that the supply train had been sighted just as they had hoped. It was moving slowly along the road, guarded by a small force of mounted soldiers and by archers riding in the wagons. Clearly, they had not expected to meet the Riders so early in the year or so far south. Verenya's strategy had worked so far.

Since the wagons would be stopping for the night, the Riders calmly lay down to rest also. They were up before dawn again, moving down to the road to find a good place for an ambush. There were plenty of crooked little draws and concealing hills from which they could watch unseen. Verenya sent a small group across the road to create a cross fire. Once settled in their positions, they let the horses browse a bit and found themselves a bite to eat. At the speed the wagons moved, it would take an hour or two for the supply train to pass them, and meanwhile there was nothing to do.

Rellai looked down at the road with interest. It was perfectly flat and smooth, completely without cover. One could see down it for miles. To one of the People, it looked like a death trap. Anyone foolish enough to travel on such a thing really was asking to be shot at.

Soon the best and sharpest ears in the group reported a rumble of wagons approaching. The archers stood ready, and the rest of the Riders stood to their horses' heads. Back in the third rank, Rellai could not see anything, but he saw the arrows fly and heard the screams and shouts of dismay from the road. Many of the guards fell in that first flight of arrows. Then the archers stood aside and let the Riders charge through.

It was so much less orderly than the practice games. At first Rellai could see only the rumps and backs of the Riders ahead of him. Everyone shouted at the top of his lungs, and the horses screamed. There was a lot of jostling and shoving. Rellai crashed into his first soldier before he realized that the man was an enemy. Both their horses staggered, and the soldier's stroke went wide—luckily, since Rellai was in no position to parry. He struck back clumsily and knocked the soldier off his horse but could not see if he had killed him; the press carried him on past. He pulled the bay's head around to get to the edge of the melee, and a man on foot stabbed at him with a pike. The bay reared up, and Rellai slashed the man's neck without thinking twice. He heard someone yelling that they should pull back and did so. Then it seemed that the fight was over.

All around the wagons, the soldiers lay dead. Some of them had been shot in the wagons and sprawled across their seats. Some of them were still alive; the Riders went around and cut their throats. They shoved the dead drivers out of their places and cut the horses loose from their harnesses. Then they paused to bind up their own wounds. No one had been killed; no one had been seriously hurt. Two horses had been lamed by cuts and had to be put down, causing great sadness to their riders. But the humans had fairly minor gashes and bruises, which had only to be cleansed with fiery chah and bandaged.

They loaded as much of the supplies as they could onto the extra horses and drove them north into the hills again till they came to a good, defensible resting place. Then Verenya granted time for them to feast on the southern food: wheat bread, salted beef, and dried fruits from the rich orchards of the coasts.

Rellai had expected more of a celebration. Instead, they sat around munching their food soberly though appreciatively. Shin laughed silently at the idea that it was a victory feast.

"Victory? This is closer to disgrace. We outnumbered them. Of course we won. It was like shooting ducks on a pond. The shame of it is that we should lose two good horses. We should have come out of that fight unmarked. Some people were sloppy. Speaking of which, young hero, you nearly made me cry when I saw you charging into battle waving your blade around like a five-year-old with a wooden toy. You were completely uncovered. I nearly shot you myself just to teach you a lesson. Do you want us to sing in the death song for Rellai that he died playing the fool?"

Rellai looked humbly at the ground. "Elder brother, I'll be more careful next time," he murmured.

"This isn't a game, you know," Shin remarked. Then, dismissing the subject, he cut himself another tasty slice of smoked meat.

7

The journey to the besieged city would take another three or four days. They could have gone faster by the road, but it was possible that the Rivermouth would be sending more parties of reinforcements, so they stayed off it. On the third day they crossed the road and bore east toward the coast. The men of the Iron City had engaged the besiegers on the north; the Riders had to fall on the enemy from the south, where they would be least protected. Thus, the main force of the Rivermouth would be caught between the anvil of the Iron City and the hammer of the Riders' charge.

Rellai was pleased when at last he had a chance to go out with a scouting party. None of the small scouting groups had reported seeing anything, but it was pleasant to ride freely, exploring the country, rather than keep to the steady pace of the host and the packhorses. If they saw a hare or a prairie hen, they would shoot at it for sport. Fresh meat was always welcome, even though they had plenty of food at the moment. Risse and Belian were with him, along with Shin to keep an eye on them, and Dai and Moros, two of Teyala's friends from the Crimsonvine.

They had just been running down a hare; Dai and Risse had both missed a shot at it. Then the lucky creature had escaped by running into a patch of thorns they could not ride through. They pulled up their horses, laughing and teasing each other. But the horses seemed restless; they pricked up their ears, and Rellai's bay stallion snorted. Shin threw himself off his horse and pressed his ear to the earth.

"Get to cover," he ordered them. "Someone's coming."

They led the horses quickly into the ravine where the thornbushes grew. Shin and Rellai crawled up the ravine to the hilltop and searched the terrain before them. About a mile away they saw a small group of horsemen, maybe five or six, like their own.

"What do we do?" Rellai asked. "We could wait till they pass by and ride back. They'll never spot us."

Shin shook his head. "No, the earth speaks of more riders than these. There is a large force coming, not too far off. These are like us, a scouting party. If we let them pass, they may happen on our main force. They may already have found our trail. We'll be within sight of the city walls today. If any of them get back to their masters, they could fall on us from the south and catch us between themselves and the city. We must try to draw them after us."

"Do we kill them?" Rellai asked.

"Not if we don't have to," Shin said. "I'm hoping they'll follow us closer in, where our friends can help us. It would be best if we could take them alive and find out what mischief they are up to. But whatever happens, they must not live to carry back news."

They led their horses up to the hilltop; when they saw that the others could see them, they mounted in haste as if surprised and galloped north and west. The others followed. The Riders let the soldiers catch up little by little to encourage them. It seemed like a game. Shin paced them cleverly, keeping the soldiers just out of bowshot but not so far behind that they would give up.

"I'm going to have to let them catch up," Shin called. "I hoped we'd be in range of Ilin's group by now, but I don't see them. It's up to us."

Guiding the horses with their knees, they put arrows on the strings. As the soldiers came within range, they exchanged shots, but to no effect on either side. The soldiers drew rein slightly and dropped back. Then they called out—a hail to someone ahead. Turning again in his saddle, Rellai saw another group of soldiers on their left flank, closing rapidly.

Then they were running for their lives. The horses were tiring. Risse and Dai brought up the rear, firing shots to keep their pursuers off a little longer. At that range they had little chance of wounding anyone seriously. With a lucky shot, Risse brought down one of the horses, and its rider went flying. But they were still outnumbered two to one.

Shin pointed to a bluff half a mile away. "We'll make a stand there,'' he panted. ''Get something at our back—best we can do.''

The horses labored up the slope, their coats dark with sweat. With a sharp cry of pain, Belian jerked in his saddle, an arrow through his thigh. He clung to the horse's mane but was jolted off and fell. Rellai slid to the ground, pulling his own mount to a halt. He slung Belian over his horse and ran beside him, steadying him so that he would not fall off again. He was somewhat protected by the horses that ran on either side of him, but his lungs were bursting as he staggered toward the bluff and his back winced from the thought of sharp edges coming ever nearer. At last he caught up with the others. He dumped his friend near a heap of rocks and hacked frantically at the arrow. When he pushed the shaft through, the leg bled freely, but it was not the bright red blood that meant sudden death.

Belian's eyes were bright with shock, but he asked for his bow. ''I have to return their gift,'' he whispered.

They ground-tied the horses in front of them to give them a few more minutes of protection.

''The horses!'' Shin ordered them. ''Shoot their horses!''

The return volley struck Rellai's big bay, which plunged and screamed, then crumpled to earth with blood pouring from his nostrils.

''Forgive me, brother,'' Rellai called. He stretched one hand earthward in a wordless prayer. They had so few arrows left that he had given his to Risse, who was the better archer. He waited, gripping his short spear, looking for one of them to come close enough to provide him with a target.

The enemies rode back and forth, taunting them, dashing closer to take a shot and then retreating out of range. They wore heavy breastplates and leather leg guards, making them hard to wound. The Riders had only a few rocks and the bodies of their horses to protect them.

Dai and Risse brought down two more, but Belian never had a chance to pay the soldiers back for his wound. He was too weak to loose an arrow. Then both sides had run out of arrows.

''Heads up, they're coming in,'' Shin roared. They closed together in a desperate little knot as the soldiers charged them.

It hurt Rellai to kill the horses, but he had to bring the Riders down. Teeth bared in furious disgust, he tore open two of them with his spear and saw them reel and founder. Moros dragged one of the Riders down with a weighted thong and stabbed him when he fell. Rellai stabbed the other under the edge of his cuirass.

But Belian had been ridden down, and when Rellai yelled for Shin, he got no answer. Out of the corner of his eye, he saw the old fighter fall forward over Belian's body. Dai and Moros were dueling fiercely with the three who had killed Shin. They were pressed shoulder to shoulder; Moros seemed unable to use one arm. Rellai heard Risse's shout of triumph as she cut down her opponent. Maybe they could still do it. But the next thing he heard was a cry of anguish from Dai. Moros had fallen. Dai attacked her slayer in fury, but he was unprotected from the soldier on the left. He staggered back against the wall and slid to the ground, badly wounded. Two of the three soldiers he had been fighting turned on Risse. The other one seemed to be hurt. He backed away from them, toward his horse.

Time seemed to be stretching out for Rellai; he had time to see what was going to happen, yet however fast he moved, he was too slow to catch up with his anticipations. He saw with anguish that Risse was trying to fight two at once; the sword was not her weapon, and she was already tired. There was no room to maneuver. The two who were attacking him had pressed in so close that the fight had become a kind of deadly shoving match; no one had room to swing properly. It would have been funny, but Risse's ragged breathing was loud in his ears, and he could not get to her.

He set his back against the wall and held them off at arm's length, his long blade threatening them so they paused for a moment. The glint of their eyes, dark and bright beyond the sword blade, triggered something in his mind. The ragged edges of his awareness gathered into one smooth flame. He seemed to be looking down on the fight from a height. From up there he could see how all the moves could make a single pattern. There was a fault line, as in shaping flint. He had only to strike it and the sharp edge would shape itself to his direction. He understood that he was experiencing *harrarne*, the other way of seeing which he had entered before only at rare times, with Shernhalla. He felt calm and watchful. He needed only the wit to pick the right moment.

He feinted once at the man on his left, then lunged with his short spear at the one on the right. It did not matter where he hit him as long as he hit him. The spear point ripped the soldier's thigh; he screamed and staggered back. And Rellai, still stretched low, sliced the other soldier's knee with a backhand stroke. His leg gave way, and Rellai killed him with a second blow.

But the one he had speared was not finished yet. As Rellai straightened up, the soldier gathered himself for a last effort and drove his dagger upward. Rellai saw it coming and felt as if he were struggling for an endless age to pull himself up and out of the way before he felt the shock of the blade biting into his flesh. The soldier had tried for the blow that slips under the ribs to the heart. He had missed his aim, but Rellai staggered, right hand convulsively pressed to the wound just below his ribs. He saw the bigger of the two soldiers fighting Risse turn to him with a triumphant look. He had no strength left to fight with. He knew he would have one move, and only one. Completely open to attack, he looked straight into his enemy's hatefully pleased eyes. He felt the muscles gathering to strike, felt his enemy commit himself to the blow, and swayed just the hairbreadth needed to let it pass harmlessly by. He did not so much strike in return as hold out his blade in the right place for it to slice open the white neck between beard and collar. The soldier seemed to lean into the blow like an animal led to the slaughterer.

Then Rellai let himself slip to his knees. Surely Risse could deal with the other one. She had to.

He heard the desperate gasps and grunts of struggle, the clash of metal on metal, and the scuffling of feet in the gravel, then her victorious "hai!" With great effort, he raised his head to look at her. For a moment he met her eyes, still bright with determination. Then her eyes went blank: still open but with all thought gone. She sprawled on the ground beside him, the feathered butt of a deep-driven arrow in the hollow between her breasts. He felt a bursting agony in his own chest and tasted blood, then his sight seemed to darken and he understood nothing. The darkness retreated and left him staring at the dust; he was supporting himself with his right hand. Another arrow shaft transfixed his right shoulder, but he could not feel anything there. He looked up.

Beyond the dead horses and the bodies of his friends, the last soldier stood with a third salvaged arrow on the string, ready to finish his kill. He would escape; he would return to his host to boast that he had shot down the flower of the People shamefully, like so many rabbits. Rellai strained for the one eye of clarity among the roaring currents that threatened to sweep him away.

He still had one move left. One move; there was always just one move more.

He slipped the *khalestri*, the last weapon, from the back of his neck. The little gilded knife flew like a swallow diving and buried itself in the enemy's eye.

It was very quiet then. Rellai wanted to rest, but he still had things to do. He had to gather up his friends' weapons and ornaments so that the enemy would not dishonor them. He started to crawl toward Belian. Dragging himself just a few feet made his head swim. He stopped and thought and realized that he could not do it. He had strength for one more thing. He apologized to his friends' spirits in case they were still near him and begged them to help him. He knew they would understand that he had to warn the pallantai, and he could not go without Risse.

He sat up and whistled; the effort made him cough, which hurt him very much. But Shin's horse came to the call, and one of the other loose horses followed, nervously anxious for company. Rellai was glad of that; the heavy saddle the soldiers used would make his job easier.

He lifted Risse and laid her across the saddle. He did not try to touch the arrow. The horse snorted and danced with fear at the strange burden, and Rellai clung to the pommel, struggling to remain conscious. He secured her to the horse as well as he could. He had to pause after every movement to catch his breath and let the darkness clear from his eyes. He called Shin's horse by name. It bowed as low as it could for him. He leaned across its back and somehow managed to get into the saddle. He passed out while he was doing it, but when he opened his eyes, the horse was still standing patiently immobile, making sure that he did not fall off. Reaching behind him, he fumbled the burden straps loose and used them to tie himself in the saddle. He knotted the reins of both horses to his mount's neck strap. Lying forward over its neck, he told it to go.

It started off and slowed to a stop several times. It knew he was not secure in the saddle. He was too weak to smack its flanks. He laid one hand against its warm, smoothly pulsing neck.

"Go, brother," he begged. "Please go home."

He pictured the camp and the other horses, grass and grain and kindly hands. He renewed the memory of slashing, sharp, frightening things and the evil smell of blood all around.

"Run!" he whispered. And the horse began to run.

Rellai endured, still willing the horse to run; each step was like another knife driven into his ribs. Soon he was delirious and would have dismounted, but he could no longer remember clearly how to do it. All he wanted was to lie still. It got dark and stayed dark, even when he had his eyes open. There was nothing left but pain and hanging on.

When he felt hands loosing him and lifting him off the horse, he struggled faintly. There was torchlight in his eyes; he could not get away from it. They lowered him to the ground; it hurt in spite of their gentleness, but at least he was not moving anymore.

"Ayei, Taurhalisos!" someone exclaimed softly. "It's Deronh's Rellai."

"Is he living?" another voice asked. "Where are the others, then?"

Rellai tried to answer them, but he could not.

A new pair of hands came then, hands that were cool and light and moved swiftly over his body, bringing some ease with them. They held a sodden cloth to his lips and let a cold, bitter-tasting drink wet his mouth.

"Warn Verenya," he whispered. "There are soldiers coming from the sea."

He thought he had spoken, but he looked at the faces around him and they seemed not to have understood. Despairing, he struggled to form the words again. But one of those hands rested on his lips.

The other voices seemed very far away, but the new voice spoke as warmly and clearly as if it were within him, not just in his ears.

"Don't try to talk, little brother," it said. "I can take your thoughts, if you permit."

It was an effort to keep his thoughts focused, but not as hard as moving his lips. He relived the terrible things he had seen, and when it was done, he found that some of the pain had been drawn from him. He was very tired.

"Messengers have gone to Verenya to tell him all," the voice said. "You have finished your work. Now we are going to move you into the camp and care for you."

But still he clung to the healer's hand. "Risse," he said.

"You brought her back to her people," the voice said. "Surely you have done well. Surely you have made yourself very tall. Now rest, brave rider, heart brother of ours."

The praise was good, but there was so much sadness and pity winding around it. He did not know why. All for a few wounds. But he was very tired.

He was never really awake for a long time after that. People made him drink things; they did things to him that hurt. He seemed to be riding all the time, even in his sleep. He was looking for Risse. He could not find her. It seemed to be twilight always on the plains where he was riding, and there was always a fiery ache in his side. He was tired almost to death and wanted to lie still, but he could not stop. He tried to explain this to the dream people, but they always faded away again and left him alone on the great plain.

At last he came back from a long quiet sleep and found himself lying on the ground. A fire flickered before his eyes. He explored the unusual sensation he felt and realized that it was comfort. He was warm, and he did not hurt. He lay still so as not to awaken the pain again and tried to think where he might be. He smelled horses and heard the quiet sounds of them moving around. He heard voices and thought they were speaking Thanha. But he could have been anywhere. Soft footsteps approached him.

A familiar impression shaped itself in his mind, unmistakable as the smell of horsemint. "Deronh," he whispered.

Then the Rider had flung himself on the ground next to Rellai and was hugging his legs, still afraid to touch his bandaged torso and shoulders. Deronh was beaming as Rellai had never seen him do before.

"It's true, then, it's true, you really will come back to us," Deronh said. "Healers don't lie, but it's been so long that you lay without speaking, without moving. After every fight I feared I'd come back and find you gone."

"How long?" Rellai asked.

"The Lady's lamp has come and gone and come again. And each day was a hundred years of winter."

Rellai basked in the warmth of Deronh's presence. But there was something missing.

"Risse," he said. "I must go to her. Or is she already well enough to travel? She doesn't seem to be here."

Deronh's whole body winced with anguish, giving Rellai an answer he refused before it could be spoken.

"No!" he cried. "It can't be. I brought her back!"

"You brought her body back, to be given back to earth by her own people. It was all we could do. She had taken the Road to the North. No one comes back after an arrow through the heart. Think, paliao, and you will know she is dead."

"No," Rellai cried again. And in his heart he struck Deronh for telling him that. His weak arm barely moved, but Deronh felt the blow. And Rellai felt Deronh's great sorrow and understood that it was true: Risse was dead.

"I'm sorry," he mumbled. "Forgive me, I didn't mean it." He hardly knew what he was saying. But Deronh forgave the insult instantly, as he would have forgiven a colt that kicked because the girth pinched.

He pressed Rellai's hands to his face, and Rellai felt the tears falling on them.

"I would have spared you this, paliao," Deronh said. "If only I could. It is very hard. When you lay wounded and sick with fever, some people said to me that we should not trouble you further, that your heart was on the road already and we should let you go. But I begged leave not to go with the war host, and I sat with you day and night until you began to mend a little. I am like you, you see. I could not let go of one that I love."

Rellai let his fingers weave into Deronh's rough mane and was a little comforted. But when the healer came to him and wanted him to eat, he could not do it. He drank a little tea with honey, but the thought of food made him sick. He turned his face away and watched the grass moving in the wind. He could not think ahead. His mind only journeyed back over the plain to where Risse lay. He would never see her grave. It lay somewhere under the long grass.

He heard them talking about him, but he did not pay much attention. One day Deronh showed up with a bucket of water and one of the twisted-grass strops they used for washing down the horses.

"Sit up," Deronh said firmly. "You need to get cleaned up."

"Why?" Rellai protested.

"To show respect," Deronh said, sitting him up and propping his back against rolled saddle blankets. "Your hair should be cut, anyway, and it's a good thing. You could never get the knots out of it now."

He had warmed the water, but Rellai's teeth chattered by the time he had finished. His head felt strangely light and cool after the long hair had been cut short. With Deronh's help, he donned his new clothes and wrapped himself in his cloak to get warm.

"I'll tell them you're ready now," Deronh said.

"Wait. Who?"

But Deronh had gone.

Rellai sat up as well as he could as the others approached. First came Alvala of the Waterbird. Her hair had been cropped, too.

"My thanks are due to you, Rellai," she said formally. "You slew the slayer of Risse, the child of my heart. Her honors were few, for she was very young. Yet I beg you to accept this in memory of her. And when you are healed, together we will make her a deathgift."

She kissed him and moved on, leaving the little ivory horse in his hands.

Those who had been closest to Belian and to Dai and Moros followed her. They laid precious ornaments in his lap and kissed him, begging him to help avenge their dead. The last was Verenya himself. He had dressed in his best; knotted around his graying hair was the head cloth Grandmother had woven with her own hands. He put around Rellai's neck a chain of heavy gold worth twenty horses in the city where it had been made.

"Shin and I were beshani, many summers ago," he said. "He did not die alone; he had good brothers around him. And the one who spilled his blood will never boast of it. These things ease my heart. Later we will eat together, and you will tell me how my brother died. And when you have healed, together we will make him a deathgift."

The kiss he gave Rellai had the weight of the gold in it: a gift and a burden at once. When they had gone, Rellai sat with head bowed, searching for strength within himself. The honors laid on him could not be refused. He would have to set his feet once more on the paths the living followed, though it seemed to him that there was only weariness before him.

Deronh came back with a bowl in his hand. "I leave you for a moment and you collect all kinds of useless trifles," he teased, but Rellai could see that he was very proud.

"Now eat something. You look like last year's ribs, all chewed clean of meat." Rellai found that now he could eat.

8

He was back on a horse within a week. The healers watched him carefully, but when his breathing remained sound and he did not begin to cough blood, they let him do as he liked. At first he was so weak that he could scarcely hold up the reins. He rode a little way from the camp to exercise alone with his weapons. He was ashamed to be seen in his condition.

Deronh told him about the aftermath of his ride. They had sent messengers to let Hadhla know they were delayed and had laid an ambush for the soldiers from the Rivermouth.

"They came by sea from the harbor at the river mouth," Deronh said. "That was bold—loading horses onto ships. But they couldn't send a large force that way. We outnumbered them again. Even so it was not an easy victory. Since they didn't have to carry their own weapons all the way, they armed themselves heavily. Even the horses wore metal. And they were well trained. They fought well. If they had caught us by surprise, with more enemies at our backs, we would have lost much blood. As it was, we destroyed them, but they spoiled our attack on the siege force. Hadhla didn't get his lightning strike. We have been harrying them, dividing their attention and cutting off their supplies. When Hadhla thinks they are weak enough, we'll attack them again in force."

"That battle I will ride in," Rellai said.

Deronh looked up for a moment from the bridle he was repairing but did not say anything. Rellai understood from his reaction that he was no longer a young one in their eyes. They might fear for him, but they would not try to turn him aside.

He was well enough to ride in a night raid a couple of weeks later. They did not have to do much fighting; they had some of Hadhla's spies to guide them through the trenches and caltrops. Then they mounted and galloped through the tents, shooting fire arrows into them so that when Hadhla's ground forces arrived, the camp was pandemonium. It also occurred to Rellai to cut the picket ropes as he went by, and the others who followed him stampeded the extra horses. They pulled back quickly and reassembled on the plains outside to enjoy the spectacle of panicked men and horses colliding in the flame-lit dark.

Afterward, he could not sleep for a long time because of the twitching and aching of his strained muscles. But he had stayed on and done what was necessary. He drove himself even harder, hefting his sword till his arms felt like wet rawhide. It was lucky that he had taken the arrow in his right arm; it hampered him in using his bow more than anything else, and he did not want to ride with the archers in the next fight.

Summer drew on; the grasses flowered, and the damp ground dried hard and dusty. The unaccustomed heat of the south beat down on them till they felt like bread loaves baking on a hot rock. The Riders began to chafe and grumble and spent their evenings throwing the seven bones and their days riding races, betting away the spoils they would win if they ever put an end to the tedium. One stifling afternoon, messengers came from Hadhla's camp.

"I've heard there's sickness among the siege forces," Deronh said. "Could be this is Hadhla's time. Hope so. I'm tired to death of sitting here."

"That big man speaks for Hadhla; he's no errand runner," Rellai said. "He had gold around his neck and signets on his fingers, and he walked like a captain. They are talking about something important."

The lowlanders stayed in Verenya's tent for a long time. After they left, runners came around and told the Riders to gather at the evening fire for news.

The word was that they would mount a full-scale attack in two days' time. The rumor was correct; the springs that the Rivermouth soldiers had been depending on had dried in the hot weather. The water was scant and foul, and there was much sickness running through their camp. Conditions in the besieged city were becoming unbearable, too; Hadhla had decided that the siege must be broken.

The Riders were cheerful at the thought of action. They were suddenly busy taking care of all the repairs and improvements that they had been putting off. But Rellai thought that Verenya had looked grim as he told them the news.

"He knows it won't be easy, that's all." Deronh shrugged. "Those people have their backs to the wall now. They're already dying of sickness. If they let us break through, they'll be slaughtered. So they'll fight to the bitter end. They've got nothing to lose.

"Also, Verenya knows that the city master will spare his own at our expense whenever he can. But it doesn't matter. Verenya won't throw us away. The rest is just fighting."

As Rellai checked and rechecked his tack and weapons, he thought of Shin and missed him. He missed Belian, too. For a moment the memory of Risse brushed his mind, and the strength seemed to drain from his arms. He clung to his horse's mane until the feeling passed. Then he went back to checking the horse's hooves for stones. There was a taste of blood in his mouth, and he found that he had bitten into his lip, but he could not remember why.

The battle began before dawn. Rellai left behind his bow and his light spears. He had the short stabbing spear, the long sword, and his body knives. He found himself in the first rank, riding with the heavyweights, with scarred warriors of Shin's age and those younger fighters who were big and reckless. Down the line he saw Lindhal, mounted on the brother to his own big bay that was dead.

They left their fires burning to give them a few extra minutes before the watchers in the siege army realized that they were not in camp. Some of Hadhla's men came with them bearing planks to help them get over the trenches before the enemy lines. Once there, they abandoned any attempt at secrecy. They poured over the ditches in full cry, some of them disregarding the planks and leaping across. By the time they reached level ground, the defenders were scrambling from their tents. They formed a line that was ragged at first but strengthened rapidly until it was many men deep.

Against that dim mass, indistinct in the gloom, the Riders hurled themselves as if at a wall. Their archers rode on the flank with a covering volley, but as soon as the charge broke against the enemy ranks, they had to cease fire. It was impossible to tell friend from foe in the tricky early light. Hacking his way through the enemy, Rellai found himself swallowed up and surrounded. Only his mount's bucking and kicking kept him from being stabbed in the back. The others, wiser than he, had avoided being drawn in. He was on his own.

Fast as he cut them down, new heads rose like mushrooms out of the mist. His arms wearied and ached; his sword hilt was slippery. He could not see any way to get out of the situation except to outlast them, and he was not sure he could do that. They kept trying to kill his horse, and he knew that he would be dead as soon as they got him on the ground. He pulled his mount back on its haunches, forehooves flailing, and sliced at the soldier who had tried to slip under the horse's belly. As he pushed ahead into the space he had just cleared, he spotted another horseman ahead of him. In the growing light, he could see that it was not one of his people. The man wore a breastplate with an unfamiliar design.

Rellai decided that the man made as good a mark as any. With renewed determination he spurred onward. The horseman was surrounded by a guard of men better armed and arrayed than the others. When they spotted Rellai, they immediately went for him. There were five, and two of them had long pikes that kept them beyond his reach. He was jockeying furiously for position, trying to dodge the pikemen while one corner of his mind reflected calmly that this had been a mistake, when a well-angled arrow felled one of his opponents. The archers could see to aim again, and some friend of his among them had seen him and risked a shot. Rellai knocked aside the first pike and trampled the man wielding it. The second pikeman was hampered by his own comrades. He had no helmet, and Rellai cleaved his skull in passing and wrenched his horse around to face them again. He found that he had come to the edge of the crowd, and there was room to turn.

There was also room for the enemy horseman to charge him, scattering the foot soldiers from his path. Rellai caught a blow on his sword that jarred his bones to the shoulder, but with his right hand he planted the spear in the enemy's thigh. No green soldier, the man reeled but turned his mount and prepared to meet another charge. Rellai turned faster; he drove his horse brutally into the other and smote the rider down by main force. The man was dragged a few steps as his spur caught in the stirrup, then his horse plunged free and left him lying motionless on the ground. With regret, Rellai realized that he would have to leave his spear lying there, too; he dared not dismount to retrieve it. He caught up with the riderless horse and found a spare lance sheathed behind the saddle. It was not as sweet in the hand as his spear, but it would do. He heard hallooing nearby and saw a small group of Riders coming toward him.

"What took you so long?" he shouted. "I thought I was going to have to mow down the whole host by myself."

"You're lost," they jeered in return. "The real action was all back there, after you left."

Gratefully, he closed up and rode along with them. He realized that he was dripping with sweat. He had no idea how long the time had been; by the look of the sun, they had been fighting for a couple of hours.

The foot soldiers they saw ran from them; some of them did not run fast enough. The Riders worked their way back toward their starting point, hoping to meet one of the captains who could tell them what was happening. The camp was strangely silent. Most of the fighting seemed to be over, and there were many dead lying on the ground.

"Look, the roan stallion over there," one of them called. "That must be Varo from the Crimsonvine. He'll know."

Varo hailed them as they caught up with him.

"Heavy riders who aren't hurt are re-forming over there by the tents," he said. "Hadhla is pinned down over in East Camp by the last big company these people have. What's left of this lot has surrendered. Get over to the east and break their backs, and we will have earned our pay for the year."

Rellai did not like how weak he felt. He denied the weariness and reached for his strength in the way Shernhalla had taught him. He felt his heartbeat steady down; his arms and legs tingled and then felt very light. His head cleared, and everything he saw became as sharp and bright as the patterns in a weaving. The tiredness was still within him, but only as a faint warning, letting him know that his new energy would not last forever. He was in harrarne, the hunter's mind. It amazed him that he could do it deliberately. He was grateful for Shernhalla's endless pitting of him against hunger, cold, and repetition. He had not known before that he was learning a weapon skill, but now he held the weapon in his hand.

They heard the shouting and confusion of battle from a long way off. A pitiful remnant of mounted soldiers met them and tried to hold them off the beleaguered siege troops, but the Riders crashed through them and galloped on. They hit the infantry like an avalanche, at full speed, and cut them down like reapers in a ripe field. The Riders whooped and screamed, and dust rose in clouds and caked in their hair and on their horses' flanks.

The faces of the men they trampled were masks of dirt set with red-rimmed eyes and white teeth. Rellai felt the sting of various minor cuts and blows, but nothing really seemed to touch him.

Shin was wrong, he thought. It is a game.

The game was soon over. The remnants of the infantry backed together, shouting something in Giristiyah. At first Rellai paid no attention, but the words were familiar and he suddenly recognized them from boys' fights long ago.

"It's surrender," he shouted. "They want to give up."

Some of the Riders laughed.

"Tell them we'll take them one on one if they don't want to die like animals," Varo said. "They can't surrender to us. We don't have any use for slaves."

Hadhla apparently did, though. One of his aides arrived on horseback in a great hurry and barked something at the enemy soldiers, who promptly threw down their weapons.

"Thank you very much, we'll take charge of this," he said to Varo.

Rellai wondered if Varo was going to kill him, but the Rider thought better of it. He slowly turned his back on the city man without appearing to have heard him. There was utter contempt in the gesture, but Hadhla's servant took no notice of it.

It seemed the battle was over. They moved back toward the city gate where Verenya had set up a lance and was gathering the Riders back together. A troop of archers passed them going the other way.

"Hai, Rellai!" one of them called. "We're going down the road to hunt strays. Want to come?"

"I don't have my bow," he called back.

"We'll find you one," she said. "There's plenty of weapons the owners have no more use for."

He caught a stray horse, left his own with Varo's band, and went after them. It was strange to ride in the heavy war saddle. He got a captured bow, too, longer and heavier than what he was used to. It was awkward on horseback but powerful. They followed the fleeing soldiers down the road, shooting at them, and he practiced till his aim was accurate. They could have killed them all, but Rellai suddenly wearied of the game.

"There's no honor in this," he said. "Killing sheep is harder."

He pulled up and let the column go. Some of the others continued in pursuit, but most of them caught Rellai's mood and stopped. They went slowly back down the road, stripping the bodies of gold and good weapons. Rellai counted at least a dozen he had killed there himself. He had a good bundle of spoils.

When they returned to the field, they helped to gather up the dead and wounded and carry them back to the camp. They left it to Hadhla's men and the people from the newly freed city to kill the enemy wounded and those who lay sick in their tents. Verenya did not want his people to risk catching any of the lowland diseases.

Rellai rode back through the field looking for the horseman he had brought down. He was not sure how many of the men on foot he had killed, but he was curious about the rider. He cut the straps on the man's heavy breastplate and opened his shirt. There was some kind of amulet around his neck, which Rellai left alone, and also a pouch with gold and silver money in it. The coins had pictures on them. One had a ship, one had some kind of a fish, and one had a man's face. Rellai admired them and wondered how they had been able to make them so small. The man also wore many jewels, including rings with large clear stones and one of plain gold that had writing cut into it and was flat like a signet. Rellai gathered it all up and asked Varo to give it to Verenya. It seemed too much to carry around on his own person.

When he was done, he realized that he was tired. In fact, he was exhausted. His mouth was dry, and his clothes were damp and clammy. He was cold for the first time in weeks. He climbed back on the unfamiliar horse and rode slowly back to camp. There he took the horse down across the trampled mud to the little trickle of a stream where they watered and went a little way upstream for water to clean himself. He found that some other first-year Riders had tended his other horse for him, as if he were a seasoned warrior, and some hot stew was keeping for him in the bottom of the pot.

"What's your count?" someone asked him as he ate.

He thought back on his confused struggle in the mist and tried to reckon accurately. "Five hands that I know of," he said.

"Talao!" the questioner exclaimed.

"It's a start," Rellai said. They put his attitude down for modesty, a good thing in a young one.

When he had finished eating, word came that Verenya wanted to see him, and he went to the captain's tent.

Verenya was looking at the signet ring Rellai had taken.

"This man you killed was the second in rank of the siege

captains,'' he said. ''This ring gives him authority; he was brother to the master of the Rivermouth city. You bring down big game in your first hunt.''

''I hope I have not disturbed your councils in my ignorance,'' Rellai said. ''I thought only to bring him down because he was above the rest.''

Verenya dismissed the problem with a flick of his hand. ''We had no use for him. What Hadhla wants, let Hadhla hunt. It was well done. I will keep this ring, but the rest is yours, with much honor.''

Rellai bent his head, the brief Thanha sign for ''no.'' ''Keep it for the sake of that one who was your besha,'' he said. ''Make gifts in his name. I have no need for it.''

''I thought you would want it in memory of your own friend,'' Verenya said. ''But I thank you, if you are satisfied.''

Rellai's face was smooth as stone. ''When the smallest child in the Rock wears enemy gold in her name, then ask me if I am satisfied,'' he said.

Verenya watched him leave the tent. He had feared for the child Rellai, thinking him too dreamy, too sensitive to survive. But he had become all pallantai, skilled and fierce, and Verenya feared for him still. He thought of Grandmother's words: ''He is my gold knife, with an edge of steel.'' And he was glad that he was not Asharya. He had no wisdom for Rellai.

Rellai had found the wisdom at the edge of a blade and decided that was good enough. People waited by his sleeping place at night, and he enjoyed that game and slept warm afterward. A distance grew between him and the others of his age. They cared for his horse and brought him food as if he were their elder. His pack was heavy with gold and fine weapons. No one questioned his place when he rode in the front rank with the best of the pallantai. He danced with his enemies and killed them when the dance was over.

After the siege was settled, he went with the group that rode south and fought several skirmishes with the remnants of the Rivermouth forces. When the Rivermouth city was bottled up inside its gates, they left it to Hadhla's men and headed north again. It was time to take their pay and go home.

Rellai looked forward with the others to hot food, to plenty of water, to drinking around the fire and sleeping soft. Yet he felt curiously empty and without purpose once they had crossed the mountains into the safety of their own territory.

In the quiet days before the Singer came he took to hunting alone again. He went to the hills of long grass where he and Risse had wandered together. But when he saw the small white flowers blooming underfoot and smelled their elusive scent, he felt the slow pain tearing at his heart again. When he trod on them, he felt like a murderer. For the first time, the thought of the men he had killed was a burden to him. He had blood on his hands and the taste of revenge in his mouth, and he did not feel at home in those hills anymore. He forded the river where the dark water growled among the stones and hunted in the broken country on the other side where no flowers grew.

He came in from the hunt one day and found Hilurin standing in the great hall with his baggage piled around him. To his surprise, the Singer recognized him.

"Ah, it's my namesake," he said. "Do you think you might do me the kindness to help me unpack these things?"

The Singer had a place apart, near Grandmother's. Like hers, it was a chamber truly separated from the hall, where there was privacy within walls. Rellai found it too quiet and too enclosed. When he had helped the Singer arrange his gear, the little room had become crowded. Yet in his own way the Singer lived as sparely as any of the People. His only possessions were the tools of his art: musical instruments, spare parts, writing materials. Rellai looked curiously at the books; he had never seen any in the Rock.

"Thanks, young man," Hilurin said. "Might I impose upon you further and ask for some tea? I'd be pleased to have you join me."

Rellai was inclined to take offense at being asked to run errands. But he reflected that he was still the youngest of the junior warriors and that it was hardly a disgrace to share tea with the Singer. What he truly resented was the hint of amusement in Hilurin's eyes, as if the Singer knew exactly what he was thinking and was simply trying him out like a new flute.

When Rellai put the bowl of tea in the Singer's hand, Hilurin raised it in courteous salute.

"Congratulations," he said. "The Asharya tells me the Crimsonvine would like you to be one of them. If you accept, Varo will have you as one of his own fellowship. You have done great things this summer."

Rellai bowed his head, thinking. That was the way it was always done. The captains went to Grandmother and discussed with her the placement of the young pallantai. Then the offer was made discreetly, so that no embarrassment to anyone would result if the arrangement did not work out. The Crimsonvine had a good name, and to be one of the dozen or so who slept and ate with its leader was a very great honor.

"Why are you telling me this?" Rellai asked bluntly. "Why are you the messenger?"

"Because I have a message of my own for you," the Singer answered. "Last year I wanted to teach you music. They told me you had yet to learn war. Now I think you have learned something about war. I have asked the Asharya to lend you to me this winter."

"I am grateful for the honor," Rellai said stiffly. "My thoughts now are about weapons. I think of killing men and taking what is theirs. I don't have any need for music."

The Singer did not seem at all insulted. "Don't decide yet," he said. "Wait until after the feast. Come and talk to me then."

"I'll do as you ask," Rellai said. "But I don't think my answer will change."

"Understood. Now there is one more thing. I can choose one to help me at the singing, to hold my cloak, to accompany me. I asked for you, and your Grandmother has granted my wish. The singing will be held in a hand of days. Come to me tomorrow and I will teach you what to do."

Rellai ran up to the grazing ground to settle his mind. He was angry that he had been given away to the stranger without his consent. Yet with the same hand, Grandmother had given him a good place among his people and great honor. He decided to serve the Singer with a good heart until after the feast. Then he could forget about the man. After he had become one of Varo's barhedonh, no one would be able to make him do what he did not want to do.

After the evening meal he sought out Varo to say that he would accept the offer. He had counted over the others in the fellowship. He liked them all well enough, though he knew them only as a child knew the elders who came and went. He looked curiously at them as he passed among them, wondering what it would be like to have them at his right and left hands for as long as he lived. They looked back with some amusement and moved courteously away so that he could speak with Varo alone.

Varo extended his hand silently, and Rellai touched palms with him. He liked what he saw in the older warrior: a certain graceful daring, a quick mind, boldness, yet not without subtlety. And not to be known all at once, either. Varo gently disengaged himself from Rellai's scrutiny. His name meant "shadow."

He offered Rellai chah, and Rellai was pleased that he had had some experience with the powerful drink during the summer campaign. He was able to swallow it without a blink.

"So you think you can live with us," Varo said.

Rellai gave the Thanha nod: a quick upward toss of the head.

"I hear that you will be helping the Singer on the night of the feast," Varo said. "We'll send for you when you are no longer needed there."

He dismissed Rellai with a touch of his hand. "Till the feast, then."

Rellai went out to the hills again. As he passed by the upper end of the hall, he heard music sounding faintly from the Singer's room. The tune paused, retraced itself thoughtfully, and continued again. Without sight of player or instrument, it sounded as if the notes were live things with a living will, shaping themselves as he listened. As he wandered, they kept returning to his mind, where they gradually took on new life and began shaping themselves into a new and different form.

On the night of the feast, the weather was uncertain. Shadows walked; flesh and blood turned insubstantial in the shifting light. Stars gleamed like curious eyes and then were hooded by thick veils of cloud. Restless winds tugged the flames high into the air and then beat them flat against the ground.

Rellai had taken off his shirt so that his scars would show. He was still shy of painting them. He hardly needed to; between the old ones on his back and the new ones still blue-white on his arms and belly, he looked as if he had been fighting for years. He shivered in the chilly wind, and the chains around his neck jingled and cast off sparks of firelight. A flash of long legs or a sweep of dark hair would catch his eye, and he would turn around with his heart jumping, to see nothing.

He was glad when the drumming started. He wanted to lose himself in the dancing. The others were there to grieve and to be healed. He did not want to feel anything.

The Singer came out to them. Rellai had helped him put on the black paint made of ashes and had taken his cloak for him. But the old man did not seem like the same person, with his lowland accent and his slightly ridiculous court mannerisms. There was a power in him.

Rellai danced hard, his eyes shut half the time, and did not know that he had come around to the head of the circle until someone put a willow branch into his hand. The long, whippy branch was painted red, and the Singer was striped with red where they had struck him with it, laying their sorrows on him. Rellai had never danced that part before, having lost no one and suffered no wounds. He stepped out to face the Singer; the old man looked him in the eye and sang out a line to him in challenge. The tune was the one that had haunted him for days.

The willow dropped from his hand unnoticed. The drummer's not as good as I was last year, he thought. Then he entered into the music and was lost. At first he and Hilurin flung the tune back and forth between them. Rellai could see the notes patterned like sparks against the darkness before they were sung, voice meeting voice like blade on blade in battle. Hilurin retreated and retreated until Rellai was singing alone. He had lost all awareness of himself. He lived in the lines of fire that the music drew for him. And then the pattern was complete and it was finished.

He was standing in the Singer's place. His chest was heaving; he was slick with sweat. And people were staring at him as if the Mountain Spirit were standing behind him: with fear and wonder, almost with adoration.

Someone held a cloak for him as if he had been the Singer. He turned to Hilurin, bewildered.

"You did well. Go on, now," the Singer whispered.

The two who had brought the cloak put their arms around Rellai's shoulders and drew him away. In his heightened state of awareness, he knew them by touch, without seeing them: Shallas and Nin, from the Crimsonvine. They took him into the darkness of the Rock. He could hear breathing. The spicy and throat-choking smell of *gebrith* smoke was thick in the air.

"Take," someone said. A pipe was put into his hands. He could see the ember glow for a moment as he drew on it. He choked and drew again. His head spun, and he felt as if he were floating. The others appeared to him like points of light, embers glowing in the dark. He could put a name to each one. They came in close to him and ringed him like a circle of fire. They touched his palms, and fire bloomed in his hands and trailed upward along his arms.

He woke up looking up at the sky. He was lying out in the grass. Someone had laid a blanket over him. He sat up on his elbow and grinned. There were a lot of other bodies scattered around him. The sun told him that it was still early in the morning. He had aches he could not recall acquiring, and he smelled strange to himself. He rubbed a hand across his chest and found that most of his ornaments were gone. He was wearing only the chain that Verenya had given him and his ivory horse. After thinking it over, he recalled giving the others away in the dance.

He saw Shallas slowly trudging up the hill toward him: a stocky, deliberate woman, one who never hurried herself but who could endure forever. She had been a farm woman until soldiers had killed her husband and carried her daughters away. They had left her for dead, but she had survived and headed slowly northward to join the People. She still limped. Rellai remembered the faces of her children as if he had known them all his life, and he could have found his way back to her farm without a wrong step.

She carried a jug in one hand. When she reached him, she poured liquid into a bowl and handed it to him.

"Tea," she said. "You'll need it."

He pushed aside the droplets of melted honeycomb that floated on top and drank. Scalding hot and very sweet, it revived him.

"Thanks," he muttered. He found it hard to look her in the face; he had remembered other things about the woman and the previous night that embarrassed him.

She went on her way. He was finishing the tea when Varo came and sat next to him. Rellai offered him the last few swallows in his bowl. Varo had dark circles under his eyes.

"That was a most unusual night," he said. "I have welcomed many brothers, but it was never quite like that." He fixed Rellai with a piercing look. "But you know that, don't you?" he asked. "You remember those times as well as I do."

"Not all," Rellai stammered. "Not everything. Only what was in your mind when—when I—and this doesn't always happen. After the singing, and the dancing, after the gebrith—that's different."

"Maybe," Varo said. "But I am not a fearful man, and I see danger in you. I think I am going to give you a new name. It's too confusing to have two people called Singer. You will be Khalle from now on—the Edge. Until you become Singer yourself."

It was a good name, a name with honor.

"I accept," Rellai said. "But I'm not going to be Singer."

Varo did not argue with him; he rose and led the way down to the river.

There they stripped him to his scarred skin and scrubbed him in the cold, purifying waters. All down the banks of the river the pallantai were washing themselves and putting aside the night. He became one among many, joined with them in the river. When he stepped out and put on the new clothes they had brought for him, he felt empty and clean and ready for a new name.

Then he went upstream and found the Singer. The old man was not supposed to be seen until the evening fires were lit. In courtesy, someone had to look after his needs until then. Everyone was still fasting, but a jug of tea and a blanket had been sent for the Singer.

"So, I can't call you 'namesake' anymore," he said. "You are Khalle now, I hear."

"A warrior name," Khalle said proudly.

"I wonder," the Singer said. " 'Edge' has more meanings than are found on a blade. At any rate, I will have the pleasure of your company for one more night. You will sing the Elassyon with me tonight. I am an old man. My voice might fail, and that would be a disgrace. With your assistance, no one will notice."

Once again Khalle was nearly provoked into rash words, but once again he yielded to the old man's wishes. Hilurin had washed off most of the body paint, but there were traces of black around his eyes and on his back where he had not been able to reach.

"If I am to stand beside you," Khalle said, "you'll have to get the soot off your face at least. With respect, barasha, it's back to the river for us."

The benefit of serving the Singer was that Khalle could be alone for a while. The old man sat wrapped in a blanket, either dozing or withdrawn into his own thoughts, and did not pester Khalle with any more probing or provoking questions. So Khalle curled up in the other blanket and rested, glad to be away from comment and curious eyes.

At dusk they returned to the Rock. Khalle looked over the Singer's shoulder, out past the fires into the shadows where the People gathered. The song of setting free was simple and time-hallowed. It had been the same for a hundred years. Khalle sang without thinking about it, letting his voice weave gently over and under the Singer's melody. As he sang, he became aware again of his brothers; they came to mind as faces flower out of darkness at the touch of firelight and fade again into shadow. He felt them opening to the touch of the music, felt their grief wash over him like the rush of shadows. And he drew them to himself with his voice and heart, into the harmony that existed for a breath, only as long as he was singing.

The music ended. People left the dancing ground quietly in little groups. Their faces were washed with tears, but there was peace on them. They were returning to their hearth fires, to each other's arms.

Khalle and the Singer were left standing alone.

"You don't cry for her," Hilurin said.

Khalle shook his head. "It's better if I don't think of her."

"When you sing, you think of her," Hilurin said gently. "That song you made last night—the one they're calling 'Lament for the Flowers'—they'll be singing it for a hundred years. When all the gold you won is lost under earth and the names of all the men you killed are forgotten, they will sing the lament, and it will ease their grief. And she will live in it—your voice and her memory, never parted.

"Now tonight, you changed nothing. The music stayed the same. But no one will ever sing it quite that way again. You can't not do it, do you see? No one can make you sing, but you have to sing."

"I understand," Khalle whispered. "You don't have to keep talking."

"All right, then. They're waiting for us inside. You will get an old man some wine, and then run and play. I'll have enough voices to help with the drinking songs without you."

9

After struggling against it for so long, Khalle spent the best winter he had ever had in the Singer's company. He learned that there was training for the voice as well as for the hand and eye. He learned to play the thamla to accompany himself. Drums he already knew; the Singer showed him something about the flute and the bowed *serian* that they danced to in the lowlands.

"But you won't use them much," he said. "Your gift is in your voice, and you can't sing and play these at the same time."

Hilurin taught him to read so that he could play the music from the books. Khalle never got to like reading, though. To him it seemed a strange and unnatural thing. The words and notes were nailed to the page like hides pegged down to dry. They had ceased to live.

Between learning all those things, keeping up with his weapon practice, and doing all the ordinary jobs that fell to one of the young pallantai, Khalle had no time to get bored that winter. He spent time among the horses with Deronh, and he hunted with his new barhedonh. But he always came back to the small room and the old man's music. Hilurin told him many stories about the world beyond the mountains, especially about the courts of the city masters and their captains. Of Hadhla especially he spoke, and the intrigues he had seen in the Iron City.

"Hadhla has a son, you know," he said one day. "The child was always sickly. Most people thought he wouldn't live to be a man. Now, one might surmise that such a bull-beast as Hadhla would have get everywhere, but apparently this was not the case. Still, a persistent rumor that could not be quenched held that he did have another son somewhere, a bastard born of a Somostai priestess, who abandoned the boy rather than turn him over to her clan.

"The strange thing is that the Somostai apparently believed this nonsense. When it seemed certain that the master's son—his name is Dona, by the way—would die of the lung sickness, they came to the master. They told him some cock-and-bull story about how the bastard child was sucking away the life that should have belonged to his true son and said if he didn't find the other one and turn it over to them, his son would die. I never did hear that they found another son. However, Dona did recover, and he's now—oh, a few years older than you, I'd say. Man-high, even for a lowlander, eh? Well, it just goes to show you must never take Somostai at face value. Their god does not condemn lies, only disobedience."

"Why are you telling me all this?" Khalle asked irritably. He hated thinking about the cities, hated the reminder that he had been born there and not in the Rock.

"There is more to being Singer than a sweet voice," Hilurin said. "Do not be childish. You cannot afford to ignore things because you find them distasteful. You must hear and remember everything. You are the Asharya's eyes and ears. You will let her decide what can be ignored. And after she has decided, you'll make the people understand, you'll give them one heart so they can move together.

"Now, pay attention. It's important for you to know more about the Somostai than your childhood superstitions. Have you ever wondered why they are tolerated in Erech Tolanh? Masters do not take kindly to powerful, secretive opponents—and the Somostai have often opposed Hadhla."

"I never think about these things," Khalle said proudly. "They are not necessary to a warrior." In spite of himself, he was beginning to be curious.

"Perhaps not, but someone has to do the thinking around here. Ignorance is nothing to be proud of. That is one thing you could learn from the Somostai."

Khalle was shocked. "I have nothing to learn from those evil animals!"

"Nonsense. Even an enemy can teach you. Gold is not the only spoil to be taken. That is precisely why Hadhla tolerates the Somostai. They have subtle and curious minds and have spent many lifetimes of men exploring the properties of metals and substances, and even of flesh and blood. Whatever they find out, they write down in one of those books you despise, until they have amassed a great store of knowledge. Some of that knowledge is very useful to the master.

"And they have been useful to us as well. When Hadhla wanted to make war on us, they dissuaded him. Not because they are friends of ours—but they are curious about us. They think we might be useful to them someday.

"Power is not in high walls and many soldiers. Power is in the pattern, and the Somostai understand the dance of power very well. If you wish to be useful to your people, you must try to learn that dance, too."

"Where did you learn so much about the city folk?" Khalle asked.

"Where do you think I spend my time when I'm not with you? Do you think I go to sleep in a cave? I am highly regarded in Erech Tolanh. They call me the Harper there, not the Singer. I have been Grandmother's eyes and ears there for many years. I tell you these things about the master and his son from personal observation—I know the boy. And it's important for you to remember this, even if you forget the rest: If Hadhla loves anything, he loves his son. This knowledge of his nature may be useful to you some day. And when he dies, the son himself will be for the Thanha to deal with. You must learn his moves, for he will be your adversary."

The Singer began to drill Khalle in reading an audience, in noticing the least change of expression or mood, and in the ways of shaping their response to flow in the direction he wanted. Using those techniques, Khalle learned that Hilurin hated the city master, too, and that the old man had learned something about the master's plans that frightened him. But Hilurin's way of thinking was not like the others, and Khalle was not able to discover what it was that the old man feared.

Days were lengthening, but the snow was still on the ground when the Singer called him away from the evening hearth.

"I'm going away tomorrow," he said abruptly. "There are horsemen coming with a message for the Asharya, and I will go back with them."

"But it's still winter," Khalle stammered. "Why are you going now?"

"These horsemen will carry an offer from a great lord to pay me well if I come to sing at his daughter's wedding," Hilurin said. "And if I go, I'll find out things about this summer that Grandmother needs to know. You must take great care of yourself this year. I won't be seeing you till the autumn, and there's so much for you to learn. If you get your throat cut now, I'll never forgive you."

"I'll help you pack," Khalle said, but the Singer waved him off.

"Go finish your meal. I'm not completely decrepit yet. I can manage. Don't worry, I won't leave without saying good-bye."

Khalle could see that Hilurin wanted to be alone, so he let him go.

He went up to the Singer's room when supper was over. But Hilurin was not there. He made himself comfortable and waited. It was dark when Hilurin finally showed up. Khalle heard him moving around, finding a candle.

"What are you doing here?" the Singer asked when it was lit.

"I wish you weren't going," Khalle said. "I never wanted to do this, and I haven't been so easy to teach. I wish now I'd listened to you better. I'll miss you."

"Oh, enough, enough," Hilurin said crossly. "I'm not headed for my funeral, you know. Save the sad songs till you need them."

He began shuffling through the papers on his shelf. "I'm leaving some of this music for you," he said. "You need the practice."

"Hilurin," Khalle said shyly.

"Well, what is it?"

"You never ask me for anything. Let me stay with you one night."

After one astonished look, the Singer came and sat down next to him. He heaved a long sigh as Khalle put his arms around him, and Khalle thought he was going to accept.

"No, no, and no," the Singer said. "First of all, I think it would be good for your character if someone says no to you, just once, so you'll know what it feels like. Secondly, you Riders are never more dangerous than in love. You would break my heart for sure, and I'm too old to get over it one more time. And thirdly, well, thirdly just because."

Khalle heard the pain in the old man's voice and tried to trace it to its source, thinking he might persuade him. Suddenly he sat bolt upright in shock.

"Grandmother!" he exclaimed. "You were her lover."

"You have astonished me twice in as many minutes," Hilurin

said. "How did you guess that? No, never mind. I suppose you couldn't explain it to me.

"Yes. I was born in the Rock, strange as that may seem to you. I had to leave, for reasons I will not explain just now, and don't try to find them. I don't want anyone but myself inside my head. That is one reason I left, I suppose."

Khalle settled down again, hoping he would go on. Hilurin absently stroked his hair.

"I am not able to be one with these people, not for long. Only in the music, for a time. I could not live with them year in and year out. I had to go away. But I cannot altogether leave them, either.

"You don't understand, do you? Maybe someday you will. One gets scars in this game as in any other."

Abruptly he pushed Khalle away.

"You are a terrible temptation," he said. "But I suppose it won't do to send you stumbling back to your hearth in the dark. You can stay if you promise to let me sleep. Kindly remember that I am an old man and need my rest."

The horsemen arrived at early dawn, before most people were awake. They were not invited to stay and showed no inclination to do so. They wore the hated armor of Hadhla's soldiers. Khalle felt sick at the sight of them. To his surprise, Hilurin greeted one of them warmly.

"Ah, young master," he said. "Come here. This is the youth I told you of."

The young man dismounted and put back his hood as he walked stiffly up to them. Khalle saw keen blue eyes, black curls cut short in lowlander fashion, and a head carried arrogantly high.

"This is Khalle, of the Crimsonvine. His gifts are many; do as he says and you may possibly survive the summer. Khalle, I leave him in your charge. Care for him as you love me."

He sprang onto his horse with the ease of a much younger man, and his escort moved out, leaving Khalle to stare at the stranger.

"You know my name. I do not know yours," he said. The stranger stared at him, and Khalle realized that Hilurin's last words had been spoken in Giristiyah. He switched languages.

"I am the master's son," the stranger replied. "They call me Dona."

"What are you doing here?" Khalle asked. His face betrayed nothing, but he was shocked.

"It has been custom, in some families, to send a son to hunt with the Riders for a summer," Dona replied somewhat stiffly. "I cannot say why, for I know nothing of your ways. The Harper tells me you are skilled in war. I am here at my father's wish. I had thought I was expected."

That reminded Khalle that courtesy was due even to the enemy. "No doubt you are expected, by others wiser than I," he said. "But since I am the first to welcome you, let me offer you some breakfast."

He sent the horse off with a small boy and took the stranger to a hearth and found him a hot drink and food.

Small children, who were always the first to wake up, hung around just out of reach but close enough for their murmured comments and laughter to be heard. The profound respect they had for Khalle did not extend to the stranger.

"What are they saying?" Dona asked.

"They talk about your clothing, your horse—him they like. They wonder why you cut your hair—if you are in mourning for someone, or if you did something bad and your people cut off your hair and threw you out. They think maybe that's why you are here."

"I cut my hair because I am no woman," Dona said angrily. "How is one to tell, among you?"

Shallas was passing by, on her way to breakfast. She snorted. "Come to my sleeping place tonight, pretty boy, and I'll show you," she said.

"See here, old mother—" Dona began.

"Who are you calling mother?" Shallas snarled. "Your mother has four feet and no manners."

Before Khalle could warn him, Dona lunged at her, and she threw him. He tried to get up, and she flipped him again. He landed hard and writhed silently for a minute until his breath came back.

He came back to Khalle and sat with lowered head. Everyone ignored him. That was truly an insult, but he did not have the sense to resent it.

When Shallas had finished eating, he approached her again but kept a respectful distance.

"I was rude and foolish," he said. "I hope to learn better."

Shallas still did not deign to address him, but she observed to a friend, "He is not stupid. There is hope for him."

Dona accepted that without pressing for further recognition.

"I cannot make my hair grow faster," he said to Khalle afterward, "but perhaps you would be so kind as to point out other things in need of alteration."

"Change your clothes," Khalle said. "Also clothe your tongue otherwise. Some of us speak your language, but it tastes bitter to us." He spoke harshly, but his heart was moved toward the stranger in curiosity and the beginnings of respect.

He took Dona to find spare clothes, and as they went he pointed out the names of people and things in Thanha, just as Teyala had led him about, long ago when he first had come to the Rock.

Grandmother sent for Dona as soon as he was dressed. Khalle waited; he felt responsible for the stranger because of what Hilurin had said. After some private conversation, Grandmother asked him to come in, too.

"Hilurin has asked me for a favor," she said. "We are to have a guest this summer. I need a brother to this guest, one who will be his right-hand friend and make him feel at home. Because Hilurin has been a teacher to both of you, I think you belong together."

Khalle was too well mannered to let his protest be heard, but his whole body shouted it for Grandmother to read. It was his first year as an adult, a year of learning to know his barhedonh, a year to enjoy his freedom. To spend it instead nursemaiding an ignorant, arrogant lowlander galled unbearably.

"I ask you because I have need of you," she said to him in Thanha. "We must not let this boy die. We would gain his father's hatred forever. Someone must be with him who can keep him safe."

"Why is it me?" Khalle asked.

"Because you are the best," she answered. "Others have wiser heads, more experience. But I have no other pallantai like you. If you fenced with the Soul-eater, your beshani would bet on you to win. You are true steel. You will never fail me. If you are with him, my heart will rest easy."

She touched his hair in a gesture of favor, and he could only bow his head.

"Honors and burdens are given with the same hand," she said gently. "They must weigh even in the end.

"Now, one thing: Do not make a guest of him. Hadhla wants him to learn of us. That suits his purpose. We will make him suit ours. Teach him, indeed. Make him one with us. Snare his spirit with our ways, so that even when he sits again in his father's city, he will never be able to leave us. Do you understand?"

"Understood," he said.

But the awe that fell on him in the presence of Grandmother's complex wisdom vanished as soon as he left her.

"Understand one thing," he said to Dona. "If I must look after you, you will do as I tell you. You will learn our speech; I am not going to be your interpreter. You will learn to live as we do. If that means scars, if that means cold and hunger, don't look to me. I'll keep you alive, but I won't make it easy."

He pulled off his shirt. "See these marks? That's what it cost me to be Thanha. It will cost you something, too."

He had worked himself into a passion. He would never have spoken so to one of his own. It would have meant blows between them. But Dona shamed him with a soft answer.

"*Peranne,*" he said. "I understand. You see? I've learned one word already. I won't be a burden to you for long."

Within a week, Dona's presence was not news anymore. He kept quiet and stayed in Khalle's shadow, and the others began to accept him. They called him Telhirya, "Young Wood," because he was as tall and thin as a willow whip. After the first day, he always kept his temper, so they stopped teasing him. But no one made friends with him. He was courteous but distant, and Khalle puzzled on how to fulfill the Asharya's command.

He tried Dona's skills and found them oddly inconsistent. Dona could ride passably well with his own high saddle and spade bit, but on the light Thanha horses he was stiff and uneasy. In swordplay it was the same: he had mastered every move with great correctness, but he had no grace or fire. Khalle could disarm him with ridiculous ease, because he always knew exactly what Dona would do next, and Dona could never anticipate Khalle's moves. He could hit a fixed target with a bow, but when it came to hunting rabbits, he seemed to lose his eye. Out in the hills he was deaf and dumb. His feet crunched heavily, without any sense of the ground. He walked bolt upright with no thought of cover, and trail marks and weather signs seemed invisible to him.

"Look with your eyes, man," Khalle said in exasperation. "A person would think you'd been locked up in a room all your life."

"That's not far from the truth," Dona said with his slow smile. "I have been always within walls, you know. Always guarded. I've had more teachers than a whore has glass beads around her neck, but I see they taught me precious little.

"Hardly their fault, though. I don't think I have it in me to be a warrior."

They were sitting by the hearth fire. Dona had a book of paper, like Hilurin's but empty inside. With a pen he sat and wrote in the book almost every night. He did it with a care and thought that he gave to nothing else.

"Why do you bother with that?" Khalle asked. "What does it say?"

"I write down what happens, so I can remember it when I am far away. Here—this part tells what you said to me today about how to find tracks on hard ground. I can read it again and think about it. Those letters there are your name."

"I know it, I can read," Khalle said. The letters stood out clear and black against the thick smooth paper. On the side of the page Dona had drawn a deer track, and below that Khalle recognized a sketch of his own face.

He tore the page out and thrust it into the fire. Fire wrote black and red letters on it, and his face crumpled and disappeared.

"You write down what I say, but you don't learn it," he said fiercely. "You want to take my face back to the city with you, shut up in this book, but in your heart there's nothing. What use is it for you to come here?"

"Give me a little time," Dona said.

"It isn't time you need. You can't buy knowledge from us piece by piece, like glass beads. You have to take what's offered."

But Dona stared into the fire in stubborn misery. Khalle left him and went to look for someone to spend the night with. He was angry without knowing why, and Hilurin was gone. There was no one to give him advice about the stranger.

10

Again the warriors went out very early in the spring. Hadhla's plan was to press the attack against the Rivermouth city. The Riders were to strike southward, opening up a path for Hadhla's army. His foot soldiers would begin a siege against the city while his cavalry and the Riders harassed the countryside around it and prevented any rescue. There was some fear that the Rivermouth might have hired the People of the River or the People of the North Hills to defend them; the People of the Rock disliked fighting against their cousins. But apparently both groups were busy with other concerns.

Khalle had a bad feeling about the master's son. Dona's skills had sharpened, but he still fought like a lowlander. He felt the cold keenly, and Khalle knew that he had trouble with his stomach over the Thanha diet of beans and horse milk.

Dona was all right in the first few skirmishes, raids on border patrols and isolated outposts, as they worked their way down into Rivermouth country. But the first time they ran into solid opposition, there was trouble.

A large troop of Rivermouth men stood off a group of Riders in a narrow valley. They had chosen their position well and hung on to it stubbornly. Hadhla's men had taken the long way around over the hills and were already pillaging the farmlands beyond. But still the Rivermouth soldiers stood their ground.

Khalle joined an attack against one end of the line and took Dona with him. After the first clash, he looked around and saw that the lowlander had jumped off his horse and was trading blows with a swordsman on the ground. More foot soldiers were gathering; soon he would be hopelessly outnumbered. The main charge had left them behind. As Khalle watched, someone with an ax dispatched Dona's horse. Swearing, Khalle wheeled and galloped back to the spot. He spent his throwing spears on soldiers who tried to cut down Dona from behind. He had to fight his way through in brutal haste, taking cuts and blows that never would have landed if he had not been in such a hurry. And when he got there, Dona hesitated, reluctant to retreat.

"Jump!" Khalle roared.

Dona grabbed the burden strap and managed to scramble up as Khalle spurred his lathered horse away from the battle. Their only immediate escape route was a precipitous climb up the side of the little valley. Thrown spears rattled around them.

"Your bow," Khalle yelled. "Put some fear into them if you don't want to be crowmeat."

They were pursued for some distance. Finally the cries behind them ceased. The sun was going down, and Khalle had no idea where the rest of the host had gone. The horse was limping.

"Get down," Khalle ordered. "He's strained himself badly. I have no desire to see him ruined because of your stupidity. We'll have to walk, and may the Lady cover us if we meet more of your lowlander friends!"

They found a path going back down. The foothills before them twinkled with dying fires. Off in the distance, Khalle could see a circle of fire that marked the Riders' camping place. The sweat started to dry, and he was chilly. He could feel Dona shivering beside him.

The breeze brought an acrid smell of smoke close by. The horse shied at a shape in the dark that turned out to be a broken gate. The house on the place had been burned, but they came to a shed that was intact.

"We might do better to rest up here until morning," Khalle suggested. "The horse may be all right then. And there's less chance we'll get caught when we can see than there is now that any fool could blunder into us on the road."

Dona made no objection. Khalle set him to build and tend a fire while he rubbed down the horse and foraged. There was enough hay scattered and trampled to make a meal or two. There was meat enough, too, from the animals that had been butchered and left. The farmer lay near his gutted barn. Khalle did not look for the rest of the family. He trudged back to the shed with his scavengings, his bruises aching sorely.

"What did you mean by that remark about my stupidity?" Dona asked him in a low voice.

"Let it lie," Khalle said. He wanted something to eat and a warm sleep. He did not want to talk.

"No. I want to know."

"I mean you fight like a little boy with a stick," Khalle said in exasperation. "Rule number one: Never get off the horse! You don't think. You act as if you are alone. If you want to get killed alone, that is your business. But you are going to get us both killed if you don't learn something about war. You have no sense-of-the-people at all. Why didn't you come when I called you? When a brother comes to rescue you, you run! You don't invite him to die with you."

"Sense-of-the-people!" Dona said. "Look around you. Is this what you call having a sense-of-the-people? These people are all dead, destroyed by you and your precious people. You are barbarians, renegades—" He had slipped into Giristiyah epithets in his anger.

"Renegades, are we?" Khalle shouted. "It wasn't us that did this. We only kill to live. It's you city people who slaughter for money, while we do the real fighting for you. We risk our lives so you can get rich. You are sheep-killing dogs, killers for sport! Yes, dogs and the relatives of dogs."

Dona laughed bitterly. "Watch your tongue, wild boy, when you speak of your father."

Khalle froze. "What do you mean?" he said quietly.

"Come on, don't play stupid, barasheli. You know as well as I do. Didn't Hilurin make sure we both knew? Have a little respect for your older brother."

Before Dona had finished speaking Khalle was in midair, yelling "No!" He landed on Dona and rolled him over and over, snarling like a wolf as he punched and kicked. Dona had barely enough skill to defend himself from the blows. Khalle fought with himself inwardly as he realized that he dared not kill or even seriously hurt the master's son. He lay half on top of Dona, arms and legs tangled, pushing the other's face into the dirt as he tried to master his rage.

"You're lying," he hissed. "Hilurin lied."

"I'm not—lying," Dona gasped. "The Harper doesn't. Has never lied to me. Heard stories. 'S true."

Khalle slammed Dona's head harder into the ground, hard enough to evoke a grunt of pain. It was as if his anger and his need were a knife that parted Dona's heart.

He sorted through scenes like a man running down a long

corridor past many rooms. They cut the little dog's throat, and warm blood sprayed over his face.

"Will he get well now?" his father's voice said from the shadows. But still he woke up choking, unable to breathe.

He lost the mock fight to the gatekeeper's son. The next day he watched as they beat his sword master till the man fell to the ground unconscious.

The Devourer's holy fire reflected in the staring eyes of the bound kid. Its hair was white; its perfect little hooves tried to kick, to leap away, but could not.

"Your father is the chosen one," the silky voice of the Somostai said. "You are highly favored by the Destroyer of Flesh. Your hand must make the sacrifice." An age of time seemed to pass before he could lift his hand and obey.

He lay in bed with the girl—in one hand the money, in the other, under the sheet, the knife that pricked her.

"Yes, yes, they say it's true," she whispered hastily. "I heard she was a priestess, I saw the one they said—but it was long ago. I don't know what happened to her son. Oh, dear kind master—please let me go. They will kill me if I say a single word."

She stuffed the sheet in her mouth, but he could hear her crying in a tiny frightened whisper as he closed the door behind him.

"Let me go," Dona said in a stifled voice.

Khalle rolled off him. "I'm sorry," he said.

Dona sat wiping at his face. His lip was cut, and he was streaked with blood and dirt.

"You hate Hadhla," he said. "I can see why."

Khalle was shocked. It had not occurred to him that Dona would be able to look into his thoughts, too.

Dona felt him flinch and laughed, then winced himself as his lip started bleeding again. "I know Hilurin was right now," he said. "I'll tell you what else I heard.

"Somostai have many powers. Some are like yours, or so they say. They claim the Destroyer has given them power to see the inmost hearts of men. They claim healing powers. Mostly I have seen their power to destroy. They taught Hadhla to make a liquid that burns, and many other things they say the Destroyer has sent them for the destruction of his enemies. Certainly the dog sacrifice did not cure me. But then, I am not so sure they wanted me to get well.

"Hadhla has powers of his own: uncanny ways of knowing

how to put pressure on a man or a situation to shape it to his will. The only thing he didn't have was sons. Well, he had me—a poor creature, sickly, marked for the Dark Land most likely. What I heard is, Somostai decided to give Hadhla what he most desired, but on their rein. They would send a woman, one who had the qualities they wanted, and order her to get a son off him—as one breeds a good cow to a prize bull. This boy would have Hadhla's touch and whatever of their own they could put into him. And then, maybe when I died, they would let Hadhla know they had him. Maybe they would give him back to his father. But his soul would be theirs forever."

Khalle shuddered violently.

"Yes, the Soul-eater," Dona said. "Even the Free People fear something, don't they? And it's strange, isn't it, that once this boy had slipped through their fingers, I started to get better? As if they decided to let me live, after all.

"Anyway, there's no doubt in my mind anymore. You are that special thing they hoped to create. You have all his power and something more. And you can be ruthless, as he is. The weapon comes to your hand, and you strike. Yes, you are truly my father's son."

"You may not be good with weapons," Khalle said, "but your words are hurtful." He sat in silence; he could not argue, and there was no adequate apology. "Hadhla values you more than me, if that is any comfort to you," he offered finally. "He would have sold me to the Somostai to preserve your life. As it happened, my foster father found me first."

"Consider yourself fortunate," Dona said. "Hadhla values people as he values his money. They are counters to buy him what he wants."

"I wanted to punish you because you were Hadhla's son," Khalle admitted. "Now I find out I'm the same as you. Why don't you hate me? It would be fair."

"Hate you? I envied you. You saw what it was like to be the master's son. Hadhla used people on me like tools, to shape me. If I failed to achieve the form he wanted, he would break the tool. I've had plenty of whores and courtiers, but never anyone to trust. I suppose I hoped we could be friends—since I own nothing you want and you have nothing I can take away from you, we have nothing to fear from each other. But now I see that wherever I go, I must still be the master's son. Still, I would like you to know that I didn't mean to get you killed today. I only wanted to show you that I wasn't a coward, even though I'll never be a Rider."

"You're no coward," Khalle said, surprised. "You've got courage, all right. You just don't have good sense."

Dona raised his eyebrows. "You talk to me about good sense? After charging through the front lines today with me in your wake and no weapons but your sword and a loud yell?"

"That was stupid," Khalle admitted. "I'm the one who nearly got us killed. I got angry because you spoke too close to the truth. Hilurin says the man who gets angry at the truth will be a fool all his life."

"And his life won't be long." Dona finished the saying. "Yes, he used that one on me, too."

"Why didn't he tell me who you were?" Khalle said.

"Who can understand him! Perhaps he knows us both too well. If he had introduced us properly and said, 'Now, boys, you are brothers, so I want you to kiss each other and be friends,' wouldn't you really have hated me then?"

Khalle laughed. "I'd have shot you in the back on the next moonless night."

"Indeed."

"A truce?" Khalle offered.

"Agreed." They touched hands.

They shared a cloak that night. Dona had always slept alone, but his bedroll and baggage were lost along with the horse. For all his aches, Khalle enjoyed the good warmth of brotherhood. As he was falling asleep, he heard Dona chuckle behind his shoulder.

"What is it?" he asked drowsily.

"Hilurin," Dona said. "Old fox. He did this on purpose. I don't know, when I see him again, if I should make him a feast or kill him."

"You make him a feast," Khalle said. "Then I will kill him."

"No, I think I must do the killing. He wants to make a Rider of me, let him enjoy the first benefits."

At sunup the horse was somewhat recovered. Walking and riding in turn, they caught up with the Thanha rear guard by midmorning and were remounted. The Crimsonvine sent up a cheer when the two finally rejoined them.

"You look terrible," Nin told them. He looked at Dona. "Did the horses step on your face while you were sleeping?"

Dona, whose face was lumpy and strangely colored, laughed freely as Khalle had never heard him do before. It was surprising how quickly his city-bred brother learned once his whole strength was no longer concentrated on keeping the People out.

The problem of the day was their approach down into the valley to catch up with a large body of Rivermouth infantry who were trying to intercept Hadhla. Going by road would be swiftest, but Varo was afraid that the Rivermouth men might have split up to prepare an ambush where the road skirted high hills on its way down.

Dona pushed his way closer to the captain. "With respect, *olani*, I think there's no fear of ambush today. They fear dividing in the face of the Riders more than anything else. They look for safety in numbers. They'll all huddle together, expecting an attack from you. They certainly won't go scrambling up the hills, even if it's the most sensible thing to do."

Varo looked at him with new respect. "How do you know this?"

Dona shrugged. "I guess, I don't know. But it's a good guess. Remember, I know these people. They don't think the way you do."

His guess turned out to be correct. They had no trouble on the road. Varo included Dona in his councils from then on, treating him like a seasoned warrior, not like an outsider who was there on sufferance.

"It's true I never campaigned," Dona explained to Khalle. "But I have heard all my father's counsels since I can remember. There is a book in my memory with pictures of all the cities, their captains, their victories, and their mistakes. In bed as a child, I used to fight out my father's wars with toy soldiers. Later I studied them with maps. I can tell you what Odrach of the Rivermouth eats for breakfast, and how he crossed the Morsshe on rafts the year of the floods."

Khalle listened to his stories and, in return, practiced with him outside the camp. He taught him some of the simplest of Shernhalla's lessons. He tried to show him how to see through the opponent's eyes, how to step inside his moves. As Dona's skill improved, Khalle worried over him less but kept the awareness of him always in mind, ready to catch him if he fell. Dona remained as he had been, somewhat quiet and reserved, but people started to warm to him. They liked his way of taking a joke, and his steadiness. Khalle, who had spent much time alone since Risse died, found his heart taking ease in Dona's presence. They called each other *kestri*—"my right-hand friend."

In only one way did Dona remain aloof: He did not play the game of delights with anyone. On nights when everyone was celebrating, he slept alone.

In the end they took the city. When the last sortie had been crushed, the Riders watched Hadhla's troops undertake the last struggle at the gate. A messenger came from Hadhla after the Riders had been pulled back.

"He wants me to ride with the city forces when the gates are opened," Dona said. "Come with me, Khalle. You can see for yourself how the Somostai break down the walls."

Khalle remembered his childhood terror of the priests, but he was too proud to let Dona see that he was afraid. Dona was recognized as soon as they drew close to the siege lines, and Khalle was amazed to see how the cityfolk treated him. Gray-haired captains ran up to touch his stirrup and ask if they could serve him in any way. Khalle perceived that they did not serve him only out of fear; clearly Dona was respected and liked among his father's slaves. The bearing that might have appeared arrogant among the Riders seemed natural and right—if any of the lowlanders' ways could seem right to Khalle.

They rode along the edge of a trench where many of the priests were directing work on mighty engines. The horses shied nervously from the strange smells and shapes. The priests had always looked alike to Khalle, but seeing them up close, he was surprised to note that they were of many different ages, some as young as himself. A few were even women, but where men and women Riders wore their hair long, the Somostai all cropped their hair alike. They worked with the discipline of an army. Unlike the others, they showed little more than polite deference to Dona. Their request to move back behind the trenches was as brusque as an order.

"This is not a show for the sake of amusement, master's son. Our skill is far more dangerous than the edge of your sword and will crush the ignorant and unwary. So please you, retire to safety and leave us to our work."

They used the running fire that Dona had described. A huge thing like a giant's slingshot cast it into the city, and the flames rose high. They also used what looked like a thunderbolt that blasted the wall so that part of it crumbled and the rest began to burn. Even back beyond the abandoned trenches, the Riders could hear the screams from the doomed city, and the horses smelled the fire and shifted uneasily.

Khalle's skin crawled.

"He is calling up demons," he whispered to Dona. "He asks for demons from Ar-Ravanh's hell. But the Destroyer gives nothing without taking back. What is he going to ask from the master for the lives that are put in his hand today?"

Afterward they went down into the city and rode through its streets. Even partially destroyed, it was far greater and richer than the Iron City. Dona pointed out the tall houses and the rich ornaments—but Khalle only smelled death. He felt as if the houses would fall into the narrow street and crush him. He begged Dona to leave.

"My father is here," Dona said. "I must go and see him. He'll want me to feast with him tonight. He'll be proud of what I have become. And it's all due to you. Come with me. He can be very generous in victory."

Khalle panicked. "Never," he said vehemently. "If he thinks I'm dead, that's the best I can hope for from him. I never want him to know I live."

"Go down to the harbor, then," Dona suggested. "Wait for me there at moonrise."

The tide was out, and there was space to breathe on the mud flats next to the river. A long smudge of smoke hazed the stars downwind. Khalle rode out until he came to the sea itself. The horse snuffed at the salty water and snorted. The waves were barely breaking on the shore, and the water had lost its color with the fading of the light. He could not see the tumbling green and blue he had heard of; he sensed only something vast and darkly shining that sighed in its sleep. He saw lanterns rocking on the water where the fleet from the City of Gulls had anchored. He was contented to watch for a long time, till he heard Dona's footsteps on the beach.

"He's pleased, very pleased," Dona said. "He's also drunk, very drunk. I see Verenya is sending in a couple of groups to keep watch tonight. It's just as well.

"I told him I had a friend. I said you were a Rider, and too proud to come within walls. At first he was going to give me something for you. Then he looked canny and said you might come to him, and he would reward you."

"What does he want this for, anyway?" Khalle asked. "He

has one city. No, two. City of Gulls is as good as his since he 'saved' them last year."

"The Iron City is poor," Dona explained. "On the shoulders of the mountain, all we have is the mines. Hadhla needed a seaport so he could trade the things we make without paying. City of the Gulls gave him that. The Rivermouth is a port, too, but more important, there are those farms all up the river valley. And there's timber for ships. With three cities, he will rule the whole south coast."

Khalle snorted. "And then?"

"It's the master's nature to seek power. He has to get more, always, or he'll end up with less. Look at it this way. Because of the war here, there won't be war in the Iron City. The farms burned this year, but if Hadhla rules, there will be many years of peace for them. Power is like a backfire that burns in a circle, spreading outward. There's still fire, but it's farther away from you the more powerful you are."

"Look up there," Khalle said. "There are the hearth fires of the People, up there in the plains of heaven." He was tired of talking about the ways of those who lived within walls.

"Somostai say the sky is not a plain, but a sea like the one before us," Dona told him. "The stars are islands floating in the sea, like the lanterns on the bows of those boats. Maybe each one lights a ship full of passengers, people like us."

The very idea gave Khalle an unbearable sense of vertigo. "You're untied in the head," he scoffed.

"I speak in earnest," Dona said. "It is said among the Somostai that our fathers' fathers journeyed across those dark seas. That's why Hadhla will never be master of the Somostai, no matter how many cities he may conquer. They remember the secrets of our birth, and we have forgotten. Nor will they ever loose their grip on those secrets. If it came to their ears that I knew even this much, they would probably have me killed in spite of anything Hadhla could do. I should bury this knowledge deep." He sighed. "But I can't help wondering if it's true. I suppose I'll never know."

He gazed out into the night without speaking, till Khalle felt that his brother's spirit had already traveled far from the shore where the tide lapped at their horses' feet. He waited patiently till Dona turned back to him. The master's son touched his arm.

"Let's make a vow in honor of the occasion," he said. Khalle could tell that he had been drinking with his father. His voice was husky, and he smelled like wine and the incense that cityfolk burned at feasts. "Let's vow to each other that when we're old men, when we're no longer needed—you by your barhedonh, and I by my city and my war host—that we'll slip out one night and go a-voyaging. To the mountains or to the sea—it doesn't matter where, so long as it's new, and far from here, and undertaken for no other profit than our own amazement."

"Remind me of it when my hair is gray, and I'll surely go with you, if I can still get my old legs around a horse."

"No, no," Dona protested. "You must vow solemnly. Otherwise you'll find yourself occupied with watching a pot of beans boil or some other important task, and you'll send word that you can't come." His words were light and joking, but Khalle felt his distress.

"I vow, then." He laid his arm around Dona's shoulders. "What sour thing have you tasted at our father's table? Something troubles you."

Dona shook his head impatiently. "Conniving and calculating without end," he said. "My life is an endless practice field. I must think of it as a journey with a destination, or I grow too weary. Never mind—now I have something to look forward to. Look—the heavens approve our plan. There's a shooting star."

Far to the south, a bright spark was moving steadily across the horizon.

"That's not a shooting star," Khalle said. "It's moving too slowly and too steadily. It's not fading. I don't know what that is. I never saw anything like it."

His hair stood on end, but the thing, whatever it was, passed into the haze and disappeared.

Dona made the homeward trip with the Riders instead of going back north with his father. He was there at the feast and the dancing, but in the night he somehow slipped away. Khalle felt his presence around somewhere, but in the celebration he forgot to look for him. In the morning Dona was there, smiling slightly and looking just as usual, while the others were moaning and groaning.

He received many gifts and honors, with warm glances from the other pallantai. His hair had grown respectably long and gleamed like obsidian; ornaments shone around his neck, and he had learned to move with the graceful pride of the People.

But he came to Khalle the next day and told him that he was going away.

"I must go back to my father. Will you ride with me as far as the pass?"

Khalle assented in shock. He could not believe that Dona would really leave. But they rode together, and the day passed, and Dona showed no signs of turning back. They made camp and sat on the hill above their fire, star watching.

"Why go back?" Khalle asked. "What is there to go back to? Here with us you have freedom and everything a person could want."

"I have to go. It's my—well, I don't believe in fate, but it's what I'm best suited for. Some people have the hand and eye for the bow, others for the sword; Deronh has the horses, and Hilurin has music. I'm the only one who really sees what my father is trying to do. Except Somostai—I think they understand, but what they want to do with it is the wrong thing.

"Hadhla is an evil man in many ways. I only blame him for the unnecessary evil that he does out of stupidity. He is what he has to be. But what he is building will outlive him, and it will not be evil if I have the strength to carry out what I foresee.

"Instead of little cities locked within their walls, fighting each other every year, laying waste to what little they have, we could have a wide land at peace. And then follows trade and travel—and there are so many things we don't know, places we haven't seen. Imagine, we could send ships east—not up the coast, but out to the islands I've heard of, and beyond . . . And the Riders could take some of my people west and north, over the Great Wall." He sighed. "I'll never get to go, of course. But I can send someone. They can bring me back tales of everything they hear and drawings of everything they see.

"But all this depends on Hadhla's bloody wars and dirty intrigues. The other masters are just like him, jealous and suspicious. They'll never agree to peace until they're forced to it. So he's forcing them."

Dona's words gave Khalle the same uneasy feeling that he got from thinking that the stars might be islands in a vast sea.

"I don't understand you," he said. "You think of things that are so far away. I think of what I know and what is close at hand. I think of my brother, that I need you and that my people need you. How can you leave us for things that may never happen?"

"Think on this, then," Dona said. "What do you think will happen to your people when Hadhla's wars are finished? You'll be a weapon that may turn in his hand. He'll break you in two."

"Let him try," Khalle said. "We destroyed a city before, when they turned on us."

"Maybe you could defeat Hadhla alone. What if three cities come against you, united? And how will you live, when no one pays you to fight for them anymore?"

"I don't know. The pallantai never think about those things. It's up to Grandmother and the captains to decide." It was a thought that had never entered Khalle's mind before, but suddenly it seemed logical and real.

"In Hadhla's plan there is no lasting place for you. In mine there may be. The People need me more in the city than here."

Khalle's heart said "But I need you here." He was too proud to say the words out loud.

Dona embraced him. "A piece of my heart will stay with you, paliao," he said.

"You're still here, tonight," Khalle said. "Will you leave us without a single taste of sweetness?"

His fingers traced Dona's wrist and touched his palm, but Dona pulled back.

"Don't press me, brother," he said. "Do you think it's easy to say no to you? It's best for me to leave here with nothing that could bind me to any of you, not even a single night. Believe me, it's best." He stood up abruptly and picked up his cloak. "Let's sleep. The fire has burned low, and the nights are getting cold."

11

At the first light, Dona tied his few possessions behind his saddle, embraced Khalle, and rode away.

"I'll send you word when I can," he called.

Underfoot, the grass crackled with frost. Khalle rode back to his own people with a heavy heart.

Hilurin left, too, soon after. He said he had an errand and would come back before the pass was closed. Instead he sent back the messenger who had gone with him. Grandmother told no one what the message said, save that something was happening in the Iron City and that Hilurin would be staying there till spring. Whatever the word was, it lay on her mind like dark clouds over Stormfather. She was often ill that winter and seemed much worn with the worry she would not share. Often she asked Khalle to sleep at the foot of her bed. His presence seemed to reassure her.

And so it was that he was with her when it came.

By then it was spring. The smell of new grass was maddeningly sweet to men as well as horses, and the moon-washed night air was as cool as river water, but not too cold for two or three to share a cloak and keep each other warm. It was a poor time for a young man to be kept inside the Rock, away from his beshani. But she called for him often. Amusing herself, as he thought, she would sometimes ask him to tell her the dreams of other sleepers or to see if he could sniff what weather was in the air. Because it was the Asharya's request, he tried, and more and more often he was right.

That night he felt the nightmare that awakened her even before she called him. He uncoiled himself from his blanket and struck a light.

"Grandson," she whispered.

"I'm here, Asharya."

"Listen! Listen for me."

"To what? Weather? What is it? I don't understand."

"Not weather. But something coming, or someone. Try to hear."

It had become easy for him to hear the low babble of dream talk from the sleepers in the great hall outside. With an effort he got beyond that, into the currents of darkness and moonlight, out into the sleeping plains till his senses were lost in the vagueness of distance. All was still.

"Nothing, Asharya."

But even as he said it, he felt something on the edge of his awareness. It was very far away, very faint, but it tore the night like a distant, unearthly scream. A sickening giddiness seized him as he tried to follow it; he shuddered and was once again aware only of the sleeping place and the warm yellow flame of the lamp.

"What is it?"

"Asharya—I can't say. Surely nothing! It was—seemed—high in the air, but sharp, not like a cloud, and no bird could—I must be dreaming."

Her bony fingers closed around his wrist, but there was no reassurance in the touch. "No dream. Hilurin warned me. It's the weapon against which there is no defense."

"An attack? Now? Then let me wake the captains, let me warn—"

She cut him off with a gesture. "Be quiet. You will not be here. You will go to Erech Tolanh now, and fast. Go to Dona nav'Hadhla. You have promises with him, isn't it so?"

"Dona Telhirya was my friend," Khalle stammered. "The master's son is a stranger to me."

"Never mind. He has a heart for you. If there is any help for us, he will get it from Hadhla. Now go."

He threw himself on the ground beside her. "I don't understand! My people are fighting, and you want me to run away? Asharya, don't do this to me!"

"Did I tell you that you would be the weapon closest to my hand? If I'm down, I let my knife fly—not leave it in the sheath while my enemy rides over me. In you, too, there is something against which there is no defense. Now run!"

Without a word of parting, his heart in turmoil, he ran. The Rock was rousing behind him, but he ran without pausing for anyone. All the while, his sense of something terribly wrong was growing like the sound of that distant scream in the air. Uphill to the grazing ground he sprinted; he whistled up a horse with the last of his breath and headed her east at a gallop.

He was only a mile or two from home when it came: first the quiver of the air crowding together ahead of it, then a flat black shadow across the stars, then the scream it made as it stooped and swooped high again, like an eagle striking; and after that came the fire. The horse shrieked and reared in terror of something that was not so much a sound as a wall of angry air. Khalle was flung off and rolled head over heels on a hillside that shuddered under him.

In his fear he reached back to the Rock—and he died. He was crushed, he was torn, he was choking, he was burning. He screamed his throat raw with the agony of a thousand deaths, but he could not even hear himself in the roar of the fire.

It stopped. Suddenly there was a heavy stillness around him. He heard a small, irregular noise and recognized it at length as his own breath. And that was how he knew he was still alive.

He clawed his way to his hands and knees. He looked back. The shape of the Rock had gone. In its place stood a column of unearthly fire. And when he sought for his people, there was nothing, not even a death cry. They were dead already, burned and buried where they lay. The feeling for the People that had been as much a part of him as sight or smell was gone, as if his eyes had been torn out. The door to home opened on a blank wall.

He dragged himself over to the mare and found that she was dead, too. The hide was still smoking where hot splinters of metal had torn into it. It seemed that some of the fire from the sky had struck great fists into the ground nearby. Indeed, there was no defense, nor was there any return blow he could give to make this invincible enemy come back and strike him down, too. Only one thought lived in his mind: He had been told to go to Erech Tolanh, and he would go there.

He saw something moving against the light of the fire. Some of the loose horses had escaped and were fleeing in his direction. His lips would not shape a whistle, but he got his fingers between his teeth and managed some kind of a noise. They turned toward the security of a familiar sound. He caught one of them, mounted, and rode away east, with the pyre of the Free People still burning at his back.

Dawn whitened the peaks ahead of him as he struck the trail leading up to the pass. He had stopped once or twice to drink, but never for more than the few moments it took to splash water into his mouth. Dawn on the lowlands pass always brought back to him the night he had first come to the People, carried before Deronh and wrapped in his cloak. He took his belt and beat the horse savagely, driving it up the steep rocks at an insane pace. Only when the little stallion stumbled and squealed in protest did he remember that they were born of the same mother, the great plain, mighty and endless. He thought of Deronh and was ashamed, and he slid stiffly off the horse's back.

Ahead lay only the rocky passes. He realized that by the time he had forced his mount up them, at the end of that night's riding, he might as well cut its throat. And there was no comfort waiting at the end of the road. He turned the horse's head back to the west and waved it away. Then he tucked the long rider's sword across his back and started to run.

That was a very small deathgift for a great heart like Deronh, but it was all he had. Deronh would not care about the blood he would spill for the others. The horseman had probably gone north by then, anyway; he would not have waited once all the plain of stars was free to him. But if he was still near enough to care, maybe he would see one of his horses going back home and be made happy.

Khalle's breath came and went harshly and evenly in time to his climbing feet; his eyes, dry from riding all night, stung with the wind. The wild, grieving tune of Tyrel's Song rose and fell in his mind. He felt again the smooth vibrant wood of Hilurin's thamla sounding under his hands, as if he were playing it again on the night of grieving for the dead. The deathgift for Tyrel and her companions had been terrible: a whole city laid waste, so they sang it, and one from every hand of warriors had never come back. What revenge, what song, for a thousand dead? The enormity of it stopped the music in his head.

"The names of my dead will never be sung. There's no hearth to sing them by, no ears left to listen. But there will be a revenge. By my name, by my soul, there will be a revenge."

There was no answer; the winds whispered and sobbed in the crooked passes, bringing no words he could hear. He listened carefully all the same. And he was attentive and grateful to every sharp stone and stumble in the path. They kept him high up in the trance of prolonged effort. Without small things to sharpen his awareness, he could go in deeper and deeper until he was running in his sleep.

He was half-asleep, anyway, by the time he came to the drop where the trail fell down the side of Old Cloudy to the city road. The rising breeze from the valley brushed against his face, and he woke up instantly. It was all wrong. It smelled like burning. Or was it that he just could not get that smell out of his nostrils? He leapt and slid down the mountainside to where he could catch a glimpse of the city.

A low black cloud fanned out from the broken walls. Erech Tolanh had been burning for some time. The road below him was deserted. Khalle had not thought there was anything left he could still care about, but his heart choked him with sudden fear for Dona. He had to find him whether the master's son could help him or not.

He got down to the road and broke into a run again. It was easy going on the smooth road. That nagging urge for speed drove him too fast. He had been riding all night and running since dawn, and to get there at the end of his strength would be as bad as never getting there at all. He was coming close to that end.

Fallen stones at the city gate blocked his way. The walls had come down for a long stretch on both sides of the towers. Nobody had come in that way as far as he could see. They had merely knocked it down and left it. He had to climb over; the gateway was nearly impassable.

The city stank of ashes and fear; it was a place of defeat, full of broken things and dangerous to be in. Reckless with his haste, he danced over rubble and tumbled Giristiyah bodies. He heard the footsteps coming barely in time to vault over the remains of a house wall. Burned timbers crumbled under his hands.

He crouched, trying to pant silently and to ease his legs, which were cramping fiercely. The soldiers were not Hadhla's men, not from any other city force. They were cropheads, black-robes—Somostai. They were going somewhere; they had business; they were not terrified. He noted that, but it did not help. He knew that Somostai could not have caused all that destruction. Such power was beyond them or anyone else he had ever seen. He would have liked to kill them all the same, but he did not have the time to waste. As soon as their backs went by, he was off. There was fire still at the heart of the city, where the Great House stood, and his fear pulled him toward it.

He could hear sounds of fighting as he approached the center. But the noises were scattered and random: small groups still skirmishing, not the roar of intact forces meeting.

From some distance away he could see that the Great House was not exactly standing any longer. The old stone fortress side was still relatively intact, but most of the west end—gilded timbers, colored slates, all the stuff of Hadhla's boasting—had come down. Fire still crackled around him, and thick drifts of smoke obscured his vision. The shacks at the edge of town had burned quickly. At the center, the fire had more to feed on: tall strong houses, built of solid oak, paneled with sweet, resinous *cuyirlin*, and stuffed full of chests and hangings. The master and his friends had built themselves a fine tomb: smoke for a monument, their feast a barbecue for dogs.

He worked his way grimly around to the fallen end of the house. The tough soles of his feet smarted from stepping on still-hot embers. He wished he had his boots. Where the house had fallen lay a man-high layer of treacherous litter, still smoldering. Around that, the shell of the house still stood where the wall posts had not yet given way. Inside, the fire burned on with a low, steady roar. Even as he watched, another section of the roof caved in. A flurry of sparks went up, and fire danced triumphantly along the gable ends.

How to get in there? He was almost certain that Dona was dead. Or if he was alive, what help could he possibly give? But Khalle held stubbornly to his purpose. While he was on that trail, he was still Thanha. At the end of that, there was nothing.

Swearing at the scorching debris, he picked his way around the jagged end of a stone wall. Eddying smoke caught in his lungs and made him cough. He climbed over half-burned barriers of unidentifiable junk and found himself in the gutted keep of the house. There was a dark doorway in the wall, and within it he found stairs going down. He felt his way downward in the dark. The air was stifling, the stones just short of searing, but there was no fire there. At the foot of the stairs, he came out into a room that sounded large and high. He felt his way along with one hand on the wall. Then he came back into a narrow corridor, turned a corner, and saw light ahead.

High windows let in daylight. There were many rooms down there, but they seemed little used. Nothing in them caught his attention. In places, parts of the wall had broken inward, leaving large gaps of daylight high up. And in one of those half-destroyed rooms he found Dona.

At first he did not know what he was looking at. Dona lay facedown, his body twisted, where he had fallen when the room had been shaken apart. Khalle crossed the room in one spring while the recognition was still registering. He seized the body and turned it faceup. A faint sound of pain told him that Dona still lived. He flinched from his own heedlessness. No part of Dona's body was whole enough to bear touching without pain. His face was as white as glass; already it had the unchanging look of the dead.

Khalle cut the thongs that held Dona's arms bent behind him, and Dona groaned again. His eyes opened, and his lips moved soundlessly. *Water*.

"I'll find you some. It's me, Khalle. I'll get you water."

He laid Dona down as gently as he could and ran back down the hall. He cursed himself for not having a water bottle, for stopping to drink along the way and not getting there earlier. His own mouth felt cold and dry.

He charged through the abandoned rooms like a crazy man, scattering things as he went. At last he found some kind of storeroom. He shattered the necks of the big clay jars with his sword and watched useless goods spill out onto the floor: oil, honey, peppercorns. Finally he found one jar that held beer. He dipped some into a jug and raced back to Dona with it. He raised Dona up and gave him a drink in the palm of his hand. Dona could not swallow; he wet his mouth and let the beer run out the corners of his lips. Khalle, holding his brother, tried to sort out his wounds and see what needed healing. He was overwhelmed by too many things gone wrong.

"I'm dying, little brother."

Khalle could not have heard the words if they had not been palm to palm.

"No, Dona! I'll find you a healer."

"No time for that. Listen."

Khalle felt rather than heard Dona's impatience—to have waited for so long and have no strength to speak.

"What is it, brother? Who did this to you? Tell me! I will make them pay—ten for every finger of your hands!"

Dona was silent for a long time.

"The Rock," he said finally.

"The Rock is no more," Khalle said.

"They said so. Barasheli—I was wrong. All a waste, everything I came back to do. Hadhla's dead. Somostai . . ."

"Somostai did this?"

"Strangers with them . . . stars that move . . ."

His voice faded, and then he opened his eyes and made a final effort. "Was you they wanted, Khalle. They thought—my kamarh. If they hurt me enough you'd come. They wanted me to summon you, but I wouldn't. They were afraid, but I don't think they meant to kill me, just to make me call you. But the roof fell. They ran. I waited."

"Wait for me a little longer."

Dona pushed him away, a feeble touch he could barely feel. "No. You are the last of the Rock. For them the price of blood. For me—only find them. Find out why."

"Please, barasha. Killing I can do, but no more promises. My heart is dead inside me."

"Khalle. Find out. Who. Ask them why. Live till you find them. My deathgift."

"All right," Khalle said at last. He barely heard his own words, but he knew that Dona was no longer hearing with ears, either. He sat in the dark with his brother, listening to his heartbeats.

"Still watching stars, paliao?" Dona asked sleepily. "Come lie down. It's cold as hell tonight."

Then there was silence. Khalle came back from it slowly, and he was cold, though the room was stiflingly hot. There was blood on his hands; he marked his face with it. But he still could not go. He could not leave Dona within walls, without any honors. He took off his ear stones and his ivory horse, the only ornaments he wore, and put them in Dona's hands, and he hacked off his long hair and let it fall by the body. If anyone returned there, he would know that a Rider lay there and that someone was grieving for him.

That was all he could do. He turned then and groped his way back to the earth above. When he stepped back into the open, people were waiting for him. There were too many of them. He ran. But he was hampered by the debris, turned aside by unexpected walls still standing. They knew the place better than he did.

They had guessed which way he was going and sent people to meet him. Across the courtyard, white, dazzling fire was eating the stones of the Great House. It had a color and a smell like no fire he had ever seen before. Stairs still rose to part of a balcony that way; beyond them was the fire, but that was the only way he could run, so he backed slowly toward them.

A few of the soldiers had seen him glance that way and had already moved to cut him off. They circled him slowly. He wanted to rush them and get it over with, but he moved back instead, waiting.

Be sharp, he told himself. They want something from you still, or why don't they call for archers?

He licked his lip and tasted blood and salt.

One more fight—the last, so make it good.

In a way he was happy, because he would not have to keep his promises. They would take that burden off him.

No one wanted to be the first to come after him. Finally one of them gave an order, and three men closed in cautiously. He lunged and got the slowest of them in the belly. But he had to expose his back to do it. The second slashed at him and laid open his head before he could drop the man. He felt the third man come up behind him and tried to twist aside as he pulled his sword free. He moved too late; he felt the blade from behind grate on his shoulder bone and sink deep into the bunched muscles below. The arm jerked in fiery numbness, and he helplessly watched the sword drop from his hand. He fell and rolled out of reach, thinking quickly even as he scrambled for distance. The burning stairs were his only retreat. More soldiers were coming into the courtyard. Soon they would overwhelm him by sheer numbers.

The big man who was giving orders shouted again. "Don't kill him!"

Khalle spared a glance for him. He had cast aside his black cloak, but the cropped hair marked him unmistakably as Somostai. Khalle gave ground again, panting. The man who had cut him moved after him warily, keeping between him and the bodies so that Khalle could not get another weapon. He still had his knife, but he could use it only once, and after that he would be empty-handed. Blood ran through his soaked head cloth and over his face, blinding him, and down his arm. Soon he would be too weak to stand. And then what? What did they want from him? To drag him away like a pig for slaughter, to take him apart inch by inch like Dona? The stairs were the only way to run, and beyond them there was only the fire.

He leapt for the bottommost step, and they were too slow to stop him. Once he had gained height on them, they were afraid to follow him up the steps. But he had no weapons. They only had to gather their courage and rush him together, and they could take him. The man who had cut him already ventured onto the first step. The others were closing in behind him. Khalle had reached the balcony at the top; he had nowhere else to go.

He looked around wildly for something, anything, to take up and fight with. The top post of the stairs looked back at him: a stone face, the likeness of the Eater. The tongue lolled between its teeth, and the eyes were empty holes. But the face was cracked across, and pieces of the pillar were scattered across the buckled pavement. He leaned against the pillar and felt it shift, but he had only one good arm to push with.

"You don't have me yet," he panted. He ripped off his head cloth and flung a loop around the pillar. Twisting his good hand into the strip, he threw his whole weight against it. He felt the rasp of stone against stone as the pillar shifted, toppled, and crashed down the stairs, shattering as it fell into chunks that crushed arms and legs and left a jumble of bodies between him and his pursuers.

The man who had cut him had evaded the falling stone and was still coming. Eyeing the man's sword hungrily, Khalle let him come. He scuffed a heap of rubble together as he gathered the head cloth to a manageable length; he had enough control over his damaged arm to grasp a stone and drop it into the sling. At that distance he could cast right-handed and still not miss. His enemy dared another step or two, and the unhurt ones behind him began to pick their way over their moaning comrades. Khalle whirled the sling and let fly.

The sharp stone flew wickedly true, striking the swordsman's forehead with an audible crunch. As the man crumpled, Khalle leapt on him, breaking his neck with a well-aimed kick and wresting the blade from his dying grasp. The others moved back when they saw that he was armed again, but the big crophead urged them on from behind like a master of hounds whipping his unwilling pack. They pressed in on him, shields lifted high, hoping to pin him against the stone railing. One armed, unarmored, he had no hope of defending himself. He attacked them instead, with exulting rage—but not without cunning. Raised shields exposed thighs; those who fell, hamstrung, would not rise, and the second rank tripped over them. The next to face him turned to protect his leading leg and left open the soft space between rib and hip; Khalle's sword gutted him like a slashing tooth.

But there were too many. He stabbed, shoved, and slashed,

reveling in every cry of pain he could draw from them, but still they pressed him. He could not find room to swing. If they had meant to kill him, they could have had him then. His strength was running out in dark lines that streaked the stones underfoot.

The sword's weight dragged at his arm, but he lifted it for another stroke. That time the edge sliced into steel and stuck, and before he could wrench it free, it was twisted from his hand. A score of hands had hold of him before he could move. He thrashed in their grip, but the pain of their grasp on his wounded shoulder took his breath away. Leaning back suddenly, he freed his legs for a moment and kicked one of them over the edge into the flames. That was the way he had to go, taking as many of them with him as he could. If he could. Otherwise they would take him back to whatever fate they had in mind for him, maybe the same one they had been keeping for him all those years since Deronh had found him on a rock in the place of the Eater.

Ayei, Taurhalisos! he cried silently. Do I have to die so afraid?

And then the strange and deadly scream in the air came back. The soldiers looked up involuntarily. He did, too—and he was caught. It had the same shape and feel to it as the thing he had felt in the air over the Rock. It went so fast, a thing like a crack in the world, down which he slid as helpless as a bare hand down a blade's edge. His enemies were somehow safe inside it, the real enemies, as far beyond his reach as the sky, while he died among the rats in a ruined city. In some other existence he felt hands grasp his arms and heard the babble of voices as he stood dumb as stone. With an effort that tore all his senses, he wrenched free and leapt with his last strength toward the alien fire. And fell. And fell. And fell.

12

Dark. Blinding cold. He tumbled loose from everything. There was a flash of strange faces, of walls. The gray curved walls flickered across his eyes, punctuated with stabs of that unearthly cold. Again and again he thought he flung himself away from those walls, only to find himself leaping into them again. Still he heard voices, but they jerked on and off as if someone kept clapping hands over his ears.

Djiziskhrais its—hweirdid—goingdown—

He was still falling. Those others were falling with him. The fire was still waiting for them far below. He could feel it reaching out for him; the steel seed around him gathered itself to bloom into a flower of fire. Pure terror consumed him.

He hit with such a shock that the pain trailed the impact and he felt nothing. He was lying on the ground. Fire licked at the sky, but away from him, not behind him or around him anymore. His lungs wrestled silently with immovable air. He groped for his knife but could not reach it. Everything was gone. Then the darkness was the familiar bloody black of overwhelming pain.

Hands and voices again. He thought he was back on the steps; he tried to fight them off, but only his eyelids moved. They had no faces. No. It was cloth wrapped over everything but the eyes. The babble of their voices would not resolve into Giristiyah or anything he had ever heard. Maybe he was dreaming. He remembered leaping, but nothing after that. How had he come so far from home?

Dark eyes looked at him over the mask, and he tried to speak to them. But his mouth was too dry with the tormenting thirst that was on him; the words made no sound. Those eyes staring at him were the last thing he saw as awareness faded away from him.

Dr. Janet Logan stared at the naked man on the stretcher. He was patched with blood dried dark and with blood still slick and bright, and he was blackened with ashes. He looked dead, his eyes sunken shut and his mouth hanging open. But he had spoken to her. She was almost sure he had.

"Hey, Captain Quack! You going to help me out here or what? This isn't the only wienie at the roast, y' know." Jackson jabbed his needle vigorously through the ragged edge of the wound. "I mean it, Janney. Grab dirt or check out. Fuck, another bleeder. Suction!"

She moved automatically to assist him even while she stared.

"What happened?" she asked. "When I heard the explosion, I grabbed my shoes and was halfway here before my beeper went off. But I still don't know what's going on."

"Who does? Looks like one of the hi-fighters crashed and burned on the runway. It's still burning. Those guys, we won't find enough of them to identify. The others coming in are a maintenance crew and a transport out to North Fork that was loading up when the fighter came screaming in. Pretty bad.

"Hey, dig this. I just saw one in triage; his tags had melted."

"Jesus, Jackson, will you shut up?"

He shrugged. "Don't worry about it, we decided he was dead. Check out this guy, though. No tags; in fact, he came in bareass just as you see him. No ID at all."

He lectured her while his hands moved deftly over the body he was working on.

"His clothes weren't burned off, because there are no marks on his skin like you'd expect if he'd been burned in a pattern like that. He is burned all over, but evenly, and it's only first degree, like he was flashed on all sides at once. Except his feet. Lots of little burns there, like he'd been walking on hot debris—but we found him just lying on the runway. And another thing—these head and shoulder wounds are all dried up. Now, when did they have time to do that?"

He tied off the last stitch.

"Got to move along here. Tell them to keep him on extenders

for a few days. He's lost a lot of blood, and he's dehydrated. And if you find out who he is, flash me. I'm curious."

Janet turned the unconscious man over to the paras, but she stared after the cart as they pushed it down the hall. He had spoken to her; that was the problem. She had heard him call *Help me. I'm lost.* But he had not said a word.

She meant to go check on him as soon as she had a spare minute, but slack time never arrived. The rush of work caused by the crash had just eased off when a line of trucks pulled up, and once again the halls and wards were chaotically over-crowded.

A harassed para stopped her as she hurried toward the stairs. "Dr. Logan, would you mind stopping to see Colonel Kruger? He's giving us a hard time."

"What do you mean? Kruger is *here*?"

"How'd you miss that? Almost the whole Mike Force is here. They're getting treated for chemical exposure. He's kicking up a stink about his lab results. Says he wants to talk to the chief of medicine, but Petersen's in a meeting with some heavy from PCOM."

"Sure, why not. I've always wanted to get a look at El Cu-chillo."

She rapped on the door and walked in without waiting to be asked. The patient had the bed cranked to its most upright po-sition; he managed to look belligerent even with an IV in each arm. His eyes were swollen, and his face was sunburn-red. He cocked his head and squinted at her.

"I asked to see someone in authority. Who are *you*?"

"I'm Dr. Logan. I'm afraid the chief of medicine is in a meeting and can't be disturbed. What seems to be the prob-lem?"

"I've been through that. Thornkiller. Direct dump. We were running for home—shitheads didn't even see us. Three days to our pickup point! I haven't been able to see right since the sec-ond day, and all they give me is eyedrops.

"All these damn tests. Run my blood through the washer, stick it back in. I don't know what the f— excuse me, what the hell is going on. I can't get anyone to explain it to me."

"Well, I'm enough of an authority on Karpinski's syndrome to answer your questions. I assume they're just running you through the normal series for someone with an overexposure to thornkiller. We're trying to avoid absorption of the chemicals into the tissues. Because after a certain point, you get kidney and liver damage as your body tries in vain to excrete the stuff, and eventually your system goes berserk and starts reacting to the contaminated tissue as if it's a foreign body. That's what we call an autoimmune reaction."

She watched his eyes. They kept drifting away from hers.

He knows all this, she thought. He has something else on his mind.

"How bad is it going to be?"

"I couldn't tell you, sir. I haven't seen your tests. You could die of it in a month with a direct hit. You won't, though. That's what all the procedures were for. To wash as much of the poison out of you as possible before it gets permanently fixed. We don't know how it will ultimately affect any individual till he actually gets sick. One thing we do know: Once the autoimmune reaction shows up, you don't get better. Most cases of drastic overexposure end up that way. We've had a couple of hundred, and they're all gone or on the way out."

She had his complete attention now.

"You're talking about half my command! I could lose them all!" He pulled himself together. "How can you tell if someone's getting sick? What if they're out in the Dust somewhere when they go down?"

"If you start feeling bad, you can come in for some tests and find out how far it's advanced. There's no way to tell ahead of time."

"Well, now, suppose some chuck decides to play tough guy and ignore the symptoms?"

"We keep records of people who were exposed and pull them all in for a check after three months. It usually shows up by then. You can't fool the tests. I don't think you have to worry too much about people collapsing in the field. They die slowly."

"I see."

But it was obvious that he still had something on his mind.

"You're all computerized here, are you?" he asked then.

"Of course."

"What happens if—hypothetically speaking—if the records get lost? So that you didn't know for sure if someone had been exposed?"

"Hypothetically speaking, that would be bad for the patient; we might forget to chase after him for follow-up treatment."

"You wouldn't have any way to know he was sick."

"No, sir."

"But you can't fix it anyway."

"No."

She waited for him to speak again, but he seemed to be lost in thought.

"Was there anything else?" she prompted finally.

"No, that's it. Thank you for your time."

He had dismissed her, but she knew he had not come to the point yet.

"If you'll excuse me—" She picked up the lightpad at the end of the bed and called for Kruger's lab results.

"Leave that alone!"

The results appeared, neatly graphed; every number was in the red zone.

When he realized that he could not stop her, he gave up.

"All right, I'm a dead man," he said. "Tell me something I don't know."

"You've already seen these results."

"It was my blood. I was entitled."

"And what you want to know is how to wipe them off the database."

"I didn't say that."

She shrugged. "You didn't have to. What I don't get is why."

"I have a job to do. I can't waste time in the hospital. I can't afford to look sick. Especially after this has happened." His voice dropped. "Is there anything you can do?"

"Medically, no." She hesitated, then shook her head firmly. "No. I'm sorry."

So that's the great Marcus Kruger, she thought. She tried to settle down to transcribing research notes, but the encounter had shaken her. He practically came right out and asked me to falsify his records. I guess they're right about him. He really is some kind of fanatic. Wants to die with his boots on.

She heard him say again "Half my command! I could lose them all!"

That was the real pain, she thought. It rips him up that they're going to die. That's why he wants those records wiped. He wants to stay with them to the bitter end, as if that'll help any. "My boys." What an ego.

She saw their faces—walking shadows. They looked so bewildered when they got the lab results. They were not even bleeding, but they would be dead within months.

Shit. I can't sit here and think about this.

She set Jon's pocket box on her desk, slipped the plug into

her ear, and turned it up loud. She did not really like Medicine Shirt, but it was better to listen to their bad dreams than her own.

> By the light of burning bridges
> I see there's no one left in range.
> Their stars are rust and their guns are dust
> And the checkpoints all have changed.
> Are the shadows ahead the beckoning dead
> Or the rescue squad returning?
> Did they call my name or was it a game
> Of the flame on bridges burning?

She looked up and saw Petersen standing in the doorway. His lips were moving. She pulled the plug.

". . . step into my office for a minute? I need to consult with you."

Janet considered falling to the floor unconscious to indicate extreme surprise. Normally Colonel Petersen did not bother to consult her; he picked her brains in the hall or the lounge. Then, if he liked her ideas, he appropriated them as his own. If he did not like them, he told her she was undisciplined and poorly trained and suggested that she review the literature. Since the truly latest medical journals were twenty-two light-years behind them, she found it difficult to comply.

"Right away, sir," she murmured politely.

"There's a patient I need your help with," he informed her as she entered his office.

"With respect, sir, I hope he's not another case of quote high-stress intolerance unquote. I keep telling you there's not a thing wrong with those people except that they're tired of being shot at. It's a reasonable position, and if you want someone to tell them they owe it to themselves to go get blown up, I wish you'd pick someone a little bigger and better padded than I am. Telling lies to distraught humpers is not my idea of a good time."

"Janet, will you please stop raising irrelevant issues? This man is a unique case in my experience. He's apparently a casualty from last week's airfield disaster. I say 'apparently' because we picked him up with the others, but we've been unable to identify him. His physical ID doesn't match anything in our personnel files. He's not critically injured, but he is combative and unresponsive to the point where he's endangering himself."

"Sure, I'll take a look. I assume you already have brain scans and have eliminated the possibility of organic damage?"

"Well, now, here we come to the crux of the matter. PCOM has sent an investigator to write a report on the whole incident. There's a possibility that sabotage may be involved, and of course the presence of an unidentified man is alarming. It's important for them to be able to question him, and at this point they are still unable to communicate with him. Until his identity and status are determined, he must be kept under maximum security, and all his records are considered restricted information. You would be expected to report to Colonel Simonds and to me and keep us fully apprised of all developments."

He leaned toward her and lowered his voice conspiratorially. "Colonel Simonds told me it's possible that he's some kind of—experiment. Gene tailoring or the like. That's why extreme security is needed. That would explain some of the anomalies on his chart. That's a restricted communication, of course."

Janet's curiosity was definitely aroused. Though Petersen's a bigger fool than I thought if he buys that "experiment" garbage, she thought disdainfully. There's not a lab on this planet that could handle something like that, unless the Nupis are so far ahead of us that we're doomed anyway. "Can I see him now?"

"I'll accompany you. You'll have to have your security card recoded so you can get into the annex."

She seldom entered the annex. It normally held people admitted for tests and observation, and Petersen was quite secretive and proprietary about his special patients. Gossip had suggested that the annex patients were isolated because they were victims of bizarre chemical and biological weapons, either their own or the enemy's. Janet thought it more likely that Petersen was hoping he would discover some strange indigenous disease and make it into the medical texts.

Petersen opened the door and looked into the patient's room. "He's awake. We try to keep him sedated, but he has a peculiar reaction to some of our best medications. You'll see it on his chart."

She recognized the man who had been on the stretcher. His head had been shaved and bandaged. He was wearing restraints on his head, his wrists, and his chest; he had a nose tube taped to his face, and there were three separate patches of medication stuck to the soles of his feet. He was not fighting, but she could see that he had been pulling against the head restraint till blood oozed from beneath the bandage. There were raw patches on his face where he had apparently torn the tube loose several times. He was motionless but rigid with terror, like a horse in barbed wire.

He tilted his head back to keep the blood from running into his eyes and fixed his gaze on her, and she knew she had not been wrong. He had spoken to her. She crossed the room to stand next to him. In spite of the restraints, he moved his hand enough to lock his fingers around her wrist. His eyes focused fiercely on her face. She tried to communicate some confidence to him by looking back calmly.

The room blurred around her, and only the warm band of his fingers around her wrist remained solid. Images surfaced in her mind. They were all nightmarish: corpses, rubble, dead faces, and a stink of burning that filled her mouth like the taste of fear itself. A distorted figure that she recognized as Doug Petersen appeared. He had the cutaneous injector in his hand, but suddenly it turned from a plastic skinjet to a snake that would sink its fangs into one's arm, spreading a venom of madness.

The patient let go. She staggered as if she had been dropped. She could feel sweat prickling around the roots of her hair. The fear in the stranger's eyes was making her sick, and she could not believe that Petersen had not felt it.

"You see what I mean," Petersen said calmly. "We've tried several combinations of sedatives, but we haven't found one that works reliably. We had to tube him, because he refuses to eat."

"If the drugs aren't working, why not withdraw them?" she asked, struggling to keep the anger out of her voice. "He's disoriented already. Give him a chance to adjust to reality."

"The risk is too great. I doubt Colonel Simonds would approve it."

"You're the chief of medicine, not him. I'm not touching this if you won't back me up. At least give me a chance to prove that I'm wrong."

"I'll take one chance on you, Janet. The first time you're wrong, that's it."

"Thank you for your well-placed confidence, sir," she said sourly. "I'll order a para to stay on duty with him all night, but I don't think it will be necessary. I'm going to stay and observe him for a minute."

After Petersen had gone, she spoke gently to the stranger.

"What in the world are you so afraid of? It must be something bad to make you do this to yourself."

His eyes widened as she reached for the nose tube.

"Take it easy, now. I'm going to make this as fast as possible."

She ripped the tape loose and eased the tube out. Next she peeled the stickybugs off his feet. She checked the labels before throwing them out.

"Good grief, you've got more dope in you than Jackson's bathroom cupboard. No wonder you're feeling slightly twisted. I'm not going to let them give you any more of this. Maybe if you're not doped to the gills you'll eat. If you can just keep everything smooth for a few days, I'll get you out of restraints, too.

"Now I'm going to have someone change that dressing for you, and I've ordered you some plain old muscle relaxant. It'll help you rest. When you wake up, I want you to eat, and then I'm going to come back and see how you're doing. I won't say they aren't going to hurt you, because that wouldn't be the truth. But I won't let them hurt you more than they have to. So don't give them any excuse, dakko?"

She could hear his breathing slow down and even out. He showed no response to her words, but she could feel the fear receding.

"You're doing all right, so I'm going to leave you for a while. I'll be back."

Khalle watched her go. He could read how shaken she was by the too-straight line of her back. He, too, was shaken. Now that the fight was over, he knew how weak he was, how exhausted. The crazy voices of unseen strangers still washed around him, but they were fading, muted. He knew they were there, but he no longer breathed the breath of their mouths or found himself with dead men in their unregarded beds. He could keep them away now that he was free from the medicine that left his mind helpless.

A place as big as the Rock, he thought, stacked with broken people in racks like dried meat strips. They give you one poison to make you quiet and another poison to make you talk, and both make you come untied in the head. All are crazy, but only I can hear. Do they really not hear—or are they so strong, so strong they don't care? . . . That enemy woman. She took the snake's tooth away. She let me touch her. But she's not so strong. My enemy is afraid like me.

He felt a welcome numbness spreading over him, like balm on skin scraped raw. She had not tricked him; it was just a sleep

didn't tell me anything I didn't already know. They were last seen going north. A search team found them three weeks later, all the bodies but his. The only odd thing was a note at the end that looked as if someone who read it added it later. 'Q ref Clausewitz.' Ever hear that name?"

Jackson shook his head, then winced. "No, and I wouldn't tell you if I had. If you keep nibbling around the edges of classified information, you're going to get smoked. I don't want to hear about it. You're obsessive about this, you know. It doesn't look good for the only psychologist in Jefferson to be so neurotic."

"I don't care," Janet said quietly. "I'm going to keep looking. I don't care if I stay up all night for the rest of my life. I don't care if I get transferred. I don't—"

"Yeah, yeah," he interrupted rudely. "You don't care if they take you up to Orbital and drill holes in your brain. You'll change your mind when they get started, but don't say I didn't tell you.

"Look, sugar, why don't you just accept the fact that he isn't around anymore?"

"You wouldn't understand. I've found him before when nobody thought I could. We used to play a game when we were kids. He'd take off into the city, at random, till he didn't even know where he was. I could always follow him. It got to be a joke with us. We'd say, 'If you want to find me, just look in the mirror.' Meaning we were twins, of course, but also that all I really had to do was think about what I'd do myself, and I'd be able to figure out where he'd gone. I'm haunted by the feeling that I've missed something, that I'm letting him down."

"You haven't missed anything. It's not your fault. He's just dead. It happens."

"Come on, Jacks. Everyone's so eager to beat me over the head with the fact that he's dead. But nobody can show me a body."

"You told me yourself they sent you a bloody shirt along with his personal effects."

Jan grimaced. "Yes, with the usual tact of the bureaucracy. I'll tell you a little secret, though, Jacks. I had a sample analyzed before I washed that shirt. It wasn't Jon's blood. And if it had been, how would he have managed to remove his shirt while exsanguinating and then vanish without a trace? Riddle me that."

"Search parties aren't always thorough, especially that far into the Open Zone. Maybe he went looking for water or something and smoked it under some bushes. Maybe the lupos ate him. Shit, I'm sorry, Janney, I know it's your brother we're talking about. But be realistic. What else could have happened to him?''

Janet gnawed at her thumbnail. ''Assume the worst, then. Assume he's dead. I still have to find out who did it.''

''That's pretty obvious, isn't it? Scouts get snuffed in the Open Zone all the time.''

''It's not obvious at all. Not to me. Our parents were killed in a protest action back on Delta. It was supposed to be an accident, but after we got old enough to think about it, we never believed that. Our father had been under surveillance as a 'subversive element' for a long time. We were adopted by an aunt when we were about five, and we never did anything out of line, so our political unreliability is just a faint whiff in our files, not a real black mark. But Jon always wanted to be just like his father. Maybe he succeeded too well. The resemblance seems clear to me.''

''You mean somebody had him killed? That's stretching paranoia to new heights. With all the fire and flying death around here, who's going to go out of their way to kill a mere flunky who makes little reports for the government network?''

''Jon was better than that. He was very high, but very nervous, the last time I saw him. He thought he was on to something.

''At first he'd been interested in the fate of the first colony. He knew that officially they had been massacred by the Nupis in some mysterious way and that the inquiry was closed. But he thought maybe he was a little smarter than the official inquirers and could find out what really happened. He heard things—rumors of people seeing artifacts, traces of roads, thing like that. At first he thought he was closing in on the remnants of the first colony. But—''

She hesitated before continuing.

''You know, one of the ostensible purposes of this whole trip was to get back into space and see if we could make contact again with the people who came from Sol-Terra and the home worlds so long ago. To find out why they left our ancestors to colonize Delta and never came back. Jon and I spent a lot of time thinking about that when we were kids. We imagined a lot of things: wondrous galactic empires that would welcome us home, immortal humans who lived in peace and harmony. There was still a little spark of that dream alive in Jon. He would have risked everything to find out if there was somebody else on this planet. Maybe he went too far and found something else instead, something he wasn't supposed to know. The beauty of a war zone is that it's so easy to have accidents there.

"Jacks, you talk to all kinds of people. Do you have any idea what he might have run into up there?"

Jackson blew out a lungful of smoke and rubbed his neck wearily.

"Unlike you, I don't listen to the ramblings of crazy people. I have no need to know what, if anything, is going on anywhere else. I have enough trouble to deal with right here in Jefferson. The only thing I need to know about the north is that I should stay away from it. Bad things happen to people who go too far north. Bad things happen to people who ask too many questions. Why should Jon be any different?"

"He's my brother."

Jackson blew a smoke ring and shot it down with another one.

"So, it's your ass," he said finally.

"I didn't come up here to argue with you, anyway. I found the naked guy. Dougie Petersen's keeping him locked up in the annex."

"Who is he?"

"Well, that's the funny thing. I didn't even have to sneak up on him. Dougie handed him to me on a plate. I guess he's under pressure from the crash investigators. They think this guy is a survivor, and they want to question him. Since he isn't talking, Petersen figured maybe I could work a little magic and get him to cooperate. There's no ID on him anywhere. They have his prints, retina, blood type, but no name. Bizarre things in his blood work, too. I've never seen anything like it.

"You know, I'm getting really tired of getting assigned to soothe and inspire every humper who gets his brains scrambled. Two years of psych and a lot of neuroanatomy, and all of a sudden I'm the flippo's best friend. But in this case I make an exception. They were fucking him over to an extreme degree. It was more than the usual brainless malpractice that goes on around here. And with Petersen sucking up to this Simonds chuck from PCOM, he definitely needs my protection. Petersen would vivisect his mother for a good efficiency rating."

Jackson looked really alarmed. "Holy shit. Do you have any idea who this Simonds actually is?"

Janet shrugged. "Dougie didn't say. Why?"

"Simonds doesn't really work for Air and Space Command. He's an aide to Tony Gero."

"So?"

"So Gero is the Net supervisor at PCOM, if that means anything to you. He's the head shark of all sharks. Even General Nymann can't interfere with him. Believe me, if Gero's interested in this guy, you want to stay away from him.

"And don't try to fool me with that 'who, me?' expression. I know how pigheaded and stubborn you really are. Now you're off on another crusade to provoke Petersen till he transfers you to some firebase at the backass of beyond. And you're the last friend I've got who can tell me what day of the week it is."

"Don't give me a hard time," she protested. "If you'd seen this guy, you'd understand. They're making him crazy. They're doing him actual harm."

Jackson gave her a weary look.

"So what else is new?" he asked. "We're not healers here, my pure-hearted little friend. We're technicians. We correct malfunctions in these units and plug them back into the mighty machine."

"Stop it, Jacks. I hate it when you talk like that."

"Yeah, the truth hurts. You think you're rescuing and rehabilitating the poor lost humpers. Actually, you're just giving them another chance to get killed and mutilated."

"Oh, get off my face, Jackson. I don't see you refusing to sew people up just because they could get hurt again. You may think you'd be doing them a favor by letting them rot, but they wouldn't agree. They want help, and I'm going to get it for them, regardless of what you or Petersen or some chuck from out of town thinks about it."

Jackson sucked hard on his smoke and burned his fingers.

"Goddamn it, Janney, grow up, will you?" he said angrily. "The harder you dig, the deeper it gets. You can't get them any effective help. Even if you get them out of the hospital, they're still trapped. You can't get them out of the war."

"Well, it has to end sometime. Maybe we can keep a few of us alive till then."

"Shit. They don't even want to win. They want it to go on forever, because as long as there's a war, they have total control. 'Take back the stars,' hell. If we really did succeed in recolonizing space, we might all get out from under, and that's the very last thing they want. They'd rather jack around over who owns this pathetic little piece of real estate till we all smoke the big one. New Hope—what a joke."

Janet's anger vanished. She understood why Jackson was in

such a belligerent humor. "You went out to the goodwill clinic yesterday, didn't you?"

"Yes, I did, and yes, I lost one, and you can get out of therapeutic mode and not waste any of your empathizing on me." He ground out his roach and concentrated on salvaging the remnants. "It's the kids that get me. I figure we got ourselves into this mess, but they've been landed on a strange planet without their consent. This little guy had repeated attacks of parasitic fever till he just wore himself out. It makes me so fucking mad. Why aren't we building clean water systems and figuring out how to kill the native bugs instead of wasting our time reassembling guys who were perfectly healthy till they blew each other to shit?"

Janet sighed. "I'm starting to see what I would call borderline malnutrition, too, but of course there's an official pronouncement against noticing a thing like that. The fair-share rationing process ensures ample nutrients for all, and all that good shit. PCOM collects what they grow and issues ration cards, but you'll note the soldiers get the lion's share, and the farmers eat corn and beans. They might as well be in a labor camp. It comes to the same thing."

"Yeah, and the same thing applies to us. You know we don't really have a choice. So take my advice and don't step into the path of the machine. It will not grind to a halt; it'll just step on your head till you go pop like an eggshell and move right on over your body."

"Well, you can calm yourself, Jacks. I don't want to mess with anyone. I'm curious about this guy, and I think he deserves a chance to get well, but I'm not going to *do* anything, dakko?"

Jackson seemed to regain his usual mocking equilibrium. "We all need our fantasies, I guess. If you want to pretend you can actually heal people, that's quaint but fairly harmless."

"Stop it, Jacks. You can't get to me that easily. In fact, if you're still in the mood, I believe I'll have that drink now."

"Here you go. See, I'm a beneficial organism, well adapted to my environment. I provide the only possible escape."

13

Khalle relaxed his guard a fraction after several days when they fed him and let him sleep, and no more people came to ask him questions he did not understand. At last he was healing and getting some strength back. He started to think about getting out of there. Soon he would be well enough for whatever they had in mind, and he did not want to wait and find out what that might be.

One day they came to his room and gave him clothing. It was just like theirs but without any decorations on the chest and shoulders. That ought to make things a little easier, he thought. If he looked like the rest of them, that was good. They took him out into the hall with only one guard, who was careless and apparently unarmed. Throughout the walk he debated with himself whether he should take that chance and go. But he did not know which way was out. He decided to wait as long as he could. The moment he smelled trouble, he would move. Until then he would go along with them and hope to learn something about the strange place.

The soldier delivered him to another room very much like his own. There was no one in it but the woman who had spoken to him. He decided it would be safe to go in.

Janet chewed her pencil, waiting for the patient to arrive; the habit did not show as badly as chewing on her nails. She straightened up and put the pencil down as she heard a knock on the door.

"You want me to wait outside?" the orderly asked.

"That's okay, Nicky. I won't be needing you for another hour or so."

"You sure you don't want me to wait? I hear this chuck's kind of a weird one," Nicky persisted.

"In that case I certainly don't want you to wait," she said severely. "The less you hear, the better."

She kept an eye on the stranger during that exchange. His eyes flicked from one to the other as they spoke. Clearly, he was alert and listening.

"Come in," she said. "Have a seat." She pointed to a comfortable chair. His eyes followed her finger, but he did not sit. He took one step into the room, moving aside from the door. He cased the room, locating the corner where he would have a good view of door and window, then moved to it without turning his back on her and folded up gracefully onto the floor.

Janet smiled ruefully. "You may be paranoid, but you sure aren't crazy," she said.

He read in her voice that she was well disposed toward him. He still did not trust her, though. She wore the same clothes as the ones who tormented him, the enemies. She was one of them. He did not understand what she wanted. Why was she concerned for him?

There had been one, before, who came to him wearing the clothing of an enemy and became a brother. He would not think the name, even to himself. Those-cut-off had no names till the deathgift was paid and the mourning was finished. He put his attention back on the enemy woman. Her face had a pinched, pale look as if she were unhappy about something. She was grieving for someone, too, maybe.

She kept talking to him, undisturbed by his staring. Her voice had the same gentle, soothing quality that Deronh used on his horses. He flinched as that thought went through his mind.

There was a man who worked with horses once, but I am alone here, he said to himself. That has nothing to do with me.

Nothing she said seemed to elicit any response, not even the flicker of an eye. After a while she fell silent. She knew better than to stare him in the face, but she watched him sidelong and waited. Soon she felt him looking back at her. Behind the silence she felt uncertainty. He was studying her, trying to decide about her. When she did not say anything or make any sudden moves, he let himself examine the rest of the room. He saw the map she had taped to the wall, and his eyes lit up.

"Take a look," she offered. "Here's Jefferson, where we are.

The refinery, south of here in the desert. Real desert down there, not like the Dust, where at least there are thorns and things. Farms, firebases, airfields, settlements—still a few of those around North Fork where the bombing wasn't too bad. That's us—blue zone, the Consorso. Green Zone, the New Peoples' Union. And in between them the Open Zone, which of course means the Closed Zone. Pretty much the way it was back on Delta."

She hoped that he would recognize and respond to something in the map or her description. He examined the map closely—especially the northern area, where the mountains started—and turned away. He had not found anything he was looking for. As she watched, she wished she could get hold of a map that went farther up into the mountains. It was curious, but they all seemed to stop within a couple of hundred miles of the defensive perimeter.

Paper conservation, I suppose, she thought. They have strange ideas of how to economize.

"At first I thought he might be a civilian," she told Petersen later. "I think I can scratch that possibility. He behaves like a polvorado, what they call someone who's been out in the Dust too long. I tried various kinds of lingua on him. Sometimes people will respond to their home language better than Delteix. I tried some of the Union languages as well, but I didn't get any reaction. I suppose it's possible he's from some remote area where they speak a dialect I've never heard or that he's never learned Delteix, but that seems unlikely. It seems more as if he has simply decided that human beings are not a significant part of the landscape. What I say seems to run over him like rainwater. He knows I'm there, but it just doesn't matter. I've seen that before. They shut down all response except to a perceived threat. His level of anxiety has to come down several notches before he can take an interest in conversation."

She knew that Petersen expected her to report on every detail of her sessions with the stranger, but she told him only enough to keep him satisfied. Much of their time together was simply frustrating and pointless. The moments when he seemed to reveal a fleeting response disturbed her too much to report. She felt that she was glimpsing a pattern that should have made sense but did not. She did not want Petersen to have grounds for jumping to conclusions she had not yet reached.

I'm sure there's nothing organically wrong, she typed into her private file.

> *He has a phenomenal memory, and he listens with such intensity. Once he understood that I wanted him to speak, he easily repeated anything I said. But he never says anything on his own. He names objects now, but he won't name himself. There's something really odd about it.*
>
> *When I first saw him, I thought he was paranoid; now I'm not so sure. A lot of the people I see appear paranoid, but since someone really has been trying to kill them, I can't necessarily class that as a symptom until I know more about their situation. It looks as if he's responded to some extremely traumatic event by forgetting who he is and refusing to talk. But I get the strangest feeling that he hasn't forgotten anything, that I'm teaching a frightened stranger words he never heard before.*

The mysterious Colonel Simonds never came to hear her reports. One day, however, Petersen told her that Simonds was not pleased with her rate of progress.

"But we *are* making progress! He may not be talking spontaneously, but at least he has shown that he's capable of speech."

"Colonel Simonds feels that he's well enough for more intensive work. And since this isn't really your field of expertise, he asked me to consider turning him over to a specialist from the hospital in North Fork."

"I don't think that would be a good idea at all. Most of what I've been doing is a process of establishing trust. He's acutely aware of his surroundings. Change them arbitrarily and you could drive him back to a deeper withdrawal."

"He's planning to come next week to evaluate the patient himself. If you want to convince him your work is significant, I suggest you move fast."

Janet went to her office the next day with a feeling of defeat.

The worst of it, she thought, is that I know it's my own fault. I played it safe. I didn't take any chances, I suppose because I've been afraid to find out. I don't know which would be worse—to be right or to be wrong. If I don't take the risk, though, I may be blowing his only chance to communicate with a human being before Simonds takes over.

She did not try to talk to him. She sat quietly and tried to sense his presence as she had once been able to sense Jon. She held her own awareness calm and open, like a hand that he could reach for if he wanted to. She could feel him listening, too, wondering what she was doing. After a few minutes, she seemed to see herself through his eyes. Her chair and desk became strange, uncomfortable artifacts. There was no point in them. They insulted him, holding him off beyond barriers as if he were a wild animal. She longed to get up from her desk and sit with him on the floor. She was not sure if that was her desire or his.

This isn't happening, she told herself. You're totally losing your objectivity. You should get out of here right now and go tell Petersen you bit off more than you could chew.

No. To hell with Petersen. To hell with objectivity. To hell with everything that's correct and doesn't work.

She went and sat on the floor facing the stranger. She nearly touched him, but he tensed all over, and she withdrew her hand.

At least she finally had his full attention.

"You know, I'm not technically qualified to do this," she said. "I don't have a lot of techniques like the ones they'd use on you in North Fork. They let me do this because nobody else wants to talk to crazy people, and I don't mind. You see, I want to know how it happens that we can talk to each other at all. That's what I set out to study. There's a whole world in every person, and these sounds we make are the only picture of it we can have. Like telemetry from the starprobe. Stories from the unknown worlds."

She held his eyes; she held his attention with the words, while with the sense she could not define she traced the shape of his defenses.

"I tell people a lot of stories in here. Sometimes you can enter into a story and find there what you can't say on your own. And if that doesn't work, well, it passes the time, anyway.

"I want to tell you a story. You might want to pay attention, because nobody on this world or any other has heard it yet.

"My father was a newsman. He traveled to the worst places on Delta, trying to find out the truth and bring it back for people to see. We went to the airport to meet him one day, my mother and Jon and I. Jon and I are twins. Were twins."

She saw the stranger's hand move. He held out his first and second fingers pressed together. He understood.

"Two alike. Yes. Two." She licked her lips and continued. "Well, it wasn't any of those far-off places that got him in the end. There was a big crowd at the airport. I thought they were all there to welcome my father. I told you I was very young. When they started shouting, I got scared. And then there were the riot police. With all the special gear they had on, I didn't know if they were human or what.

"Someone in the crowd started throwing things. We saw the police begin to move, but we couldn't see when they actually hit the front rank. We felt the shock and heard the screaming run back through the group like a wave. Then the crowd began to move. A mass that size has undertow. We were torn apart. I couldn't find my mother."

She felt herself trembling. She could see the people so much taller, all strangers, pushing and trampling. She could hear them screaming. She was falling. She blanked out the images with a great effort and forced herself to speak on in dry, carefully chosen words.

"Part of the crowd stampeded down a passage that was closed by a locked gate. Twenty-seven people died there. My mother was one of them. My father came off the plane and looked for her everywhere. When the police ordered the survivors to clear the area, he didn't move fast enough. Rubber bullets aren't supposed to kill, but when they hit you in the head, sometimes they do. They always said it was an accident. It was a scandal in the news for a while, but nothing could be proved.

"I guess I fell, and that saved my life. Somehow I rolled or scrambled to the edge of the crowd. We were kept in protective detention for a while, till they could find an aunt who came and got us. She was good to us, but from then on our family began and ended with us. We didn't take a chance on anyone else."

He was not watching her; he was staring at nothing. She wondered if he had heard her at all. She continued doggedly.

"That's not the point, though. There's something else that I never told anybody. I lost my mother. I called for her, and she didn't answer. Instead there was an emptiness. A great silence that would never answer again."

He was so silent. She wanted to grab him and force him to look at her.

"You've heard that silence, haven't you?" she asked. "It rings in your head forever. You can't get it out of your mind, that emptiness where they go and don't come back."

She stopped again. Who's talking crazy now? she thought. Unprofessional. I should stop this right now.

But she had him. She could feel it; he was listening. She clenched her fist. Nothing's crazy if it works, she told herself.

"I knew she was gone," she said. "But Jon—I could *hear* him." She looked for words that would reach the stranger. There was no word for the sense that was close as a touch. Jon's frantic crying had pulled her from the aid station; she remembered running across the asphalt heaped with bodies, tugging at their limp weight till she found Jon huddled underneath.

He was listening intently; they were both so intent that neither noticed how he had reached to touch her arm with his fingertips.

"For months he screamed with fear when he saw a helmet, a uniform, a stick, even a pair of shiny shoes. We stayed together, though; we never lost each other again. Until last January. Now he's gone; I don't know where. Maybe I'll never know.

"That's the real reason why I became a doctor and started studying how people talk to each other. It wasn't to further the knowledge of mankind or get a good job. I wanted to raise the dead and find the lost. A crazy reason. I've spent a lifetime maintaining a low profile so no one would ever find out what I really thought.

"I've never told this to anyone else, but I have to talk to you because I think you can hear me, and no one but Jon has ever been able to. You can be found if you want to be found. You can answer me."

For the first time she looked directly at the stranger.

"My name is Janet. I want to be your friend."

Shocked, Khalle had to will himself motionless. A touch, light and fleeting like thistledown, had caught him in his hiding place. She had used his own tricks on him. Caught up in her tale, he had listened unguarded, open to her voice and eyes. He was still safe. He must be; she did not have the skill to take his thoughts. But he had seen her story. He did not understand it all, but he saw the shining death bird, the soldiers, and the bodies on the ground, and he tasted the familiar ache of old sorrow. When the images faded, his fingers still rested on her arm; in her eyes he saw the small guarded light, burning fiercely in a wide darkness. He wanted to hold on to the silence that was so much safer than speech, but he had to learn their language: how to ask why.

"Zhanne," he said. *It is shining.* He was startled again by his own voice and pulled his hand back hastily. But he had spoken to her.

There was a rap on the door, followed by more insistent knocking. She looked at her watch and realized that more than an hour had passed. They were probably worried about her, shut in with the maniac. It was a good thing she had locked the door. She scrambled to her feet in order not to be seen with him and went to let Nicky in.

14

Khalle knew it was dangerous to linger there, but still he hesitated. The woman had offered him help. He longed to accept what he needed so badly; there was so much he would have liked to ask. Yet he feared to reveal himself further to her. "Every question gives knowledge about the questioner," they had taught him. It seemed better to keep quiet and listen.

He knew he had been wrong to stay when the two strangers came to his sleeping place. They wore cumbersome clothes, but underneath, the bodies' shape said weapon training. Something smelled like metal and danger. There were cold thoughts in their eyes. The dakta-soldier fawned on them, but he was not afraid of them—and that, thought Khalle, is because he's a fool.

"This won't hurt you; it's to help you relax," the bigger of the two said, smiling.

What would not hurt him? What was the weapon? He strained to understand. One of the medikh moved behind him, and as he turned toward her, she pressed something against his neck. It stung briefly, and he tried to brush it off. It was insect-sized, but it felt like cloth, and it stuck. His hands had become clumsy; he could feel the medicine-poison spreading through his body.

"We just want to ask you a few questions," the man said pleasantly.

Khalle tried to breathe easy, but he could feel perception sliding from his control. The walls and floor became meaningless; he did not know anymore exactly where he was. There were too many positions clashing in his mind. The voices were coming back, too, like waves washing over crumbling sand. He could hear them crying, almost as if they were real people: *It hurts. I'm afraid.* So many of them.

The men were speaking to him, asking; the words reverberated in his head with their meanings half a step ahead of them. Neither one made any sense to him. He saw the fire-from-the-sky ship burning again. *Why aren't you dead?* That was what they wanted to know. *How can you be alive? You shouldn't be.* There was no good answer to that one.

Their voices were not so smooth anymore.

"We know you can talk, and we intend to have some answers. You might as well make it easy. You can start by telling us your name."

He could barely make out their faces. He could not tell which direction he was really seeing. One way he saw walls, and another way he saw floors, a close-up of someone's arm, a frame, a window; one way nothing but darkness and the suffocating knowledge of being blind forever. He felt the cold sting of alcohol and the ripping pain where they washed his burns; someone was eating, and someone was retching, and someone was fast asleep, seeing men like tiny black ants scrabbling across a vast red plain—a dream within a dream.

"You will respond to questions. You will look at me when I speak to you."

Someone put a hand on his face and jerked his head around. The response was no longer under his control. He uncoiled in a multidimensional lashing out of rage. He could not tell what he struck or where, but he felt things shatter, and that was all he cared about. For an instant he was weightless in the eye of his fury. Then a thing with a cold metal taste smashed into the side of his face, and he collided with a hard surface that turned out to be the floor.

Warm blood ran into his mouth, and he hugged his own personal pain; it chased the shadows out of his head.

That's good, dogfuckers, good! he thought fiercely. Hurt me again till I know where you are, and I'll cave your heads in!

A lot of people had come into the room, so many that every time he struck out he hit someone. Every grunt of pain and surprise gave him fierce satisfaction. But there were so many of them, and their weapon was the poison that made his body betray him. His arms and legs were too heavy to lift, and even their blows seemed far away.

Janet heard the noise and came running. By the time she

reached the heavy double doors to the annex, internal security guards had sealed off the hall. They waved her back, hands on their unslung rifles. She could see them mouthing "Sir, you can't come in here" through the glass. Other medical personnel had arrived before she had, but they were headed the other way, toward the main hospital. Several of them seemed to be injured. She paused by the doors, trying to think of a way to get in. As she hesitated, two men who did not look like the others passed her. One was in uniform; he was limping and held one arm pressed protectively against his side. The other wore a plain suit and had a bruised and bloody laceration over his eye. Wondering who they were, Janet focused on them curiously and caught a snatch of their conversation.

"What do you make of that?" the one with colonel's insignia asked.

"It can't be all put on," the other said. His voice was cool and smooth, unruffled by the confusion. "But we've heard him be rational with the woman doctor, so why does he stop talking now? It seems somebody has gotten to him. It's possible he's been blocked against questions. Or maybe he's actually psycho. But that doesn't mean he's not programmed. There's no doubt in my mind that he comes under the Clausewitz definition. It's imperative that we find out how he got here and what he's doing here. We need to take him out of here, somewhere we can really work with him."

"Dakko. I'd love to have that sucker under restraints. He's broken my fucking ribs."

Janet remained invisible to them, but she was alight with a single thought as a lit torch was enveloped with a single flame: *They bugged my office.* She had been used as a weapon, and she had been stupid enough to let it happen. The men who passed by did not realize that war had just been declared.

She tracked Petersen down after an hour of anxiety.

"What's happening to the man in the annex? Why haven't I been allowed to see him?"

"Be reasonable, Janet! He was asked a few simple questions, and he went berserk. He's dangerous."

"A few simple questions. Who are these people, anyway?"

Peterson looked uncomfortable. "Specialists. I told you Colonel Simonds was coming to interview him. Mr. Smith is an analyst; he works for Space Command, and he's here to assist with the crash investigation."

"And by whose authority are they monkeying around with my patient? Don't you think a consultation would have been in order, at the very least? I wasn't even informed. I found out after the damage had been done. Your so-called specialists may have undone a month's painstaking labor through a few minutes of incredible negligence. This man is in no condition to be interrogated. But now that it's happened, the worst thing you could do is deprive him of treatment. I need to start working with him right away, or we may lose everything we've gained."

"Well, it's not really in my hands anymore," he said. "They've requested a transfer for him. He's going to a special facility where he can get intensive therapy."

Janet was stunned. "On whose recommendation?" she asked finally.

"In cases like this, a recommendation isn't really necessary."

"Where is he going?"

"To North Fork. Now, look, Janet, I know you feel proprietary about this case, but you must see the advantages for the patient. They'll do everything possible for him up there."

"They'll do everything possible, will they? Is what happened this morning a sample of that? They couldn't care less about him as a person. He's just a program they want into."

"That's enough!" Peterson said. "They've arranged a transfer for him in two days, and that's the way it is. The discussion is closed. I want you to stay away from him until then; you obviously have lost your ability to be objective about this case."

Janet took a step closer to him, and he backed away involuntarily.

"Oh, really," she said. "I wonder if anyone has objectively considered the possible results of coldcocking a man with a barely healed head injury. Do these specialists want him to arrive coherent and able to communicate, or do they just want a warm body? It's quite possible his skull has been refractured. Someone should be monitoring his condition very carefully. Maybe you would like to do that yourself, since you can be more objective about it. After all, you're the one who will have to explain to your 'specialists' why they get a comatose gork to ship."

"All right. All right. Go ahead and monitor him. Just make sure you report any change to me. Do not treat him without consulting me. I'm going to put that in writing. And make damn sure he's all right for transfer. You want the responsibility? It's yours."

* * *

She took a deep breath before she trusted herself to look at him. There were bruises in too many places for it to be accidental. Someone had struck him repeatedly with a heavy object. The welt across his face was the worst. She turned his head carefully to check the old injuries, and his eyelids did not flicker.

Another big favor I did him, she thought. Found out how to sedate him.

As she had expected, the bruises went on down his ribs and back. At first she felt sickened by the brutality of the beating, but then she noticed the pattern. His arms and sides were badly bruised, but he had protected himself from serious damage.

Drug him, slug him—he just never stops fighting. That's his language, she thought despairingly. They'll kill him long before I ever get him to speak to me another way. Madre'dio, he must have been fighting since he was born. Some of these scars are so old.

She had never had a chance to examine him that closely. She shook her head over the old wound under his ribs. It was a miracle he had survived that one. The scar was really ugly; the surgeon must have been amazingly bad. The minor scars were the most intriguing, though. Slash marks covered his forearms—knife fights? Inside both wrists the skin was mottled and puckered, like cigarette burns on an abused child, but worse. He clenched his fists, even in sleep. She uncurled his fingers gently and looked at his hands. The sides were hard and callused, which made sense. He had obviously been trained in unarmed combat. His palms were callused, too, in a pattern she could not account for. It did not fit with holding a tool. A hammer, maybe. A baseball bat? She curled her own hands into that position. It would have to be something long and heavy. And the skin was tougher on the left. He was left-handed.

She checked his fingers; the knuckles were bruised and cut, but nothing seemed to be broken. She frowned and looked again at his fingertips. There were calluses there, too—familiar ones. He played the guitar. It had to be—there was no weapon she had ever heard of that one fired with one's fingertips.

Her grip tightened on the stranger's hands. Words were not enough to reach him, and he could not feel her touch.

Music is a language too, she thought.

She took the pocket box from her lab coat and set it by his head. The music was faint but very clear.

By the light of burning bridges I read the writing on the wall:
There's smoke on the wind and I'm running blind
And I'm riding for a fall.
Is it my luck that's running out,
Or is it the tide that's turning?
The only light on the road tonight is the light of bridges burning.

The stranger opened his eyes and looked at her. He was as stone-faced and silent as he had been at first, but the music had awakened him. She had no idea what was in his thoughts, but she caught the flavor of them, and they were unmistakably strange. Like that blood workup—every single thing in his record was almost normal, but when they all came together, the total was something strange. Like music—each note was familiar, but when they came together, they made a tune that had never been heard before.

"Oh, my God," she whispered. "How could I have been so stupid?"

He's not a civilian, and he's no damn experiment. He isn't one of us at all. That explains the funny blood and all the other things they wouldn't let me see. It explains why the drugs didn't work and why he won't speak Delteix or any lingua that I've heard. He's human—but he's not our kind of human. What Jon was looking for has come and found me.

She knew then what she had to do.

Protest memos won't do it. No amount of going through channels will help. If I don't take the risk, they'll destroy him.

I know who you are. Trust me. I want to help.

Khalle thought he was dreaming. The woman touched his palms and spoke to him with her heart as open as one of his own people. She offered help.

Never taking his eyes from hers, he searched her face and thought for a clue to her. He went carefully. He had no wish to reveal himself to her, and she seemed so quick to understand. Why would she turn against her own kind?

He saw that she was indeed a kind of healer. Also, he saw her working with many strange machines, but he let those images go. They confused and frightened him—pictures in his mind that he had no words for. It seemed clear that her people were like the Somostai. They loved things and gained from them a secret knowledge that gave them all their power.

He called up the picture of the two men who had questioned him and felt the red glow of anger in her. He showed her the doctor with the poisoned needle, and she hurled the image from her as she had hurled the needle. Captains who do not protect, healers who will not heal—these things make her angry, and she looks for a new city to serve. That he could understand.

He made his decision. He would trust her, far enough to accept the help she might give. He would give her his name.

But he could not find the word that meant "Khalle." She frowned and tried to repeat it. "Halley?" It was a sound without meaning. Her mind did not run on weapons, but she knew music. He had felt that when she touched his hands. She had been close to the word he needed then. He reached for it with supreme concentration.

Sing, he said carefully. *Singer. That's me.*

With the effort of speaking the strange language, he slipped out of rapport. Echoes of music faded from his mind.

> Do you reach a hand from the promised land
> Or the shore of no returning?
> The only light in your eyes tonight
> Is the light of bridges burning.

"I have to go away for a while," she told him out loud. "I'm coming back, okay? Maybe you'll feel better when I do."

She collided with Petersen as she hurried out into the main hospital.

"Well? How is he?"

"Thanks to you and your bully boys, he's regressed totally. I can't get a thing out of him. Congratulations—you've produced a really wonderful case of iatrogenic catatonia. Oh, don't worry, I'll keep trying, but even I have to sleep every once in a while. Don't let anyone beat him up while I'm gone."

She pushed past him rudely.

Once again she headed for Jackson's instead of going home to bed. She found him up, running a copy of a videodisc. When he saw her come in, he popped it out of the machine and slipped it casually out of sight.

"What are you watching?"

"Just running off some pornoflix for the troops. Wanna check one out with me?"

"No, thanks. Listen, Jacks, have you been afflicted with otomuralism since you moved in here?"

He looked startled, then laughed. "No. I made damn sure of that. Why do you think I live in this rat trap? Of course, there's no guarantee that some buggerbutt isn't skulking across the street with a big ear, but we're about as safe as we can get. So what kind of secrets are we talking about?"

"I want to do some business with you."

"Aw, fuck. Damn it, Janney, you disappoint me."

"What's the matter?"

"Well, it's been really nice knowing one person who didn't want me to deal them some kind of shit."

"Idiot! What makes you think I want to buy drugs? I need clothes and gear for a big man, taller than you but not quite as hefty. And a few things for a little guy. I have a list here. And I don't want to have to sign for them anywhere or leave any record of the transaction. You can eat the list when you're through."

"Whoa, wait a minute, I'm not in the haberdashery business. I specialize strictly in recreational self-abuse. I'm afraid I can't help you with this particular fantasy." His fingers touched his neck absently.

"Well, I'm pretty sure you can. You know, when you lie outright, you're fairly convincing. But when you're just kind of stretching the truth, you rub your neck. It's a habit you should get out of before somebody else notices."

"Oh, Christ," Jackson muttered. He went ahead and rubbed his neck anyway.

"Just what is it that you think I can do for you?" he asked carefully.

"I don't think, I know. This business of yours is a big cover-up. Oh, you do really sell people drugs. But you're using the money and contacts to run another kind of network. People put any weird behavior down to your well-known profession and don't suspect whatever else you're up to. I'm not sure exactly what that is, either. You deal in supplies of various kinds: food, gas, medical stuff, maybe weapons.

"See, there's something odd happening with inventory shrinkage in this area. It's pretty well covered up, but if you look at all the records, there's a pattern. Computers are very good at looking over all the data and establishing a pattern, and I'm very good with computers.

"I'm not asking for much. I don't even want you to do it free. I've got the money; I just don't want it traced to me."

"Now, what if I tell you you're crazy?"

"Oh, you won't do that."

"Or else?"

"Jackson! You're hurting my feelings. I'm not threatening you; you're my friend."

"Oh? You're gonna trust me? This wasted old bum with bloodshot eyes? Jackson the permanently pumped?"

"That's an act. Well, mostly an act. Personally I think you could ease up a little and still maintain verisimilitude." She leaned over and patted his arm. "Come on, do it for the glory. Haven't you ever wanted to say 'up yours' to PCOM? Now you've got a chance to snatch their bone right out from under their slavering jaws."

"Sweet jumping Jesus. 'A big guy'? You mean that flippo from the annex? What are you planning to do with him? You know if he gets caught they'll pump him dry, and it'll be your ass on a skewer."

"Leave that to me. You just get me something for him to wear besides hospital jammies, and I'll make sure he disappears."

He rolled himself a smoke with elaborate care, remaining silent for several minutes.

"All right, I'll have the stuff delivered," he said quietly. "Jesus. And I thought you were safe to hang out with. Now tell me the whole story. Why did you decide you had to move this guy, anyway?"

She told him what she had heard and seen but left out her silent conversation with the man who called himself Singer.

"Okay, I know this Simonds," Jackson said. "But who's Smith? What does he look like?"

"A suit person, not in uniform, not in a lab coat. Medium-sized, short black hair. Very tidy in kind of a creepy way. I just saw him in the hall. He was shook up and angry—not loud, but you could feel the air crackling. Strange eyes." She shivered. "They're a real pale gray, almost transparent. Cold."

"Smith, my ass. That was Gero himself. I have to hand it to you, kid, you sure know how to pick your enemies.

"Well, now that you've dragged me into this and exposed all my secrets, I guess I might as well go whole hog and do it free of charge. One good turn deserves another, and I might need a favor one day myself, read me?"

The day shift had not yet arrived when she returned to the hospital. She headed for her office, then changed her mind. If they had bugged her therapy sessions, they might be picking up her keyboard, too. She went to the clerk's office on the second floor instead. The clerk was late as usual. In five minutes Janet had accessed the medical records and the phone connection to central personnel in North Fork and made a few changes in each database. She fixed Kruger's records, too; it no longer seemed very important. Let him do it his own way, she thought. Then she tracked down the faint whispers leaking from his plugs and found the orderly named Lopez leisurely mopping a distant hallway.

"Get a cart and come to my office. I have to move some things down to storage."

He muttered under his breath but followed her. As soon as they reached the storage vault, she turned to face him.

"Nicky, I've got a proposition for you."

He laughed nervously and backed off a step or two.

"Get serious," she said. "It's not that kind of a proposition. I hear you're trying to transfer out of here."

"No shit. I've been trying for months. They say I'm not suited for other duties."

"Where have you tried to go? Would you go up-country if that was all you could get?"

"Watch me, I'm gone. If I wanted to be a fucking hospital flunky, I could have stayed back on the world and done it."

"I've got a deal for you. I can fix it so you get out of here. The only thing is, I'll want you to take something with you."

"Oh, no, now I've seen everything," he said scornfully. "You tell whoever sent you to say this that I ain't biting. Listen, I got busted for drugs once already. You know what happens if I do it again? I get sent down to Dusty River, to the labor camp. For the duration. Forget it. Excuse me for saying this, sir, but you are the lamest narizota I ever met, and I met a few."

"Will you stuff your face in your mouth a minute and listen to me? I can arrange orders for you if you take someone along."

"Who?"

"The guy from the annex."

"The weird one? El loco?"

"Yes. And you'll have to make sure he passes for normal. Because if anyone starts asking questions, they'll trace him back here and probably catch you, too. That's why you'd be going up north. Out in the Dust, there are no snoopy eyes.

"And it wouldn't be forever. After a few months, as soon as

he gets things figured out, you can split up. I just want you to help him get away from here. After that, he's on his own."

He squinted at her in puzzlement. "Why are you doing this? What's in it for you?"

"This man is a package that shouldn't be opened by the wrong people." She stared at him as coldly as she could and saw comprehension and fear dawn in his eyes.

"You trying to tell me he's some kind of agent?"

"I never said or implied anything of the sort. You might want to remember, though, there are wheels within wheels here. You might be better off in the Dust than staying here, now that we've had our little talk."

"Okay. It's a deal."

"Orders to Kruger's Mike Force for the two of you will arrive in this afternoon's fax batch. Gear will be dropped at the loading docks in a package labeled 'Laboratory Supplies.' Are those words too big for you?"

"I can read!" Lopez said indignantly.

"Well, if you have any problems, there's a logo of three orange triangles. Take the stuff with you when you go to clean up tonight. Get him dressed, walk out, and get on the bus to the airfield.

"I have here a message to be personally delivered to Kruger. There's nothing in it that will incriminate you if it's opened, but Kruger's smart enough to know if you tamper with it. It will be beneficial to your career with him if you pass it on as is."

She turned back with her foot on the first step of the stairs. "You want to remember one other thing. This gives you something on me—but don't forget that your file determines what happens to you, and I'm very friendly with the data center. Do you understand me?"

He nodded. The feeling of frightening someone was strange to her.

You're the one who should be frightened, you fool, she said to herself. If this goes bad, you're the one who's going to Dusty River. Or worse. But she really did not care.

She went back to Singer's room to tell him the news.

The boy will come for you. She showed him Nicky again and knew that he remembered. She wanted desperately to explain to him where he would be going and what he should do, but she could not do it out loud and got hopelessly confused trying to communicate across the barrier of an alien mind and language. She had to give up. *The boy will tell you*, she assured him.

"God, I hope you understand," she said helplessly.

He stared at her for a long moment with those midnight eyes, frowning slightly. He reached up and took her hand again.

Why?

Into his mind came the fences and the spiked wire again; seen from low down, as if from a child's eyes, they seemed impossibly tall.

Because of the wire, he heard her say. *Because no living thing should live behind the wire. I can't give you freedom, but I give you a chance to run for it. So go!*

She did not want him to go; she wanted to ask him to come back.

And don't come back, she emphasized. *They'll hurt you. Stay away!*

He let go of her hand, but she could still feel his eyes as she walked away.

"He's still sedated," she told Petersen, "but he's responding to sensation, and I feel confident there's no brain damage. The scans look all right. The only way to be totally sure would be to stop the medication and let him regain consciousness naturally. I didn't want to take that step without your approval."

"Your good judgment seems to be returning," Petersen said. "There's no way I'm going to have him conscious again while he's in my hospital. As long as you're sure there's no actual trauma, I'm going to let them worry about his state of mind. Our responsibility has ended. Read me?"

"I plan to file a protest against Simonds's handling of this whole thing," Jan said stiffly.

"Do that," Petersen said. "It'll do you good. In fact, let me see it when you're through. I may want to add my name, if you can word it temperately. Can't have them walking on our heads, can we?

"Now, why don't you take the day off? You've done a good night's work. Actually, I'm glad you called my attention to the fact that someone should observe the patient. That will put us completely in the clear if anything does go wrong. Good thinking."

"Thank you, sir."

She stayed away from the hospital all day, and that night she went to Jackson's long-running party, where she could be seen by many witnesses to be far from Singer's disappearance. Around the time he and Nicky would be leaving, she drifted to the edge of the crush and leaned her head out the window for a touch of fresh air. She listened, holding her breath, and heard no disturbance. She imagined two new shadows fading into the night and lifted her glass to them silently.

Jackson sidled up to her, leaning close as if he were whispering endearments. He was clearly nervous.

"Just what is so fucking funny?" he muttered. "What has finally cracked a smile on the face of the android doctor from Planet Purple?"

"I'm listening to the merry crackle of burning bridges," she said. "It's such a heartwarming sound."

15

Singer waited with the boy soldier near the loading docks, where the wagons-that-roared came and went. He could see the sky for the first time in weeks, but a dusty haze glowed with the lights of many buildings, and he could not pick out a single star. He moved to strip off the dark glasses that covered his eyes but thought better of it and left them on. The woman had told him not to be seen. He tugged at the strap of the bag that held his new belongings and checked automatically for his knife. At least he was armed again.

The boy shoved him with an elbow. "Wake up, this is our bus."

Singer did not like actually getting into the *bus*, but once he was inside, it jerked and bumped pretty much like any other wagon. He wanted to ask Nikei where the horses were, but he had not seen any and did not know the word.

He forgot about it when they stepped out onto the flat pavement. He remembered the place from many bad dreams. There had been a fire there—a big one. Against the darkness, lights ran off into the night in straight lines, showing how immense was the place the strangers had built. He stared, disoriented, till Nicky had to shove him up the ramp with the others. He found himself in the belly of a great beast that thundered and shrieked. A mighty force pushed him back against the webbing. He pressed his hand against the wall beside him. It was smooth and gray. He had been in a similar place before. He was fighting a rising panic when Nicky spoke to him. The effort to understand was a welcome distraction.

"I knew a guy once who went flippo when he got on the

transport,'' Nicky said cheerfully. ''Dumb shit couldn't handle watching the ground go away. Picture what happened when we got on the shuttle and went off-planet.''

''Planet?'' Singer asked.

''You know, off-world. Worlds? Like Alpha, Beta, Gamma, Delta, right? Jesus, you are brain-damaged, aren't you?''

So there *is* more than one world, Singer thought.

''Want to look? Come on, let's go forward. I ain't been on one of these things since I got here.''

Singer undid his belts and scrambled over the knees of the people next to him, earning a barrage of curses and insults, and wriggled forward down the narrow aisle. At the bulkhead they could look into the pilots' compartment through the thick glass bubbles that were the only windows. Singer looked out into a sea of darkness sparkling with solitary fires and tried to understand how lost he really was.

When the dawn came to meet them, he realized that they were flying north and east of where they had been. The flying thing jolted down onto another flat strip, and he ran with Nicky and the others across the field to more buildings. The new place felt to him like an armed camp. He glimpsed some of their defenses, and he saw them carrying weapons—the intricately shaped clubs that were not clubs, that fired shaped metal. Nicky had shown him how to take them apart, both the small one and the long one, and how to load the cases full of metal pieces. They looked like bird arrows more than anything else—blunt, heavy, and darkly shining—but inside each one was a mouthful of fire to make it fly. To pass the time while he and Nicky sat on another bench and waited, he tried in his mind to take the weapon apart again and put it back together. He had nearly done it when he lost track of one of the parts. Without thinking, he put a hand on Nicky's arm to better tap his thoughts for what was needed. Nicky jerked away from him instantly, with a confused burst of unpleasant responses. Singer had a hard time sorting them out, but the gist was clear: One did not touch other people. He thought of old times wistfully. If Nicky had been his brother, they would have lent each other a shoulder for a pillow and stayed warm and comfortable in a strange place. Instead, there was a hard bench, hard wall, hard floor, and weariness. In his mind he crumpled the weapon into a tangle of scrap and turned his thoughts to the people around him. He noticed that not all of the strangers were dressed in the same dull-colored clothing.

A few of them wore shirts that flashed sparks of light from mirror fragments sewn to the cloth with crude but gaudy stitching. Those shirts were embroidered with signs he could not recognize and were decorated with feathers and scraps of bright cloth. He wondered if the shirt wearers were honored above the others, if they were the true pallantai. He got Nicky's attention again and indicated them with a questioning look.

"Yeah, they're believers," Nicky said. "What about it? You mean you never heard of Medicine Shirt, either? They definitely left you in the bag too long.

"Well, it don't mean a thing, anyway—just one of those things the polvorados get into. They believe in the music, all those songs about magic and the old gods. You wear the shirt and you'll live forever, bullets can't touch you. Some of the stuff I hear is spooky—they say the shirt has to be washed in the blood of a man before it really works. But it's just talk, mostly. They wear them in town to look real hard, but they're too smart to wear them out in the brier patch. Or if they do, they turn them inside out so the mirrors don't show."

Finally a man in an ordinary drab shirt approached them. "You the replacements from Jefferson?"

Nicky jumped up. "Yeah, we're for Guijarro—the Mobile Force."

"Yeah? Well, Kruger's got the Mothers working for Harlan now. I hear there's a big push north coming up. You hear anything about that?"

"Shit," Nicky said disgustedly. "That's just great. Out of the briers and into the wire."

"How about you?" the man asked, glancing casually at Singer. "Heard anything?"

But Singer was thinking about something else and did not answer.

"He's got this head injury," Nicky said hastily. "He kind of spaces out sometimes."

"He should fit right in with the Mothers, then," the other man said. "Half of them haven't learned to eat with a knife and fork yet."

They climbed into yet another kind of machine where one sat down and it sped down the road. Singer wondered if they ever used their legs. I'll get powerful muscles in my hind end among these people, he thought. He tried to estimate the distance they were traveling but found it hard. The machine ate up the road like a galloping horse, mile after mile.

It was nearly dark by the time they arrived at their destination. The place was a camp: row on row of tents, more than for the siege against the Rivermouth. But they beleaguered no city; they had been set up with geometrical precision in the middle of nowhere. And that was only a small portion of their forces. Again Singer was baffled and frightened by these people. Their power was so immense and their goals so hard for him to understand.

The camp was new; the scars in the dry earth were still raw. Reddish-yellow dust was everywhere; it puffed around their boots and powdered their clothing. The driver of the traveling machine let them off near a clump of buildings, pointed out to them which way they should go, and roared off in a cloud of dust. As they trudged along the path, their way was suddenly blocked by a group of half a dozen men who came out of one of the buildings. Singer noticed that they wore shoulder ornaments on their plain-colored shirts, and he was not surprised when Nicky stopped in his tracks and saluted them.

The man in the lead seemed about to pass by, then he paused and looked them over more closely. "What's this?" he asked.

"T-Spec Lopez reporting to First Mobile Force, A Company, *sir*!" Nicky announced. "With a fax for the colonel, sir."

Singer noticed the extra emphasis on that respect word, as if Nicky were afraid that Singer would forget about it. He had been told how important their rituals of rank were to them. The *conel sir* accepted the fax with a nod but made no move to read it. He was older than the others; his hair gleamed silver, and he wore an eagle badge on his hat. The others gathered around him the way the captains walked with the Asharya when she walked: half-deferentially, half-protectively. Maybe this was the barbarian Asharya. Singer looked him over carefully.

Kruger looked back. He noticed that their uniforms were still new and well creased. The little one was practically quivering in his effort to make a good impression. The big one was standing straight but easy; he had not even come to attention. He was wearing shades, but the silver-haired man had a feeling that behind them, he was staring.

"Take off those glasses!" Kruger barked.

Singer was surprised to hear himself addressed in such a fashion. It took him a minute to figure out what was meant. Meanwhile he did not move.

"Take them off!" Nicky whispered without moving his lips.

He sounded frantic. So Singer took them off. It was too dark to wear them, anyway.

Kruger saw the long scar on the replacement's face and the places where the hair still had not grown back over his stitched skull. Kruger was tall, but the new man was taller. He stared down with an intensity that barely escaped insolence.

"And what do you do, Singer?" Kruger asked.

Singer could tell that he had done something wrong. He had aroused curiosity. They had told him what training he should claim; *riharra*—a scout—they would make him. But he could not remember the words. He had to say something.

"I fight, no?" he said, daring a gesture toward the still-fresh bruises on his face.

Fortunately the white-haired man chose to take it as a joke and laughed.

"You do that," he said dryly. "As you were." And he passed on.

Nicky blew a huge sigh of relief.

"That was who?" Singer asked.

"Shit, that was only the boss man of this whole camp. Marcus Aurelius Kruger. They call him Mackie Messer in Heimat, where he's from. That's El Cuchillo to you and me. He knows more about down and dirty than anyone. And you have to be making little jokes. Listen, you just keep quiet and let me do the talking."

The man has a good name, Singer reflected. *Makho Chi*, Mack the Knife, he translated to himself. There was power in him. He knew that was bad, really—it only made him a more dangerous enemy—and yet somehow he felt more at ease to be back under the eye of a real captain.

The incident lingered briefly in Kruger's mind. He was annoyed because they were sending him the bottom of the barrel instead of the qualified replacements he needed. The equipment problems were bad enough: flaming, stinking gasoline-powered vehicles and antiquated projectile weapons. Now he was getting questionable personnel, too. That kid had probably never seen combat. The big one must be a class-3 citizen to judge by his lousy Delteix. The camp rats made good fighters, some of them, but they were erratic at best, and this one seemed pretty far around the bend.

He opened the fax in private. It was from the hospital, and he feared they were already calling him back. It was signed by the

Dr. Logan he had spoken to, but it said only, "Lab results lost due to data entry error. Return at your convenience for retest." He wondered why she had changed her mind. Possibly this was a covert request to favor those who had brought the message. He resolved to treat them like all the rest, but he would keep his eye on them.

The tent they walked into was empty except for one man sitting on his bed, plugged into his pocket box. Eyes closed, he was nodding in time to music they could not hear. Singer thought that maybe the man was praying, until he took his plugs out and the music trickled out of them for a minute.

The man waited for them to say something.

"Hi, you got any extra beds?" Nicky asked.

"A few," the man said dryly. "Those two over there are free." He waited till Nicky dumped his gear on one of them, then added, "Those were Rader's and Po'boy's. Po'boy had the biggest feet you ever saw. Last Tuesday he stepped on a mine and blew himself and his buddy to shit. You two just make yourselves at home."

Nicky looked nervously at the bed, but he was embarrassed to move his things. "We're looking for a guy named Pablo Saldivar," he said. "He's supposed to recycle us."

"You're looking at him," the man said.

"Oh. Well, I'm Nick Lopez."

Saldivar studied Singer for a minute. "Does your chico here have a name?" he asked. "Or do you do the talking for both of you?"

"That's Singer. We were in the hospital in Jefferson," Nicky said. "He had some real bad head wounds and he's been kind of disoriented. But he's still sharp when it counts."

"Well, we'll see about that," Saldivar said. "Now, if you'll excuse me."

He plugged himself back in and ignored them. Nicky went to look for food. Singer lay down to rest. He had caught the fact that the bed belonged to a dead man, and he almost asked the brother to lend him some strength. But the one who used to sleep there was no besha of his. Singer wondered where these people went when they died. There was no Road to the North for them. It would be a long journey home across that sea of night.

He wished that he could hear the music Saldivar was playing. He studied the man and felt respect for him. He was quiet and calm in his movements; not a large man, he was compactly muscled with square, blunt-fingered hands. He had the kind of face that weathers early but then remains unchanged, so that it was hard to say how old he was. If I could hear his music, Singer thought, I would know his mind.

16

Time passed quickly; Singer kept quiet and watched what the others did. A lot of it was impossible to understand by looking, especially the things Nicky could do with talking machines and boxes full of fire. But other parts of their war seemed much like his. He went with Saldivar and some of the others into the tangled hillsides, and they found no fault with him. They never met any of their enemies, which disappointed Singer. He was curious to see what the others would be like. But they found many traps, clever beyond belief. Everything became deadly around these people. Fire rained from the sky, and a million tiny knives could explode from the earth like angry bees. Still, the country was much like his own, though it was dry and overgrown with thorn thickets instead of tall grass. Soon he could read the small signs of man-made disturbances as if they were written with a brush and ink and then he felt safe again—much safer in the bush than back in the camp, where he felt staked out for death like a tethered goat. After a couple of weeks, Saldivar said to him, "Take it away, callado," and let him lead.

Nicky helped him practice with the new weapons, and he came to understand what it had been like for Dona, working outside the camp, trying to learn from a scornful boy who spoke a strange language. In a way it was not so different from the bow and spear; all was in the eye. True, the bow did not kick one back or deafen one. On the other hand, an arrow could not punch holes through things one could barely even see. He learned to cherish the rifle, but his hand went first to his knife, and he felt empty without his own weapons.

On one expedition he marked a thicket of young trees that

grew where the ground held a trace of dampness, then went back later and cut some straight poles. He hid most of them in a good place where they could season but took one back with him. It would only make a cityfolk bow, a stave bow, and a green one at that, but it was something to be working on. He brought it into the tent with him in the evening and shaved it smooth with his knife. He turned it over and over in his hands until he had pared away every knot and scar. He could not find any leather thongs, so he lashed the ends and grip with boot-laces. The bowstring was another problem: no sinew, no horse-hair, no silk. He ended up using a filament they had that was clear like sinew but tougher and less elastic. The filament cut his fingers when he drew the bow, so he took apart a glove to make a finger guard.

The arrows were crude but not hard to make. He had a collection of arrowheads made from different odds and ends of metal that they had thrown out. He stole a small file that worked better than anything he had ever had for shaping the points. There were no feathers, but he glued on strips of a stiff, thin substance like scraped horn. Nicky called it *pahlastika*.

Saldivar, in the tent most of the time that Singer was working on his bow, never said anything; he seemed absorbed in his soundless music. But occasionally Singer would look up and see him watching. The day Singer finished the bow, Saldivar took off his plugs and watched him bend and string it. The pull was nowhere near the strength of the Thanha war bows, but it would do for small game. Singer then unstrung it and stowed it between his bed and the wall, wrapped his tools carefully in a bit of rag, and stashed them, too.

"That's something I never learned," Saldivar said. "What are you going to do with it?"

"Hunt," Singer said. "Need things to make a better one." He did not know the words, so he crooked his fingers next to his head.

"Horns?" Saldivar said. "I hate to tell you this, but there are no buffalo out there. When are you going hunting?"

"Tomorrow."

"Just like that. You're just going to walk off by yourself."

"Sure. You show me already how to not die. It's okay. You want to come?"

Saldivar laughed. "Sure, I'll come. I'll even sign us both out. I'll say I'm retraining you. Are we taking Lopez?"

Singer shook his head. "Too noisy."

* * *

Singer woke up when the sky was just starting to lighten. He collected his equipment and stood at the end of Saldivar's bed till Saldivar started and sat up.

Beyond the perimeter wire, Singer traveled swiftly and almost silently through the half dark. Saldivar soon fell behind but was never out of earshot. Singer did not wait for him, except once when his stretched-out senses caught the faintest gleam of light. It was a single silver blink, not the spatter of leaf-shine. He stepped back cautiously and tilted his head back and forth to catch it again. There was a wire just a couple of fingerwidths off the ground. He let Saldivar catch up and showed him where it was.

Some way down the path, Singer signed for Saldivar to step back. He strung the bow and aimed an arrow that parted the wire. There was a flash and a *whoof* that left his ears ringing. The crackle of expiring fire and the rattle of tree fragments raining back to earth went on for a long time. They pushed on faster in case the makers of the trap were waiting to see what it caught.

As soon as he saw a chance, Singer left the path and followed a twisting trace that looked like a deer trail. It headed downhill; if it was a game trail, it should lead to water. Dawnlight stole over their shoulders as they came to the edge of a grassy dip in the hills. Singer crouched in the brush and watched for a long time with an arrow nocked, but the meadow seemed empty. The grass swayed, and a rabbit on its way home sat up and sniffed. The arrow hissed over the grass and caught the rabbit in midjump.

Singer waited to see if anyone out there had noticed. Then he crawled out into the grass to retrieve his kill. Nothing moved but the leaves. There was no sound but the morning birds. He shrugged and strolled back upright with the rabbit.

"Think we're alone," he said to Saldivar. He whistled to himself as he gutted the rabbit. The knife they had given him was really not bad: a little too short and heavy, maybe, but it held an edge well. He cut out a piece of turf, tucked the offal underneath, and pressed the turf back over it. He popped the heart and half the liver into his mouth and offered the other piece to Saldivar.

"Back home, you could get sick that way," Saldivar said.

Singer went on chewing. Saldivar looked disgusted.

One more thing I did wrong, Singer thought. But the warm, bloody liver tasted so delicious that he finished it anyway.

"Where we going to now?" Saldivar asked.

"Downriver. You know that wet place? Might be birds there."

They were too late to set up a blind at the shallows where the river spread out, but Singer knelt in a clump of reeds and waited while a few scanty flights of water birds winged over them. When a group came close enough, Singer drew, tracked their flight, and loosed, all in one smooth arc. A single bird broke its flight and tumbled, flapping, into the water.

He offered the bow to Saldivar. "You want to try?"

Saldivar turned the bow over, getting the feel of it. "I don't know, it's been a long time."

When another handful of birds flew over, he tried a shot. The homemade arrow rose, passed them, and plunged into the water. He had been leading them as if he had been holding a shotgun. Singer handed him another arrow.

The sun was fully risen. The birds had vanished among the reeds; he could hear them calling to each other. His boots and trousers were soaked. At last a lone bird circled the water and descended directly in front of them. It grabbed air with widespread wings, turning its pale breast toward his arrow. He pulled the bow to its full extension, took a deep breath, let it out halfway, and loosed the arrow. The bird fell, knocked backward out of the air.

They splashed into the water to pick up their birds amid the flapping wings and alarmed cries of the other flocks.

"They're called what?" Singer asked. Both had webbed feet and flat bills. The smaller one had iridescent blue-gray feathers; the one Saldivar had brought down was brown and buff with a longer tail.

"I dunno. They're all ducks to me," Saldivar said.

Singer put them in his pack with the rabbit.

They climbed upstream, avoiding the sandy margins of the streambed where bootprints would show clearly. The river had diminished to a single shallow channel, but the wash on either side showed how it would flood in the spring. Singer stopped to examine crumbling footprints around one water hole. They were old, but they showed the divided hoof that meant a horned animal.

There was a steep, rocky hill with good cover not too far from the water hole. They climbed into the rocks to a spot where they had a good view on three sides. Saldivar took out a case with little tubes in it and pressed it to his eyes.

"There are your buffalo," he said. "Next thing to it, anyway." Singer looked and saw brown animals, too far away to distinguish horns or hooves. Saldivar handed him the tubes. He looked through them.

"Ayei," he said softly. His eyes had traveled ahead of his body, as they did in dreams, and followed the animals. He could have put out a hand and touched the hairs of their coats. They were small brown deer with simple curving horns. He could see each blade of grass they were chewing. He handed the glasses back to Saldivar reluctantly. "Long running to catch them," he said. "No time today."

"Yes, and I wouldn't recommend going out there. We might meet something that would shoot back. There shouldn't be traps so close to camp. They tell us there's no activity in this area, but it ain't so. I have had a bad feeling about this trip up north. Somebody is up there waiting for us."

Singer gathered small dry wood and built a hot, smokeless fire. He skinned and cut up the game, made a willow hoop, and scraped the rabbit hide while the meat cooked.

"You must be part Montaraz," Saldivar said jokingly when their first hunger was satisfied.

"Maybe." That was a pretty safe answer to almost anything, Singer had learned.

"No offense intended. My grandmother was a mountain woman. Fierce old lady. Where you from, anyway?"

Singer shrugged. "Someplace I'll never see again. I don't remember those things. The past is gone."

Saldivar brooded on that for a while. Then he nodded. "I read you. I used to talk all the time about 'back home' this and 'back home' that. It was a major recreation. Now all those guys I used to talk with are gone, and all I've got's this collection of useless data about people who don't exist anymore. It ain't worthwhile, making friends with some new boy so I can remember how much he loved his moto long after he's dead and gone. You get so you know you're alone and it's better just to leave it that way."

He sighed and fumbled in his pocket for a battered metal tin. "Smoke?"

The twisted paper he offered smelled spicy, like gebrith. He lit it with a smoldering twig.

Singer sucked the hot, resinous smoke deep into his lungs. It did not have the sacred power of gebrith, but it was not unlike it. He felt his vision expand and clear, as the glasses had magnified his eyesight. He did not want that vision; he wanted to be left alone. But fortunately there was no one within his range: There were animals and birds, movements of cloud and wind, but no people, except the stranger next to him.

"This is good country," he said wistfully. "Dry, yes, but there's game, there's water, if you got eyes. Could go and keep going, got no reason for turning back."

"Don't think I haven't thought it," Saldivar said. "The back of beyond looks better to me every time I think about this ratfucking run we're headed for." He took another drag of smoke. "I've heard of some who did it," he said. "There are stories. Of course, they're all listed as MIA, but the stories get around.

"They say there are people living in the hills. They say there are cities far to the north, oceans with ships on them. I hear these stories, but no one can tell me where they start."

His voice trailed off dreamily, and Singer thought that the smoke was carrying him away. But he suddenly fixed Singer with a very sharp look. "What do you think? Ever heard anything like that?"

Singer just shrugged.

"Well, I'll tell you what I think, cofra. I think Kruger believes it, for one. The man's obsessed with moving north. Ever since last year. There's no other reason for him to accept a shitsuckin' assignment like this one. These hills are crawling with Nupis."

Their shoulders were just touching as they leaned against the rock. Singer felt, like heat from a coal, the deep anger that Saldivar kept covered up with his dry, quiet speech and deliberate movements.

"When you going home?" Singer asked.

Saldivar watched thin tendrils of smoke dissipate on the wind. "Home?" he said finally. "It's like you said: That's gone. There's nothing for me on the world, even if they'd let me go back. I just wanted to live through, get my land grant, retire. Do a little hunting and fishing. Maybe even do a little farming. I could, you know.

"But by the time I arrived, they'd already declared martial law. There were no more elections, and the laws were whatever PCOM said they were, so you couldn't appeal for your rights. Not that I would have, anyway; I got that knocked out of me on Delta, being a C-3. I got here just in time for the bombing. They pulled all the civilians they could reach back into the protective perimeter. They take them out in armored trucks every morning to work the fields. So there's not much chance to desert, unless you want a short, lonely life. There's nobody out there. Anyway, after the bombing they said the situation had changed. Our original terms were revoked, and we were in for life. 'Till the war ends' is how they put it, but I'm not so sure that's ever going to happen. Not in my lifetime.

"Y' know, what's really smokin' me isn't that they lied to us; that's standard. But they're throwing us away, and I don't know why. Rolling us down the gully like a worn-out tire. I don't like getting trashed."

Singer got up abruptly and started putting out the fire. He could not stand to be in such close contact with the stranger anymore.

They chose a different path back and went quickly, without speaking, a body length apart, one a little ahead of the other. Singer really wished he had left the strangerfolk gebrith alone. The sharpened awareness it granted him made him feel exposed on every side. Gebrith was for darkness, and for friends, not for the flat afternoon light that made a solitary target out of a moving man. He thought of asking Saldivar why he did it, but all he had to do was look at the other man to know the answer. Gebrith could not distract Saldivar; nothing could. He was walking under the knife all the time. The world had become a book of signs that would read him the story of his death someday. The smoke did not blur his concentration, but it put some of the colors back into the sky, let him see something in the grass besides the footprints of death.

Saldivar signed to Singer to come near and sank down into the grass. He did not have to say anything; Singer could see for himself where previously straight stems had been bent and where the sandy crust of the turf had torn under the pressure of heavy feet. There was no clear trail, but the hillside had a dappled look that said it had been walked on.

"When you think?" Singer asked.

Saldivar shrugged. "Three days?"

"How many?"

"Too many. Shouldn't be anyone here. Damn." Saldivar squinted at the traces, chewing his lip. "Damn. I guess we gotta."

"I say no," Singer said. "This smells bad."

"Look, they're waiting for us," Saldivar said. "I know they

are. Now or next week or whenever. Am I gonna just walk into it like a city boy into cowshit? I gotta *know*."

They began working their way uphill again. It was slow going. After an hour or so Singer decided that they were right, that the others they were tracking had indeed been headed in that direction. They had to be long gone, because he got no sense of their presence, and the smells he picked up were stale ones. Nevertheless, he had a growing feeling of uneasiness; somewhere there were watchful eyes. Suddenly he knew the eyes were *there*, they had found him. He threw himself sideways, grabbing for Saldivar as he fell. Dirt spit at him where flying metal bit the ground. They scrambled for cover, belly down in the dry, crumbling dirt. They reached a shallow gouge in the earth, with clumps of twisted brush spreading out from it. Saldivar tried a quick look over the lip of the depression and hugged the dirt again as shattered rock fragments flew past his cheek.

"Ah, shit," he said wearily.

They tried a couple of ways to escape from their position, but the sniper always followed them. If they kept their backs flat to the slope, under cover of the brush, he apparently could not see them. If they moved, he could.

"He's got to be in those trees, north of us. That's the only place high enough to overlook all this. We're at the far edge of his range, but still inside it. He had to try for us now, instead of waiting till we got closer, because there's a lot more cover just uphill from here. All of which doesn't help us at all. We're fucked."

"Be dark soon," Singer suggested.

"No good. He'll have a night scope for sure. We'll be blind, and he'll see better than he does now. And it's possible he has a radio and can call in help. We could spot his flash in the dark, but I can't get my head up enough to get off a shot, anyway. No, I don't want to wait him out. He'll win."

"Wait for the almost dark," Singer said. "Not for us to see him. For him to see you. Don't matter if you hit him. Make him look, is all. He thinks we'll run for cover. You hold his eyes for a few blinks and we'll see who's blind."

"What are you going to do to him, throw rocks?" Saldivar asked.

Singer touched his arrows.

Saldivar opened his mouth, could not think of a counterproposal, closed it again, and thought for a while.

"You be careful," he said finally.

The descending sun pulled the colors out of the landscape, and shadows crept out of hiding. Singer nodded to Saldivar and rolled down to the edge of their cover. Saldivar slid his rifle over the top of the ridge and fired into the trees. The response was immediate. Singer heard Saldivar hissing curses to himself as he ducked another spatter of gravel.

Then he was sliding and scrambling through the brush. Saldivar fired again, and Singer saw the flash of the sniper's answering fire: in the trees, as they had thought, maybe two body lengths from the ground. Singer tried to stay low, but he did not bother too much about cover; there was none that could protect him adequately if the sniper spotted him. Speed was the important thing.

He had crossed the dry wash north of them and was heading up into the trees. Once out of the sniper's sights, he slowed to a silent stalk, one or two steps at a time, each taken with full attention. He skirted the clump of trees to place it between himself and the dimming glow of the western sky. The sniper was well hidden. Even with some idea of where the attacker was, Singer could not find him. He stayed perfectly still for long moments, waiting for some betraying sound or movement.

And it came. He heard a faint rasp of boot heel or rifle stock against a branch, and something that was not a twig in the wind shifted against the light. The sniper was trying for a new position that would give him a better angle on Saldivar.

Jump! Singer willed his companion silently. *Move!*

The sniper fired again. Singer could not tell if Saldivar was hit, but he saw what he had been looking for: a triangle of shoulder and back exposed between tree branch and trunk.

He heard the *thunk* of the arrow striking flesh, then a slow tearing of branches, and finally, the body meeting the ground. There was silence. He ghosted up to the place, not taking for granted that the enemy was dead. In fact, the man was not, though he lay very still. He was bleeding heavily and had smashed himself unconscious in the fall. His rifle lay close to his hand. Singer searched him for other weapons; no ornaments or money were evident.

Saldivar arrived in a few minutes and looked the sniper over briefly.

"Well, that's it for him," he said. "Too bad we can't ask him any questions." He fired once more, and the man's skull disintegrated. Singer swallowed. The casual destruction that these people held at their fingertips still disturbed him.

"The rifle's yours," Saldivar said. "That scope's worth its weight in gold if it isn't smashed. Let's move. We've been making a lot of noise."

They had a couple of hours of hard traveling before they were back in familiar territory. They approached their own perimeter very cautiously; the guards were nervous.

"Why don't you stay home at night like a good boy?" Mooney complained after he recognized Saldivar. "I'm going to ground you permanently one dark night."

"Not if we see you first," Saldivar said. "And we always do. Hey, if you're still interested in a starlite, we've got one."

Bates, their squad leader, stopped them as they headed for their tent. "The captain wants to see you."

"Now?"

"I wouldn't make him wait if I was you."

"Saldivar, where the hell have you been?" the captain demanded.

"Just a little routine training mission with Singer here, sir."

"Don't you know better than to stay out after dark? Are you crazy? You could have been shot coming back in, even if there wasn't anyone out there. You recon people are under orders, too, you know; you can't go roaming around the countryside like you own it."

"Yes, sir. We would have been back earlier, but we ran into some trouble."

"What kind of trouble?"

"We found evidence of large-scale troop movements, and while we were following up on that, we ran into a sniper who was watching the trail."

"What happened?"

Singer showed him the rifle.

"I want to talk to the colonel about this, sir," Saldivar continued.

"Make a report and I'll see that he gets it."

"I know you will, but I really want to talk to him myself."

"Do you seriously think he's going to cancel this operation because you saw the bogeyman?"

"I'd like to talk to him," Saldivar repeated stubbornly.

They sat outside the colonel's bunker, waiting to be called in. It was late, but the lights were still burning inside.

Saldivar rubbed at his suit but succeeded only in smearing the dust around. His face was powdered with red-brown dirt, too, with lighter areas in the squint creases around his eyes and mouth. Singer imagined that he looked pretty much the same himself.

Colonel Kruger ignored their disheveled condition, keeping a straight face that won approval from Singer.

"Well, Mr. Saldivar—and Mr. Singer, isn't it? Yes, you had something urgent to report to me?"

Saldivar told him the story. Singer did not listen. He was watching the stranger Asharya. Kruger's eyes were a cold, faded blue, like river ice hiding whatever might move behind them. He was spare and thin like an old knife that had been used and resharpened till it was worn away from its original shape.

"What is your recommendation, Mr. Saldivar?" He had a flat, ironic way of speaking that made it hard to tell whether he was taking them seriously.

"Well, sir, I'd say this proved that our reconnaissance is totally inadequate. I think if we really checked it out, we'd find that the enemy is here in force and we'll be walking into a trap when we move north."

"Have we not been 'checking it out'? Isn't that your job, Mr. Saldivar?"

"Excuse me, sir, but what we've been doing isn't worth shit. We've been patrolling the edges of our own camp like a troop of Pioneer Youth. We were specifically ordered to avoid doing anything that might promote premature contact, and that includes long-range recon, which is the only thing that could tell us what to expect. It's fucking nuts, sir, I'm telling you."

"Since that's your opinion, Mr. Saldivar, it might interest you to know that Operation Long Shot was planned by General Harlan himself. He requested that I carry it out. I have been working very closely with him, and I have his full assurance that we'll get air support and reinforcements if we need them. Does that satisfy you?"

Saldivar made a helpless gesture with his hands. "I guess it has to, doesn't it?" His voice was tight with frustration.

As he followed Saldivar to the door Singer looked into Kruger's face and saw the colonel's eyes contract faintly, as if with pain. He saw that Kruger believed everything they had just told him and was not going to do anything about it.

"I don't understand it," Saldivar said to him. "I wouldn't have bothered to talk to anyone else. But Mack is different. I never heard anything but good about him. Harlan! What is this

Harlan shit? Mack hates old Bungalow Bill Harlan. He got in deep shit with him a few months ago for penetrating too far north. So why is he running this trip for Harlan now? I don't get it. He should know he can't trust Harlan. He should know."

"He knows," Singer said.

"Then why? I want to know why."

Singer took a long hot shower, the only thing these people had that he really envied. Saldivar produced his precious bottle of chah and offered him a drink.

"To the next buffalo hunt," Saldivar said. They drank in comfortable silence.

"Something I've been wondering," Saldivar said finally. "Out there—I could swear I heard you right next to me. You said 'Move it!' or words to that effect. I jumped all right. I thought you were long gone—scared me half to death. And a round came through right where I'd been lying. It would have nailed me for sure. Half a shake later, you pushed our friend out of his tree house. How did you do that?"

Singer just shrugged.

"You don't talk much, do you?" Saldivar said.

"Maybe not," Singer answered.

17

When the day of Long Shot finally arrived, Singer could feel the mood in the camp shift, like wind pushing off a cloud bank. There was fear, but also relief to be moving at last. Singer cleaned his rifle over and over again. His fingers ached for his bow; he had to leave even the clumsy makeshift one behind. He sorrowed for the sweet weight and clean balance of the blade he had lost, wondering if fire had spoiled its temper or if it lay just where he had dropped it, waiting for a new master.

He rode with Saldivar, Mooney, Nicky, and the others in their group in a new kind of machine that looked like an enormous reedfly with rotating wings. It was not as frightening as the other flying things because he could see out and watch the country crawling past below. He still missed his own weapons, and he missed the feel of a good horse, but otherwise he was not concerned about what would happen. He did not care who got killed, and he had no intention of getting killed himself. He would find out how they fought and take a few lives if he could do it without danger. The time for the big payment would come later, when he found out how to hurt them badly, how to spill their dearest blood. Picking off a few foot soldiers was not worth his life—so he told himself.

He could feel Nicky shivering next to him; the boy's eyes were wide and bright, and his talk was loud. Singer was used to feeling stupid next to Nicky's quick tongue and sharp wits. Now he could see that there were things that Nicky had never done before.

It was a long ride. Singer got tired of watching dry hills scroll by and went to sleep. They had been up early. He woke when they started to come down, spiraling in tight curves. He gripped his gear and tested all his straps. The pilot was yelling for them to jump almost before they touched down; he pulled away while they were still scrambling away from the door.

But it was quiet except for the *lop-lop-lop* of the flying machines coming in to drop other teams. They had been dropped on a hilltop in the open. They had a good view of the broken country around them. Flat-topped hills thrust up out of eroded ravines. Thorn brush and spiky dry-land grass clung to the upper slopes. In the ravines and around the feet of the hills, close thickets of cuyirlin alternated with open groves of sweetbean trees; Singer did not know what the strangers called the plants. The broken hills rose gradually, joining together till they formed a mesa overlooking the sands to the northwest. Singer understood from the maps that Kruger would be landing up there and that the regular soldiers would follow. They would build their camp there, where they could see any movement in the desert. It was up to Singer and the other rangers to comb out the brush country and make sure no enemies were waiting there to destroy the new camp.

Bates pointed them down into the ravine; they moved in with Saldivar in the lead, the others spread out behind him, Singer trailing. The brush clinging to the sides of the gully soon rose over their heads; Singer could hardly keep the others in sight as they pushed through the twisted branches. They reached the bottom of the gully without seeing anything. The roar of the flying machines swelled and faded unceasingly behind them; most of the other two companies must have arrived by then.

Brush gave way to trees and then to bare, hard-packed red dirt as the gully opened out and passed between the craggy hills. Suddenly they heard a scatter of shots on their right, and then the hills seemed to explode. There was continuous fire all around them, explosions and cries. They hugged the ground. Singer could not tell who was shooting at them; the noise was deafening and seemed to come from everywhere. Nicky had scrambled in close to him, and though he could see the boy's lips moving constantly, he could not hear what he was saying.

Saldivar was shouting to get their attention.

"Up there," he yelled, gesturing toward the hill west of them. "They're up there—we've got to get to better cover."

The trees ahead of them burst explosively into flames.

"Fuck, they've got laser cannon," Bates yelled. "Lopez, call for air strike on that hill."

Nicky just shook his head and dug his fingers into the ground. His lips kept moving, and his eyes were squeezed shut.

"Lopez, goddammit, you heard me," Bates roared. He pounded the ground in a fury. He could not reach Nicky from where he lay.

"Singer, tell this fucking posy if he doesn't get on the radio *now* I'm going to tear his fucking dick off and stuff it down his throat," Bates said.

Singer reached over and shook the boy. "Nikei," he called to him.

"Get your hands off me," Nicky gasped. He fumbled for his radio gear. "I can't raise him," he said in a moment.

"Get it right, you little fucker," Bates said.

"It's no good, they're gone," Nicky said.

"Then get headquarters. Air support! Where's our fucking air support?"

"I can't, there's nobody. Shit. The freq is all jammed up, and nobody is answering."

The noise level doubled; they could not hear him speaking anymore, though he was shouting by that time. They looked up and saw one of the vitos coming down the ravine behind them. The pilot was trying to pick up speed and lift out of the field of fire, but the ship listed crazily. It lurched past them and crashed in the rocks beyond. One man rolled out the door and tried to run but was picked off before he had taken three steps. The gunner hung halfway out the door, groaning.

"We gotta help them," Nicky said. The others did not bother to answer. The guns on the hill were starting to concentrate on the downed vito. It was suicide to move.

But Nicky started crawling out of the brush. Singer seized him by the ankle, but the boy kicked him away. He had his courage between his teeth, like a colt that had grabbed the bit and intended to run with it. Cursing in all the languages he knew, Singer ran after him across the open space. They both made it as far as the wreck and crouched behind it, listening to the whack of bullets biting into the frame in front of them. The windows that had not shattered in the crash grew lines of stars with holes in their centers. The sharp-smelling slime that fed all the machines was puddling in the dust.

"Gimme a hand," Nicky gasped. They eased the gunner to the ground. He continued to groan quietly, as if it were a task that required his full attention. Nicky crawled in through the door and lowered another semiconscious man into Singer's arms. Singer dragged the man out of the way. He tried to follow Nicky but dropped to the ground again as more bullets sank their teeth into the carcass of the machine. He had a bad feeling, very bad. He tried to figure out what it was—something to do with the smell?

"Nikei, na-se!" he shouted. "You come out!"

Nicky's head appeared, and Singer reached up and grabbed him and pulled, and the vito blew up.

Singer had no way of understanding what had happened. He was rolling over and over in the middle of a fire, he thought, and all he could hear was screaming. He was holding on grimly to something that hurt him. His head cleared, and he stopped screaming, but the noise went on. He realized that it was Nicky he was clinging to, rolling him in the dirt and trying to beat out the flames that clothed his body. The boy's face was blackened and raw, and he screamed with every breath. Bright seams of blood welled where flying metal had clawed him. Every time he screamed, it was Singer's own name he heard—Nicky calling on him for help like Belian with the arrow through his leg. And he was falling into the hell of Nicky's pain; he could not get away. He put his hand on the boy's heart and stopped it, like snuffing a candle between two fingers.

Then everything became very cool and distant. With cover from the smoke from burning fuel and metal, it was not too hard to rejoin the others under their pitiful bit of protection. He stripped off all his gear except the belt with the grenades on it and turned that to hang on his back with his rifle. He thought about taking off the heavy boots, but his feet had grown too soft for the thorns and rocks. He brushed ash off his seared hands and shuddered. That was Nikei.

"Singer, what do you think you're doing?" Saldivar asked.

He could barely hear the words; his ears were still shocked by the force of the concussion.

"Vaharainne-de," he answered stonily. "They have died."

He meant the people on the hill.

"You come back here!" Saldivar shouted.

Singer concentrated on the problem. The problem was to run in under their fire until he was too close under the hill for them to see. It was the sniper problem in another form. He picked out his route. Stealth was no use; he would have to run for it. He heard the people behind him open fire to cover him. One of them popped a smoke grenade to add to the rolling cloud from the vito. Dodging at full speed through the thick smoke, he reached the steep, undercut face of the hill before he expected to. He moved around to the west, climbing as he went, to come at them from behind. A good crack took him twenty feet up. After that it was mostly finger and toe work; it was difficult in the thick-soled boots to place his holds neatly and make no noise.

He climbed as fast as he could; reaching the top, he was about to pull himself onto the summit when he remembered the traps those people liked to set. They might have filled the ground with nests of steel bees. He scrambled sideways along the rocky edge. They were dug in just below the top of the hill, partly protected by an overhang. There was no way to get at them directly. He found a ledge where he could cling by one hand, armed the grenade as they had shown him, and lofted it up and into the exposed opening.

He clung to the rock till it was quiet again and then vaulted in, finding his knife in his hand instead of the rifle. There was no one left to fight. One man pointed something at him, but before he could do anything with it Singer had jumped on him. Two more were alive, but barely. The others were dead, as if he had smashed them against the rocks with a giant fist. But he had not touched them. It was not enough. Under the cool distance there was something roaring, a fire; it roared to be fed and would eat him if he found it nothing else to consume.

Someone climbed noisily in behind him, and he whipped around. It was Saldivar, and if Singer had had the rifle, he would have killed Saldivar before he recognized him.

"You all right?" Saldivar asked. As soon as he saw that Singer was not bleeding, he turned his attention to the weapons.

"All *right*," he said with quiet satisfaction. The enemies had one of the flame guns and one of the guns that spoke many times—Singer had seen them in the camp, but he had never handled one—and some other kind of thing like a big tube with packages. And down below them, on the hill to the east, was another group of enemies with fast-talking weapons trained on their friends. Saldivar loaded the weapon and fired, and they went flying, tasting what it was like to be defenseless.

Another wedge of flying machines came in low and swooped down the valley, blowing back the long grass where the pinned-down soldiers were hiding.

"Take this," Saldivar ordered. He left the gun to Singer and settled the rocket launcher against his shoulder. The magic fire in it swept to its target in an eyeflash and blew the machine apart in the air. Its twin tried to swing around and lift away from them, but Singer held tight to the gun that jumped in his hands like an animal and kept it aimed until the machine slid sideways and flew nose down into the hill.

"This valley is clear now," Saldivar said. "Everybody that can has to move up into higher ground."

They found Bates and Mooney already heading for the mesa. There was a ragged group of others around them, pulling in from the surrounding hillsides.

"Kruger's here," Bates said to Singer. "He was on that vito. You and Lopez pulled his nuts out of the fire for him. Shoulda left well enough alone."

But Kruger was there, and they followed him up the slope, running crouched over, dragging the wounded and leaving a trail of their dead. They gathered just below the exposed summit, sixty or seventy of them, maybe a third of those who had landed. They had no supplies and little ammunition left.

Then Singer began to hear that unforgettable protest of the torn air that warned him that the fire-from-the-sky ships were coming. For a minute he thought it was the air support Bates was waiting for but then realized that they were coming from the wrong direction.

The knot of men around Kruger was moving up again, waving the rest of them to follow. They made a final effort and had reached the top when the hillside below them again burst into flame. The ground bucked under them as if the rocks wanted to bolt and escape. Fire surged and roared, sheathing the trees and stretching up to devour the air above them. Even their enemies ran away from what they had done. It was not much use to run. The top of the mesa, which looked bare from below, was covered with waist-high, bone-dry brush. Only the sands on the other side were safe, and they could never outrun the fire that far. Kruger ordered them to dig a backfire, and some of them began to scratch at the dirt and tear at the tough bushes.

Singer lay flat and stared into the twisting, liquid mouth of the fire. Curses and prayers in the names of many gods writhed together in his mind like clinging smoke. The smell and sound of the flames tore at memories that would destroy him from within before they wrapped their red cloak around him.

They have called up a demon, he thought despairingly. A gift from Ar-Ravanh to destroy us all. And he had handled the fire weapons himself; the fire had his blood on its mouth. The fire moved toward them in wide, lurching strides, like a blinded giant.

Singer's palm rubbed the earth in the old prayer: "We are one flesh. Preserve me." But the earth herself was burning. Only the Wind Horse could help me now, but he is grazing far from here.

He stood up. He had to get as high as possible. There was a

rocky tooth sticking up not far away, and he climbed as far up it as he could go. He stood there, precariously balanced, and spread his arms out wide. There was not a hint of moisture in the scorching air, but there was always wind somewhere, a cold breath turning in the sky high over the desert, where the fire ships flew. He reached out to the white streamers of the Wind Horse's mane, cold with the snows of far-off mountains. He could feel them turning toward him, turning as a man's thoughts circle in the bounds of his skull. Was it possible to be one mind with the wind? For a moment it seemed so; then white fire tore apart the web of contact and hurled him back to the ground. He wondered why he had not known before that it was so much easier not to breathe. This was his last thought. But as it faded, he felt a cold breath against his face and knew that the Wind Horse had come for him, with shining hooves to tear and trample the fire.

He dreamed he was dead, and it was a hard waking. It hurt to breathe; it hurt worse to cough. He knew he was bleeding. It was night.

Someone lifted his head and made him drink; Saldivar, it was.

"Asshole, don't you know you're supposed to keep breathing?" The words were angry, but the voice was full of concern.

He saw himself illuminated by a flare of white light, tumbling to the ground, shot and bleeding. He saw Saldivar pounding on his motionless chest and breathing into his mouth. Bates had tried to pull Saldivar away, but finally the body choked and gasped for air. Then the two of them had dragged him along with them, fighting the savage, gritty wind that was flattening back the fire. He realized that he was seeing Saldivar's memories.

"What happened out there?" Saldivar asked. "What do you think you were doing?"

He saw himself with lightning nailing him to the rock, a perfect target, his shirt whipping around him in the sudden wind.

"Tried to make it stop," he whispered. "Was too big." There was no way to explain what had happened. "Shoulda left well enough alone," he said, but Saldivar did not seem to understand. He gave up and shut his eyes.

"Don't you know any better than to pour water into him, with a hole in him like that?" Bates said. "It's a waste, anyway. He'll be dead in a couple of hours."

"Shut up," Saldivar said fiercely. "Singer is not going to die. Singer is going to be all right."

"Sure, you're going to carry him all the way home."

"They'll pick us up tomorrow."

"You'll be waiting for that bus a long time," Bates said. "Make sure you got exact change."

"Shut up," Saldivar said again.

Singer heard them arguing far above his head. He knew that Bates was right. After the fire came the cold and the dark. He was drifting down into it.

After a long time he felt someone lifting him, jostling him.

"*Nalassnon,*" he protested weakly. "Lemme alone."

"Shut up," Saldivar said. He held a cup to Singer's lips again; Singer tried to turn his head away, but the liquid ran down his face and it was cold, so he gave in and drank it. Saldivar pulled him against his shoulder and wrapped a thin blanket around them both. A little warmth seeped into Singer's deadly chill.

"You're going to be all right," Saldivar repeated.

Saldivar knew he was being stupid. Singer was going to die. Someone that crazy couldn't survive. But he held on to Singer even more tightly. He was tired, so tired of losing.

He had strange dreams. He was conscious of the cold sand, of his thirst, and of the ache in his legs where Singer lay across them. But at the same time he was dreaming. He dreamed he was climbing a steep hill in the dark. The rocks were sharp and slippery. He was carrying someone or leaning on someone, he was not sure which. He heard someone in sharp anguish trying to breathe, but he could not tell if it was he or the other.

He heard them climbing down; their footsteps went away in the dark, leaving him there. His breath was white in the air. He was cold, but he was not going to cry. He began to sing so they would know that he was not afraid. The man swung him up onto his horse, and they were riding, riding; when he came to, the pain in his side was red-hot, harder than he had ever imagined, but he kept riding. They lifted him down; they tied his hands and feet; they kept asking him: Where was he coming from? Where was he going? What was his name, what was his name? I don't know. I don't know. I don't know. No! The blows kept falling; they were hitting him, hitting him, hitting him; they were going to kill him, and he was running, but he could never get there in time. He could smell the fire, and then it was all around him and he was burning. He tried to scream, but he only twitched in his sleep without letting go of his hand. Don't let go of him, don't let go; they were through the fire, and suddenly the cold returned: absolute cold, dark beyond darkness, nothing left but not to let go. He did not let go. And all the time they had been climbing the hill in the dark; they were unbearably tired; even the air was sharp and painful. Not much farther now; don't be afraid, he heard, and then it started to get easier. Slowly the ground leveled out, and there was enough light to see by as he turned and looked into his face. Somebody said his name.

"Palha?"

Saldivar did not know where Singer had found out that his first name was Paul; nobody called him that. And he had a funny way of saying it, with a breath at the end. But he was talking.

"Get this off me," he said, fumbling irritably with the soaked dressing on his chest. "It's wet."

"Leave that alone!" Saldivar carefully unwrapped the layers. The wound underneath was still an ugly thing, but it looked as if it had been healing for a couple of weeks and would probably be all right.

Singer abruptly doubled over in a spasm of coughing. He spit up a lot of red-brown garbage, but when he finally lay back, he breathed easily.

"How did you do that?" Saldivar whispered, gazing at the healing wound. "What's going on?" Cold fingers walked slowly down his back.

Singer looked at him with a tangle of feelings—fear, wonder, amazement—that almost turned into a smile before he caused all expression to vanish from his face.

"Told you, leave me alone," he said. "When you get real sorry, remember I told you."

That was all Saldivar could get out of him.

Singer foraged in his garments and produced a bar of chocolate and a bag of raisins. He handed half the candy to Saldivar and wolfed the rest of it.

"Eat," he said. "You'll be tired. Bad dreams, no?"

Bates stared at them with undisguised disbelief. Singer ate raisins while Saldivar strapped his chest again and bandaged his burned hands and wrists. His shirt was shredded, scorched, and stiff with blood, but he had nothing else, so he put it back on.

"Medicine Shirt," he said to Saldivar. "Bullets lose their power."

"I didn't know you were into Medicine Shirt," Saldivar said. It was his favorite group; he had a whole string of their tabs for his box, but Singer never listened.

"Ah, Palha, I know them all by heart," Singer said.

"And who told you my name?"

Singer gave him that twisted smile again. "I know," he said.

The moon had risen, and the tired survivors were waking up and getting ready to move again. A messenger came and told them that Kruger wanted to see them. He had camped under a dune with the remnant of his staff. His face was badly bruised, but he seemed to be otherwise intact.

Obviously, he recognized them. Saldivar had a wild, fleeting fantasy that the colonel was going to apologize, but he did not refer to their earlier meeting.

"Mr. Singer, I'm told it was you who rescued me," he said.

"That was Nicky. He's dead," Singer said brusquely.

"Well, I'm sorry to hear that. I deeply appreciate what the two of you did. I'm told also that you and Mr. Saldivar blew the Nupis off that hill so we could move out of there. I appreciate that, too.

"What I need now is people who know this area. I don't think anyone is coming to pick us up. The Nupis started a brushfire that's still burning in those hills, and they're camping out around the edges to pick off anyone who comes looking for survivors. We don't want to go back the way we came. And we don't, at this time, have a functional radio. We're going to have to walk home."

Saldivar looked out over the moonlit desert, reconstructing in his mind all he knew about the terrain between them and safety. Without thinking, Singer put a hand on his shoulder and shared the picture. It was a good picture. Palha remembered where there was water and cover, the shapes of hills and the prevailing winds. He thought like a Rider.

But there was too much empty space.

"I've never been out here," Saldivar said. "As you may recall, we had some very clear orders not to attempt penetration of denied areas. I'm not sure exactly how far west we are. My best guess is it would take me maybe four days to get back. For all of us, it'll be at least a week. If we can't find water, we won't make it.

"What I'd do, sir, is get them moving right away. Stay as close to these bluffs as possible. Keep walking till dawn and then find some shade and keep still. Send most of the scouts out looking for water. Maybe we'll find some before you all die of thirst."

18

Singer put his arm in a sling and went out with Saldivar. Mooney stayed behind to help work on the radio equipment. The water scouts had extra canteens. Singer borrowed a couple of spare T-shirts and carried them along.

The obvious place to look for water was back in the hills, but they did not dare go back there. Instead they cast westward, in a wide sweep ahead of the march the others would be taking.

The moon went down, and it was dark for a while; then the sand flushed with dawn. At first the warmth of the sun was pleasant; soon it weighed heavily on them, pressing out all the moisture in their bodies.

Singer took the T-shirt he had brought along, tore it, and tied it around his head. He pulled a flap over his mouth to shade his face from the sun. The sand was not really granular; it was more like baked-dry dust. In some places it was caked hard and abrasive as rock; in others it was soft powder that gave underfoot and puffed up to cling to sweaty skin and irritate eyes and nostrils. Saldivar fashioned a head cloth like Singer's and found that it helped to keep the dust out of his throat.

Both of them had a half memory of having seen a dark line, like a fold in the desert or a line of dunes, and that was what they were trying to find. By the blazing midafternoon they had spent as much time as they could afford before turning back, and there was no change in sight.

"Well, what do you want to do?" Saldivar asked.

"No point in going back without water," Singer replied. "Maybe some of the others found some."

"No. Not unless they went to the hills. Maybe not there. Did you see water on the way in?"

"No, but it's stupid to keep on like this till we drop." Saldivar swallowed with difficulty and felt the dust scratch in his throat.

"We've been coming down a little and a little. Look back and see. Maybe soon it goes down. That's where the water will be."

Saldivar wiped his eyes and looked back. They had been coming down a long, very gentle slope. They kept going, and the slope increased; after another hour, the flat pan broke up again into buttes and sand falls that crumbled down to a wide dry wadi. There was some vegetation under the bluffs, though there was no water in sight; the sand must be damp somewhere below the surface.

"Shit, and me without my shovel," Saldivar said wearily.

Singer had uncovered his face; he turned thoughtfully in a circle, sucking air through his open mouth. He followed the wadi north and climbed among some gray, pumicelike rocks that had been uncovered by the wind. Saldivar groaned inwardly but followed him. The rocks had a porous, abrasive texture and scraped off skin every time he slipped. Singer looked back at him expectantly.

"Smell it?" he asked.

Saldivar thought Singer was crazy, but in a minute he caught a breath with a green, damp taste to it. Deep in a crack between rocks, where the hungry sun could never touch it, there was a dark pool of hoarded water. They climbed down to it and drank. It had a dank, still taste, but it was cold and free of sediment. Singer wet his head cloth and let it drip over his face. They filled a canteen apiece and lay in the shade, sipping luxuriously every few minutes.

"Is there enough for everybody?" Saldivar asked.

Singer nodded. "Seen it before—the rock drinks up water. It's full with it; will soak out till the rock's dry. Should be enough."

He leaned his head back against the rocks and closed his eyes. His face was pale and drawn; he looked as if he still had a fever. Saldivar decided they should wait for an hour or two, until the sun's worst heat had passed.

"How are you doing?" he asked. "Want me to check those dressings for you?"

"No. It's all right. My hands hurt, is the worst."

"Well, I got a little pill here that should take care of that in no time."

Singer looked at it suspiciously. "Is this going to make me strange in the head?" he asked.

Saldivar laughed. "I wouldn't recommend taking two or three of these," he said. "But you're already strange in the head. I doubt if one will make it worse."

He wanted to check the chest wound; he was afraid it would start bleeding again. But Singer insisted that it was all right. He was not coughing; he just looked tired out. He sat quietly with his hands stuck out stiffly in front of him. Saldivar could tell that he was in a lot of pain. He thought he would try some conversation to distract him until the pill started working.

"You and Lopez were tight, huh?" he asked tentatively.

Singer rolled his head back and forth.

"Didn't know him," he said shortly, as if the question bothered him.

"Well, shit, I don't understand you, man," Saldivar said. "You want to go up a cliff against a laser and a rocket launcher over someone you didn't even know? That's crazy. You could get killed."

"I killed Nikei," Singer said. His voice seemed to be coming from a long way off. "I didn't mean for it to happen that way. He was just a kid."

"What are you talking about? You did the best you could."

"All the young ones died. Nothing I could do would ever be enough."

Saldivar did not understand, but he heard the desolation in the other's voice. "Look, Singer—no, come on, look at me—your job is to stay alive. There's nothing worth dying for. So okay, you're the magic man, you're unkillable, but don't push your luck. It's stupid. Nothing more. Just stupid."

Singer heard the far-off echo of a voice saying "Do you want them to sing that you died playing the fool?" Saldivar saw a little life come back into his face.

"And another thing. You don't want to think about everything too much. What happens, happens. Thinking doesn't make it any different or any better. Just let it roll."

"I hear you," Singer said. Some of the tension went out of him.

Saldivar thought for a while before saying anything else. He wished he had something to smoke. There were things he wanted to know about Singer, but he knew that Singer did not like questions. Singer might be messed up at the moment, but that did not necessarily make him any easier to handle. He finally decided that it was as good a time as any.

"I saw what happened out there," he said softly. "You called the wind, didn't you? I saw the lightning come down to you. I saw something strange about you when we smoked together, but I thought I was hallucinating. Who are you, Singer? What are you doing here?"

He held his breath waiting for an answer, but there was none. Singer was asleep. Saldivar sighed.

"Later," he said. "You know I am going to get to the bottom of this."

He shifted over a little to let Singer lean against him. Normally he could not stand to have anyone within a foot or two; it just made him too jumpy. But Singer was different. It was right for Singer to stay near him. That was where he belonged.

They filled all their canteens and backtracked. The sun flared like a torch in a sky the color of aluminum. But there were no sandstorms, no gunships swooping out of the sun, no trace of any hostile movements. They picked up the trail easily and caught up with the rest of the group at twilight. They were camped in the lee of a dune in a demoralized huddle of ponchos and shirts propped on sticks and rifles to provide a little shade. Singer and Saldivar came down the duneside in a cloud of dust and were greeted by a dispirited chorus of whistles.

Kruger sat under his improvised canopy with the captain and Mooney, who was still trying to fix the radio equipment.

"We got it," Saldivar said briefly. They dumped the canteens at his feet.

Kruger's eyes opened wide with surprise. "Thank God," he said. "Get a couple of medics and have them pass this out to the people in the worst shape; stretch it as much as you can. How far did you have to go for it?"

They told him, and he raised his eyebrows again.

"It's a long walk," he said. "I guess we'd better get started."

His lips were peeling in little flakes, but he had not looked twice at the water.

It took most of the night to get back to the wadi, carrying the wounded survivors on makeshift stretchers. There was plenty of water for everyone, seeping slowly from the spongy rock. Kruger let them sleep most of the day. When they woke up, they drank their fill again, filled their canteens, and moved south, following the course of the dry riverbed. Kruger had decided to stay near water for as long as possible and cut back to the east only when Saldivar thought they were close to safety. They were very hungry; the miscellaneous provisions they had been carrying had all been eaten.

For three days they traveled south. Mooney still worked on the radio whenever they stopped for a rest, but he said privately that he did not think it would ever work again. On the second day, they had to dig in the riverbed for water. The water was there: four feet down, scant and muddy. But on the fourth day, tough grass and thornbushes reappeared on the banks. They were descending again. When they came to a fork where the wadi joined another riverbed, they saw water flowing—ankle deep, as thick and brown as coffee with cream.

Kruger sent a party across the river to investigate the other side, putting the captain in charge. Their spirits were raised by the sight of grass and water, and they hoped they would find something to eat. Instead, Singer smelled ash. He thought it was a trick of the mind; he would never be able to get the smell of fire out of his head. But they stopped in amazement at the edge of a clearing. They were looking at a farmyard, or what had once been a farmyard. They proceeded cautiously, but it seemed empty. The adobe buildings were mostly blown to pieces. The barn had burned down—that was what Singer had smelled—but the ashes had been cold a long time. Marsh hay, Singer supposed. They found some carcasses in the ashes. One of them was a human body, probably a man, and they found others: two more men, a woman, and a child.

They split up to search the buildings for food. Singer and Saldivar and the captain headed for a shed that looked as if it might have been a corncrib. But behind the barn, Singer heard something, a familiar sound, a sound of life: a muffled snort, a shuffling of hooves. There were two horses picketed in the saw grass. One of them pricked his ears and nickered after a rustle in the grass. Singer circled and flushed the fugitive out of the grass. It was a boy, not big enough yet to aim the heavy pistol he waved at them. The captain shot him before Singer could grab him.

Singer gave the captain a disgusted look and spit on the ground. "Stupid," he said.

Saldivar thought so, too. The captain would have hit Singer if his shot had missed; Singer could have disarmed the boy easily enough.

The captain flushed. "He was armed, in case you hadn't noticed," he said. "Maybe you think it only makes a little hole if you get shot by a kid. Or maybe you just wanted to wrestle, huh? Maybe you miss your little greaser buddy."

Singer looked as if he was about to jump the captain, but he just took a deep breath and let it out slowly.

"I don't like you," he said quietly. "I don't like you and I don't hear you." He turned his back deliberately and bent over the crumpled body.

The horses jerked at the end of their ropes, eyes rolling in fear at the shots and the strange smells.

"Hey, here's our fresh meat," the captain said. He dropped them neatly with one shot apiece.

And Singer whipped around with the dead boy's pistol in his hand and blew his face off. He waited for the body to stop twitching and then spit on the ground one more time. Then he gathered up the boy and laid him carefully with the horses.

For a minute Saldivar thought that Singer was going to cry. But when Singer turned around, his face was stony except for the crazy light behind his eyes.

"He shouldn't have killed the horses," Singer said, as if that explained everything.

"Whatever you say," Saldivar said. "Cool down now, okay?" He tried to keep Singer looking at him as he moved carefully closer. Singer still had the gun in his hand. "You want to give me that now?"

Singer handed it over without any fuss, and Saldivar realized with a twinge of shame that it had never been in Singer's mind to hurt him.

The others came running to find out what was going on. Bates took a look at the two bodies on the ground.

"The captain forgot to look both ways," he said.

"The kid had a gun," Saldivar explained unnecessarily.

"Well, ain't that a bitch," Bates said. "Now we'll have to bury the sucker."

They did not take too much trouble over the burying. Bates sent a couple of people back to get the rest of the group. Some of them started a fire and butchered the horses. Singer, whom Saldivar watched closely, did not turn a hair. Now that they were dead, he had turned his back on them. While the meat cooked, they scratched a hollow in the ashes and put the captain in it with burnt timbers to cover him. No one asked any more questions about how he had died.

While the rest of the group was still sitting around the fire eating horsemeat, Kruger called Singer and Saldivar to meet with him in one room of the house that was still standing.

"They had a radio. Mooney is trying to reach the base now. Meanwhile, I'd like your opinions on why these people were here, who killed them, and why. You've had a chance to look around; what do you think?"

"Are they Nupis?" Saldivar asked.

"Probably. There are only a few items of clothing in the house; they look like cut-down Union uniforms. That pistol the boy had is standard issue. But what were they doing here?"

"My guess is they are runaways, free-lancers," Saldivar said. "It would make sense, if you assume the Nupis are colonizing over there to the west. These people ran away—deserters, or maybe they ran from a forced labor farm. I don't know how they run things over there. They came as far as the desert and couldn't go any farther, so they found a place to homestead and hoped they wouldn't be spotted. They obviously knew how to farm. They were able to lift stock from somewhere."

He fell silent.

"Who leveled their homestead?" Kruger prodded him.

"My best guess is that it was their own people," Saldivar said. "It was a search-and-destroy operation. They don't want little enclaves of renegades sprouting up on their perimeter."

He chewed the corner of his lip and avoided Kruger's eyes. He was wondering if the same thought had occurred to his own superiors. Maybe there were similar little farms somewhere, populated by people like him, only with more guts—people who had kept on going. Maybe those people were dying, too. When he glanced at the colonel, he saw that Kruger's eyes were on the ground, as if he were having uncomfortable thoughts, too.

In fact, the colonel looked as if he had been dead for a week. He had big black circles under his eyes, and the bruises on his face had not even started to heal. In between black and blue marks and peeling sunburn, his skin was white and slack.

Mooney came out of the corner where he had been fiddling with the radio. "I got them, sir! I got some firebase on the edge of the hills, and they put me through to HQ in Guijarro. We're way out at the far end of their range, but they'll be here by morning."

Kruger pulled himself together.

"That's good," he said, but Saldivar thought he looked more worried than ever. "Pass the word, but quietly. Let them know we'll have to wait quite awhile. Mooney, I want you to stay glued to that radio. Listen in case Guijarro tries to communicate again, and check other frequencies for traffic. Bates, Saldivar, Singer, I want you three to stay close to me. I want regular sentries, but I also want you to rotate guard duty tonight. Wake me up right away if you hear so much as a gnat fart. We aren't going to blow it this close to home."

"If I watch, then I pick the sleeping place," Singer said. It was the first time he had ever spoken up in a meeting. "This place smells bad." Kruger finally agreed, and Singer took them out to the edge of the meadow where the horses had been. It was too near the brush for Saldivar's taste, but Singer seemed to find the farmyard more unnerving than snakes or wild animals.

The night wore away. At moonrise it was Singer's watch. The fire where the others slept, near the ruined house, had burned down to dim embers. A little red light close at hand showed that the radio Mooney hugged was still patiently fishing for sound in the unruffled night air.

Palha.

Saldivar thought that Singer had touched his arm, but when he looked up, Singer was sitting motionless several feet away. He was listening.

"Something coming," he whispered. "Not the vitos."

Saldivar shook Kruger's ankle to wake him up. At the same time, Mooney crawled over to them.

"Colonel, I'm picking up chatter," he whispered urgently. "It's some lingua I can't read."

Before Kruger could say anything, they all heard it. The jets swooped on them out of the sky. Once again, the earth shook and fire flowers burst from the ground on black stalks. There was nothing they could do but hug the ground until it was over.

The noise stopped. The fire-from-the-sky ships were gone, untouchable as always, leaving nothing behind but smoke. Kruger started running toward the rest of his men. Singer followed slowly; he already knew what they would find.

Almost all the people who had been sleeping around the fire were dead. Whatever parts of the buildings had been left standing were destroyed. Half a dozen men came out of the shadows, miraculously spared or not too badly hurt. That was all that was left of them.

"Fill the canteens," Kruger said. "We're leaving here."

"Sir, what about our ride out of here? Shouldn't we wait for them?" Mooney protested. "Maybe they're still coming."

"They aren't coming," Kruger said. "You can bring the radio, but don't use it again."

They did not understand what Kruger was doing, but they were stunned. None of them wanted to stay there. They moved slowly to follow his orders. The farm well had been filled in by one of the explosions, so they had to use river water for the canteens. They had found a sack of ground grain in the barn earlier; one man dug among the timbers till he found it. They brushed the grit off a few chunks of horsemeat and slung them in a spare shirt. With those supplies and their weapons, they headed out into the desert again. Kruger had Mooney aim them for the firebase he had picked up on the radio, and they started walking toward it in a straight line.

They made only a few kilometers that night. Kruger walked like an old man, stumbling and wavering until Saldivar asked if they could stop. They threw themselves down on the sand and slept as if they were dead.

The next day was not much better. Kruger was clearly ill. Saldivar gave him two pills from his private stash and then a third, but the colonel still moved painfully, stiffly, as if it hurt excruciatingly to bend his joints. Singer worried. He stayed as far away from Kruger as he could; the barbarian Asharya walked in a nightmare landscape that Singer did not wish to share. The others moved like sleepwalkers. Singer remembered the dream he had seen in a dying man's mind in the hospital: the ant-men crawling across an endless desert. If this went on, they would all die.

When they stopped again to rest, he went reluctantly to where Kruger sat bowed with his head in his hands. He lightly touched the older man's shoulders and his knees. What he felt there astonished him. The joints were swollen tight and burning, and all through Kruger's body was the same burning, as if the body were tearing itself apart in a vain search for an invisible enemy. Slow tears ran down Kruger's grizzled face; he hid them, but he could not stop them. They were the tears of an Asharya who had thrown his own children away.

Kruger tried to shake Singer off.

"This only works if you let me," Singer said.

"What is this, the laying on of hands?" Kruger asked testily. "I already tried your friend's home remedy; it just about killed me."

Singer felt the fierce barricade in the old man, like that spiked wire they used, and the fear behind it. Almost he liked the old dog, still snapping to the bitter end. Almost he wanted to find a way through the barrier, but he reminded himself whose dog this was. He did not want to know anything about a sickness that made a man's body devour itself. He was no healer. He just wanted Kruger well enough to walk home.

Kruger did not know what Singer was up to. Some kind of hypnotism? Singer held his gaze for a moment, but then he looked away and his eyes unfocused as if all his sight were in his hands. His fingers probed the joints where the pain was worst. At first it hurt more. But Kruger kept remembering Singer's eyes, as dark and cool as deep water. A pervasive feeling of comfort, of being taken care of, spread over him, and the pain eased as if his tired body were soaking in a clear running stream.

When he opened his eyes, it was morning. The survivors were sleeping in a huddle, trying to keep warm. As soon as his glance fell on Singer, Singer sat up and looked back at him. He looked like hell. But Kruger felt easy and alert, better than he had in months, since the first symptoms had settled in.

"We keep moving now as fast as we can, as long as we can," he said. "We rest only when we have to. We're on the way home."

He was able to keep up with them again. When he got tired, Singer always seemed to know and would come and lend him an arm till he got his breath back.

Singer could see the men's spirit strengthen now that they had their Asharya back. Kruger encouraged them, drove them on. They hit the hills before their water ran out again, and when they were within a day's travel of the firebase, Kruger let Mooney use the radio again. They would sit down and wait for guides rather than risk being shot as they walked in.

Saldivar propped up his legs comfortably and busied his hands rolling a tiny joint from his last crumbs and seeds. He had been saving it for the end, one way or the other.

"Mind if I ask you a personal question?" he said to Kruger. "Doesn't it bother you that every time we call for a pick up we get shelled?"

"I think we're safe this time," Kruger said absently.

"This time! Oh, that's great. Just think, all ten of us may survive. Till next time. Damn. I told you this was going to happen. Why didn't you listen to me?"

"You're out of line," Kruger said.

"You're damn right I'm out of line, and I'm never getting

back in. We were butchered, and you know it. You were waiting for it to happen. Bates said it: he said we should have let you die, and he was right. You aren't worth a rat's fuck."

"Mr. Saldivar, because of your excellent performance as long as I've been acquainted with you, I'm going to pretend you never said those things. I don't advise you to repeat them. Go back to the Dust where you belong and stay there, and keep your mouth shut."

He was not angry, but he would not meet Saldivar's eyes. He got up and limped away.

Vitos came and landed in a clear area in the valley. The sky was blue, and grasshoppers chirped in the grass till the sound of the rotors overwhelmed them. No one shot at them. They flew over the little firebase and went on to the big camp at Guijarro.

Saldivar and Singer walked into their tent with Bates and Mooney. There was plenty of room, since no one else had come back. Singer checked his hiding place. The bow was still there, but the green wood had stiffened. It was not much use anymore; he would have to make another one.

Singer cleaned up as well as he could, trying to shower without getting his bandaged shoulder wet. He and Saldivar were sitting around in clean clothes and bare feet, taping up their blisters and finishing the last of Saldivar's precious bottle, when a messenger leaned into the open door.

"The colonel wants to see you, Singer."

"Fuck him," Saldivar muttered.

Singer started laboriously to put his boots back on, wincing as he tried to cram his swollen feet into the battered footgear. He compromised by carrying the boots with him.

Kruger's eyes widened at the sight of his bare feet.

"Where are your boots, Mr. Singer?" he asked.

"They hurt," Singer explained. It did not occur to him that anyone would order him to damage his feet.

Kruger controlled his tongue with a visible effort and asked him to sit down.

"As you know, there's not much left of this force," the colonel said. "It will take some time to rebuild it."

He paused for Singer's assent, but Singer did not realize that he should respond. Kruger found his silent gaze disquieting.

"I'll be giving all of you temporary assignments until I get something worked out," Kruger continued. "Probably we'll continue to work with the 3rd Battalion while we're getting back up to strength. Now that we know there's a sizable enemy force occupying the highlands, we'll have to dig in here and try to clean them out.

"But you aren't fit to go back to the Dust yet, even on close-in forays. What would you think of working for me, at least until you get full function back in that shoulder?"

"Can't do it," Singer said. "It's no good for me inside walls."

"Look," Kruger said, "I can't send you anywhere in the field with that wound. It has to be inside. The only reason I'm asking you instead of telling you is that it's kind of a personal request. I need someone I can rely on."

It took great effort not to lower his eyes under Singer's dark, steady stare. "It won't be for long," he said unsteadily. "A few months max. Just till I can get us back in some kind of shape."

Singer knew what he was talking about, and unwilling pity dragged at him again. And he himself needed rest, concealment, and information that the barbarian Asharya might show him the way to.

"All right," he said.

"That's good. Now that that's settled, all of you are getting four days' leave in Jefferson to recuperate. I want you to have a checkup at the hospital while you're there. Report to me when you get back."

19

Saldivar and Singer traveled through most of the night, hitching rides with water trucks and convoys on their way back to Jefferson from the uplands. When they pulled into the city, it was still dark, a couple of hours before dawn. Stiff and yawning, they ambled down the deserted streets.

"No point in turning up at the hospital now," Saldivar said. "Wish I knew someone in town."

Singer stopped. "Not going back to the hospital."

"What is it with you? Who's going to look at that hole in your chest?"

Singer was already working his way into concealing shadows.

"All right. Stop. Come back here! We won't go there. Got any other suggestions?"

Singer considered. "There's a doctor. Logan, they call her."

"A woman? I might know her; she sewed me up one time. I know where she lives, if she hasn't moved."

When they came to her building, Singer led the way around the back, looking for windows. The building was only two stories high, like most structures in a place where there was infinite room. It was easy enough for Saldivar to climb up and loosen the window catch once he understood that was what Singer wanted.

"You're going to get me arrested," he complained, but he opened the window and slipped inside. He caught Singer's wrist and helped him through the window; Singer's long legs jammed halfway inside and nearly toppled them both onto the floor.

"Who's there!" someone gasped. Then, a moment later, incredulously, she said, "Singer?"

"Yes, me."

A light went on.

She had been sleeping on top of the covers with an old blanket around her. She was wearing an old shirt and a pair of gym shorts. Her short dark hair stuck up spikily like an awakened child's, and her round-eyed alarm turned suddenly to a look of exasperation.

"I told you not to come back," she said. "Shut the window. Come on in."

She turned her back modestly and pulled on a pair of trousers.

"Now let me look at you. You got yourself cut up again. Damn. You're going to have more stitches than a quilt. Listen, are you in some kind of trouble? Is there something you need right away? Speak up if so."

Saldivar thought that she talked to Singer as if he were a wild animal she did not want to alarm. Singer seemed not to mind it.

"No trouble," he said. "We want to sleep with you."

She burst out laughing. "I think what you mean is that you want a *place* to sleep, dakko?"

"Dakko," Singer said agreeably. "Also, this stranger has more words under his tongue now. He wants to see your face and say thanks."

"De nada," she said. "The pleasure was all mine. Hm. These clips look pretty good. The edges are knitting up nicely. You won't need stitches if you're careful and don't break this open. Who fixed it for you?"

Singer nodded toward Saldivar.

"You did a good job," she said. There was a pause while they looked each other over.

She noted the deep-bitten lines at the corners of his mouth and the thick bar of mustache—worn not to hide any weakness, she decided, but to keep the world at a distance. She observed how he braced himself protectively when she touched Singer.

"My name's Saldivar," he said. "I remember you. You saved a couple of fingers for me a few years back."

"Sorry, I don't remember," she said.

"Well, I do, because they were my fingers. It was during the bombing, right after I got here."

"May I?"

She took his hand and turned it over, flexing the joints and examining the scars.

"I think I do recall, now. I didn't really have much to do with this. I was just assisting Jackson. Surgery isn't my specialty."

"You're the one who came around afterward to see how I was. I appreciated that."

She looked at his face again. "I remember you without the mustache. You were the one who had nightmares, weren't you?"

"Yeah, I had casts on and I couldn't move, and I kept waking up and thinking I was still buried. You used to come by and sort of remind me of reality. When I was on my feet again, I wanted to buy you dinner, but you said you never went out with patients."

"Hm. Well, if you could see most of my patients, you'd appreciate the wisdom of my attitude." She let go of his hand. "Are you guys hungry? No, no—just sit on the floor, if you don't mind. That way if anyone's watching, they'll only see me, and I'm up at night all the time."

"Why would anyone be watching you?" Saldivar asked.

"I try not to give them any reason," she answered evasively. She started going through the refrigerator.

"I'm afraid I live on P-bars and ice cream mostly," she apologized. "Looking at carved and broiled humans all day sort of reduces my appetite for big pieces of meat."

Saldivar did not have much enthusiasm for what she set out, but Singer crunched his way though a double handful of raw vegetables. He tried the ice cream and sneezed at the cold like a surprised cat. He persevered, and a look of dreamy pleasure spread over his face as the first mouthful melted. He ate the rest of it without talking, slowly wiped his mouth with his fingers, licked his fingers, and wiped his fingers on his pants. Then he took the blanket off Jan's bed, rolled himself up in it, and went to sleep.

"God, I wish I could do that," Saldivar said.

"Do you still have trouble sleeping?"

"Not all the time. We've been hit a lot lately."

"Were you with Kruger when he ran into a load of thornkiller a few months ago?"

"That was the first time. How did you know about that?"

"I saw Kruger when he came in. What happened?"

"We were up past North Fork that time—pretty far past. It could have been an accident. We were running for home, we weren't where we were supposed to be, maybe someone just fucked up and dumped it on us.

"So we put ourselves back together, and then we get assigned to Harlan. We get moved north again, this time up past Guijarro. Kruger had a deal with Harlan that we would get air support. There was no air support, there was no pick up. What there was—twice—was strikes against us, and they knew exactly where we were. Three companies went up there, and except for Singer and me and a few others, there's hardly anything left of us. There's an official explanation for everything, but I can't accept that it's an accident anymore. Somebody's trying to kill us, and they damn near succeeded."

Janet chewed on a thumbnail. "I'm not saying you're wrong, but how do you figure they could cover up something like that?"

"It's not that hard." Saldivar shrugged. "The first time, the pilots didn't even have to know we were there. Ground troops have been dumped on before. Just another accident. The other times—someone had to have leaked our position to the Nupis. Which means it was a heavy that did it."

"It must be a big secret if they're willing to take such strenuous measures to preserve it. How could they conceal something that important for so long?"

"Who's going to find out? Military personnel go where they're told. Civilians need a permit to travel, and anyway, you'd have to be out of your mind to go through the Open Zone if you didn't have to."

"What about the pilots who fly recon over the northern perimeter?"

"Check it out—Net fish get all those routes. The Net is tight. They don't talk."

"My brother had been talking to pilots just before he disappeared. He was a video man, and he had gone up past North Fork not too long before you ran into trouble there. He tried to get Kruger to talk to him once. He thought Kruger knew something, or suspected something about the Open Zone that had been kept secret. It's possible the same people who tried to kill you were the ones who got to him." She glanced sideways at Saldivar. "How much do you know about our friend in there?"

"Hey, he's my teammate. What else do I need to know?"

"Well, one thing you should know is that it's not safe for him to be here. There are people looking for him here."

"What for?"

"I don't know for sure, but I don't think they mean to do him any good. He was in the hospital here."

"So?"

"So he wasn't ever exactly discharged. I think they'd like to get him back. You've got to take good care of him."

"I take care of him just fine," Saldivar said stiffly. "You want to stop beating around the bush and tell me something straight out?"

"I can't. I don't know anything for sure. I think he may have something to do with all this, but he doesn't talk about it. Maybe you've noticed."

I want to trust him, she thought. And I have to trust him if I expect him to trust me. But how much has he seen? How much will he believe?

For the first time, it occurred to her that the small favor she had done for Kruger might have had a large effect. If I'd let those lab reports go through, they could have pulled him out for medical reasons. That would have neutralized him, and they wouldn't have had to go after him again and kill off all those other people. But without Kruger, where would I send Singer? I've got to have more information! I'm not like Jon; I can't get pilots drunk and pick their brains. I'm going to have to go after the PCOM network. Madre'dio!

Saldivar interrupted her train of thought. "Why are you worrying about him, anyway? Are you—" He was about to say "his girl," but it did not seem like the right word.

"I'd like to think I'm his friend," she said. "But there's more to it than that. Impossible things happen when he's around. Maybe you've noticed that, too. When I started believing the impossible, I started to hope again. And I knew I'd do anything to keep that hope alive. There's something in him that calls to you. Do you know what I mean?"

Saldivar remembered the touch of a cold wind on his face, parting the smoke like a sword out of nowhere, and the feel of Singer coming back to life under his hands.

"Something like that," he said softly. "Anyway, if he trusts you . . . When I was in the hospital before—"

"What is it?"

He turned away abruptly. "Nothing. I'm too tired."

"Go ahead and sack out. You can have the bed; I don't feel like sleeping right now, anyway."

"The doctor has bad dreams too?" He was glad of a chance to change the subject.

"Sometimes."

"You still dream about the bombing?"

"Not exactly. It's more like remembering the bombing brings back some other things I don't like to think about."

"You have worse things than that to remember? I don't envy you."

"You're from the Zona del Tregua, aren't you? I've heard people talk about the Tregua, and they make New Hope sound like a picnic."

Saldivar reached automatically for a smoke before remembering that his pocket was empty.

"Listen," he said. "Nobody is from the Tregua, any more than people are from hell. They're all from somewhere else and looking to get back there. We're not all camp rats. My father had a skill. He tried to live decent. But the waiting, year by year always thinking he'd get his application stamped and we'd get out . . . My friend sold stolen junk. He got caught, and they said it was corrective labor or enlist and volunteer for off-planet. They made it sound good—you get out of camp, you serve out your term, and they'll give you your own land up here. So a bunch of us all signed up together." A shadow crossed his face. "I'm the only one left."

"Your parents?"

"Who knows? They were never much for writing, anyway. I guess they died while I was still in the freezer." He tried to laugh. "I'll get a land grant for sure. They didn't lie about that. Lay enough of us end to end and the desert will bloom, all right."

" 'Every thorn will have its rose/Red as a drop of blood,' " Jan quoted.

" 'Blood Roses.' You like Medicine Shirt?"

She shrugged. "My brother did. I listen to them a lot now because it's all I've got left of him."

"I thought you must be a believer," Saldivar said. "You're wearing the shirt."

She glanced down. The ripped shirt she was wearing had been painstakingly embroidered and sewn with feathers and mirrors. The largest mirror, a little bigger than a scope lens, had been stitched into the pocket over the heart. It was cracked.

"No, this is Jon's. He wasn't a believer, either. This was his idea of a joke—also a way to fit in with the polvos he hung out with. I wear it now, and I listen to his music. Sometimes I feel as if he's listening, too. The music seems to have a life of its own in it. It's like the wind that comes in from the Dust. It has voices of its own, and it carries you along—not where you thought you'd go but where the wind is blowing."

Saldivar felt the chill that had sometimes warned him when he was being watched. He thought it was strange how her words seemed to harmonize with his thoughts, as if they were following the same line. He spoke without thinking. "The wind came out of nowhere when—"

She leaned forward again, her dark eyes alight and watchful, as if she were anticipating what he was going to say. "When what?"

"Nothing, I don't want to talk about it now. God, I'm tired." He rubbed his hands wearily over his face. His eyes felt as if they were full of tiny needles, but he could not keep them shut. "I can't come down. You got anything to drink? Some pills?"

"Drinking is bad for you," she informed him. She turned the edges of his shirt back and laid her hand on his chest. The touch was cool and delicate and made his skin shiver. He took a deep breath involuntarily.

"Don't do that."

"Why not?"

"Now, why the fuck do you think not?" he glared at her.

"It's better than drugs."

"With an ex-patient?"

"You were never my patient; you were Jackson's. I came to see you because I wanted to."

She waited a minute, and when he did not protest again, she started to unbutton his shirt.

Saldivar woke up with the low sun at the window blazing into his eyes. The bed seemed luxuriously soft and warm, and he could smell coffee. Looking around for his clothes, he saw Singer still curled on the floor next to the bed. Janet sat at the kitchen table. She looked up from her keyboard as he came through the door.

"There's a cup for you in the heater."

"Thanks." He paused, feeling awkward. "Thanks for everything, I mean."

"No hay de que."

"About the hospital—I don't remember too clearly, but I have this feeling that you were there a lot."

She shrugged. "I didn't sleep any better back then than I do now."

''Why wouldn't you talk to me when I was back on my feet?''

''I was afraid to.''

''Afraid? Why?''

''Why were you afraid to tell me what you meant about the wind?'' She locked up her keyboard. ''I thought maybe you'd like to go to Jackson's when Singer wakes up. He's always got a party going. He'll feed you and give you a chance to refill your stash.''

''If people are looking for him, is that smart?''

''Jackson is good with all kinds of narizotas. We'll be safer around a lot of people than we are here.''

Saldivar was about to warn her not to wake Singer unexpectedly, but she did not try. She looked intently at the sleeping man until, with a sudden intake of breath, he sat up.

20

The party was in full swing when they arrived. Jackson greeted them at the door, wearing a grubby scrub suit. It was hard to say if the stains were human blood or juices from the barbecue.

"Janney, baby," he said, falling heavily on her neck. "It's great to see you. Let me get your bodyguard drunk and then we can get down."

Janet disentangled herself while trying to signal over his shoulder to Singer that she was not being attacked.

"These are friends of mine, Jacks, so kindly get out your under-the-bed bottle, not the usual gastric lavage. They have news about the Mobile Force and Harlan's 3rd. Try bribery if you want it—large steaks to begin with."

Saldivar was still eating long after Singer had swallowed all the beef he could stomach. Sated, Singer listened with half an ear while Palha bargained with Zhanne's big-bellied friend for the smoking herb. It was the first time he had heard anyone bargaining, and it was interesting, but it still seemed wrong to him. Things like gebrith should not be bought and sold.

Near him, a game started up. Someone was throwing the bones. He watched intently till he thought he understood the game. The counting was different, and they played with only two chunks of bone, but the idea was similar. He nudged his way into the circle. When his turn came, he was eager to test himself against the defender, who seemed to be a player of some power, having amassed a big heap of other people's money and ornaments in front of him.

Singer still did not understand their money, so he kept laying down paper until they seemed satisfied. The other man threw first. Singer was puzzled. He could not feel any kind of force being exerted. He took the bones in his hand and shook them to get the feel. There were six ways to get *shi*, that was seven, and only two ways for *mente*—el-leven. He decided to work his way through them all. Slowly the pile of goods crossed the floor to him. He had to lose some of it back once or twice to reassure the other player. In the end it was all his. He was baffled. There was no resistance at all; the other man let him throw whatever he wanted. He had stopped throwing with the People long ago because he won too often, but this was ridiculous.

His opponent searched his belongings for something else to bet. He had already lost the arm ring that told him what time it was. He had a case with a shape that was not completely unfamiliar. Singer pointed to it.

"You want to play for my guitar?"

The man opened the case and took out a stringed instrument that thrummed faintly as it struck the edge of the box. It had too few strings to be a thamla, and it was curved and not cornered, but Singer's heart leapt toward the sound. With a decisive gesture he indicated that he would gamble the whole pile for the instrument.

"You're on," the other man said enthusiastically. Singer rolled a one and a three; then he went up through the numbers, skipping twelve, and back down again to a double two.

The others stared at him. He had deliberately taunted them, trying to make them oppose him, but they had not done anything. It seemed they had no feeling for the bones, just as they were numb and blind in so many other ways.

He slowly collected the money, leaving a pile of rings and other objects. "Take these," he said. "I don't want them."

He picked up the instrument and tried it hesitantly.

"Show me how to play and I give your money back," he said to the other player.

"Believe me, I'd like to, but I can't. It's not even mine. I won it from a friend. Thanks for giving my watch back, though. That's the last time I shoot with you, boy."

Singer felt Saldivar at his shoulder and handed him a wad of bills. "Take this, it don't fit in my pockets."

He tried to play the guitar, holding it flat on his lap like a thamla. Saldivar took it away from him.

"What's the matter with you? That's no way to do it. You have to turn it on, for one thing."

He started tuning the instrument; Singer understood after a minute what the intervals were supposed to be, took the guitar back, and fixed them. Saldivar did not have it quite right.

"So play something if you know so much," Saldivar said.

Singer moved closer, till their knees were touching as they bent over the guitar together. He started to play, and Saldivar recognized the opening chords of "Burning Bridges."

"You sing," Singer ordered him. "I can't get the words, so fast."

"What do you mean?"

Singer just shook his head and kept playing. The music seemed to lure Saldivar, challenging and wooing him. He picked up the tune, under his breath at first. He had to raise his voice to keep up when Singer began harmonizing wordlessly. By the end of the song, half the room was listening or joining in, and Saldivar was doing his best without hesitation. He figured no one could hear him, anyway. The music flowed from one song to another as if it were a live thing like a river searching for a way half-forgotten. The force of the current carried him with it and pushed aside all obstacles. He found himself in the middle of "Black Sun"; he was drumming wildly on a set of metal boxes, and the rest of the party was either dancing or pounding on any available surface. The noise was tremendous. Saldivar's throat was raw, but he could not hear himself singing anymore. In fact, he was not sure that he was singing. Everyone was shouting. In the most crowded corner, a fight had broken out. He saw fists flying, and a man's shirt tore apart, but without any sound that he could hear, like tissue paper parting. He knew there was something wrong with the situation, but he could not stop drumming. The music demanded that from him.

> Black sun, smoking mirror.
> The hummingbird drinks from a crimson flower.
> The hummingbird has eyes of stone.
> Smoking mirror, black sun.

"What the fuck does he think he's doing?" Jackson shouted into Jan's ear. "That's the guy from the annex—I never forget a scar! And that's Gary Sanderson getting the shit kicked out of him over there. More noise and the golpos will be here!"

"He just showed up, Jacks. I told him to stay away. I thought he'd be safe here. And I wanted you to get a good look at him, in case he needs help again sometime."

Jackson groaned. "Oh, I love the nice way you say 'help.' You make it sound like cucumber sandwiches and tea, instead of my ass on a skewer. Anybody who cheats with dice like that doesn't need help from me."

"Jacks, I don't think he's cheating. He's not that kind of a guy."

He gave her a sharp look but dropped the subject. "The point is, this has got to be stopped before anybody gets disassembled. I don't need the heat. I could use a little help myself."

He muscled his way through the crowd and dragged the combatants apart. The press closed up behind him again like honey after a knife. Janet slid between dancers as far as the middle of the floor, where Singer and Saldivar still sat facing each other. She touched Singer's arm, and the bitter energy that surged through him stung her like a shock. He did not seem to recognize her. His eyes were fixed on some distant point.

She shook Saldivar's shoulder. "Pablo! You're starting a riot."

He turned and looked at her, and the pace of his drumming slowed slightly. "Huh?"

"Play something else." She searched for something he would know. "Play me 'Blood Roses.' "

He grinned. "Sure. Hey, cofra—follow me."

The music changed course slowly into minor chords and complex, subtle rhythms. Singer's voice still flashed in and out of the somber melody like a fish leaping in a heavy sea. The partygoers who were quarreling hesitated and dropped their hands, losing their train of thought. The song came to an end. Janet took a deep breath and was surprised by how much she needed it.

"I forgot how much I hate crowds," she said. Her voice trembled.

Singer spread out his hands. His fingertips were bleeding. "Long time," he said.

Jackson reappeared, breathing heavily. "I want you to know I had to break out my last six cases of beer to keep these people from taking my place apart. This is your fault, Janney. If it's going to cost me six cases of beer to get you to my party, you better come straight up to the bedroom next time."

"Sorry, Jacks, we were just leaving," Jan said meekly.

"Oh, no problem. I'll get it back one way or another. Bring the chico back any time. Just don't let him play for money."

The stars were fading; the air felt cool after the hot room.

Singer walked in the middle with his arms around their shoulders.

"Kestri, andri," he said, and laughed. Then he put a hand on each of their heads and made them cross over in front of them.

"Kestri, andri," he said again.

"What are you talking about?" Saldivar asked.

"East hand, west hand. Sun-goes-up is the side for fighting. Brother's arm is the best shield, they say. Sun-goes-down is the side for laying down the fight. But they say watch out for the west-handed man, because he goes to a fight like he goes to the game of love, and when he plays the game with you he'll take your weapons and all and leave you with nothing but the skin you got born in."

"We call it left-handed," Jan said.

"You play like a son of a bitch," Saldivar said. "Left-handed or not. Where did you learn to do that?"

"I'm Singer," he said, as if that should have been obvious. He had come to know Saldivar well enough to know that calling his mother a female dog was a compliment, not a death challenge. Still, the question plunged him back into silence again, and they walked a few blocks without speaking.

"Who is smoking mirror?" he asked Saldivar.

"Funny you should put it that way. God of Texico, long ago. Or that's what the Montaraz still believe. Hummingbird is his brother, the god of war. They drink the blood of warriors. Medicine Shirt has its darker moments."

Singer nodded. "A song for the Destroyer. A good song for the destruction of a man."

"Take it easy, it's only a song."

"Have you a friend following?" Singer asked Jan.

"No, why?"

"Someone walks this way with us."

"I don't know anyone who lives in this part of town." She shrugged. "Coincidence."

"Didn't you say someone might be watching you?" Saldivar asked.

"I'm cautious, but I'm not paranoid. If someone is following me, he'll stay away as long as you're around."

Singer remained silent the rest of the way home, and Saldivar could feel his watchfulness. It made him nervous.

"Singer's usually right about things like this. Was there anyone there you didn't recognize?" he asked when the door had closed behind them.

"Oh, sure, but they were all friends of Jackson's from out of town. They're easy to spot. The only real stranger was that pilot everybody wanted a piece of. Jacks must have something devious in mind for him, because he's not the type who usually shows up at the party. Hombre non simpatico, apparently."

"Who is he?"

"His name is Gary Sanderson. I know that because he appears on an interesting personnel roster as a civilian meteorologist. Actually he works for the Net. The last I heard, he was on a classified flight schedule in the north. Now he's supposedly attending a special school on high-altitude photo analysis, here in Jefferson.

"Funny thing about that flight schedule. They were using hi-fighters, and that normally means reconnaissance. But what were they looking at up there? Of course, they can be used for bombing, and supply records seem to indicate a short run of precision strikes in the northern zone, sometime last spring. But the objectives—that information is so heavily shielded that I haven't found a way into it yet."

Singer put his hand on her arm.

"Precision strikes is what?" he asked. The picture came clearly into his mind before he had finished the question.

Fire from the sky.

He turned to Saldivar. "Wait for me. I'll come back."

He eased out the window and dropped. Saldivar jumped up to follow him but stopped at the window. As far as he could see, the streets were empty and still. Not a shadow moved to tell him which way Singer had gone. He smashed his fist into the windowsill in frustration.

"Do you think you can catch him if he doesn't want you to?" Jan asked. "You might as well relax."

"You don't know him the way I do. He's gonna get himself in trouble." He could not help remembering how Singer had shot the captain without a second thought. It had not occurred to him not to.

"I know one thing about him. You can't make him do anything he doesn't want to do. If he's looking for trouble, you won't be able to keep him out of it." She paused. "Did you ever have a dog?"

"What the fuck does that have to do with anything?"

"Just tell me."

"Shit, no. In the Tregua they weren't pets, they were vermin. Big excitement was watching the golpos hunt down dog packs and fry them."

"Me, either. I had a friend who did, though, or thought she did. The dog had long legs and a sharp muzzle and a bushy tail. After it ate the dog next door and tried to eat the neighbor, she learned it was a lupo. Lupos aren't like dogs. They don't accept a master. They'll be loyal to you insofar as you convince them you're the top lupo, but even then you can never persuade them to do anything that goes against their nature. You can live with them, but you can never tame them. You have to respect their limits."

"So what's the moral of this little fable?" Saldivar asked bitterly.

"If you want to be friends with the lupo, you have to become a lupo. You can go out to where he is and become like him, but you can never make him be like you."

Saldivar laughed without smiling. "If you think I can growl and Singer will roll over, you don't know him very well."

"No, I think the best we can hope for is to be accepted as members of the pack, junior members who have to be protected. Maybe he'll do for our sake what he won't do for his own, and stay alive a little longer."

As he paced the room, she caught his hand and tugged at him to sit down.

"You should take better care of this. There are plenty of people waiting in line to hurt you. Don't do it to yourself."

He let her detain him. He thought of rolling himself another smoke, but he knew he had smoked too much already. He told himself he was worried because Singer was going to get himself in trouble, but he was angry at himself for not being in shape to follow, and more than anything else he was angry because Singer had gone off without him.

"Pablo, do you want to tell me about the wind? It might be important."

"I don't know if I can tell it so you'll understand. It seemed as if he called the wind. I know that's impossible, but I believed it at the time. There's a power in him. And when he got shot, I was sure he was going to die. I held him all night and had the strangest dreams. In the morning he was better. Like you saw him."

"You mean you think you healed him?"

"Oh, no. No way. He healed himself. But he *leaned* on me.

I don't know what to call it. I was there with him. Sometimes, when I was in the hospital before, it seemed like you were there with me like that. Not just next to me, but *with* me."

"Yes. I know what you mean. I felt that, too. I suppose that's why I came around so often, because you could tell if I was there or not. Some people don't know the difference. But I wouldn't see you afterward because I'm a coward. It was all right while you were flat on your back. But once you were up again, I didn't want to know if it was real or not. It can be frightening to get too close to people."

"Truth." He sighed. "It can be."

She touched his hand. "Don't worry, Pablo. If he told you he'll come back, he will."

Saldivar realized that he had been asleep again when he heard someone come into the room. It was Singer. Saldivar struggled to focus his eyes and find his feet.

"Where the hell have you been?" he snarled.

"You found him, didn't you?" Janet asked.

Singer smiled, and Saldivar remembered what Janet had said about lupos. Death seemed to have come into the room with him, a black, bittersalt savor that hung in his garments like smoke.

"Asked him some questions," he said pleasantly. "Then he tried for his gun. That was a mistake. He could have lived a whole handful of breaths longer. And every breath is sweet to a dying man."

"Why?" Saldivar asked.

Singer's smile faded. He could see that they were upset with him. When a brother got angry for no reason, the polite thing to do was to leave him alone till he came to his senses, not embarrass him by staring at his bad temper. He went out to the little kitchen and cleaned his knife carefully. He found Jan's fire lighter and made a little ash; then he cut parallel lines on the inside of his wrist and rubbed ash into them till they darkened and stopped bleeding. The dark, ridged scars would make a permanent record of his vengeance. At least anyone who saw his body would know he had been trying.

After thinking about it, he made marks for the captain he had killed with the small gun and for the five men he had killed with his own hands after Nikei died. That brought his count up to nine. The others he and Palha had killed with the fire weapons blurred together in his mind, and he did not even know how many of them there had been, so he left them out.

Palha followed him into the kitchen and sat on the table. His presence was still violently agitated.

"Why did you do it?" he asked again. "Don't you know what will happen when they catch you?"

"If they catch me, there will be a welcome for them," Singer said, checking the edge of his knife for nicks. "This man killed friends of mine. He had to die. Is he your brother? Why all this trouble over a stranger?"

"The law," Saldivar tried to explain.

"Spit on a law that makes my brothers' blood cheap," Singer said. He had to turn his face from Saldivar; he was too angry. He calmed himself with an effort. Palha was afraid; that "law" had power in his mind. Frightened people behaved badly. Perhaps Palha was afraid for Zhanne, too; his reproach was understandable if Singer had thoughtlessly endangered a friend.

"I was careful and quick," he assured Saldivar. "We'll be gone with the day, and Zhanne was never there. Nothing to fear."

"I've been thinking about this," Janet said to Saldivar. She was leaning against the doorway, fiddling with a much-bitten plastic pen. "I don't like it, either, but he may have done us a favor. Space Command has short-term quarters about half a mile from here, so he could have been on his way home. But I know the Net bugged my office a while back. It's possible Sanderson was coming here to check me out. What if he'd showed up and we'd had to deal with him here? Without you guys, I would have been in trouble. With you here, it could have gone several ways, all of them bad. He could have figured out who Singer was and reported him. Or he might have ended up dead, and then we would have had a body to get rid of. As it is, Sanderson was killed on the street; could have been anyone."

Saldivar saw her logic, but he was not that easily mollified; he wanted an explanation from Singer himself. "Look, man, I don't want to fight with you about if you should have done it, but I want you to tell me why."

Singer did not look at him. "Hunting with you was good, and singing with you was good," he said. "I like to think about doing those things again one day."

He refused to talk further about it.

Janet had brought Saldivar's pack from the other room; she

rummaged in the cooler and cupboards and dumped her remaining candy bars and fruit into the pockets.

"This is for you to eat on the way back. I gave you some soap and stuff you might be able to use—no personal comment intended. I don't want you to go, but I think you'd better, before they find Sanderson."

"What about you?"

"I'll do all right. I've been careful; I'll just have to be more careful. Keep in touch, but do it cautiously."

She helped him on with the pack and kissed him quickly. "Take care of yourself, Pablo. Come back, dakko?"

"Dakko," he muttered, warmed and embarrassed.

Singer lifted her off the ground and kissed her enthusiastically. "Thanks. Gracias. Danke."

She studied him for a minute and then gave him her secretive smile. "Riolnabe," she replied.

Singer's face became expressionless. "Good-bye," he enunciated carefully.

They caught a ride with a load of medical supplies for Guijarro.

"She's strange," Saldivar remarked as the cluster of buildings that made up the town shrank away below them. "Different."

"You liked her all right," Singer teased him. He held his closed fists out to Saldivar as if they were playing the hide-the-buckle game. "You two are both like this—you don't show your hands to anyone. Who knows what's inside?" Suddenly he struck his palms together and laughed when Saldivar jumped.

21

Singer saw Saldivar off to his new unit the next morning.

"Bates will be pissed that he can't have you back," Saldivar said. "He said since you weren't dead yet, he might as well get some use out of you. That's as good as a medal, from Bates."

Singer smiled but did not say anything. Saldivar did not find much to say, either, as the plane loaded up. To himself he said that it would be good to get back in the groove again, on his own. But after they lifted, he put his hands to his belt a hundred times, feeling as if he had left something essential behind. Singer had never said much, but he had been talking all the time—with his eyes, the way he sniffed the air, the way he moved. When Saldivar turned around to touch that constant presence, it was not there.

Singer told himself that he was glad to see the outlander go. But at least half the gladness was a sorry kind of pleasure because he knew that sometime soon he would call down trouble on himself, and he wanted Palha safely away.

The first time Singer stood in front of Kruger's desk, the colonel wondered if he might have made a mistake. Having Singer around turned out to be more like adopting a large wild animal than assigning an extra man to his staff. Singer moved so quietly that Mack had not realized just how tall he was. But whenever he stood up, the room became too small. His uneasiness at being inside was perceptible and added to the claustrophobia for several weeks, until he finally got used to living on the base.

His size was not the only thing Kruger had to put up with. The colonel slept in the HQ building; he had arranged it that

way so he could be alone and so his spells of sickness would be less conspicuous. He had not intended to have Singer stay there, but he found him sleeping on the floor outside his door one morning. He persuaded Singer to set up a cot in the outer room, but he could not persuade him to leave.

Singer was unfailingly courteous on his own terms, but he had no concept of military decorum. He usually remembered to salute officers other than Kruger and to wear his boots during his official duty hours. The rest of the time he lived in a single set of recon camouflage Dustrags, washed and worn till they were soft and shapeless, a pair of shower clogs he would kick off and leave whenever he wanted to move fast, and a head cloth that kept his lengthening hair out of his eyes. He called Kruger "Con-el" when there were other people within earshot and "Makho" when there were not. Kruger gave up trying to correct him. It seemed undignified, since he was the one who had asked for the situation in the first place. What could he do if Singer continued to ignore his reprimands? Throw him back in the brier patch?

Kruger had originally intended to make him a clerk on the intelligence staff.

"Can't," Singer said, looking politely away to show that he was sorry for giving an unwelcome reply to the older man.

"What do you mean, 'can't'?" Kruger said. "You can't type? You can't file? Can't tell A from B?"

"Yes," Singer said.

"You can learn," Kruger said. As far as he was concerned, that was the end of it.

Singer's eyebrows rose slightly in an expression Kruger was soon to know well. It meant that Singer was not going to argue, but the colonel would find out for himself.

He never became a clerk. During the day he usually stayed close to Kruger. He learned immediately when Kruger got up, what foods were good for him, and every other aspect of his routine. If the colonel forgot his watch or his sunglasses, Singer would produce them silently at the right moment. Kruger began taking him to most of his meetings when he found that although Singer never took notes, he could reproduce long conversations verbatim.

He did most of his real work in the cool of the evening, when he took off his boots, picked up his guitar, a baggie of Saldivar's grass, and extra cans of fruit that he lifted with Kruger's connivance, and went visiting. He spent many evenings with the

recon patrols, listening to their stories and complaints. When it got around that a word to Singer could catch Mack's ear anonymously and without retribution, they told him many things.

When he got bored, he went out with them for a day or two. At first Bates was the only one who would take him along. But the word also got around very soon that Singer did not trip over his feet and was a valuable companion. Out in the Dust, under cover of the night, Singer asked a lot of questions. He kept their secrets, and if they guessed any of his, they did not say. They taught him what he wanted to know without asking him what he would do with the knowledge.

Bates liked damage for its own sake. He did not care how messy or noisy an operation was as long as he could see his enemies dead and their possessions ruined. He was glad to teach Singer how to do everything he could do. But Singer modified it to suit himself. He took pleasure in the well-made pattern: in charges precisely placed, in the least possible charge that would create the necessary effect, in ambushes that herded the enemy like sheep and positioned them for the killing blow.

Eventually teams that were short a man or just new and nervous started asking him to come along, but by then he turned most of them down. He had found out most of what he wanted from them. Kruger needed him more often. The colonel was taking three different kinds of pills; Singer carried them around for him, because Kruger did not always remember what he had taken when. He had always been thin, but he was down to skin and bones. He had bouts of nausea that he tried to conceal. Singer scrounged and bribed to get candy bars, fruit juice, and pop for him—the only things he could keep down. On hot nights Kruger could not sleep. He stayed at his desk as long as he could pretend he was working; after that he tried to read, or at least to hold the book in front of him and focus his eyes on it. Soon he was going to increase the dosage again, and he was not sure what that would do. He was already experiencing moments of disorientation, short periods when his memory stopped working and he could not recall exactly what he had been doing.

He had read all the nonclassified reports on the normal progress of the syndrome. Joint inflammation and low-grade fever were the first symptoms. Blood tests would show an elevated white count and proteins in the blood. Nausea was a symptom of liver and kidney damage. Death sometimes resulted from that damage, sometimes from pericardial inflammation. Treatment was palliative. Once the autoimmune response had been trig-

gered, there might be remissions of varying depth and length, but there was no cure. Three hundred some cases had been reported; two dozen were still alive in the hospitals. The longest survival rate was a little over two years. Kruger had a feeling that he was not going to beat the record.

There was a soft sound at the door, and he looked up from his book to see Singer politely shuffling his feet in order to be heard. Kruger tried to look casual and not grit his teeth.

"What are you doing up?" he asked gruffly. "I didn't call you."

"Music," Singer said, holding up the guitar. "Do you mind?"

"Go ahead. I'm not really concentrating, anyway."

Singer sat in the doorway and played softly, tunes with no words to them, full of minors and unfamiliar harmonies. His fingers wandered and hesitated, choosing the chords he wanted, but the music always kept moving. The plucked notes seemed to be sounding in a larger space, a dusky plain where the winds blew cool between the stars and the waving grass.

Kruger realized that he was falling asleep when he felt Singer half lifting him and helping him to his bed.

After that it seemed that Singer was always awake when Kruger was. He did not always play; sometimes they just talked. It felt like talking, anyway, though Singer did not say much. Those midnight hours seemed to Kruger like the sessions of an exclusive organization with only two members. They carried him back to the years when he had been as young as Singer and had had friends he could stay up all night with, talking.

"What did you do before you joined the army?" he asked once.

"There is no before," Singer said. "Always been fighting, always been here."

"It does feel like that sometimes," Kruger agreed. "I got my start in the Tregua. I was in Eldorado, Haven, the border action, you name it. Mostly drylands, after that first six years in the jungles. Never got past light colonel, so I spent a lot of time out in the field. They finally promoted me when I volunteered to come up here. It was that or early retirement—or an attitude adjustment, I suppose. But I'm too old for that.

"No regrets, really. I never wanted to end up an Oberst Oberarsch driving an armored desk chair like H— ah, like half the people here. I'll tell you what I miss, though. They had these things called hot tubs—ever been in one? I could sit and soak in one of those forever. I feel like I'll never get the grit out of my hide. Even going swimming would be great.

"If I ever got my grant, I know where I'd go. There's a settlement called Wiesen, up by North Fork. There are a lot of people from Heimat there, and it's beautiful country. Hot in the summer, but there's rain, and it cools off in the winter. Even snows a little, but not too much. I'd build a cabin by the creek and spend the rest of my time fishing."

Singer played a run of notes that sounded elusively like a fish splashing but vanished too quickly to be caught.

"What do you miss most, Singer?"

Singer stopped playing for a minute. My life, he thought. But he could not say that.

"Horses," he said finally. "And women."

"It'd be good for horse breeding, in the North Fork country," Kruger said. "When you find yourself a woman, come look it over."

"Sure," Singer said gently. "Maybe we will meet on the Road to the North. Maybe so." He sounded tired.

"I'm keeping you up too late," Kruger said. "We should both turn in. By the way, don't forget tomorrow to have guest accommodations set up for General Harlan. He is finally favoring us with his presence."

Singer pricked up his ears at that news. He knew that Kruger had been trying for a long time to get Harlan to come out and review his newly reformed force. Harlan did not want to come, since he rightly feared a storm of questions about his lack of support for Operation Long Shot. Kruger had already deluged Harlan and his superiors with every kind of official form and protest in existence and a few that he had invented. It had not done him any good so far. Singer wondered why the general was showing up.

Singer was at Kruger's shoulder through the tour and inspection and, as usual, sat in on the meeting that followed. Kruger had introduced him as his field intelligence liaison. He was wearing his shades and his most impassive look, but he could see Harlan looking at him suspiciously. There was no way to disguise the scar on his face. If the men who had questioned him in the hospital had described him to anyone, he might be in trouble sooner than he had planned.

Harlan and Kruger discussed strategy for the new campaign

for some time. Singer paid marginal attention; he did not really care how they organized themselves, but he thought that the knowledge might be useful in his dealings with the scouting patrols.

He felt Kruger bracing himself.

"This is all well and good, sir," the colonel said. "But I have a very basic problem with the operation."

"What's that?" Harlan asked.

"The survivors of Long Shot wonder if any plan that includes outside support is reliable," Kruger said. "That group includes myself."

"What are you implying?"

"I'm not implying anything." Kruger's voice rose until by the end of his statement he was shouting. "I'm stating, as I have officially done without receiving any kind of satisfactory response, that we didn't get the support promised us for Long Shot, and that as a result, the operation was a disaster and the casualty rate was completely unacceptable. I'm not marching my command out on a bridge again for your ops boy to cut the ropes out from under us."

"We can't engrave promises in stone for you or anyone else," Harlan said. "It was a judgment call. We received intelligence from a very reliable source that the airfield at Jefferson was a target for a night bombing. We had to recall all available air to protect the field. We're working with limited resources here, and you are no more entitled to them than anyone else."

"And did this attack ever materialize?"

"That's not the point."

Harlan looked meaningfully at Singer. Kruger excused him with a gesture.

Singer went outside and sat down against the back wall. From there he could hear almost as well as if he were inside the room.

"Now, Marcus, I have to tell you that your obsession with this grievance is being seen by a lot of people as an attempt to cover up your own blatant disregard of proper procedures. I would certainly never go as far as a court-martial myself, but I feel I should inform you that it's been discussed."

"What are you talking about?"

"Marcus, I didn't come out here to deliver a rebuke. I frankly think you've suffered enough, and the fine job you've done in rebuilding and preparing for Operation Ant Trap ought to cancel out old scores.

"But if you must know, you did tread a fine line on disregarding orders. General Nymann believes it was primarily unwise long-range intelligence missions—which you were specifically warned against—that triggered enemy awareness of your movements in this area."

He held up a hand to silence Kruger.

"More serious, however, is the fact that you were overeager in the actual attack. You received orders to send in reconnaissance only and not to commit the full force until you received favorable reports from them."

"Bullshit!" Kruger exploded. "My orders were to deploy my entire force as speedily as possible, relying on air cover while I secured the area."

"I think you'll find that a check of the record shows your memory is faulty, Colonel," Harlan said smoothly.

"My staff can—" Kruger started to say, then stopped. He realized that the tattered few who remained of his staff were hospitalized in North Fork. No one left alive had actually seen his orders.

"When I was a boy in Heimat," he said heavily, "we had a constitution, as I recall. A man couldn't be convicted without evidence, or punished before he was tried. Not even in the Bund. Soldiers were proud men when I was young, not slaves."

Harlan laughed uncomfortably. "I'm not sure where this conversation is going, Marcus. We still have a constitution, you know that. Unfortunately the current emergency has forced the suspension of some procedures we might otherwise prefer, but as an old soldier you should understand that."

"The current emergency? Some of those young men who died recently spent their whole lives in the current emergency. Tell me, what kind of government makes deals with the enemy while using the existence of that enemy as an excuse to make war on its own people?"

"Marcus, I warn you, you're treading on dangerous ground here. I'm an old friend, but I can't listen to open treason."

"So asking questions is treason now?"

"Marcus, I know you're no traitor, because I know you're not responsible for what you're saying. You're very naturally distraught. You're weakened by illness. You need a rest. I think I was able to make them understand that. I spoke up against this talk about court-martial and reprimand," Harlan continued. "I decided to come out here personally and talk to you. There is a graceful way out of an awkward situation."

"Is this where you hand me the pistol and leave me alone in

my office?'' Kruger asked. Singer saw the picture in his mind very clearly, the gleaming metal weapon with its nose against Kruger's head, and his muscles tensed, ready to charge in and yank the Asharya out of harm's way. He recognized in time that it was a word game the two of them were playing. But Kruger's voice was as tight as a drawn bowstring. His life was bet on that game.

Harlan chuckled again. ''My God, Marcus, calm down. You're confirming my feeling that you've been out here too long. You're seeing shadows behind every bush. All I'm here to propose is that you take an early retirement.''

''No.''

''It's no disgrace. You've been putting yourself on the line for nearly thirty years, here and back home. That's long enough. Be fair to yourself and your people and admit that you've done all you can. If you don't want to retire completely, at least think about coming back to Jefferson. I could find a place for you on my staff, make good use of your experience. You could take a promotion on retirement, too. You could finally make general. Think about it, Marcus. Don't force me into all this unpleasantness. Nothing is official yet. It doesn't have to happen if you and I can reach a reasonable accommodation. Will you at least think about it?''

''I'll think about it,'' Kruger said heavily. ''How long?''

''I think I can stall Planetary Command for a couple of weeks. Let me know as soon as possible.'' The tones of his voice deepened, rich and kindly once he thought he was winning.

There was silence. Then Harlan continued, in a lowered voice. ''By the way, what's the background of that liaison? Singer? Is that his name?''

''Nothing out of the ordinary. He's one of our class-3 citizens, obviously. Why?''

''No particular reason. I thought I might have seen him before somewhere.''

''It's not likely,'' Kruger said dryly. ''He's spent most of his time in the field. You might have seen his name on the list I sent in. He's up for several commendations, one of the few who's not getting them posthumously.''

He called for Singer, who appeared after a suitable interval indicating that he had been elsewhere. Kruger told him to call the forward observation post and confirm that the general would be visiting later in the afternoon; then he took the general, the general's colonel, and his two majors to lunch. Singer sat around under the scrawny shadow of the HQ building, watching the air simmer above the traveling machines. There was no one else out in the blistering noon.

He slipped the package out of his shirt and turned it over in his hand. As a weapon, it was lacking in beauty: some wires, some cord-that-burned, a small, heavy-soft chunk of fire food. Bates had taught him how to make and use the thing, but it still did not speak to him. It was like all their devices; it had no outward grace and did not complement the speed or strength of the hand that wielded it. If it had any beauty, the beauty was all in the mind where the pattern for it was created. And suddenly he gasped and jerked his hand back, nearly dropping the thing. For a minute he had seen it as a pattern, a pattern of fire. Strange, very strange, and not something he wanted to think about. But it decided him. There was a certain fitness in using that weapon against them, like killing a man with his own knife. He attached and adjusted the package and went to get cold beer and be seen by many people.

He was lounging in the shade again when the parade formed to take the general up the road. His pose betrayed only the same mild interest as the others who were watching, but one finger thoughtfully traced the scar on his face. He froze when he saw Kruger beckon and Mooney jump into the back of the general's machine. Kruger himself was riding in another moto with his own officers.

They drove through the gate and some distance up the road. Then the traveling machine exploded. Singer was the first to reach them afterward, sprinting down the road with his boots dragging at his feet like dead men's curses. The machine was not really destroyed, just twisted and crushed. It lay on its side, burning merrily along with the body of one of the majors. The general and the other officer lay in the road. Singer ignored them.

Someone had dragged Mooney out from under the machine. It had thrown him and rolled on him like a dangerous horse. Tangled metal had torn him open, and he bled to death too fast to be saved.

Singer retreated to the top of the hill. He took the *gitarra* along, but he could not sing. He could see the lights down below where Mooney's brothers were drinking without him. He did not want to join them. He had killed their friend.

No friend of mine, he said to himself. He was nothing to me. But that was not true. He had eaten with and watched for him while he slept. Mooney had taught him his own weapon skill. How long does it take to make a stranger your brother? Forever! he answered himself. They come from beyond the night to steal our earth and sky. They left my people burning in their graves. They are not human. They are my enemies. As long as wind blows and fire burns. All of them.

He took his knife and made three more cuts on his arm. The small pain was soothing; it distracted his mind. There was need for another mark. Four men had died. Four enemies.

All of them? that tormenting voice within him asked. What about Palha, then? What about Zhanne, and the knife con-el? Go ahead. Kill them. It would be easy. They trust you.

He snarled silently and threw down the alien knife. There would be no score for Mooney.

There was still the other major. If he had not felt sick and decided to stay behind, there would not have been room for Mooney. Singer left the *gitarra* and the knife behind and paid a visit to the hospital. It was a single long, low building; the place where they kept the dead was at the far end, neither locked nor guarded. Inside it was dark. Singer could smell the sharp scent of the plastic the bodies were wrapped in, but the death smell seeped out, too. He had to use his hand light and puzzle out the names tagged to the plastic to find out which one was Mooney. He thought he would rather leave his friend's bones to be eaten by foxes and bleached clean by the sun then to lie there in the dark like stinking garbage. It made him sick to be there.

The building was only one story high, but there was a ventilation space above the ceiling. He stood on the sink and pulled himself up into the dusty space. Gripping the slender beam with his bare toes, he crawled to the room where they were keeping the major. He moved a panel aside and looked; the man was sleeping facedown. He let himself down at arm's length so he could drop quietly. He listened; there was no one else in the room and no sound from the hall outside. He clamped a hand over the man's face, put a knee in his back, and snapped his neck. Then he pushed the man's head hard into the pillow till he stopped moving. He took the flimsy metal necklace that was the only ornament most of those people wore and climbed back into the ceiling. He left the tags on Mooney's body; he had meant to tuck them inside the bag with him, but he did not want to touch it.

It had been neat, quick, and silent; he had disturbed nothing and left no traces behind. Now there were four marks, as there had been, and Mooney had a trophy to show that he was a man of dignity in someone's eyes, not just a bag of offal. But Singer felt very sick as he slipped back up the hill. As soon as he had laid hands on the man, he had known that something was wrong. He had heard the major's surprise and panic so clearly that he had thought for an instant that the man had called aloud for help. His last fragmented thoughts and the relentless terror that continued till the end were carved into Singer's memory. He gasped for air as if he had been suffocating himself.

I can't keep them out of my head, he thought wildly. It's like the drug, only there is no drug. It's coming back by itself.

He felt as if he needed to wash. He wished himself deep in Thunder River, where the cold, singing water could wash all his memories away like rags. But there was no river where he was, only the ubiquitous dust and the sound of alien voices from the camp where the party was breaking up. He picked up his guitar and his knife, feeling that they had both failed him, and went back down to the road.

He ran into a couple of other men on his way through the camp; that suited him, since he wanted to be visible far from the hospital.

"Hey, Singer," they greeted him. "What do you think? Was it a mine, or did somebody light up the general? I hear tell the old man did it himself. What do you think?"

"That's shit," Singer said.

"Hey, what's smoking you? Oh yeah, Mooney was a friend of yours, huh? Well. No offense intended, but that's still got to be a max, squeezing off on Harlan. Sorry about Mooney."

He was half hoping that Kruger would be asleep, but the old man was still up. The desk and walls were bare, the wastebasket was full, and half a dozen sealed boxes were stacked next to the files. Kruger turned around, and Singer smelled chah.

"Sit down, son. I've been waiting for you."

Singer sat, hardly paying attention while he tried to assimilate the meaning of the word Kruger had just used.

"I wanted to tell you myself. I resigned, tonight. I'm packed. The investigation team for General Harlan's death will be here tomorrow morning, and I'll be going out on the return flight. I'm on medical leave as of now. I'll be officially retired as soon as the paper goes through."

"Why?"

Singer thought of all the hours he had spent trying to keep the old man's soul and ruined body together. Now he was quitting, just like that.

"I'm sorry," Kruger said quietly. "I don't think I understand just what-all you've been doing for me, but I appreciate it. I can't pay you back the way I'd hoped, because I'm not going to live that long.

"They've been on me to resign for some time now. Harlan came down to 'request' it again."

"Harlan is gone now," Singer said.

Kruger shook his head wearily. "This goes a lot farther than Harlan, and it won't stop with him. Some son of a bitch is trying to kill me, and he has just about done it. A lot of other good men got dusted in the process. That made me so mad, I resolved to live till I found out who it was. I haven't succeeded. I think now I might have done better to leave it alone. I thought I could protect what was left of my men by fighting back. If I could have found out who . . . But if I'd just accepted that I'd had it and quit, maybe they'd have left the rest of you alone."

"Why they wanted you dead?" Singer asked.

Kruger poured himself another drink and stared into it. Finally he seemed to come to a decision.

"Son, I'm going to tell you this because I want you to be able to protect yourself. But I forbid you, I forbid you absolutely to get involved. Understand me? I know you, Singer. If you thought you knew who was responsible, you'd appoint yourself judge and jury and eradicate the bastard. Wouldn't you, now?"

"Maybe," Singer said.

"You know damn well you would. Get this straight right now; I don't know who it was and I never will know. This is strictly supposition."

"Understand," Singer said.

"How much do you know about the history of New Hope?" Kruger asked.

"Nothin'," Singer said.

"Frightful." Kruger shook his head. "Unbelievable. A generation without history. You must try to learn to read, son. Try not to spend your whole life as a humper."

Singer shrugged. "Only thing I know."

"I know, son, I know." Kruger sighed. "Well, the first colony was composed almost entirely of civilian scientific personnel and their families. They vanished without a trace, and that was the opener for the bloody mess we're involved in now. The Union had planted a colony just after we did—or just before, if you read their histories. We accused them of wiping out our first group, and they replied that this was an obvious provocative statement to justify grabbing the planet they had discovered. The next ship up contained civilians and equipment for economic development. It had been sent before the word got home. But the one after that was a troopship. And so it has gone. After an exchange of bombing, I think the heavies on both sides must have decided neither of us could survive much of that. So we're in a standoff. We've got the Open Zone between us, and both sides prowl it unceasingly, looking for some advantage to sink our teeth into. That's where you and I come in.

"Well, now, as I've prowled the border for the last ten years, I've seen enough strange things to convince me that maybe the first colony is not all dead. Maybe they and probably others currently listed as MIAs are being held in the north somewhere. Last year, before the shit went ballistic for me personally, I was much farther north than I had any right to be, in hot pursuit of a bunch of Nupis who seemed to be heading for sanctuary in what should have been empty territory. We ran into a road, a fucking road in the middle of nowhere. That night we saw air strikes of major size off to the north of us. For sure there is somebody up there.

"The next day we were spotted by enemy recon and had to run for home. We had almost made it when we walked into a shitload of defoliant—you know what that is? Right. They said it was an accident. A couple of platoons had to be put on extended medical leave, and twenty men came down with Karpinski's syndrome, of whom I'm the only one above ground. From there it was all downhill. I believe there are enemy installations up north that we're not allowed to go up against for some kind of twisted policy reasons. I'm convinced that one of the things we'd find if we did is the original survivors of the first colony. Someone is willing to commit murder to keep us from doing that."

"Why?" Singer asked again.

"I don't know. Maybe the survivors have some kind of knowledge that they don't want made public. Like exactly what happened to the first colony. If it turned out they really were massacred by the Nupis, and we could prove it, it might lead to another war back home. I don't know. Whatever it is, I don't think it's PCOM who's really back of it all. Their minds are just not that complicated. I think it's someone in the Net, and I think they are working with the enemy. They're accepting, even authorizing, the death of their own men as the price of keeping this secret.

"I'd love to know the answer, and I never will. And neither will you, so don't even think about it. I'm telling you this so you can stay clear of anyone from the Net and keep your mouth shut. Transfer south, if you can; it's safer. And forget you ever knew me."

Singer did the trick with his eyebrows that indicated complete skepticism. He overdid it so Kruger would notice it and laugh, and he did, but the laugh died quickly.

"I'm sorry, Singer. I know you think I'm quitting. Well, I am. When the investigation team gets here . . . they asked me to give them a list of potential suspects. I told them I had 1,500 men, any one of whom could have done it in his sleep. What do they think I'm running here, a gardening club? It'll be a witch-hunt. I can't, I won't, preside over it.

"The other thing is that Harlan was right, much as I hate to admit it. I've had it, Singer. I can't take it anymore, even with your help. I've always been a field commander. Pushing pins into a map is the most I'm good for these days. I can hardly walk. I'm taking so many drugs, I can't tell my ass from a hole in the ground." He squinted dubiously at the bottle on his desk. "I shouldn't be drinking this stuff. I'm destroying what liver I've got left.

"I'm dying, Singer. It's time for me to get out of the road and go do it."

There was a silence.

"You tried," Singer said finally. He touched the old man's shoulder and felt that what he said was true. He could part the life from that body as easily as snapping a dry grass stem. He withdrew his hand carefully.

Kruger cleared his throat. "Is there anything I can do for you before I go?"

Singer thought for a minute. "Two things. You let me take you to North Fork tomorrow."

"You don't need to do that."

"I take you where you're going," Singer insisted. "Second thing is, put me back with Bates's team."

"Didn't you hear me? I said get out of here. Go south."

"No. There's nothing for me south. After you're gone I go back to the Dust and it's okay."

"All right, then, I'll see you tomorrow." He wanted to say good-bye and thanks, but he could not seem to find appropriate words. Laboriously he pulled himself out of the chair and hobbled to his bed.

Singer knew that Kruger wanted to do it by himself and did not try to assist him. Instead, he appropriated the rest of the bottle and drank it all. It made him slightly numb, and that helped a little. He barefooted down the road, tossed the empty in a long arc that finished up with a smash against somebody's wall, and listened to the resulting commotion for a few minutes.

"Paliao doronn'a," he said to the night. "My heart is turning black." He lay down on the floor across Kruger's doorway and went to sleep. He kept dreaming that he was strangling somebody, and when he rolled the body over, it turned out to be Dona. He woke with a jerk and sat up in the dark, trying to find something else to think about. He could hear Kruger's uneasy breathing in the next room. There had been something not quite right when he had put his hand on the old man's shoulder. Kruger had been telling the truth about how sick he was, but not about everything. He had not given up—that was it. He said he had; he was withdrawing, but there was some faint hope he was stubbornly holding out.

Old fox! Singer felt very slightly better. Completely silent in his bare feet, he stole into the room. The desk top was bare; there was nothing on the shelves. But the old man's fancy coat hung straight and stiff, on a hanger on the edge of the door. In the pocket was something folded: a sheet of that thin, flexible paper that would not tear or get wet. He took it out into the moonlight and unfolded it. It was a piece of a map, with no strangerfolk writing to identify or explain it. It showed more ridges, maybe a river, and several circles marked in with a pen. He thought he might recognize the ripples and angles at what could be the southmost edge of the map, but then again, one ridge looked much like another. He replaced it carefully in the pocket, though there was not much chance that it would help the old man find what he was looking for.

The transport arrived early in the morning; the air was still chilly, and no one thought it odd that Singer kept his chin tucked into his collar and his cap pulled down tight. While Kruger greeted the investigation team and the acting commander, Singer supervised the loading of the colonel's personal effects. He recognized one of the investigators from behind and at a distance.

It was the cold-eyed one from the hospital. His hands wanted to fly to his knife. Instead he walked slowly around the transport, sat down on a pile of containers, and pretended to sleep with his cap pulled over his eyes.

All his other senses were wide open, and he knew, with relief, when they went inside and closed the door. There were medical personnel on the transport; they had brought a chair with wheels on it for Kruger. Singer thought that was an interesting idea, but he could tell by Kruger's indignant resistance that the old man considered it a disgrace to get into one. He placed himself between Kruger and the man who was trying to ease him into the chair and bestowed on him in one look the anger he had not been able to take out on Cold Eyes. The man backed off.

Singer heard him talking to someone behind his back.

"What the fuck was that?"

"That's Kruger's chico. Don't mess with him, he's a complete animal. Mean as an E-dog and just about as smart."

It annoyed him to be compared to an animal, but he did not let it really register. He was at Kruger's shoulder, ready to catch him if he fell but willing him not to. The old man walked strong and steady up to the ladder. They had a hoist to carry him inside.

The transport was not like anything Singer had ever seen. It had large windows and padded seats instead of slings that left grid marks on the passengers' backs. A woman came around and offered them drinks.

"Swing low, sweet chariot," Kruger said. "Lord, I must have done the right thing for once. I never rated this kind of treatment before."

Singer saw that he was trying to make jokes to hide the pain. His face was dead white and beaded with sweat. Another medical person came down the aisle with a skinjet. Singer snarled at him without thinking; only Kruger's hand on his sleeve stopped him from throwing the man against the wall.

"It's all right," Kruger whispered.

Blinking nervously at Singer, the doctor went ahead with the shot. Kruger's tight mouth relaxed, and his eyes drifted half-shut.

"That's heavy . . ." he muttered. "Don't hurt them, boy. It's their show now." He seemed to sleep. Singer wanted to touch him and find out what he was dreaming about, but the strangers were watching, so he sat and wondered till the transport started its descent. Then he did wake the old man up.

"How long?" he asked.

It took Kruger a minute or two to focus on the question. "Oh. Who knows? You remember what Bates used to say? 'What's the half-life of the half-assed?' Um. Sometimes there's a remission with first drugs. 'S late for me, but maybe. Could be six months."

On landing they did not even try the wheelchair. They brought a stretcher, and Kruger made no fuss as they lifted him into it. He tried to stay in focus as the hoist stopped. He thought Singer wanted to say something. But Singer only stepped back and gave him his inimitably bad salute. It looked more like a jaunty invitation to personal combat than a gesture of respect. He smiled to himself, and when he looked again, Singer had vanished.

22

Singer walked from the airfield to town. He did not need to ask for directions; he just headed for the building that towered above the others. The walls went up higher than the Rock, higher than the towers of the city, higher than anything that side of the mountains. There were five layers of windows, and the building covered the whole block where it stood. He could not walk around it, though. The drive that circled it was surrounded by a wide flat area where nothing could move without being seen, and that in turn was bounded by a high strong fence topped with spiked wire. The only entrance went through guarded gates protected by concrete baffles. Singer went to the nearest building that had a good view of the place. It was some kind of office; no one tried to stop him in the lobby. He climbed the stairs to the top floor and found a window by the stairwell where he could get a good look at the building.

From what Bates had taught him, he believed the fence was electrified. There was no cover anywhere nearby. Entering seemed impossible by force and unlikely by stealth. And even if he did get in, how would he find the people he wanted?

Well, he had to get in, so he would get in. And after that, if he failed in his revenge, he would be dead, so he would not care. But he did not like the thought of failing utterly, being dragged out like a dead dog and forgotten. He had no brothers left; he wanted his enemies at least to remember him.

A big man came out of the stairwell and gave him a sharp glance. "Looking for something?"

The man was a sergeant; Singer had a certain liking for sergeants because the stripes on their sleeves reminded him of the water bird symbol of the Lunalva barhedonh. He ducked his head sheepishly.

"Yeah, guess I'm on the wrong floor," he said, and went back down the stairs.

He walked slowly into town. His clothing was hot and heavy, and his boots hurt. All about him were places selling things, people on the streets who did not wear uniforms, even trees and green plants growing. He saw a door across the street that looked like the entrance to a tavern and recalled that he had plenty of money. It made him nervous to go in there without Palha to show him how to act, but surely one tavern must be much like another.

Inside it was dark and cool; it smelled like a tavern, except for the mouth smoke the outlanders took with them everywhere. He asked for the same kind of chah Palha liked, and they gave it to him in a glass with lumps of ice—clear, like glacier ice. It was amazing.

And he was overcome with shame that he was sitting there in one piece and drinking chah while his job was still undone.

I can't find them, brothers, he said to the shadows in the corner. I have learned their words, but I don't understand their meanings. Their faces are hidden. They kill from far away with a look or a word. The warrior who kills is only an arrow guided to an unseen target by another's hand. They live in a maze of rules, but they behave like animals: no brotherhood, no manners, no honor; they forget their friends as soon as they are dead. No, worse than animals, for they devour their own kind.

I confess to you, my brothers, I am afraid. Their numbers are endless, their power is endless, and I am alone. They are not human; I will never understand them. Yet—yet—when I think on this and I look on Palha, or my sad con-el, the blade turns in my hand and says to me, "How shall I spill the blood of your brother?" Who, then, am I betraying?

Ayei, I sometimes think I died when you left me. I am walking in the Soul-eater's cold hell no path leads out of, and I feel his black teeth chewing on my heart.

He shivered and swallowed the rest of his chah. It was good cold; it went down quickly that way. He called for another one, and when they brought it, he lifted it in a toast Bates had taught him: *Go die, you bastards!* He wished that even one of them could sense his hate. That would be preferable to such solitude.

As he gulped the chah, he looked up and met the eyes of a young man sitting at the bar. The eyes were gray and clear, and they flinched as they met his, as if from the shock of a blow—as if they had clearly perceived his thought. Singer rose slowly and made his way toward the stranger. Before he reached the bar, a thickset man took the next place and draped his arm drunkenly over the young one's shoulders. There was an exchange of words, increasing in volume, whose meaning Singer did not quite catch. Then the thickset man flew backward off the stool and landed on the floor with a thud that shook the walls. Singer got a clear view of the objecting party for the first time: short white-blond hair, tall and slender body. The man on the floor had good taste, at least, but Singer was surprised; he had observed very quickly from their thoughts and joking taunts to each other that offering pleasure to another man was the worst possible insult among these strange people, worse even than suggesting that their mothers were animals.

Singer had planted himself in the thickset man's empty seat before he thought about what he was doing. He set his empty glass down to be refilled and said to the stranger, "You want a drink?"

The blond youth glared at him, and he realized that she was a woman. He could feel the thick man coming up behind him but kept his back deliberately turned.

"Get your ass offa there," the man said. Singer ignored him.

"You, asshole, I'm talking to you," the man shouted, and grabbed Singer by the shoulder to drag him off the stool.

Several things happened simultaneously. Singer dropped and spun, striking the man's grip aside with one hand and driving the other hand deep under his ribs. As the man went down, Singer stepped back and kicked him in the face, snapping his head back. Something crunched.

The weight of Singer's boot twisted his knee painfully as he followed through on the kick. He was distracted for a moment, and by the time he was square on his feet again, shouting and clenched fists had erupted all along the bar.

All right, if you want a good reason to fight, I'll give you one, he thought. Punching and shoving, he fended off the press of bodies like a mariner hacking wreckage off the bow. The thick man was lying on the floor, being stepped on. The malevolence coming from him, like heat from an iron stove, had ceased with his consciousness. Numbed by good chah, Singer found the boiling stew of blows given and taken exciting rather than disturbing. Backing to avoid tripping on his victim's legs, he bumped shoulders with the tall woman.

He had never felt such pure hatred. It burned through him like another drink of chah, fiery and invigorating. Above the din he could hear her, in a high-pitched battle yell, inviting her enemies to perform many unseemly acts.

"Hai yai!" He applauded her enthusiastically.

Someone hit him hard; he turned in time to avoid taking it in the belly, but the blow bruised his ribs and cost him a breath. The man who hit him tried to get past him to pull his friend out from under the brawlers' feet. He gave up the attempt and concentrated on Singer.

"You chickenshit faggot, I'm gonna kill you," he panted. "You hit him when he wasn't looking. Let's see you do that to me."

Singer loosened up his guard a little, deliberately, but not enough that the man would know it was a come-on. Then he laughed at himself, because it was clear that he was wasting the subtlety. The man attacked him in a mighty leap. Singer met him with a smile and his empty hands. The man flew over the bar, hit the wall still rising, and slid down it in a jangle of broken glass.

The woman was in trouble again. Some stranger had bent her backward against the bar and seized one wrist in a hand the size of a ham hock. Singer was clearing the way to her side when he noticed that she was groping with her free hand for something behind the bar. Just as he reached her, she smashed her attacker in the side of the head with a full bottle.

At the same time, the bartender leaned over the man who had hit the wall and stood up, shouting something. Singer finally read his lips: "He's dead. This one's dead."

The woman pointed back behind the bar; there was one of the red-light signs that meant one could get out. Singer vaulted over the bar; at the last moment he changed his leap so that his feet hit the bartender in the chest instead of smashing his face. The woman followed him through the door.

She took off running as soon as they hit the street; she cut between buildings and dodged around corners—and she was fast. He was not sure why they were running, but he stayed close behind her. At last she struck a path through a field of weeds; it led to a riverbank where she finally slowed down.

"Why you running?" he asked her.

"The golpos, fool," she said. "Why'd you have to kill him?

They're going to be all over my ass now, wanting to know who you are. That was fucking stupid."

Singer was offended.

"He put his hands on me," he explained. "He asked to be dead."

He moved closer to her; she had a purple mark under one eye and her nose was bleeding. He could see her heartbeat shaking her ribs. He put out a hand toward her.

She jumped back, ready to strike him if necessary. Fire blazed in her eyes again.

"Go on, make your move," she snarled. "You wanted to buy me a drink, didn't you? Think I owe you one, right? A little freebie? Well, I didn't ask for help, and I don't owe you a thing."

Singer backed away, spreading his hands out pacifically. "Didn't think you did," he said.

"Oh, sure. You guys are all alike—tiny pork brains running down the same goddam gutters."

"What I think, maybe you're hurt," Singer said. "Your nose is bleeding."

She sucked her lip and tasted blood, then wiped her face messily on the back of her wrist.

Singer took off his shirt, dipped it in the river, and handed it to her. She looked at him suspiciously, but she accepted it and gingerly washed away the blood, keeping an eye on him at all times.

"Thanks," she said grudgingly. "That does feel better. Okay, so why did you come to help out, then?"

Singer did not know how to explain. The woman was like barbed wire; he felt as if his words would only get him snarled up. He turned his shoulder to her.

"Look," he said.

Her eyes became very wide and clear. She moved closer and touched the tangle of old scars on his back, which looked as if the skin had been inlaid with pale wire.

"We had a dog once that looked like this," she said. "Tell me that's not what I think."

Her fingertips were leaf-light. They paused in the act of withdrawing.

"Oh, no," she said.

The touch he felt then was untrained but ruthlessly powerful. She tore the memory out of its grave and dragged it into the light. His breath choked in his throat as he felt again the weight on him, the humiliation of not being able to fight back. Their kisses had driven his lips against his teeth, and his mouth was full of blood. There were five of them, laughing in the dark. The stars were cruelly bright, and no one could hear . . . him? He realized that the memory he had been living was not his.

Her eyes were clear and pale as rain and only a handbreadth from his. Her fingers dug painfully into his shoulders.

"How did you—" he began.

At the same instant, she said, "What did you—" and they both stopped.

She let go of him and sat down against a tree.

"I'm sorry," she said. "I thought you were more of the same. You understand, huh?

"I hope you did kill that sorry son of a bitch. I'm glad you did. But it won't do a bit of good. There's so many more just like him. Bastards set us on fire, and we're gonna go on burning till we burn right out." She lowered her head to her knees. "Jesus. Will you look at me? Twenty-three years old and still getting into fights in bars."

Never will I understand these people, Singer thought. For him the fight had been a few moments of pure happiness. For her, it was shame and a disgrace. Crazy as the city women who thought they were ruined if a man saw their legs.

"Twenty-three is not too old to fight. You're still strong. Come on, we do it again and I won't help. I'll bet all my money on you and win."

Her face was smeared with tears, but she wiped her nose again and laughed instead of crying.

"First things first," she said. "They said someone was coming. You must be the one I was expecting."

She pulled a small wrapped package out of her shirt and held it out to him.

"*Who* said?" he asked her, alarmed.

She gestured impatiently with the package. "The cards. Here—pick one."

They were little squares of stiff, shiny paper with some kind of design on them, all alike. He pulled one out at random and handed it to her. She turned it over.

"The Sun," she said.

The paper showed a picture: two golden-haired children, a boy and a girl, riding one horse; behind them, rays of light. He touched the image with his finger. It was well done; it was bright and clear and very small, like a memory of a time that no longer existed.

"What is it?" he asked.

"What do you see?"

"I see you and me. I see the Wind Horse. A good journey. But this is a picture of beginnings, and my journey goes to an ending."

She pulled herself upright as if she had reached a decision. "Ow. I must be getting old. I'm sore and I'm starving. I'll buy you dinner. I do owe you that much. And you can buy me a drink."

When he ventured a bracing arm across her shoulders, she leaned into it and did not show her teeth at him.

She took him through back streets to a small market where they did not see any police. It disturbed him strangely to see that the townsfolk bought and sold, planted and harvested just like real people. The food he had seen so far had come out of metal containers like everything else. She bought something wrapped in greasy paper from a stall that smelled like spices and frying oil. He bought every size and color of fruit he could find—there were so many—and a brown bottle of some liquid that she told him would be good to drink.

Laden with packages, they went around behind the market to a place where there were a lot of buildings like big, windowless boxes. They did not look like places to live, but then, he had never been able to figure out what these people thought desirable in a living space. Most of the places he had seen were *timmoi*, the kind of shelters one made when one was out hunting or on the way to a war.

Up the peeling side of one such building ran a line of metal rungs. She put her bag in her teeth and climbed the ladder to the rooftop.

"I got a place above the warehouse. There are stairs inside, but I like this better."

They ate on the rooftop. From there Singer could see the airfield not too far off. The late sun soaked into his body. It gleamed on the woman's pale gold hair and her smooth-muscled brown arms. She ate with her fingers and her knife, like a woman of the pallantai.

The squashy packages turned out to be spiced beans rolled in thin bread, enough like resh to make him homesick. The woman broke pieces from the same loaf with him. They drank from the same bottle in a new way she showed him: Take a piece of the sour, aromatic fruit called lime, dip it in salt and bite it; take a drink of chah.

"They claim it's tekiya," she said. "They do grow corn, but there's no maguey here that I've seen, so how can there be a worm in the bottle? But I've been down so long this tastes like up to me."

Singer did not know why there should be a worm in the bottle; the liquor tasted strange enough already. Everything was strong-tasting but good—he took more pleasure in this one meal than in a month of too-sweet or too-salty soldier food packed in lumps like cold mush. His tongue had been happy; it was getting numb as the new kind of chah flowed over it.

"Why were you hating those chucks in the bar? I heard you. Kind of a waste of charge. Like using a flash gun to kill roaches. Not that I haven't been tempted to—nothing else seems to work."

"I saw you look at me," he said.

"Yeah, I'd been expecting someone like you. Then suddenly there was a voice. 'Go die!' I've had impressions before, but nothing like that." She laughed.

"What made you look for me?"

"I told you, the cards. Did you see those kids in the market?"

Singer shook his head. He had seen them, but he had not paid them any attention.

"They feel about you and me the way you feel about the chucks. We can buy all the food in the place with our pay. They don't all have such an easy time getting enough to eat. PCOM comes around and fair-shares everything they grow, at the controlled price. Then they have to sell the rest of it in the dirty market to break even. I see things like that happening and I start to get a bad feeling. You can see changes coming. And I'm getting bored. Itchy. I don't want to spend the rest of my life driving humpers around the sky. So I asked myself what to do, and the cards showed someone coming. So I've been waiting for you.

"Come on inside, and I'll show you what I mean."

She opened a square door in the roof and dropped through. Singer looked around with interest. It was the first sleeping place he had been in that looked as if someone really lived there. Janet had nothing of her own in her room except the books he could not read and a dead plant on the windowsill. This woman had covered the walls with pictures: horses, suns, flowers, and what the People called "eyecatchers," the circle designs that pulled one's gaze into their heart. The most compelling of those had no definite pattern. It was a simple sphere of white and brown and cloudy blue, hanging in absolute black.

"Looks beautiful from here, doesn't it?" she said. "Probably this place looks just as good from a couple of million miles out. The planet's always greener on the other side of the sky."

And he understood, with fear and great wonder, that that was how solid earth looked from far away—like an island that diminished with distance. One could sail around it and leave it behind. He could not help thinking of one whose name could no longer be spoken, one who had dreamed with so much longing of journeying on the ships that traveled only mortal oceans of water. If he had known that one could sail among the stars—

They had the power for the great voyaging, on that sea where the stars are harbor lights, he thought. And they used it only to come here and take your life.

He tore himself away with difficulty, turning to the woman who was asking him to sit on proper cushions by a low table.

She took out the little pack of cards again.

"Do you know what these are?" she asked.

He shook his head.

"Some people call it fortune-telling. I don't look at it that way. I don't think your fate is written anywhere, except maybe in your own heart. There's always a choice you can make. But I think the cards are a way of showing yourself what's inside. They help you see the choices clearly."

Singer nodded with quickened interest. That could be why they had no skill with the bones. To them, the bones were chance only, just a game. This was the first hint he had had that they had other ways of seeing.

"They make a pattern, and I'll tell you what I see."

Her spine straightened, her breathing slowed, and he matched his own to hers. When his muscles were beginning to relax into peace, she shuffled the cards and dealt them out in a great wheel, turning them over one by one.

He had come so close to her that he could sense her disturbance.

"Oh, oh—this is where you're coming from. Nine of swords: fear, despair, pain, and cruelty. Well, that's pretty typical for a humper. You're afraid of your dreams. There's something inside you can't bear to look at. It would stab you like a sword.

"This one we call the Moon. You have a journey into darkness to make."

The image showed a light on the waters, a small boat rocking on the waves.

"She came to me with her light, when I was very small," Singer murmured. "I sang for her, and she sent me help."

The woman shot him a curious look. "Now I've seen everything," she said. "A Mike who has met the goddess!

"Here's your past—oh, oh. We're back to hard times. The Tower. I see outrage. I see destroying fire.

"But this one is the strangest thing of all. The Fool—he's stepping out into the abyss, but he's smiling. He's free."

Singer picked up the card called the Tower. The Rock was burning. How could the stranger know?

"Fire from the sky," he said. The bodies were falling. He picked up the card next to it, the one that closed the circle: the future beside the past. That figure was unarmed and barefoot, like a young one in his first year on the wisdom road. He stepped into emptiness confidently, as if he knew the Wind Horse would come to carry him. He was smiling. The hair lifted on Singer's neck as he studied the picture. It reminded him of something he did not want to remember. Maybe it meant that death would set him free, on the Road to the North. But that thought left a heaviness in his mind, as if he were missing the point.

"Does that help any?" she asked.

"Don't know," he said slowly. "The pictures tell the truth about what happened before. But the future—I don't know. Where did you learn this art?"

"Back home," she said. "Dylan's girl, Miriam, taught me. When she moved on, she left me the cards. For a long time after she was gone, I couldn't get anything but sadness out of them. I was just a kid then."

"What was that bad thing that happened?" Singer asked. He half hoped the men were still around so that he could kill them for her.

She looked at him strangely. "So I wasn't hallucinating," she said. "That was a long time ago. It's a long story."

He stretched his legs out in a way that indicated that he was not going anywhere.

"After my dad died—well, he wasn't really my father. At least, I don't think so. He never said. I guess maybe he didn't know. Ay. Maybe I should go back to the beginning.

"I'm the last of a dying breed—a commune kid. There were maybe a dozen of them, living in domes somebody else built and abandoned, in Eldorado, in the inland desert. They had this philosophy that the kids belonged to everyone, and they all taught us and spanked us at one time or another. Of course, the moms knew which ones were theirs. But my real mom went back to Occidente not too long after I was born and met a guy and they got married, and she didn't really need this extra kid from the past tagging along. So she left me with the group.

"They scraped by somehow, but after a while the well dried up and the sandal shop went broke. Some of the local kids got drunk one night and trashed our place. They tore up the garden with their sand motos and set fire to the barn, and all the goats got loose. That was the last straw. First one and then another packed up and split, and in the end there was only Dylan and me left. He was a pretty good truck mechanic, so he was never really out of a job. We moved into town and lived in a room back of the laundromat, and we got along okay till some drunk ran him off the road and his pickup smashed into a tree.

"So there I was, sixteen years old and couldn't do a damn thing. By then I knew as much about engines as he did. I'd been helping him for years. But you think they're going to hire some underage pussy to fix their trucks?

"I tried waitressing. The first guy who tried to feel me up, I shoved his chili up his nose. That didn't go over too well. I cleaned the laundromat for eating money, and that was about it.

"The young guys in town thought what you'd expect them to think. They're some pretty hard-core Old Faith folks, and they never did like our kind. They figure a woman without a man's either a dyke or a whore, maybe both. Here's this chica, she has no family and no boyfriend and no job, she's got to be turning some tricks. They kept asking, and I kept saying no. It really got them mad. So they took me for a ride one Saturday night."

She fell silent, chewing her lip.

"I guess you know the rest. They dropped a twenty on me afterward. I guess they thought it was big money, but you break it five ways and it's less than I would have made waitressing. The law laughed in my face, but then his brother's son was one of them, and he and Dylan never got along.

"I couldn't stay there after that. I hitchhiked down to Cibola, but that didn't seem far enough away. There's a Consorso base near there, and I watched the jets go over, so sharp and clean, and thought, Fuck this. So I went down and signed up. I had trouble getting him to take me, too. But I could read and write, and he was hurting real bad for his quota—nothing but camp rats and goofers—so he did in the end.

"I started out in truck maintenance. I'm a transport pilot now, and if you don't think that took some doing, think again. But I fly, goddamnit, and they don't hassle you while you're flying."

She grasped the lukewarm bottle of chah without having to look for it and took a long swallow.

Singer touched the Fool card and felt her power again. She sees truly. This will happen, but I don't know what it is.

"What did they say to you?" he asked her.

"Ace of swords, ace of wands. Wind and fire. The Judgment. Ten of swords—the end of life as I know it. And they said someone was coming who was a magician and a fool." She gathered the cards up and put them away.

"Where is he now, this someone?"

"I told you, what happens is in your heart, not in the cards," she said, not looking at him.

"Will you tell me your name?" he asked.

"It's a funny one. The group sort of made up the names, and the one they agreed on for me was Mellyn. I got a bellyful of people calling me Melons, so I go by Lyn now."

"It's a good name," he said wistfully. "Where I come from, it means 'green.' Like in the spring when the grass comes up new. On the old ways it shows up first, where the winter-dry leaves are trampled down."

"You *are* a magician," she said. "That's the other name—Greenway. We had a group meeting and decided we should all change our names to the same thing. It's what we picked. Kind of a compromise, really—some of the other suggestions were Peacefolk and Melody. It would have been worse. Dylan suggested Desertrat, or maybe Luposcat. He said that one was very mystical. They told him to go piss up a rope. He could be a rampant pain in the ass, especially when he was stoned.

"What's your name, magician?"

"You guess."

"Well, I know it isn't any bullshit thing like Snake or Smoke or Rocky or Heat or Trashman." She shook her head. "Must be the cards from before. All I see when I look at you is swords. Sharp edges. Enough sharp edges to keep out me and anyone else."

The hair rose on the back of Singer's neck. The stranger was reading his true name without even touching him.

"I'm not hallucinating, am I? I mean, I know I'm drunk, but you don't trip on tekiya, not even New Hell tekiya," she said. "You know, they used to pass the peace pipe around and talk about group consciousness, and I was just a dumbass kid. I thought it was all for real, till I found out they couldn't hear me at all. Then I thought my mom must have had one hit too many and I must have been born brain-damaged, but this is the real thing, this is magic."

"I'm no magician," Singer said. "I am a fool for sure, but you can call me Singer."

His mind told him that he had better run from the woman; she was dangerous, a healer who broke noses and laid his heart open with one stroke, a warrior who carried a sword of power and did not know what to do with it.

Moving slowly, slowly, as if he were reaching to halter a wild young colt, he stretched out his hand and touched a finger to her lips. He felt her breath on his hand, warm and steady as a wind from the south that kisses the snow off the new-springing grass.

"There's one magic, simple magic, I can do," he whispered. "Changes dark sorrow into silver rain, teaches bones to sing, and takes you where you can run forever with the wind for company. Oldest magic in the world. If you don't like it, you can fly away."

But she was still there when the sky began to pale. She smiled as soon as her eyes were open, then reached up and ran one finger down the scar on his face.

He moved her hand away.

"What's the matter? I don't think it's ugly. You've got marks all over you like God's graffiti. What's special about this one?"

He put his hand over his mouth in the old gesture, fingers hiding the scar. "It's got death in it, this one. You leave it alone."

Undaunted, she traced his ears instead. "Where did you get that, anyway?"

"The priest makes it when I'm small, to show it's no good being too beautiful. This face is for the Eater like all the rest."

She sat up in outrage. "What! What kind of priest would do that?"

"The kind we had."

"Where was that? What is this 'where I come from' riff? Look at this—you have scars on your earlobes. You used to wear earrings? Where do you come from that guys wear earrings?"

He felt her breath on his face as she leaned closer.

She gasped, and he caught her wrists and held her away from him as if she had tried to hurt him.

"There are all these faces, but it's like a wall of glass, I can't get through. No, not glass; it's fire—"

"No," he said. There was a fear in his voice that she would not have believed he had in him.

"Let go," she panted. But his grip was crushing, and he did not seem to hear her. She twisted to one side and kicked him in the stomach as hard as she could. More surprised than anything else, he let go.

"Don't you *ever—*" she snarled.

At the same moment he said, *"Never—"*

They paused, both ready to spring.

"Ayei," Singer said. "Tell me to go. This is trouble."

She grinned at him. "Seems to me I've been looking for trouble all my life," she said. "And the bigger it is, the better I like it. You're just about the right size. Speaking of which—"

She signed for silence, and Singer also heard a moto pulling up outside. He pulled his clothes on hastily.

She handed him a couple of fruits and what was left of the bread.

"Go up to the roof, but watch out they don't spot you. They'll probably leave someone in the street to look for you. You can get over onto the roof of the next building. Go down inside; there are plenty of hiding places in there. If this is the golpos, they won't bother to search there yet. I'll come get you after a while."

She swept the leavings of their meal into the trash and shoved the second glass back on the shelf with the clean ones. Singer picked up his knives and his boots and went up the ladder. He did not continue to follow her instructions. He was not about to hide in the dark. He wanted to see what the golpos did; he knew it would be best not to encounter them, but if they bothered the woman too much, he planned to put them in a box.

Their voices were indistinct from his place on the roof, but he could hear her.

"Do you have a warrant? Hell, no, you can't come in. Either arrest me or go away. Sure, I recognize him, but I don't know who he is. I never saw him before. Yeah, well, that's interesting, but it's not my problem, you know? Right. Fine. I won't be holding my breath."

Singer waited till they drove away, then went back down the ladder.

"You didn't do what I told you, did you?" she said. "Listen, now: You want to be very cool for a while. They told me that you were called Singer and that you're a dangerous man. They want to talk to you about the death of General Harlan. When they reported the description of you from the bar, it apparently showed up on some kind of Net hit list. They portray you as a psychopath running amok. They want your ass.

"You don't have to look at me funny. I don't care. Fuck Harlan, he was a grievous old fart and I'm glad he's out of his misery. But the point is this: What are you going to do now?"

Singer thought about it. The more help he received from these people, the more complicated his life became. That walled-city building sat heavily on his mind. What he wanted to do was walk into it and use his weapons to put an end to waiting and choosing. But he could hear a dry old woman's voice abusing him gently when he imagined that end. What kind of warrior fires his last arrows at sheep herders outside the walls when the princes sit safe within? Perhaps, if he could see Zhanne one more time, she could find out for him what he needed to do.

Lyn waited till she saw his conclusion settle in his eyes.

"You going back to Guijarro?" she asked.

"If I can find a way. There's a man waiting for me there." He felt her confirm the image in his mind. She shivered.

Cold Eyes. Good name.

"I haven't seen him before," she said aloud. "If I do, I'll be careful. What will you do then?"

"Think I could get a mission. They won't look for me in the Dust. That will buy time."

"Okay. That's not too hard. I'll find you a ride back to Guijarro. I think there's a vito going up there today. How will I get in touch with you when you get back?"

He looked away. "Maybe I'm not coming back. The road gets short. Don't you be holding your breath."

Her eyes blazed. "Don't you say things you know damn well aren't true. You are coming back. And I'll hold my breath as long as I damn well feel like it. Now tell me how to get in touch with you. Can I write?"

"Can't read so well," Singer explained with some embarrassment. "You go to Jefferson and find a doctor named Janet Logan." He said her name their way, *Djah-net*, so there would not be any mistake.

"Oh, ho. Your other woman?"

Singer felt hopelessly tangled up again. He could tell she was annoyed with him, but the Giristiyah idea that one could *have* a woman, but only one, baffled him completely.

"Go see her," was all he could say. "Her heart has ears. She will hear you. And she will know where I am."

23

Singer rode in to Guijarro with the vito, helped load a truck with supplies for the company where Saldivar's tent was, and rode up there without greeting anyone but the driver.

He waited in the tent until Saldivar came back.

Saldivar walked in quietly, as usual. He did not startle or smile when he saw Singer, but warm pleasure shone through his somber face and eased the tension in his shoulders.

"So, what are you doing here?" he said. "I thought you were Kruger's boy now."

"That's all finished. Told you I was coming back."

"Well, I heard you got on the bird with him. I thought you'd gone."

Singer reached out and grabbed Saldivar by the back of the neck, like one puppy biting another in play. Palha would not let anybody else do that to him. Singer shook him gently.

"Saying I'm stupid?" he growled. "They took the con-el away to die. No way I go with him there. He put me back on the team. My payoff."

Pleasure and unhappiness warred on Saldivar's face. "That's right. Mooney's gone. We've got room for you now. But—"

Singer bowed his head. He knew what was running through Palha's mind.

"I killed him, Palha. Ayei, didn't mean for it to happen that way. Saw him get in, wanted to run pull him out. But it was too late. I paid him his blood, though. That asshole major who should've smoked it instead of him. I got him for Mooney."

"Well that doesn't exactly make up for it," Saldivar said wearily. "I knew it was you. Bates figured it out, too, I think.

He ain't stupid. He recognized your little trademarks, but he didn't say nothin'.

"Why did you do it? What's it for? Don't we have enough people on our ass already? You brought a fucking swarm down on us. They've been all over here, asking questions, poking into things, trying to hang us on something.

"And what am I supposed to think about you? Are you going to blow me away sometime just because I happen to step into your sights?"

Singer's eyes narrowed as if he had been slapped. "No! Your life is the same to me as my own."

As soon as he spoke, he knew it was a rash promise, but it was too late to take it back.

"For what that's worth," Saldivar said. "It seems you don't give jack shit for your life these days. Don't you be treating mine the same way.

"What's in it for you? Are you doing this for fun, or what?" His voice was hard, but his eyes were begging for an explanation.

Singer knew he had to give him a reason, and a true one.

"You remember when you and the con-el went up by North Fork and he got the poison sickness?"

"Sure, I remember," Saldivar retorted. "But that was before you came along."

"I was there," Singer said.

The baffled anger faded from Saldivar's face to be replaced by a puzzled frown. "You couldn't have been. I never saw you."

"The fire-from-the-sky. I was there. On the ground."

He saw that Saldivar believed him.

"But—what were you doing there? How did you end up back in Jefferson?"

"That's what they asked me, and I wouldn't tell them. That's my business—find out who did that and make them eat the smoke. The pilot in Jefferson was the first. Then Harlan.

"You know the man with the questions? The one with the cold eyes?"

"Gero's his name. He's a shark."

"He knows me. If he finds me here, I'm dead. I have to go with the team. You have to trust me a little bit more."

"Okay," Saldivar said finally. "I trust you, Singer. I don't know why, when you're obviously insane, but I do. But we can't be together on this unless you trust me a little bit, too.

"What did Harlan have to do with this?"

"He lied to Makho. Makho was right, Harlan wanted him dead, and all of you. Makho wants to find out why, but he can't. I figure two chances to kill me is all Harlan gets, why or no why. Mooney was a mistake."

Saldivar paused. Sometimes he felt as if he knew Singer like the palm of his hand. Other times, like this one, he felt that he did not know the man at all. A sudden thought occurred to him.

"Are you some kind of an agent? You working for somebody? Can you tell me that?"

Singer's face was hard. "Truth: This war is nothing to me. All I want is my payback before I die. Will you talk to Bates for me?"

"Sure. I'll talk to Bates for you."

He had not felt real fear in a long time, but it touched him then, when Singer talked about dying. He struggled with the feeling. Other people had a rare, precarious place allotted to them on the sharp edge of his existence. If he let them take over his whole self, he was doomed. But somehow it had happened to him. He could do without weapons, food, or shelter; he could do without hope and he could do without a future, but he could not do without Singer. He knew that such feelings were fatal, but there was a temporary relief in giving up the struggle, as if he had stopped fighting the hook and let the current carry him downstream.

Singer waited, willing his mind to stay blank, while Saldivar went to find Bates. Palha came back with a load of gear for his friend.

"It's all smooth," he reported. "Bates says we leave as soon as it gets light. He says no fucking civilian is going to fuck with his team. You're lucky, too. This is a good mission. We finally got permission to go up there where you and I were and prove to them there's really traffic coming down that trail."

The sun sprang out to greet them as their vito rose over the horizon. There were two replacements whom Singer had not met. The big man with hairy arms was called Bear. The skinny, nervous kid who carried the radio was called Golos, after the candy he sucked on constantly. Singer was reminded so much of Nicky that he did not want to talk to the boy. Both of them looked at him curiously when they thought he could not see them, and he guessed that his reputation had been inflated while he had been gone.

Bates was wearing a pod gun. He was sweating already under

the weight of the backpack. The other teams laughed at him. "Going bear hunting? Trying to sweat off some weight? Need that to defend yourself against sand rats?" He refused to comment. When he clicked on his goggles and fixed the aiming lens on them, they finally stopped laughing.

They were being dropped with three other teams to investigate branches of the trail that Singer and Saldivar had originally found. Bates's group would be farthest north; from the air they could see the rocky mesa where Long Shot had gone down. Once on the ground, their vision was cut off by the dry hillsides that rolled away toward the desert. The ubiquitous thornbushes had not taken hold there; at first it was pleasant to move quickly and easily through the grass in the early morning light. The disadvantage was that they were completely exposed. They felt more comfortable when they took a turn under the shoulder of the hill and descended again into an overgrown gully.

Traces of the trail ran along the sandy bed of an intermittent river, which was dried to a trickle, and they followed its line loosely, a couple of hundred feet up the hillsides. They were looking for a good place to set up and watch for a few days, to find out if traffic was still running on that route.

Singer gradually relaxed; he was free and safe there, after a long time of watching and guarding himself within walls. His senses opened to the ever-changing messages of wind and sun and the small voices of animals. He checked automatically on the rest of the team. They were arrayed in their places like beads strung on a cord he held in his hand. He probed curiously at the new ones. The Bear had strength, but he was used to the strength of numbers around him. He would have to be tested before he found the confidence in himself that would make him reliable. The little one's tongue worried at his teeth, wishing for sweetness to alleviate his anxiety. Singer nearly laughed as he remembered another young one he had known who had been just the same—they had called him Little Raider because of his fondness for stealing honeycomb.

Bates was as solid and inscrutable as always, dark and bitter as barbed iron scoured clean of every speck of rust. Not a lovable man but one who could be trusted to do the job he had been shaped for. And there was Palha, dark and solid, too, but with a live warmth banked deep inside. Flint and steel, Singer thought affectionately. He could see, by the way Saldivar moved, that his friend was off balance somehow, and reminded himself to watch out for him. They rested comfortably within his awareness.

Suddenly he realized what he was doing. He stopped in his tracks so abruptly that Golos, who was nearest to him, grabbed his head and dived for cover.

"Hey! What's with you?" the boy protested, scrambling to his feet again when he saw that nothing was happening.

Saldivar heard and turned around in sudden concern. "Are you all right?"

"Break it up, girls, it ain't milk and cookie time yet," Bates growled.

Then he saw that Singer had turned white, his hand clenched against his belly as if he were in pain.

"Are you sick?" he demanded. "Have you been skipping your pills?"

Singer stared at him as if he were speaking a foreign language, then shook his head.

"Don't play games with me." Bates glowered. "If you're sick, you better say so now. I'm not gonna have you go limp on me when I need you. I'll have you extracted right this red-hot motherfucking minute if I don't think you're fit to be on the trail."

By the time he had finished his tirade, Singer had relaxed and recovered his color somewhat. He put his hand over his mouth, rubbing compulsively at the long scar.

"I'm all right," he insisted.

Bates shrugged and turned back to the trail.

Singer slogged along, head down. The joy of the morning had vanished in the confusion of his heart. His feeling-for-the-People had come back, but who were these brothers of his that he had been so glad to come back to, so eager to feel beside him? Animals. Murderers. Thing lovers spawned from metal holes. Not even human. It was his job to kill them all, and instead he was becoming one of them.

His thoughts continued to gnaw at him as they moved upstream. The banks of the stream narrowed and rose more steeply, until they were climbing and scrambling rather than walking. It would have been easier to descend to the riverbed, but that would have meant being on the trail they were supposed to be watching. As the hills rose higher, the sandy soil crumbled away from the stone underneath. They found themselves skirting a vertical face of pitted red rock. Bates considered roping up but decided against it; the rock had enough cracks and crevices to support them. They spent a few hairy moments watching Bear round the bulge in the face; the big man's bulk threatened to pull him off the wall, but they all made it.

On the other side of the curve, they encountered a narrow waterfall that plunged across their path and down into the river below. The rocks around the fall were greasy with the spray.

"Shit," Bates said. It looked as if they would have to scramble down to the bottom, ford the main channel, which was narrow but deep as it forced a way through the rocks, and climb laboriously back up on the other side.

"Too much work," Singer said. He shed the hated boots and after a moment's thought, his trousers and shirt, too. Then he free-climbed straight up about twenty feet to a place where the weight of the water curled outward from an overhang; he edged under the spume and descended on the other side. He secured the line Bates threw him, and the others pulled themselves across.

He's like an animal, Bates thought as he watched Singer's long brown arms and legs clasp the wet rock. He's like something from another world. He wondered if it was true that Singer had dusted the general. Saldivar obviously thought so.

When they reassembled and moved on, Bates came up close to Singer. "I hear you've been hunting big game again," he said quietly.

"Shooting rats," Singer replied.

"Next time, you might want to get some expert advice," Bates suggested. "That way, you don't hit what you're not aiming at. Understand?"

Singer nodded, turned away. Bates dropped back, slightly more satisfied. Singer might be a wild man, but it was clear that he felt bad about Mooney. That was good. Dusting an officer was one thing, but getting a teammate killed was close to unforgivable. He was glad it had been an accident, and he was glad that Singer was still hurting.

Beyond the waterfall, the rough red rock had been eaten away into hollows and ledges sometime when the falls had been much wider and more powerful. Looking around, Bates decided that it was as good a place as they would find for observation. All traffic on the trail would be forced to pass directly below them, yet they were shielded from sight. They would have plenty of water. The noise of the falls would cover any sounds they made. True, retreat would be difficult if they were spotted, and the masking sound of the water could work to their disadvantage as well, but he was confident that they could keep one jump ahead of anyone coming down the trail. After all, the enemy had no reason to think he was being observed.

Bates told them to set up in a bowl-shaped depression scoured out by swirling water long before. The bowl was shallow, but it would place them at an angle that made them close to invisible from below. He had Golos do a very brief commo check. Remembering the still-unexplained strafing in the desert after Long Shot, he had decided to keep radio contact to a minimum.

The afternoon dragged on, and everything seemed silent. The rock beneath them soon glowed with the heat of the sun. They doused their heads and necks and drank freely—at least there was plenty of water—but the sun beat them into submission.

"I fell like a hot rock in a sauna," Bear grumbled, and then had to explain to the rest of them what a sauna was. The whispered conversation turned to sweating in the nude with beautiful young women, or any kind of young women. Singer closed his eyes and pretended to be napping. He was still profoundly disturbed.

Because he was closed within his own confusion, Singer did not hear the sounds until they were already close. Then he jerked suddenly into full awareness.

"Hear something," he said to Bates.

They all stopped talking and listened. Bates shook his head. Then his eyes narrowed in alarm.

"Christ, you're right," he said. "Golos, get Guijarro and find out what the hell is going on."

"Not our vitos," Golos reported a few moments later. "They're alerting the other teams. They're putting a pickup on standby, but they want confirmed identification."

Bates swore bitterly. "Assholes. We'll be breakfast bits by the time they get up here." He had the farseeing black tubes to his eyes and was scanning even as he spoke. "There they are! Coming from the northwest, looks like four—no, three—light assault gunships."

"They copy. They'll send pickups and cover, but it can't be sooner than twenty minutes," Golos said. "They said avoid contact if possible and be accessible for extraction. Uh—now what?" he finished uncertainly.

"I'm not going to be the only one surprised this time." Bates grinned. "Thanks for the word, Singer."

He armed the gun and waited for the vitos.

"Hold your fire till we're sure they've seen us. This still could be a coincidence."

With a clattering snarl, the three vitos swooped down into the valley in formation. The lead ship swung toward the cliff; an explosion slammed their ears and rocked their hiding place as a rocket exploded against the rock wall just above them. Fist-sized fragments rained down on them, and flying splinters ripped exposed skin, drawing muffled cries of pain from Singer and Saldivar, who were on the far edge of the huddle.

"I can't fucking believe it! They know where we are," Saldivar shouted.

There was no doubt that the gunships had their group's position; they could not have spotted them by eye before opening fire.

"They'll sure know when I'm through with them," Bates grunted.

Another blast shook the hillside, followed by a flare of scorching heat as laser fire swept the crevices just below them.

Bates fired antilaser smoke and hit the tail of the last vito with explosive rounds as it disappeared into the smoke. They could hear the vitos sweeping on down the valley and turning for another pass. Then the fluttering drone was drowned out by the sound of rotors trying to churn their way through solid rock as the damaged vito plowed into the side of the cliff. They peered into the smoke until the gray nose of the next vito flashed into view. Bates nailed it dead on. But Singer felt the next one coming. He did not have time even to think of warning the others. He launched himself over the edge. A good part of the cliff came down with and around him as the rocket buried itself in solid stone and exploded just beneath their hiding place.

He bounced and slid down fifty feet of rock and rolled the rest of the way to the river, coming to rest at the brink, half in and half out of the water. He did not see the last remaining vito crunch to a landing on the flat top of the bluff. He did not see the men in gray uniforms jump out and load three of the unresisting bodies into their craft. He lay still; one arm drifted in the pull of the current, and tendrils of red wavered out into the brown water. The newcomers glanced down over the edge, but he was not visible from the top.

He woke up choking; the waves were slapping him in the face and splashing in his open mouth. He tried to pull himself up the bank and found that his hand slipped uselessly from the rocks. His other arm seemed completely numb. It took several tries before he could force his body to obey him and drag itself out of the water. He got to his feet, took a few steps, and fell again. Then he sat quietly as the pain settled in. He hurt everywhere. Blood oozed from scrapes and bruises. He thought that he might have cracked his ribs; he felt a stabbing pain when he took too deep a breath. He had bruised the shoulder that had been damaged before, and he had to grasp it with his other hand, as if it were a foreign object, to manipulate some feeling back into it. He knew that nothing was seriously wrong; he would be able to do whatever he had to do.

Looking upward, he could see nothing. There was no sound. He did not want to know what he would find there, but he had to go look. Shame gnawed at him as he climbed laboriously over the steep slope that had thrown him down so easily. He had failed them all. He had bailed out. It happened so fast, he thought dully. The flying machines, the fire weapons—I have no skill for these things. But he could not accept that. Bates had fought back like a real warrior. But he, Singer, Khalle of the Riders, had just flopped over the edge like a baby bird falling out of its nest. All because you weren't thinking straight, because you weren't paying attention. He had not felt so ashamed in years.

When he reached the top, he could not believe what he saw. They were gone. He had been expecting to find their bodies, warding himself against the knowledge that they must be dead. But three of them were not there at all. Only little Golos lay sprawled where he had fallen, small insects already gathering for the rich feast of his blood. The others had vanished.

He lowered himself painfully onto a stone and tried to think. They would not have walked away without him. Anyway, he doubted any of them could have moved on foot after that firebolt. What if their people had come for them and somehow he had been overlooked? No; they would have picked up Golos. They took home their dead when they could. The only possibility left was that their enemies had taken them away in the flying machines. He still did not know if they were dead or alive, although there was some hope that they were still living, since Golos, who was obviously dead, had been left. But in either case they were gone, without a trace, without a single track he could follow them by. He wondered where their own people were. Had they come already and gone away, seeing nothing but two bodies? Were they on the way? He realized that it did not matter. The last thing he wanted was to go back to Guijarro. It would be death for him to set foot there again, and without Makho and Palha, there was no reason to go.

There was no reason to go anywhere—except back to the fortress building to take his revenge in the best way he could. He had no illusions that he could make a really fitting deathgift of it, if he could even get there alive, traveling injured and alone. He had never succeeded in asking Dona's question for him—the one gift his brother had asked for.

But there was still one other thing to be done first.

I made that promise to Palha; I told him I would treat his life like my own.

Voices out of memory blamed him for putting a stranger ahead of his own kind, for running off on that trail when his own dead were waiting. But he pleaded with them.

There's time to keep my promise to you, brothers. The dead stay dead. But the living don't always stay living. Wrong it was to make friends with this outlander, and I will suffer for it, but I won't turn my back on him now. I have to rid myself of this shame. One more journey I have to make. Then, when I have kept my word to him, I will return to you.

He laid Golos straight and gave him back his weapon. He would have liked to protect him from animals and birds, but he did not have the strength. He took spare food and an extra canteen from the abandoned packs and taped up his bruised ribs as well as he could. He found a roll of candy in his search for food and left it in Golos's pocket. He scraped up the ritual handful of dust the People used when there was no time to take care of the bodies, the dust to tell the confused soul that it was all right to go on and leave. Words went through his mind: Have peace, as in your own land, for earth is one, and the Lady gathers up what she has given . . . But there were so many he had left lying with no one to speak for them; he could not say the words over this one.

"Peace," he wished him, and scattered the dust.

When he reached more level ground, he had to stop and painfully catch his breath. If Kruger's map really fit the ridges, he would find out what those circles meant; but it would be a long way.

"I'm tired," he said out loud. The pale sky and the dry earth stretched on indefinitely in all directions, and nobody answered him, so he started walking again.

24

Darkness invaded Saldivar through all his senses and devoured him. Pain came with the darkness. His inner eye, starving for images, saw it as a sluggish river, not water-bright but with the sullen sheen of slag, always tarnishing back toward darkness. Its slow current dragged him along.

He had never seen a hospital or a doctor. The officer who treated his wound told him in heavily accented Delteix that he was lucky the bone was not broken. They probed the wound roughly and dressed it, and when the leg swelled to twice its size with infection, they lanced it and washed it with antiseptic that felt like acid. It gradually healed, and the swelling went down, leaving him with sunken scars where muscle had been.

They left him always in the dark. When morning came, enough light filtered into his stifling cell for him to see the four walls, the plank bed, the bucket, and the door. But the light was always dim, and the air was bad. He guessed that he was far from the outer walls.

When they dragged him from his cell and questioned him, the light tore at his sore eyes till it seemed like only another, more brilliant form of blindness. They wore gray uniforms, but their outlines wavered, seen through painful brightness.

"You are being detained because you were found spying in territory belonging to the People's Defense Forces. We demand that you explain your presence and your intentions there."

"Not your territory. That's the Open Zone; we have as much right there as you."

The interrogator paused, then switched tracks. "We will require, for our records, the names and specialization of yourself and your friends.''

''Why don't you ask them? Where are they?''

''Your friend Taipala has cooperated with us in our investigation and has been moved to a more convenient facility where he can be made comfortable.''

''That's a lie; he wouldn't do that,'' Saldivar said automatically.

The interrogator paused again and came closer. Saldivar expected him to strike, but he did not. ''We must maintain a tone of civility in our talks,'' he said. ''We must have your cooperation. Let's talk about your friend Taipala. What were his special skills?''

''I don't know. He was new. I never got to know him. I don't know anything about him.''

''What about this man named Singer? You have known him a long time.''

''Not really. I hadn't seen him in months.''

''Yes, because he was given special duty by your commanding officer. Isn't that true?''

''I really don't know,'' Saldivar muttered. He tried to sound dumb and apathetic, but he was shocked. Somebody must have talked to them. How else could they have known a thing like that?

''You never heard what kind of special duties he had?''

''It's none of my business. I just do my job.''

''You do your job. And what sort of job did Singer do? What was his ordinary assignment with the team?''

''I don't know,'' Saldivar repeated. ''I'm not team leader. I don't make the assignments.''

''So. Who is the team leader?''

Saldivar stopped, realizing too late that he was trapped. If he told them it was Bates, then what would happen to Bates? He remembered Bates, lying on the floor of the same vito he was in, his cheek in a puddle of blood—but still alive.

''Surely you know who is your team leader.''

Saldivar shook his head reluctantly. ''I'm sorry, I'm afraid I couldn't say.''

Saldivar heard the silent guards behind him shift their feet on the concrete floor and flinched, but the interrogator stopped them with a gesture.

''May I call you Pablo?'' he asked solicitously. ''Or would you prefer Paul?''

"Call me what you want," Saldivar muttered. "You know what my name is."

"I want you to feel comfortable with me. I know you've been mistreated because you're Espanyo, and from the Tregua. I wouldn't want to awaken old antagonisms. Tell me, Pablo, as a Treguan, how can you fight for those who wouldn't even spare you land to live on? The Consorso could have resettled all of you. Instead they used your predicament merely to keep hostilities alive. Haven't you spent long enough behind the wire for their benefit? The Tregua would be free, undisputed territory if the Fokish imperialists from Heimat hadn't chosen to wantonly join in Consorso aggression. The Fokish have been a barbaric race since the preflight era. Your commander is an outstanding example—the butcher of Haven! It's not disloyalty to learn where your true interest lies. Many of your people are now citizens of the New Union, helping to build a new and better world. If you show a cooperative spirit, I can send you one of my own Treguan officers who can explain to you the history that has been kept from you. Why bring the old mistakes of Delta to a new world? Wouldn't it be better to cooperate with the future?"

"I don't know anything about politics," Saldivar said, looking at the floor. "I just don't know the answers to any of your questions."

The interrogator nodded. "Then we'll talk again later. Perhaps you'll change your mind."

He turned and left the room.

Saldivar was wondering at his luck when the two guards in the corners of the room came forward and kicked his chair out from under him.

After many beatings he had learned very little. They asked him constantly about the real purpose of the mission and about Singer. He told them the truth about the mission, but they did not believe him. They seemed so sure that Singer was part of some kind of conspiracy that he almost believed them. He could not understand what they wanted well enough to con them; he could only hug himself together under their attack like a block of ice under an inescapable sun. Every day he lost a little bit more.

When his leg was first healing, he hitched himself slowly around the four walls of his cell for exercise. After they put him in leg irons, he could not do that anymore. He tried to keep a calendar of scratches on the wall. At first the dim light told him when the days came and went. When the beatings came more often, he was no longer sure when he missed a light period.

He groped for thoughts to take refuge in, but his memories were tattered and thin. They frayed when he grasped at them and left him lying in the dark again. More and more often he drifted in and out of weary dreams for hours or days. In his brief moments of full consciousness, he knew that he was very sick.

Only one memory stayed clear: the fight on the ledge. He went over it again and again. He remembered himself and Bates being thrown into the same vito. He had seen two men dragging Bear, and his head bumping against the ground without resistance; it was impossible to tell if he was still alive. Golos had been down, motionless. He could not see Singer anywhere. He tried to remember. But Singer had simply vanished.

His hands clenched the planks on which he lay.

Be safe, he willed Singer fiercely. *Be gone. Stay alive.*

He fell again into an exhausted sleep. A dream came that was sharp and clear. He saw Singer afoot on the plains, not running light and easy through memory but grimly pursuing, driving himself. He was thin and ragged. He stopped, head raised, catching some elusive trace in the wind. His eyes had an inward look, but he was searching, searching the empty air.

He's looking for me, Saldivar thought incredulously. He tried to call to Singer, but it was a dream, so his voice made no sound. Silently he cried, *I'm here, I'm here.* He thought he heard Singer say *Palha?* The effort shattered the dream, and he found himself back in his cell.

He knew it was crazy to believe that the dream was real, but he wanted to so much that he did, anyway.

"Hurry," he whispered. "Please hurry."

He thought of Singer constantly after that; he tried to find his way back into the trancelike concentration in which he had seen him. Into his dreams crept smells of wind and sounds of water and the feel of baked earth underfoot—dreams of freedom. Sometimes he felt himself moving across the hills in a steady rhythm, as if he were being carried along with Singer though he could not see him or speak to him. Yet at the same time, he grew weaker.

One day he lay in too much pain to think of anything. Flung back into his cell, he stayed where he had fallen, without the strength to move from the filthy floor to his bed. The pain was not in his body; it was all around him like the heavy air, crushing him. The slightest movement brought savage retribution; he tried not to move, even to breathe.

Suddenly there was another presence with him. He realized that it was not a physical presence when he struggled to see—and could not stir even his eyelids. He was dreaming again.

Be still, brother, be still, a voice said close to his ear. *I dare not lose you now.*

It was Singer's voice, though he knew in a confused way that Singer was not speaking as he usually did, with spare, hesitating words. It reminded him of his grandfather breaking from Delteix into Ispanya—suddenly the voice would come alive.

Show me your hurts, Singer commanded.

Normally he tried not to think about what was happening to his body. Somehow Singer forced him to see and then took the knowledge from him. He had a brief impression of rending rage, quickly silenced lest it destroy the fragile equilibrium that let them speak to each other.

Peace, peace, Singer soothed him. *Not easy, this touching from so far. Do not fight against me. Listen. I think I have found you now. I smell the smells of men, the smoke and oil. I smell the foulness of cityfolk within walls. Soon I will come to your place. Can you show me how it looks?*

At first Saldivar could only show him the dark room. With great effort, he remembered other things about the interior of the prison: the room where he was questioned; a latrine at the end of the corridor; most important, the guard who stood at the end of the hall where his cell was, under a dim light.

Ahh, that will help. But nothing on the outside? Well, I will see the outside for myself. One other thing: They must take off those chains. Do whatever is needed. Tell them I killed a general. Tell them whatever they want to hear. This must be done soon, for I will be there soon.

Saldivar would have tried to catch hold of Singer, but he still could not move.

Stay, he begged.

Till you wake, Singer said a little sadly. *I can't find you then.*

When he became conscious again, Singer was gone.

I am hallucinating, he thought wearily. I'm really losing it. But the fantasy that Singer was out there somewhere looking for him was the only thing that kept him going.

He wrestled with the command to get rid of his chains. Was his subconscious giving him an excuse to do what he would have to do anyway or die? But he persuaded himself that it could not do him any harm to go along with them just for a few days, and if Singer did not come, well, then the whole thing was his brain disintegrating, and he was doomed anyway.

They came again, took him out of the cell, and sat him in the usual chair. The interrogator gave him a bored look. He had grown accustomed to receiving no answers and ordering another beating. But for the first time Saldivar stopped him.

"Please, no more." He did not have to fake the trembling of his mouth and hands. "I remembered something—about Singer and the colonel. He was always talking to the scouts; he'd come back and tell nobody but Kruger what they said. A general came and leaned on Kruger. Somebody smoked the general. The flash was, it was Singer. That's all I can remember."

The interrogator smiled broadly. "That's good, that's very helpful!"

Saldivar slumped in his seat, threatening to faint. It was not far from the truth.

The interrogator signed to the guards, but that time, instead of dumping him on the floor, they picked him up by the elbows and stood him on his feet.

The interrogator spoke to them rapidly, then repeated the order in Delteix for Saldivar's benefit. "Remove the handcuffs and see that he is given a good meal. When he has rested, we will talk again."

"Please, sir, the leg irons, too," Saldivar pleaded faintly. "I want to be taken to the latrine."

The interrogator considered the request and finally nodded. The prisoner obviously could not walk with or without leg irons.

Saldivar had to be supported down the hall, but once there he was able to shut the door on his guards. He used some of his privacy to try to clean his face and hands. It was a hopeless attempt, but the cool water refreshed him and made him feel cleaner.

Back in his cell, they had served him a meal on a tray. After so long in tight cuffs, his fingers were too stiff and swollen to manage the spoon; he had to lift the bowl to his mouth with both hands. To his regret, he could swallow only a few mouthfuls before he started to feel sick. He hid some bread in his tattered shirt, but he had to leave the rest.

They left him to sleep without restraints.

Late in the darkest hour of the night, he came to instant wakefulness at the sound of his door opening. He flinched, automatically raising his hands together as if they were still shackled. There was a faint dragging sound; something heavy and limp was set down. Long, familiar hands ghosted over his face, laid a warning pressure on his lips, and patted his arms and legs, pausing at the knee that was the worst of his sores.

"Singer," he choked. He thought he was dreaming again, but he could move and speak.

"Yes, me." There was a faint hint of amusement in the voice. "Be quiet; we are leaving here."

There was some tugging and pulling; he realized that Singer was putting a shirt on him and tried to cooperate. It was agony hitching the pants over the sores on his legs. The boots were the worst; he stuffed the hat Singer gave him between his teeth to muffle his pain as Singer ruthlessly jammed them onto his feet and tightened the laces.

"You can walk?"

"I don't know."

Singer lifted him to his feet. The knee buckled.

"Try again," Saldivar gasped.

Singer hoisted him again, jamming a shoulder under his arm so that his foot barely dragged on the ground. Half carrying him, Singer stepped out of the cell and locked the door behind them. The corridor was empty, and Saldivar guessed that he was wearing the dead guard's clothes. Singer took him quickly and silently to the end of the corridor, to the right, to the left, and finally to a door that opened on empty space. Saldivar felt the wind on his face and shivered; after his long confinement the air seemed ice-cold.

"Have to walk now," Singer said. Before them was an open yard, dark buildings like barracks to their left, and a row of latrines not more than a hundred yards ahead of them. Once they had crossed that space, they would be out of sight.

Singer steadied him on his feet and stepped casually out into the open. Tears of pain streamed from Saldivar's eyes. He concentrated on moving steadily, counting his steps. Singer's arm was still around him; they limped along together, like friends who had had one shot too many and were holding each other up on the way to the john. At a hundred and twenty paces, he felt Singer's hand tighten on the back of his belt. A man wearing a helmet and arm band came out of the shadows and spoke to them harshly.

Singer stopped and ducked his head submissively. He rubbed

the back of his neck as if in embarrassment. His hand snapped forward; the guard gurgled quietly and collapsed. Singer pulled his knife from the man's throat and stuck it back in its sheath. Then he lifted Saldivar by the belt again and dragged him swiftly across the rest of the open ground.

Behind the latrines, Saldivar sank onto a pile of cinder blocks and sat with his head down, trying not to pass out. The perimeter fence was more a boundary marker than a real barrier. Obviously, whoever had set up the camp had not been expecting a ground attack. Singer had cut the bottom wire on the way in. He held it open while Saldivar dragged himself through on his hands and one leg. Beyond the wire, the shallow slope up to the beginning of the brush had been singed off; there was no cover at all. He began grimly to haul himself up it.

Singer caught up with him in a hurry and lifted him by the back of his jacket.

"Stay with me," he panted, pulling Saldivar's arm over his shoulder again. "It's mined."

But he moved in a deft zigzag as if he knew exactly where he was going. They plunged into the brush at the top of the slope, and the camp behind them was still and quiet. Singer put Saldivar down, took his boots off, and hung them around his neck.

"Make us hard to track," he explained. He bent over Saldivar anxiously. "How's the leg?"

"It's good. I'm all right."

"Don't tell me lies. Waste of time," Singer said. "But we have to move. Thought we'd be covered till morning, but that soldier—they might find him before light."

Carrying Saldivar on his back, he threaded his way through the brush with incredible speed. His panting was audible, but he did not slow down. After what seemed like hours, the ground began to slope upward so steeply that he was bent nearly double as he scrambled up. He let go of Saldivar's legs.

"Hang on; it's steep," he gasped. He was climbing with hands and feet. Finally he hauled Saldivar up onto a place that was relatively flat. "Okay, roll off, but hold still. You might fall."

Singer crawled ahead in the darkness. He reached back and dragged Saldivar after him through a narrow space.

There was a *flick*, and a shielded hand light came on. Singer held it up briefly. They were in a kind of cave, a space hacked out of the thornbushes under an overhanging ledge.

"Safe, maybe," Singer said. "Been here two days." He rummaged in his pack, then set the light on the floor and propped up the pack for Saldivar to lean against. "Got water for you; also the belly medicine."

But the familiar bitterness of the drugs made Saldivar retch weakly.

"How long since you ate?" Singer asked.

"I don't know. I had some soup yesterday. I can't swallow anything. It doesn't stay down."

Singer lit a heat tab under a pan of water and shook sugar and a packet of dried leaves into it while it boiled. He added a pinch of salt and handed the drink to Saldivar.

"Salt?" Saldivar asked.

"Yes. Salt makes it more friendly to your body." He searched for more words to explain, gave it up, and shrugged.

"I get it. It's like that Hydro-Lite stuff that's supposed to rebalance your electrolytes."

"You drink it. It works."

The tea had a strange medicinal scent, but he was able to drink it. Afterward Singer gave him more water and vitamins.

"Now your leg."

"Can't it wait till tomorrow?" Saldivar pleaded. "What's the difference?"

"Now," Singer said gently.

"If you take those boots off, I'll puke again."

But he did not, quite.

Singer's face crumpled in dismay. Saldivar wondered why it looked so strange and realized that Singer had never let that much feeling show. Singer looked at the sores, but did not try to touch them.

"Motherfuckers, sons of bitches," he said. "How did this happen?"

"I don't know," Saldivar said painfully. "They beat me all the time; they used to hang me up by the ankles and—well, stuff like that. I couldn't keep it clean, so—it just—nothing ever healed up." He turned his face away; he felt intensely ashamed.

Singer rubbed his friend's shoulder the way he would rub a horse's neck to calm it down.

"Listen," he said. "You know what they want? Want to own you. Make you think you're nothing, it's their world. This world is not theirs. Belongs to the ones who want to live here. You and me."

"Philosophy." Saldivar laughed bitterly.

"Old woman told me that, first time I came home in pieces. She loved me, so I listened to her. You better listen, too.

"But tonight—you are right, can't do anything for this tonight. Has to get clean. Tomorrow we find the river and fix you up."

Saldivar thought that he would go to sleep instantly; he was exhausted. But he felt a strange kind of terror in the dark. He clutched one of the straps on Singer's pack, trying to convince himself that he was not back in his cell. He was afraid that he was dreaming again, that he would be awakened any minute by the familiar sound of booted feet outside the door. He shivered till his teeth rattled; it was so cold.

Singer rolled over and threw a protective arm around him, pulling him closer.

"I'm all right," Saldivar protested instantly.

"Sure, you always shake like a dog on ice."

"Anyway, I stink."

"You do," Singer said cheerfully. "Smell like a billy goat that is dead three days. Tomorrow, we find a river. A big river. Tomorrow. Now shut up."

Singer's warmth at his back slowly spread through him, reassuring him; at last he fell asleep.

The next day they heard the vito patrols crisscrossing overhead. They stayed hidden all day and decided to rest through the night as well; Singer had been traveling by night, but he did not want to try it with Saldivar. He waited till the hour before dawn, when a pale, milky light penetrated the brush.

Singer was carrying the pack and a rifle, so it was more difficult for him to help Saldivar. They did not go back by the steep route they had taken but found an easier descent on the other side of the ridge. Singer had brought a rope and was able to lower Saldivar down the worst pitch. They moved very slowly; Singer kept to the rough ground, finding a way through close thickets where they would be hard to spot from the air. They heard the drone of engines once or twice and once saw the dark dots in the air to the northeast, but nothing flew over them.

Even at a slow pace, Saldivar sank to the ground in exhaustion after only a couple of hours.

"I'm sorry," he gasped. "I gotta rest."

"Easy—no hurry."

"They'll spot us any minute. How come they haven't already?"

"They look where they expect us. We're too far west, but worth it to be not seen. They don't pick us up, or tracks today, maybe they'll give up, think we flew. They know you can't walk."

"Yeah, well, I can't hardly. What are we gonna do?"

Singer looked down at him; he looked thoughtful, but he was worrying. He could not see a good way to carry the pack and Saldivar. Maybe if he put the pack on Palha and then carried both of them, or maybe if he dumped the pack. But Palha needed the medicine and the extra food that was in it.

"It's not far to the river," he said. "I'll get you there."

He left the pack on his back and carried Saldivar in his arms. In an hour of heavy going, with many rests, they heard the sound of running water. The stream, which was swifter and colder than the broad river that ran through the desert, had cut into the bank, leaving an overhang that might hide them if the vitos came by. He lowered Saldivar into the water at the sandy edge.

He waded upstream a little way and came back with a handful of fat green reeds, shredded the cut ends of the stems, and got a white sap that worked up into a foam.

"This is good soap," he said, demonstrating on his own hair.

After they were both clean, he propped Saldivar's leg on a rock and started to scrub away the scabs, dirt, and dead tissue with antiseptic swabs from the pack. The running water had helped, but still the job was agonizing.

He had done half of one leg when Saldivar seized his wrist and stopped him.

"Give me a break," he said hoarsely. "I can't take any more of this."

"Maybe I don't do it right," Singer said. "I'm no healer."

"Don't you have any pills in that pack?"

Singer shrugged. "Don't understand all that's in that pack—just took your kit that you left behind. Here, you look." He splashed to the bank and laid out items in the sand.

Salidvar's eyes lit up when he saw the injector. "That! Gimme that stinger. I can shoot myself up."

He sighed heavily as the drugs took hold. "Now you can do your worst. Take your time—I'll be like spaghetti for a couple of hours."

Methodically, Singer cleaned and sprayed and packed in antibiotics. Saldivar, no longer writhing in pain, told him how to do it. But Singer's heart sank. They had hundreds of miles to go. Perhaps, now that Saldivar's wounds were cared for, they would heal. But there was nothing he could do to speed that healing, and until it happened, he did not see how they could progress more than a couple of miles a day.

"Thanks," Saldivar said as he finished up. "But you know, it isn't going to do us much good. I still can't walk. I think they cracked the bone in that one leg. And there's definitely something wrong with my knee. I can feel it grating inside, like gravel and broken glass."

Singer lifted him out of the water and wrapped him in a blanket to get dry. There was still one thing he could try, but he was very much afraid to do it. He had touched Kruger; he had lifted some of the pain off him, he had cooled the fever. That was a simple thing that any brother might try. The hard part had been touching one who was not a brother. What lay before him was a task for the greatest of healers, and he had never learned anything of that art.

Most frightening was how close he would have to come to the outlander to do any good at all. Always, with every step he took toward them, he swore to go no nearer. And with every step he was forsworn.

"Singer?" Palha said weakly. "Look, it's no good. I know that. I can't walk two hundred miles, it's just no use pretending. And you can't carry me. So you can stop worrying about what to do.

"You got me out of there, all right? Just don't let them take me back, and I'll be happy. Really. I've got no complaints.

"You'll have to say something to Jan for me. Tell her I really love her, you know, I didn't forget about her, I just got too tired. You can figure out some way to say it, get her to understand.

"Singer? Are you listening, man? This is important."

Singer had been concentrating on his own knee, thinking about how it joined together, how it worked. He moved reluctantly closer to Saldivar. He took his hand, feeling how cold it was and how faintly the blood beat under the skin.

"I hear you. Don't worry yourself. I'll take care of things."

He noticed absently how the drug was making Palha speak what he thought was the truth. He supposed they had thought their drugs would do the same with him. Only his truth would not fit into their language.

"You do something for me," he asked Palha. "Forget about the bad things. Tell me something good, tell me a place you remember with happiness." He stroked Palha's arm in a soothing, even rhythm, moving upward toward the heart.

"There was a place," Palha said. "Oh, man, it's been so

many years since I thought of this. Where the deer . . ." His voice faded into a mumble, and his eyes closed, but Singer had caught the live current of his thoughts and followed it down.

A part of him was there with Palha, in the branches of a great tree—*ohk'*, they called it. Only the faintest first reflections of the dawn reached tentatively into the forest, and the mist was still thick and cold on the stream below. There was a hunter hiding down the bank of the stream. That was the place where the deer came to drink early in the morning, and there the hunters came and would have killed many, but for small Palha, high in the tree with a slingshot and a pocket full of pebbles. The big men never understood why their prey suddenly leapt high out of the shallow water and away. One day the man who stood up and tried to shoot after them was struck behind the ear by a stray pebble and fell like a cut log. Palha plunged from the tree, sure he had killed him without meaning to. But when the man groaned and moved, Palha hurried to steal from him his rifle and his fine folding knife with its blade smooth as a new-moon crescent. No one ever found his hiding place.

A part of Singer stayed there, keeping Palha's mind peaceful and out of the way. A part of him searched deeper, matching himself hand to hand, eye to eye, heart to heart until he could think Palha's thoughts and feel his heartbeat. The deep pain sank into his own bones, wringing sweat from his face, and he turned in fear and shock as if from his own ragged flesh.

With an effort he kept steady in his thought the wholeness of young Palha and the strength of his own real body; he forced the wounded to remember what was whole. He felt the surge of heat against his hands, which were cupped above the sore. It frightened him; it felt like something that could tear itself from his control if he lost his focus for an instant. Under his hands things were happening that he could not consciously understand; Palha's heart beat fiercely, racing to cool and feed his body. Palha jerked upright and caught his arm.

"*Khuei mes'ne, te,*" he said. "No—I mean, I mean, what are you doing?"

Dizzy, disoriented from the sudden breaking of his concentration, Singer hardly dared to look.

"Your leg," he said shakily.

"Shit," Saldivar breathed. "Shit, no. This can't be."

Singer forced himself to look. The knee was still puffy, but it was covered smoothly with new skin, a strange contrast to the rest of Saldivar's body. The other sores had started to heal in a circle outward from the knee.

Saldivar scrambled to his feet and put his full weight on the leg.

"What did you do to me? What did you do?" he demanded, staring at Singer fearfully.

Singer tried to put a calming hand on him, but Saldivar slapped it away.

"Don't you remember Long Shot?" Singer asked. "I was the one hurt that time. You lent me your strength, and I got better."

"Bull, you just weren't hurt as bad as I thought."

"That was my death wound. When it bleeds into your lung, you don't go on living. You didn't know what you were doing, but you helped me. So now I do the same for you. We're even. That's all."

"No, that's not all. You can't put me off like that this time. These aren't card tricks you keep pulling. When they were beating me up, they kept asking me about you—like you were special, you were different.

"Come on, Singer! I bled for those questions. I earned some answers. Who are you, Singer?"

"You know what I am," Singer said. "You only have to look in your mind and remember."

He took Saldivar's hand, turned it palm up, and covered it with his own, palm to palm.

A flood of memories poured back, familiar as fingered pebbles, but he had never seen them before Singer laid hands on him.

He pulled away as if he had been stung.

"Get out of my head," he gasped. "You're not my teammate. Are you even human? What do you want from me?"

"One left," Singer whispered. "All I could think of to try. I'm sorry."

Singer would not look at him; that calm face no longer concealed anything from Saldivar. He understood that he had been wrong to think of Singer as impervious to the pain. He had brushed against raw places, memories like sores that would not heal.

Still he had to force the words out, one by one. Singer called him "Palha"; he knew now why. It meant "from the heart." Singer's memories had graceful words for the friend whose life had become as necessary to one as one's own, but Saldivar was unable to summon them himself.

"Will you quit being so fucking noble?" he said. "I was buried alive. You were the only—ah, fuck it, the only *man* on the planet that cared if I was dead or alive. You don't know what it was like in there. Jesus, how many times do you have to save my life before I can say thank you? Shit. I just—can't seem to—"

He was stuck. He knew that if he touched Singer, Singer would know what he wanted to say, but he could not move.

Singer rescued him one more time, wrapping long arms around him, tentatively at first, then so tight that he could feel his ribs creak. He seemed to move on through Singer's skin and look at himself through Singer's eyes: He was the strange one, speaking a strange language. But to Singer he was not a replaceable part, a collection of skills held together with guts and wire; he was valuable, necessary. That knowledge was more healing than medicine.

I'm here, Singer said in the other language. Or it could have been *I was there* or *I will be there.* Saldivar was not sure he had the tenses straight, but he understood that it was some kind of promise.

"Look at us," he said, between laughing and crying, when Singer let go of him. "Did you ever see such a couple of bony old wasted rejects? I'm going to give up being human, myself. There's no future in it."

Even as he said it, he looked up at the endless sky and drew the hot, dusty air deep into his lungs; hungry, sore, and weary, he felt that he might live forever.

Singer tossed him his clothes.

"Time we were moving."

25

Janet walked slowly back from the hospital. A night breeze fitfully stirred the dust around her feet, but it sighed and fell silent before she reached her street. The darkness seemed to press into the city, infiltrating and immobilizing. That night she wished the desert would find a way to strike back, to wipe out the town and its routines, to return the place to its original lonely wildness and forget that human beings had ever come there.

As she approached her building, a shadow detached itself from the wall and took a step toward her.

"Dr. Logan?"

She had never heard the voice before. "What can I do for you?" she replied stiffly. Her heart raced. She hoped that she sounded stuffy rather than terrified.

The figure stepped into the light. It was a tall woman in a flight suit.

"Mellyn Greenway. Your friend Singer told me to come see you. He said you would know where he was."

Janet took a deep breath as a wave of grief and unreasonable anger swept over her. Her first impulse was to push past the stranger and slam the door in her face. Maintain state, she ordered herself. Don't give yourself away.

"I don't care to talk about this on the street," she said, steadying her voice with an effort. "You can come in."

She did not ask the stranger to sit. She wanted to get it over with and invite her to leave, politely but as quickly as possible.

"You'll excuse me if I make myself coffee. I've been working for sixteen hours." That gave her an excuse to keep moving around the kitchen and to turn her face away from the stranger.

"I don't know why you've come to me. I can't tell you anything. Paul Saldivar was a friend of mine, and I know he had a chico named Singer. Their whole unit was listed as missing. They found one body, but the rest were just gone: Saldivar, Bates, Taipala, and Singer. The man I talked to searched the area and didn't find anything. If they were still alive, they'd have been seen by now, or walked out. They haven't. They're presumed dead. More than that I can't tell you. If this Singer was a friend of yours, I'm sorry. But I'm feeling pretty racked up myself, and now I'd appreciate it if you'd leave."

"Bull," the tall woman said calmly. She reached over Jan and helped herself to a cup of coffee. She dropped onto the couch and made herself comfortable. "He's not dead. Not Singer. Not till I see his body, and even then, not till I check for myself on which parts are missing."

"Look, I told you you're making a mistake. I'm not whoever you think I am. Will you please get out and leave me alone?"

The tall woman drank coffee silently and scrutinized her.

"You don't believe me, do you?" she said. "You think I'm jiving you. I can tell you things that prove I know him—and you do, too. I'd know you anywhere from the picture he showed me."

"He couldn't possibly have a picture of me," Janet said coldly. That proved that the stranger was lying: A friend of Singer's would know he hated photos. She wondered if she could defend herself with a kitchen knife.

"Now you're the one who's jiving me. You know what kind of a picture I mean. I can tell you what he looks like, too. He's got scars—here and here."

"Anybody with access to medical records could say that."

"When you're around him, you start remembering things that didn't happen to you. Is that in the medical records?

"You start understanding words that aren't Delteix, too—or any lingua you remember. Like he calls you Zhanne. It has something to do with light, no? Now, would a golpo notice a thing like that?"

Jan trembled with relief—and confusion. If the woman was not a spy, who was she?

"I'm not worried about the golpos," Jan said.

"Well, maybe you should be. He killed a chuck in a bar, up in North Fork. They came around to my place afterward but they didn't find him. He said he was going back to Guijarro to get a mission. I had a flight out this way, and I thought I'd come tell you they were after him, in case they showed up here."

"It doesn't really matter anymore, does it?" Jan said wearily. To her surprise and disgust, she felt tears running down her face. "He's gone now, and Pablo's gone with him. Just like Jon. After he went missing, I hoped and hoped, and gave up, and hoped some more. And waited. I'm not going to go through that again. So if you're not here to bug my brain, will you please just leave me alone?"

Lyn snorted. "You don't like my looks and you don't want my sympathy, huh? Well, there are things I don't like about you, either, y' know. Like that you have a good education and you're a doctor and everything, which I really respect, only I don't know about anything except the insides of engines and you're always polite and always nice whereas I'm scum. I hate people like you.

"So now that we've got that all aired out, do you think we could just forget it and get down to business?"

Janet had stopped crying.

"Your technique is very good, actually," she said with a last involuntary hiccup. "Telling the truth in a ruthless fashion is sometimes a good way to shock people out of their grooves.

"I apologize, and I appreciate that you're trying to help. But there's nothing you can do."

"Well, for starters, I'll show you right now that he ain't dead."

She reached into her shirt and pulled out her pack of cards. She shuffled swiftly and fluently, with her eyes closed as if to concentrate better on what her fingers were telling her. Still squeezing her eyes shut, she slipped the first card off the deck. She flipped it over, took a deep breath, looked, and then smiled.

"This card is Singer," she said. "Ace of cups. He's alive, all right. That's a life card."

"This is ridiculous," Jan said.

Lyn touched her hand. "Just look, okay?"

Slowly she laid out more cards, but Jan's eyes were fixed on the first one. She could feel herself plunging into the cool water pictured there, into the overflowing fountain.

Pictures. Confused memories of cold, running water, whispering a new name. That was long ago. But there was water out there in the desert, and he knew how to find it. She tasted warm, brownish liquid, rough with sand grains. He crouched warily, lapping it from his palm, under moonlight that revealed a path-

less wilderness around him. Shadow and glimmer jumbled the landscape like paint streaks on a face, and the moon invited her to walk into the maze.

That was the way Jon had gone: into trackless country. And that was the way she had started to go with Singer and Pablo: to unexplored territory with no marked roads. But they were all gone, and she was afraid to go on. She took one step forward, and she was lost. The darkness still beckoned her, but she resisted, terrified.

He was climbing, scrambling desperately. Every bone ached, and his hands and feet were cut and bruised. She went up the ladder of swords, though the edges sliced her hands mercilessly at every step. Five—six—seven—she could not hold on to the blades anymore; there was no escape that way. She let go and fell, and fell, and fell, down into the darkness.

Only one light glowed, far off on the horizon. As she stretched out her hands toward it, it seemed to come closer; it was not a light but a door, with light streaming through it. She gave in at last and stepped through.

"Say 'friend' and enter," Lyn said.

Janet realized for the first time that she had not spoken at all; she had been sitting there staring at Lyn for who knew how long. The cards lay between them: ace of cups, Moon, seven of swords.

"Amazing," Lyn said. "You used your psychology to back into it, and I used the cards. But I don't think there's a lot of difference in the results."

Question!

Janet saw a picture of Singer walking into her mind as if he were walking into his own room in the dark and laying his hand on what he needed. He walked out again, but the door was open. Light came through.

"Madre'dio," Janet said aloud. "It works."

"He showed me," Lyn said. "Showed you, too, but you just didn't know it. Once that door is opened, it can't be shut again. I guess it's always been there. We just didn't know how to open it."

"Well, then—" Janet said helplessly. "I've been an asshole," she concluded with total conviction.

"That's nothing," Lyn snorted. "At least you were polite about it. You should have seen how rude I was to Singer. I told him to go fuck himself."

They leaned on each other's shoulders and laughed out loud. Janet sobered up first.

"I've watched so many people do this in therapy," she said.

"Sometimes you can just see the light come back on, and you know they're going to make it. I would always try to look very all-knowing and benevolent. Actually, I didn't have a clue what they were feeling. I always wondered.

"What was that, anyway?"

Lyn shrugged. "Don't ask me. I never did it before. I think it's like there's some kind of a connection now, but it's not direct like a phone. The cards have always been like that for me—they tell me what I didn't know I knew. Some of it's literal, and some of it isn't. I know he's alive out there, though." She gathered up the cards carefully. "You seemed to be expecting somebody else when I showed up. You said you weren't worried about the golpos, but you're sure scared of something."

Jan hesitated; concealment was a long habit. But in her brief contact with Lyn, she had felt nothing concealed or held back. Lyn was as clear as a laser flash. Jan decided to tell her the truth.

"I'm scared of the Net. I decided when I heard that Singer and Pablo were gone that I was going to get even, come what might. But I'm afraid the fish are going to catch me before I can catch them."

Lyn grinned. "Oho, that Ms. Captain Doctor routine is just a pretty rabbit skin to wrap the baby lupo in. Tell me more while I fair-share your kitchen. I'm starving."

It took less time than Janet had imagined. For parts of the story that she hardly dared describe out loud, she experimented with showing Lyn in images they could both see. It was a frustrating and tantalizing experience, like trying to hear a conversation in a strange language.

"Hey, I'm ready for Delteix again," Lyn said finally. "It may be slow and old, but this stuff is making my brain ache."

"People think communication is easy," Jan said. "That's because they aren't paying attention. In my line of work I see how hard it can be. And 'this stuff' is really different; it's not just hearing words in your head. It's like the difference between taking pictures from orbit and actually coming down here to live, walking around the planet and entering into its biosphere.

"You know what I feel like? They shipped a lot of animals as freeze-dried embryos. When the embryos arrived, they thawed them out in a special solution, and the little buggers plumped out and started to grow. This part of me has been freeze-dried in hard space, waiting for a more favorable environment. Now we'll see if I'm viable, or if the fish decide I'm a mutant and kill me."

Lyn shook herself. "And I thought I was the weird one," she

said appreciatively. "Hey, show me this Saldivar chico before we switch out of this mode."

Janet recalled the strong, compact lines of Saldivar's body, his warm eyes and proud mouth. She tried to make the picture objective, then realized that "objectivity" in that context was like trying to transmit what was not in view of the camera. She could show Saldivar only as she had known him. She found herself blushing.

"Not much point in blushing, is there?" Lyn said.

They silently exchanged memories.

"I guess not," Jan said ruefully. "It's a good thing I like you. This would be really hideous otherwise."

"That's a question—if it would work otherwise. I think there has to be a certain kind of harmony. Like, back on the farm they used to talk about vibrations and resonating on the same level. That was mostly jive, but there is something to it."

?

The big dome, the one they called the kiva, late at night with everyone gathered in a circle. Old blankets and faded shawls drawn over shoulders. Firelight glinting on bright eyes amid tangled hair, on sunburn and stubble. Big man, grizzled hair bushing back off bald forehead, discourses slowly in his South Island drawl that is half real, half a put-on.

The child in the corner tucks her knobby legs under her for warmth, listens and wonders. Jealous of the baby nursing under one shawl, she slows her breath until it is light and even like the little one's; she touches and enters: sleepy, sleepy warmth, warm sweet milk. Suddenly she is scared and pulls away the touch. The baby flails and screams, startled into wakefulness.

"So you've been doing this pretty much all your life," Janet said thoughtfully.

"Pretty much, but I don't use it as much as you might think. When I was living with those folks, I was too young to know I was different. And afterward, there was nobody to talk to. Or listen to. I don't want to know what most people think. It's bad enough listening to the stuff they come out and say."

"Yes. It's self-protection to pretend it just doesn't exist. It gets lonely, though."

"Yeah. I never would have met you, most likely, if it hadn't been for Singer. Janney—he's, like, not from around here, is he?"

"You caught on to that, did you?"

"I looked in his head. It was none of my business, actually, but I was trying to get hold of him, and he's got no handles, you know? I saw you, and I saw Saldivar. I went farther back in the past, and I ran into this barrier. It was like a wall of fire. He wouldn't go anywhere near it, but I knew from that one look that he's not one of us. What is that block he's got?"

"When he was in the hospital, he used to wake up screaming names. But as soon as he saw where he was, he would lock up his face and say nothing. I think he saw a lot of people die. His family, or whatever he had instead of a family.

"I've worked with a lot of people who had that problem. People who had their unit wiped out, kids who lost families in the bombing, before the civilians were pulled back. There's a lot of guilt on top of grief. They feel they should have saved the others, or that they have no right to be alive when the others are gone. There's loss of identity, too. Their whole context is gone. They don't know who they are anymore."

"They get over it, don't they?"

"Usually. But what if they'd done more than just watch? What if they experienced each death as if it were their own? I don't know what that would do to a person's head."

Lyn imagined being in the truck with Dylan, feeling his skull smash against the windshield and the steering column crush his ribs, sitting there pinned and bleeding, unable to call for help.

"Stop it!" Jan commanded.

Lyn shuddered. "That could fuck you up real good," she muttered.

"Yes. He's hurting all the time, and he can't solve his problem, because if he thinks about it, he'll go crazy."

"Yeah, but we're his friends! We could help him."

"That's what I thought. Now I'm not so sure. What he remembers looks like an air strike to me. We did this to him. He can't live alone; this empathic thing he does means he needs people to trust, to form sort of a buffer zone between him and the rest of the world. But the closer he gets to us, the closer he gets to his enemies. The pressure inside just gets worse. That control he has is like a deadman switch. Sooner or later he'll get too tired to hold on to it. He has to go home, or he'll die."

"Who is he, really?" Lyn asked.

"My boss tried to tell me he was a Nupi experiment; I think that was the cover story he was given. I think Singer's people were here before we came from Delta. So you could call them aliens, I guess, but I don't believe they're true aliens. I've seen his lab reports. He's just too much like us. The best guess I can make is that they came here from the home worlds, too—maybe even before we did. Obviously, they've had time to change, to diverge from what we are. Without genetic analysis that we can't do here I can't tell if they're a different species—but somewhere we have ancestors in common. I'm almost sure of that. It's so typical of the ass-backward way we've been doing things. We spend uncounted resources and lives to get back into space, to find our kind, and when we do, our first thought is to kill them.

"But I've had enough. I'm not going to let it happen."

"What are you going to do?"

Janet stared into the dregs of her coffee as if they held a clue to the future. "Well, I'll give you the unvarnished prognosis. What will probably happen is that I'll screw up and get thrown in a labor camp. Or maybe they'll just assassinate me quietly. If they'd kill Kruger for snooping, imagine what they'll do to me. Probably cut me up for spare parts."

"What have you done to deserve all this? Must be worse than just your bad attitude."

"It's what I'm going to do. It all started out quite innocently. When I began poking around after Jon disappeared, I was looking at things that weren't classified at all. You can find out an amazing amount about operations and so forth by keeping track of supplies, for instance.

"But I kept getting in a little deeper and a little deeper, especially after Pablo told me how they'd been hit. Eventually I saw a pattern of unusual events centering on an area of the northern perimeter. Holes in the data can make a pattern, too. But the reason behind those events is very closely guarded. I found out that most security here is very sloppy. An amateur like me can find a way right through it. But this particular area is locked up tighter than the pharmacy on Saturday night. And I do have a job to do in addition to this research.

"I had one word to go on: 'Clausewitz.' It showed up in a report on Jon, and it didn't look as if it was supposed to be there. I looked it up in the encyclopedia—it's a person, a Fokish strategist of the preflight era. He is thought by some to have invented the concept of total war. He also discussed at some length the uses of war as an extension of policy. Some pompous fart on the top levels would probably think that was a clever name for a devious strategy. But the word shows up *nowhere*. I tried a general search and got shut down so fast, it practically burned my fingers. Fortunately I had taken the precaution of not using my own office.

"See, the big network runs in two tiers. Level two, at the bottom, is for all kinds of lower-echelon officers, like me. Also clerks and so forth have some access, especially for input. Level one is for the jefes—Nymann and Gero and the like, plus their staff and flunkies. Now of course there are passwords to get into various datasets; you can't have a file clerk accidentally reading the notes from Nymann's staff meetings. But every password has to be listed somewhere, and there's always the chance that an unauthorized person will get the list, and then you're right back where you started.

"So what they've done is to give each desk its own internal ID. When you ask for something—like the Clausewitz file—the system asks your desk who it is. If it gets an ID that's not on its list, it shuts you off. I've spent all my spare time for the last couple of months putting together a tool to sneak past this. It can be turned loose in the system, and it will then move itself around to keep from being spotted, all the time watching every transaction with a level one machine. Pretty soon it will have figured out the identification process. Then I can go in, tell the system that I, too, am level one, and get whatever I need."

"That sounds too slick to be true," Lyn said. "Make sure you give me a raise while you're in there."

"Programs always sound slick in theory. In practice it could explode in my face. For instance, what if there's a burglar alarm that will alert them and help them trace back to me?"

"I say do it! Burn that bridge when you come to it. Jump in and yell—you won't feel a thing. That's what they told the drop troopers when I used to drive for their training flights. But I don't see how all this is going to help Singer."

"Pay attention! It will tell me who is after him and why. Everyone who gets involved in this gets hit from behind. If we know where they're coming from, we'll have an advantage for once. Knowledge is power."

"Is that a quote from your moldy Fokish generalissimo?"

"I don't know who said that first. Probably some scrawny network tweaker like myself. Perhaps more to the point, I may find out who Singer is trying to kill and why. That will help us find him. You don't hunt the hunter. You track down his game and wait for him to show up. If we can do that, we may be able to stop him from getting himself killed. He can handle anything on two legs, but there are some things he just doesn't grok—like computers and electronic surveillance and totalitarian medical technology.

"Thirdly, I'll find out where his home is, or was. And then I'm going to help him get back there. Not just because of him, but also because that's where I'll find my brother. If I ever find him.'' She tugged at her hair till it stood up in spikes. ''I'm beginning to think that even if I'm right about Singer, I may never see Jon again. It's so unlike him not to leave any word for me. I thought I might find something in my search through the files, but nothing has turned up.''

Lyn considered the problem. ''Are you maybe getting too technical? Maybe he left you a note taped to the cooler or something.''

''Do you think I haven't looked?'' Janet protested. ''Nothing came back with his personal effects but his shirt and his collection of music tabs. Not even a notebook—I guess he took that with him.

''I kept the shirt a long time. Then I gave it to Pablo one time when he came down to visit. I got it back again a couple of weeks ago, with his personal stuff. It's kind of ironic, really.''

She went to the closet and pulled out an untidy bundle. Putting the things away carefully would have been an admission that they had not been left there by accident, that no one was coming back for them. She shoved the bundle toward Lyn.

''Here. Pathetic remnants. There's some of Singer's stuff in here, too, but none of it will tell you anything.''

Lyn unfolded the battered shirt and sorted over the odds and ends inside. She picked out a string of tabs and chose one with ocher and red swirls in the plastic. ''Mind if I put this on? I really like these guys.''

Jan grimaced. ''Yes, everyone but me. They're angry, bitter, sad. I already have those feelings. I don't need them amplified.''

''Burning Bridges'' filled the room again.

Lyn turned up the volume. ''There are a lot of ways to make music carry a message. Have you checked them all out?''

''What do you think! I know about underlays and embedding and all that stuff from working with Jon. I examined these tabs and didn't find anything. What's more to the point, I feel sure the Net looked at them, too, and their equipment is better than mine. They would never have returned them to me if they'd found anything.''

She picked up the shirt and started to refold it.

''Ouch.'' She examined her finger, where a bright bead of blood had welled up, and plucked out a splinter of glass. The cracked mirror had finally disintegrated. She tried gingerly to remove the rest of the glass, then took a closer look at the mirror. Part of the stitching that held it in place had been cut.

Lend me your knife.

Lyn handed her the knife before she had time to speak the request. Jan slashed through the threads and shook out the mirror backing with its remnants of glass. A folded scrap of polysheet had been pressed between the mirror and the backing. She smoothed it out and read:

> jly to jlx—I want to leave you this in case something goes wrong. I'd like to call you, but I don't want to use any public access. Somebody has been following me around since I talked to a pilot who told me he had flown classified missions in the north. The man was feeling well smoked because one of his chicos had gone down and they weren't allowed to retrieve him, because he was in the treaty area. I asked what treaty, and he sobered up in a flash and denied having mentioned it. I'm going as an observer on a border patrol north of here. That will let me check the territory myself and maybe get away from this fish. I'll be back to see you as soon as I can without bringing anyone in my wake.

There was a break; then the message continued in a barely legible scrawl:

> Janney, I'm lost. I'm somewhere in the Open Zone: we were ambushed and the patrol smoked it, but I'm all right. I'm afraid to go home. I think they're trying to kill me. So I'm going on farther north. I won't wait for them to smoke me off the way they did Papa. I hope you'll find this—I'm sorry—wish I'd done better. Janney, please come find me—you always did.

"Oh, God," she whispered. "He was alive. All this time, this has been sitting there, and I didn't find it."

Lyn picked up the sheet. "Are you sure this is from him? This shirt's been a lot of places since he dropped it."

"I'm sure. He always used polysheet out in the field. This is his writing. Even if someone could fake that, they wouldn't know about the call letters. They couldn't know our joke about the mirror. Why didn't I think of that? Why didn't I think! Madre'dio, I washed this shirt! If he'd used paper, I'd never have known."

"Take it easy," Lyn said. "What could you have done, anyway, except maybe to rush off after him and get yourself killed?"

Jan took a deep breath and choked off her tears.

"Well, I'm sure as hell going now," she said grimly. "Now you know what's at stake. Do you still want to come along? You know they could hang me right now for what I've already done, but you don't even know me as far as they're concerned. You could back off and be left out of it."

"I could ask them to put me back in the baggie and refreeze me, too—that would be nice and safe. You think I'm going to find you and Singer at long last, and then let you go off without me and have all the fun? Pig's ass! I'd die once just to avoid boredom. I'd die twice for my friends. All for one and one for the road, dakko?"

"Dakko." Jan's rare smile warmed her face. "It'll be good to have you along. I figure it'll double our infinitesimal chances."

"Two hundred percent of zero is zero," Lyn said. "I don't need a computer to figure that one. Sounds like my kind of party. So when are you going to turn this thing loose on the unsuspecting sharks?"

"I want to perform a small test inside the hospital network. If it doesn't blow up, I'll be ready to run in a week. After that, it will take a few days—I can't tell exactly how long—before I can set up a fake ID and use it.

"I'll call you when I'm ready to roll. We'll have to analyze the results and talk strategy.

"There's something you can do in the meantime, too. Keep an eye on your cargoes and lift anything that looks useful. We may have to head out on our own, and if we do, we'll need field rations and gear. If you can lay hands on cold suits, get them. Do you have a handgun?"

"Yeah, but I never use it. About the only things I see to shoot at are the bugs in my rack."

"Start wearing it. Get us a projectile rifle and some ammunition, too, if you can."

"Why don't I just steal you a laser cannon while I'm at it?"

"Go right ahead—you'll be the one who has to carry it."

"Are you planning to open a second front? Don't answer that. Just promise to be careful, dakko? And if you can't be careful, fight dirty."

She embraced Janet and walked away. Jan could hear her dropping down the steps two at a time, whistling with callous disregard for the neighbors. The sun was just tingeing the eastern edge of the sky.

26

Lyn found a fax waiting for her when she arrived at work. The last message from Jan had been a page of cheerful news about nonexistent patients. "The case we were both so concerned about is doing quite well—he's walking around the hospital already and should be up and running soon." The new message was simpler: a row of star and comet graphics and the words PARTY TIME. Lyn found a crew scheduled to fly to Jefferson later in the afternoon and traded flights with them. She had to promise them several cases of beer to sweeten the deal and wondered how she would come up with it. Janet did not seem like the type who would know where to find the dirty market.

She found the loaded pack on the rack where she had stashed it and stowed it under a seat behind the pilots' compartment. It seemed extremely heavy, and she hoped she would not actually have to carry it anywhere.

Janet met her at the airfield. She wore her usual stone-cold serious expression, but Lyn could feel the suppressed excitement beneath it.

"It's ready to go. Walk me back to the hospital and you can watch it run."

"Hey, it's getting dark already, and I still have to come up with three cases of Heimat beer," Lyn complained mildly. But she followed Janet down the road toward town. "I've never done so much walking in my life—might as well have joined the infantry."

They passed through the door check with a nod to the guard and got on the elevator.

"They're supposed to check my badge before they let me

through, and they're not supposed to let you in at all without stating your business,'' Janet said. ''But they never bother. See what I mean about lax security? Of course, if we had explosives in here, it might be different, but most of these chucks don't recognize danger in anything that doesn't go bang.''

Janet opened the office door and turned on the lights.

''Nice place,'' Lyn commented.

''Sorry, this isn't my office. It belongs to the chief of medicine. I didn't want to run the final stage from my desk. Ever since they bugged my office, I've wondered if they were tapping into my keyboard. I don't know if they still have their eye on me or not, but I decided I didn't want to risk it. I'm going to use Petersen's desk.''

Lyn whistled softly. ''Isn't that kind of chancy?''

''It's the safest alternative in the building—way up here on the third floor, and Petersen almost never comes in on the night shift. The hospital never sleeps, but parts of it relax at night.'' She took a deep breath, clutching the edges of the desk. ''Well, it's time to jump and yell, but I don't want internal security here with their flash guns at the ready.''

She tapped the keypad. The screen began filling with text, and Lyn heard her inner shout of triumph. ''I'm getting it!'' Jan whispered. She had attached her backpack portable to the desk; it hummed thoughtfully to itself as it copied the data.

''What's it saying? I can't scan as fast as you.''

''Here's the gist of it: Kruger and Pablo were on the right track, but they didn't go far enough. There are Consorso citizens being held somewhere, but I don't quite get where. That's an old report. Umm, apparently they got moved. Don't know where to. Central thing is what they're calling the Clausewitz accord. We have maps from orbit that show suspiciously humanlike artifacts not far from here. Investigation revealed that they were indeed inhabited by humanoids. At this point Gero was contacted by his Nupi analogue, who proposed a solution. Native presence would be strictly concealed from all personnel outside the intelligence structure, except for military heavies needed for cooperation. 'Neutral zones' would be established where any movement would be subject to air attack. No ground penetration from either side. After a limited period of observation, further measures would be agreed upon and carried out. Probably 'neutralization.' Under no circumstances is contact with the natives to be attempted, or communication with Delta about the existence of the problem.

"But they're worried the Nupis are cheating—which means they are cheating themselves, or they wouldn't know. Here! Here's the raid that got Kruger and Paul." She touched the screen to insert a marker. "That's a map—we'll print it out later," she explained. "They hit this place to warn the Nupis to abide by the accord. That may be Singer.

"This is an incredible bath of information. I wish I had all night to wallow in it."

She popped another tab into her portable. Her fingers did a little dance on the pad, and the screen went blank.

"What's the matter?" Lyn asked.

"Nothing. I just told it to skip the visual display and copy directly into my little machine. It can go a lot faster if it doesn't have to put anything up on the screen.

"You know, when I first came up, I couldn't believe these were really computers," she commented. "They don't even talk. Typing words letter by letter is so slow. I don't know how they got all this junk keyed in at all."

Suddenly, Lyn leapt for the light.

"There's someone coming!" she hissed.

They froze: Janet behind the filing shelves and Lyn crouched next to the door. Janet, too, could hear footsteps. They approached the office, hesitated, and then moved inside. As the unknown intruder reached for the light, he stepped on Lyn's hand.

She hit him in the groin, hard enough to knock him off his feet. He wheezed for breath to scream, thrashing wildly around the floor while she struggled to hold on to him and stifle his moaning.

"Hit him! Hit him!" she gasped.

Jan groped in the dark. She could feel the butt of a pistol through the flap he had just had time to unsnap. She pulled it out and clouted him awkwardly with the barrel. There was a muffled yell, and he kicked harder than ever. She felt for the right spot on his skull and tapped him once more, a little harder than she thought was right. He went limp. She dropped the gun and grabbed Lyn's arm.

"No, don't turn the light on," she ordered. "Do you have a hand light?"

"Sure. What for?"

"I have to finish this job."

Palming the tiny light so that it could not be seen, she bent over the desk. The last batch of data had been dumped into the portable. She erased what she had just done and turned it off. Then she rubbed the desk vigorously with her sleeve. She wiped the gun, too, and slid it back into the holster. Then, out of curiosity, she held the light to the man's face.

"Madre'dio!"

"What's the matter?"

"Quickly!"

Once out in the hall, she turned off the lights for the whole corridor. They headed silently for the green light marking the stairs.

"We'll go down to the bottom and out the fire door. We don't want them to have a time of exit on us."

Once out in the chilly air, Jan breathed deeply and ran her fingers through her hair till it stood on end.

"Who was that? Why did he get you so upset?"

"That was Petersen! My boss! Of all the evil luck. Why did he have to get industrious tonight? Madre'dio, I hit him with his own gun."

Lyn snorted and then started to laugh uncontrollably. "Evil luck? You have the best luck I've ever seen. Now you can die happy."

"Well, it's really not funny," Jan said repressively.

"Come on, he can't have recognized us."

"I'm not worried about that. He could never, never believe that he'd been decked by a couple of females, one of whom wasn't even an officer. It really isn't right, though. We might have fractured his skull. He could be bleeding internally. Admittedly, he was a redundant orifice, but that in itself doesn't justify hurting him."

"Next time, just shoot him. Spare yourself the worry."

Jan shuddered. "I really don't think I could. I have such a clinical picture of what even a normal round does to the human anatomy. I can stand to look at casualties by thinking of it as sort of an act of God—it just happened to them, and now I have to fix it. But when I seriously contemplate one human being inflicting such obscene damage on another, it makes me ill."

"You're in a bad line of business, then."

"I know it," Jan said sadly. "All the people I love seem to be in it, too. I guess if someone were looking down the barrel at you, I'd go ahead and blow his head off. But I'd probably throw up afterward. I'm a hypocrite."

"I never killed anybody, either," Lyn confessed. "I got caught in a stupid firefight once, and I was shooting *at* people, but I don't think I hit anyone. It wasn't altruism that stopped me, though; I was too scared to shoot straight.

"Listen, I know what it's like to feel your life being ground out like a dead butt under someone's boot heel. That won't happen to me again. I'll kill anybody who gets in my way. Innocent or guilty, he can move his ass or kiss it good-bye. I just hope to the mother of God I can shoot straight next time."

Tired and cold, they quickened their pace as they neared Jan's apartment. At the bottom of the stairs they paused and turned to each other. Both had a sudden feeling of unease.

"Somebody here?" Lyn asked.

"Yes . . . but not a guest. And yet it seems like someone I know." Her eyes widened. "Paul! But Singer's not with him. Something is wrong."

She stopped outside the door and called gently. "Paul? It's me, Janet, and one friend—a friend of Singer's. All right? Can we come in?"

A hoarse, rusty voice she could hardly recognize finally responded. "Dakko, come on."

Saldivar was crouched in a corner near the window, in the dark. He cradled his rifle in his arms, a finger on the trigger. He stared at Jan as if he was not sure he knew her. She knelt on the floor beside him and put her arms around him. He resisted her for a moment, then he put the rifle down.

"I didn't know where else to go," he said.

"Pablo, corazon, you made it. You're home."

The rest of their silent conversation resounded in Lyn's head. They might as well have been shouting.

With a great effort, Saldivar turned in her direction.

"Who's she?" he croaked in that disused voice.

"Singer's friend," she said. "I met him in North Fork. Where is he?"

Saldivar's face worked. "All the way south—we came together. Two days ago—he walked out on me. I don't know where he is." His voice broke, and he stopped talking.

Janet touched his mind as calmly as if she were lifting off a field dressing to look at a wounded arm. There was a moment of panic as he resisted.

"I have to know or I can't help," she said gently. He yielded grimly, no more than necessary.

They were only a few days out from Jefferson. They had spot-

ted the road but stayed away from it. Both of them were worn to the bone. Singer had the Dust cough. Both of them had persistent fevers that came and went; Saldivar thought they must have picked up something from the muddy water they had been drinking. Singer became edgy and withdrawn as they came closer to the end of the journey. Several times he seemed to be about to say something, but he always changed his mind.

One night Saldivar came slowly up from a deep sleep, feeling peaceful and rested. He realized that he was listening to Singer's music. He lay quiet, his eyes still shut, forgetting to wonder where the instruments had come from. After a while, Singer spoke to him.

Palha, I have something to do. I made promises a long time ago. Do not be angry. I freely unbind all ties between us. You owe me nothing; do not make me a deathgift. If you want to do something for me, please take Lyn and Zhanne and try to find a place where you can live a long time. Do not think of me too often. It is not good to walk too much with the dead; I know. Good-bye, my brother. I have loved you.

He did not understand what Singer meant. He knew he should try harder, because it was important. But the music filled his mind. It was not wild and strange like a lot of the things he picked up from Singer. It was beautiful, just very sad. As he listened to it, he saw a tall, thin girl, her face lit up as if by firelight. Her hair was a dark cloud against a starry sky. She turned toward him, though she was not looking at him, and the firelight caught on the ornament that hung on her breast. It looked like a white horse. He wanted to go after Singer and ask him who she was and why the music was so sad, but he could not open his eyes.

The music died away into a fading rhythm. It was the sound of Singer's feet, running. The rhythm died away, too. Then he could open his eyes. He leapt up; there were no stars, and Singer was gone.

Saldivar turned away from them abruptly. "I couldn't find a trail." His voice was still harsh and cracked. "I searched till I dropped. A couple of times I saw maybe traces, but they could have been anyone, a deer, a rabbit. He moves so damn fast, and he doesn't leave any tracks. I couldn't figure what to do anymore. I couldn't go back to Guijarro; everybody I know there's gone now."

"But where the hell is he going?" Lyn asked. "This shit about having things to do. I don't like the sound of that."
"That word he used," Jan said. " 'Deathgift.' What does that mean?"
"I don't know. It's just something he said."
"No, think about it for me a minute. You must have picked up more than that."
All he could see when he tried to think was the white horse dangling from the girl's neck, gleaming in firelight.
"He wanted to leave me the horse," he mumbled. "But he didn't have it anymore. I think he left it with somebody who was dead. Deathgift, it's something to do with remembering them. But he won't have any because they're all gone."
Before answering, Janet brought him a glass of cold water. He drank thirstily, and she refilled it.
"He's saying good-bye," she said finally. "He left you the only gift he could—a memory of something he loved."
"Why did he leave?" Saldivar asked. Janet heard the question—"Why did he leave me?"—and the desolation in it.
"He has been pulled two ways till he can't take it anymore," she said. "So he's cut himself a deal. He'll do what he has to do, but he'll leave us behind—safe, he thinks. It's too late for that, of course, but he doesn't know it."
"That's crazy," Lyn said flatly.
"Not to him. It's the only way he can get off the hook."
Saldivar drank again, feeling the water soak into his parched body, willing his strength to return. Janet felt his determination. *I will find him. Whatever he thinks he has to do, I'll go with him.*
"You will," she said. "You're our secret weapon. But you're not in shape to follow him at the moment."
Saldivar intended to stand up and demonstrate that he was ready to go right then, but each time he made that decision, he noticed that he had not carried it out.
She slipped her hands under his arms. He was about to protest that he did not need a little girl to help him up, but she pulled him smoothly to his feet and drew his arm over her shoulders.
"PT moves," she said, smiling sideways at him. "I practiced on 300-pound hemiplegics. Take a hot bath, get warm. I'll check you out after that, and you can get some rest."
When he came out of the bathroom, they had taken his clothes and left him an old pair of sweats that were short in the legs but clean and warm.

"There wasn't much I could do for your clothes except call a priest and have them anointed for burial," Jan said. "Now lie down. I want to take a look at you. Stop twitching—I'm doing this in my official capacity."

She examined him briefly: looked at his throat and eyes, palpated his abdomen.

"You ought to have blood tests. God only knows what kind of parasites you've picked up. Did you stop taking your medicine?"

"No. Just ran out. We were out there a long time."

"Hm. Interesting. I wonder if you've actually developed some resistance. Your liver doesn't seem to be enlarged, and it should be, by this time."

The scars on his bare legs caught her attention; they were puckered silver circles, as if some monstrous mouth had bitten him repeatedly. She turned his knee deftly in her hands and moved on to the long sunken marks on his thigh.

Her cheeks turned a bright, angry red.

"Who treated this for you?" she demanded. "Butchers! Animals!" He could feel her anger tingling through the ends of her fingers as she explored the muscles.

"Did it hit the bone? Have you got fragments in there?" she asked anxiously.

"No, it's okay, I think. My knee was pretty well wrecked, but Singer fixed that."

Janet nodded thoughtfully without commenting. She finished her examination.

"If you don't mind, I'd like to try something. You remember that shoulder wound Singer had? I told Lyn about that." She turned to Lyn. "Check out his eyes. Go ahead—touch them."

Lyn pulled her hands away almost immediately.

"Shit, that's weird." She rubbed her eyes vigorously. "That feels bad. It sort of itches and burns. But I don't know what it is. I don't want to mess with his face."

"His inner eyelids seemed to be granulated," Janet explained. "Reaction to the dust, I suppose. I think we can handle that. Put your hands back on him."

She placed her palms lightly over Lyn's on his eyelids, while he was still wondering what was going on.

It was not light that touched his closed eyes, but light was its only analogue. It was penetrating, revealing, a weightless power. It was so nearly tangible that he flinched from it as if from a scalpel, but almost before he could resist, it was gone.

He blinked experimentally. For a moment he had a disorienting sensation of looking out through three sets of eyes at once, but it faded.

"It feels better," he said wonderingly. His whole face seemed to have relaxed. The network of paler creases where the sun had not penetrated was clearly visible.

"It is better," Jan said. "Madre'dio, if only I could go and learn from the people who taught Singer and then take this back down to the wards—"

"They'd say you were crazy and lock you up," Lyn finished for her.

"I suppose so." She sighed. "Anyway, I am afraid to work on that fever. The systems for infectious disease are so complicated. Rest and food should help."

Lyn gave Saldivar soup and bread and cautioned him against wolfing it, but there was no need. He dipped the bread and chewed the moistened end as slowly and carefully as an old man. He kept nodding off in midbite and waking up with a start to realize that he was still eating.

" 'S great," he mumbled finally, "but I've gotta sleep. Haven't slept in two days. Just give me a blanket. I can roll up on the floor."

Jan folded her arms. "You're home, Pablo, read me? When you come home, you don't sleep on the floor, and you don't sleep alone."

He found that they had pulled the mattress off the bed and added cushions and blankets to make a pallet big enough for three.

"Move over," Jan told him. "If anyone wants a piece of you, they'll have to go through us first."

All the same, he laid his rifle out by his head, where he could reach it instantly.

"Just don't blow a hole in my ass on my way to the bathroom," Lyn grumbled. She sat up in bed and shared a smoke with him; they passed it back and forth until he fell asleep between puffs. He vaguely heard the women's voices going for a while but soon sank into a deeper sleep and was conscious of nothing.

He slept so peacefully, in fact, that Jan was the first to know when the men came to the door. She sensed rather than saw a dark figure moving toward them. Reaching frantically with her mind for Lyn, she rolled and swept her legs into the man's ankles, cutting his feet from under him. He fell backward on top of her. She wrapped her legs around his ribs and bit his wrist savagely. She heard a clunk as he dropped his handgun. Then it got even darker; one of the others had thrown a blanket over the intruder's face, blinding Jan, as well.

She heard a grunt of surprise and pain, and another body fell across her legs. While the second man was distracted by her attack, Saldivar found the rifle and hit him clumsily but effectively with the barrel.

Janet struggled wildly to extricate herself; she got one arm and her head free of the blanket in time to see the third man come through the window. The others were still facing the door and did not see him; against the faint moonlight in the window, she could see his arms in silhouette, raising a weapon. She felt a cold anger that absorbed her fear and seemed to illuminate the room like a searchlight. Her free hand found the cold metal of the gun. She raised it like an extension of her arm and squeezed the trigger. She grimaced in anticipation of the noise, but the only sound was a subdued *pop-pop* as the silhouette at the window vanished.

She clawed her way free of the weight on top of her and sprang across the room; her first thought was to see if the intruder needed medical aid. But when the light went on, she saw that she had hit him between the eyes and at the base of the throat. She made it to the sink in time to throw up.

"Thanks, Janney. You really saved our collective ass that time," Lyn said soberly.

But Jan was crying and shaking. "You said, 'Next time, shoot him,' " she stammered. "But I'm a doctor. I'm a *doctor*. I'm not supposed to kill people."

Saldivar held her tightly until he could feel the trembling lessen. He felt as if it had been a hundred years since he was that young. "Sometimes you don't have a choice, chica. Somebody's going to die. You just try to pick who."

Janet heaved a long sigh; he could almost feel the weight settling on her shoulders.

"Triage," she said sadly. "I know. But it's different when you do it yourself. It really is. I didn't think I could. But when I thought they were going to hurt you, I just went berserk."

"Check the two on the floor here," Saldivar said, nudging the nearest with one foot. "I don't think he's dead; I couldn't hit him hard enough from where I was. And I know this one's alive. He'll wake up in a minute. We're gonna have to figure out what to do with them."

"While you take a look, I'll lug the body out," Lyn said cheerfully. "Put him in the shower and pull the curtain. At least we won't have to look at him."

Janet examined the others and felt somewhat better when she discovered that they were still alive and relatively undamaged. Nothing seemed to be fractured.

'Yeah, but we can't leave them that way," Lyn said uncomfortably. She dropped an impressive load of armaments on the floor. "Look at all the shit I took off this one chuck. And I probably missed something. They're pros. Gagging him won't be much use."

"Yes, they're pros all right," Janet said. "So I assume that if they'd wanted to kill us right away, they'd have done so. Give me that pouch."

She ran a finger over the neatly ranged supplies and pulled out a small disposable injector.

"I thought so."

"What is it?"

"The name wouldn't mean anything; I think it's supposed to be a military secret. They started using it on Singer when syndorphin didn't work. They wanted us alive. Ugh." She shuddered.

"Lucky for us," Lyn said cheerfully.

But Saldivar met Janet's eyes with perfect understanding.

"I'm starting to feel better about shooting that one, and I feel fine about shooting the other ones up," she said fiercely. "You can gag them, too, but this will hold them as long as will do us any good."

They rolled the unconscious men onto the mattress and covered them with blankets. Lyn had finished mopping up the floor.

"We'd better get moving," she said. "It'll be sunrise pretty soon. I can take off as soon as they finish loading."

"How long do you think we have before someone notices that we haven't been delivered on schedule?" Jan asked.

"Hard to say," Saldivar replied. "These two had no radio, so they weren't expected to report. But that means they probably had a backup team waiting someplace. I'd expect them to use gas if they think there's any trouble. We don't want to wait for that."

"We better take a few minutes to pack," Lyn said. "We should take whatever's useful that we can carry. Food. All this shit from the visitors. We can stuff it in my bag. Paul, my man, you must put something on those legs. I think they are max right, but you will be thrown off the field if you go out like that.''

''I am not wearing any more dead men's pants,'' Saldivar said. ''Take the rags off the one in bed. If they don't fit, fuck it.''

He was so emaciated that the clothes hung loosely on him, but belted tight and tucked in, they looked fairly respectable.

He wrinkled his nose in disgust. ''You'd think a fucking major could take a bath every couple of years.''

Lyn wolfed the last bite of a candy bar and handed him a couple. ''Don't kick, you've been promoted. That's just the natural smell of an officer.''

''Hey,'' Jan protested mildly.

''I've got all the food that's portable, the ammo, and explosives,'' Lyn continued.

''I want to take these, too,'' Jan said.

''Hot pickles? Aren't things hot enough for you yet?''

''Just the jars,'' Jan said, dumping out the contents. ''A useful thing that one of my crazed humpers explained to me once. I'll show you later.''

She zipped her portable into its padded backpack, threw in a couple of chains full of tabs, and shouldered it. Lyn picked up her duffel bag; Saldivar took the silenced pistol and reloaded it. They moved quietly through the hall, past the still undisturbed sleepers, and out into the night.

The street was quiet, too, and it stayed quiet. When a truck passed three blocks away, they heard the tires whispering through the dust. However warily they walked, their rubber-soled feet made a sticky sound against the pavement like tape being peeled off a wall. They felt naked. In the east, clouds a shade lighter than the night sky lifted like an eyelid that would open soon and expose them to the glare of the sun.

Saldivar took a deep breath of the dry air and frowned.

''I thought it was raining,'' he said. ''I guess I dreamed it. It was raining so hard, I couldn't get up—it kept pounding me down. I'm sorry—I didn't even wake up till I heard the first one hit the ground.''

His skin prickled with fear as they hurried through the streets.

''The city's worse than the Dust,'' he muttered. There were too many hidden places, too many barriers, and no cover for a solitary fugitive. Lyn and Janet seemed alert but unworried. They reached the airfield without seeing anyone. The cargo hatch was still open; they climbed the ramp and went forward.

"All right, so we're safe as long as we're in the air," Lyn said. "But where do we go after that?"

"That depends," Jan said. "I think he'll head for North Fork. That's where his enemies are. But finding him before the fireworks start depends on Pablo mostly."

"Why me?" She could feel his wariness.

Lyn interrupted before she could explain. "Because he loves you, chuck. Yeah, I said love, so quit twitching."

He turned away, his face tight and grim.

"Bear in mind that we aren't totally sure he's the same species as us—so maybe you're even stranger than you think." She grinned. "Moreover, we're all in the same bag as far as that goes. The main thing is to find him, no?"

"How are we supposed to do that?" Saldivar asked.

"I'm not sure I can explain what I mean," Janet replied. "It would be easier to show you." She held out a hand to each of them.

"No. I don't want anyone messing with my head," Saldivar said.

"I don't want to mess with your head," Janet said patiently. "Maybe with other areas, if we get out of this alive, but your head is your own. It's just that if we want to find Singer, we have to speak his language."

The effort it took was like climbing uphill through heavy sand; slowly, reluctantly, he reached out and touched their hands.

He could feel something pulling on him. It felt like being drawn slowly into deep water—the moment of panic as he lost the feel of the ground and then the slow readjustment of balance as the new element supported him.

The first thing he sensed was Janet's presence. Singer always called her Zhanne—"shining." But to Saldivar she seemed restful and healing like water. The light in her was elusive like the light that played on water. When the watcher was patient and the water was quiet, the light would gather at the surface to reveal itself as a full circle, a face looking back. At last he stopped thinking of her as small and weak. Force could scatter the light but not destroy it.

He would not have willingly turned toward Lyn, but she beat on him like firelight on closed eyes. She was like a twisting flame: fierce, impatient, searching, burning out everything that got in her way. He had not wanted to believe that she was Singer's friend, but now he could understand it. She was swift and single-minded. Loving or hating, she would give it everything she had, and that was Singer's way.

She made Saldivar feel cold and stolid like a stone hunched in the rain. I've spent too long protecting myself. I built my own Tregua, and now I can't get out. He moved away from them; he did not want to, but their encroachment was unbearable. To his surprise, they let him go.

He stood in the old place with the ancient, illegal hunting rifle cradled in his thin arms, heavy but not too heavy for him to aim. It was so quiet that he could hear the mist gathering and falling in drops onto the wet oak leaves. He could hear their footsteps as they came toward him cautiously like young deer. They called to him. He hesitated for a long moment. Then he hooked the sling over a branch and stepped toward them, empty-handed.

They were not holding hands anymore; they had all drawn closer together till their arms crossed over each other's shoulders.

"I—" he started to say, and then finished it in the silent language. *—been on my own a long time. I didn't think I wanted it any different. But Singer—*

"The thing about Singer. He gave me back my eyes. You know how I used to go in the woods. I would sneak through the camp boundaries. They would have drilled me like a dog if they'd caught me, too. It was worth it to me to get out. That's why I came up. I thought I'd get out after a few years and have a place of my own. But after a while I couldn't even see anymore, just scan and process, like a cyborg or something. Even if I saw myself bleeding, I couldn't really feel it. It was like, 'Damage control, report!' 'Aye, sir—closing down sector C for repairs.'

"Maybe this isn't the right word, but when I was with him, I started to feel *human* again. I thought that was bad, but I don't now. Whatever happens today happens to *me*, not to some kind of machine they run till it gives out and then dump. He came and got me out of hell. Anybody who tries to hurt him again is gonna have to go through me. Not over me, *through* me."

He fell silent. Janet and Lyn closed up on either side of him in unspoken assent. They moved close enough that their shoulders just touched his, the way Singer used to do.

"It was raining," he said softly. "Raining hard—where he was."

27

Marcus Kruger listened to the rain. The North Fork weather reminded him of his boyhood. At least he thought it did. He could not really remember what the weather had been like then. It was too long ago. Truthfully, he did not like the rain that much anymore. He wanted the sweeping spaces of the highlands back, the wind-stroked flanks of those golden hills.

Times like this he missed Singer: times when every joint in his body racked him, when his gut hurt and his chest hurt and his blood seemed to crawl painfully around its circuit.

But it's not the disease that's gnawing you tonight, he thought. It's your heart that's hurting, isn't it, old man? Singer, Saldivar, and Bates. The very last of them.

You should never have let him go back to the Dust.

He looked out for you through those bad months, God knows why. Any fool could see he was in some kind of trouble. You should have done something for him.

But he was a proud boy, and silent. Not one to talk about his business, and never asked for help.

You should have helped him, anyway. It's too late now.

Ah, give it up, old man. You're hardly in a position to be helping anyone. Take the few days you've got left. Let the past go. Soon enough, none of it will matter anymore.

He knew the signs. The disease was getting worse again. Soon enough, they would be taking him back to the hospital, and he would not come out. The thought of dying did not hurt anymore. It was steadying, almost comforting. He could put aside grieving and regretting; there would be an end to it. He hung on because he hated the thought of dying so uselessly. If he could have achieved one victory to make up for the losses, it would have been all right. But there was no longer much chance of that.

The sound took a minute to register: He thought he had heard something at the door. It could not have been; it must have been branches rapping each other in the wind. He heard it again. He debated. He hated going to the door in his wheelchair, to sit gazing up at the visitor like a child, but it was not easy to get up and walk anymore.

Come on, old man, he told himself. How many more visitors are you going to get in this lifetime? Can't afford to turn them away. Maybe it's death himself, come for you in person.

Laboriously, he wheeled himself to his cane and levered himself out of the chair. His joints protested at the extra weight, but he got his balance and shuffled across the room to the door.

The face was gaunt under layers of sunburn and grime, and the Dustrags were truly rags and plastered close by the rain—but it was Singer. There was silence except for the background rattle of rain in the pitchy dark and a distant rumble of sullen thunder.

"But you're dead," Kruger whispered.

"Maybe you and me both are dead," Singer said. "But we're here. Long time been traveling to see you, Makho. You going to let me in?"

It was the voice that convinced him that Singer was really there. He reached out and touched the apparition's arm, and it was solid and real under his fingers. He stood aside and let Singer come in.

Singer stood there dripping; he rubbed a hand over his head as if he could not believe it had stopped raining on him.

"The bathroom's in there," Kruger said. "Get those wet things off."

Singer stared at him as if he had forgotten how to speak Delteix, but followed where his finger pointed. Kruger heard him sit down heavily on the edge of the tub, heard him hiss with pain as he worked his boots off. He knew he did not have any spare clothes that would fit, but he found a blanket.

"Are you hungry?" he called. "Of course you're hungry."

He dragged himself back to the kitchen for food and a hot drink.

"Where've you been? What happened up there?" he asked, leaning across the table. He kept wanting to touch Singer to be sure he was real.

Singer folded slices of bread in half and ate them methodically, two bites to a slice.

"What happened?" Kruger insisted.

"Just like last time. Somebody knew where we were."

"What about the others?"

Singer stared at the floor. "Don't know. Golos didn't make it. His body was there. Bates, Bear—they were gone, couldn't find them."

"Saldivar?"

Singer was silent for a long time. "Looked for him," he said finally. "I looked. You were right, Makho. Many days to the north, there are camps. They held him there."

"But did he—"

Singer made a small gesture that said "Do you see him? Is he here?"

"I'm sorry," Kruger said. He started to clench his fists, but he could not close his fingers and ended up rapping his hands helplessly against the tabletop.

"We have to keep fighting for the ones who are left," he said. "You saw this camp? Could you find it on a map?"

Singer nodded. "You still have those maps?"

"How did you find out about those?"

Singer shrugged. "They helped. Part I saw was right."

"Will you come with me? Will you talk to those bastards at PCOM? You're a witness. They won't listen to me, but they can't ignore you. Will you tell them?"

Singer just looked at him, and Kruger felt the tremendous weariness that he was keeping on top of doggedly, like a man riding a spar in a heavy sea.

"Sorry," he said. "You're tired. We can talk later. How the hell did you get here, anyway? You look ground to the metal."

Singer gave him the familiar don't-be-stupid look and stretched one battered foot out from under the table. "Walked."

"What? From where?"

"From the camp."

"From north of Guijarro? Are you crazy? You mean you didn't stop for medical attention? You didn't report at Guijarro?"

Singer almost smiled. "Worse than absent, Con-el. I'm dead. Remember? Wanted to stay that way."

"But why?"

"How many times do I let them try? We're all dead now, all but you and me. Would I be here if I had stopped at Guijarro?"

"But your own unit—they wouldn't have—"

"Bates. Saldivar. They were my unit. Who put that poison in your blood, Makho? You trust anyone, you are a fool." His teeth showed in a merciless grin. "Take me to see your bastards, Makho. Yes, we will *talk*."

He made the word sound like an obscenity.

Kruger cleared his throat awkwardly. "Sounds like you've got some things on your mind, too. Maybe you and I had better do some talking in the morning."

"I come from the dead, and come morning, I go back to the dead." There was a fey calm in Singer's voice, as if he had already set himself beyond discussion.

Kruger tried once more to reach him. "I'm so damn glad to see you, Singer. It's like a miracle."

Singer only grinned again. "Ah, a mir-a-cle," he enunciated carefully. "But what god is running with us? Guess and throw the bones."

He refused to take Kruger's bed; he curled up on the floor in his old way. Kruger did not get the feeling anymore that Singer wanted to protect him. If he slept on the floor, it was because he felt safer there. Kruger lay awake for some time, worrying about him. He had a strong feeling that it was not smart to take Singer to PCOM, but he wanted to so badly that he could taste it: a man who had *seen* and come back. Whatever twisted policy had made them hide the prisoners, they *could not* deny it after that.

If I turn him loose, God knows what will happen to him. He'll do something crazy, and they won't understand because they don't understand how crazy people can get out in the Dust. If I keep him with me, maybe this time I can help him.

Kruger woke up in the middle of the night and leapt to his feet before he remembered that his legs did not work so well anymore. There was a horrible snarling noise in the living room, as if Singer were wrestling with a wolf. Kruger foundered toward the door and slapped the switch. As the light went on, Singer whipped around and aimed a flying kick at his head, missing him by inches. He landed in the middle of the floor and stood there panting, still braced to lash out in any direction, slowly coming down out of the nightmare.

"Sorry," he muttered. He looked around at the walls, absently rubbing the old scars on his wrists. He looked at his hands, convincing himself they were undamaged. "I'm not—no. I dream. Ayei, dreams. Red and black." He shuddered.

"Sit," Kruger said. He knew better than to go near him yet. "I'll get you a drink."

He remembered that Singer liked bourbon and poured him four fingers. Singer drank it in a couple of swallows.

"That's good," he said. "But it don't help. Nothin' helps anymore. They can't sleep."

"Who, Singer?" Kruger asked him gently.

"I close my eyes, I see the fire, and they call my name, but I can't find them. Only the fire. Like smoke on the wind they are gone, and the fire of their going, it burns me, burns me."

He ground his fist against his mouth. He was biting the back of his hand till it bled.

Kruger touched him and felt the muscles jumping and shivering like spooked horses.

"They're gone, son. Let them go. I don't mind telling you I cried for those guys we lost. But it didn't bring them back."

Singer shook his head violently. "No. No. They want their names back. When I say the names, I will remember. And when I remember, I will die."

Sweat ran down his face like tears. His skin was hot to the touch.

"You're burning up," Kruger said. "You need help."

"There's only one kind of help I need."

He grasped Kruger's wrists. His grip was still like iron. Kruger flinched in spite of himself, though he tried to keep his eyes steady.

"You afraid of me now?" Singer asked. He laughed, and it was a frightening sound. "I am not like your kind, to throw away my brothers. No. Your own people scored on you so much better than I ever could. I take what I need by force, so you can say afterward you betrayed no one. But it won't kill you."

Kruger waited; he did not have the strength to struggle. Singer's fingers burned into his wrists like hot metal. Kruger realized, with a disturbing lack of alarm, that he felt no fear. He seemed to have lost his concentration; he was not even thinking about what to do. Instead, stray tags of memory drifted through his mind, moments of conversation with Singer, remnants of even earlier times that he had thought were lost for good. He wondered vaguely if he had had a stroke. He had already lost control of his body; his thoughts moved aimlessly, as if someone else were turning them over, looking for a clue to a pattern.

Suddenly that other eye found what it was looking for, and he was pinned down.

"Why do you call me son?" Singer asked. "Your son is dead."

They could not keep the grass down; it was already flopping raggedly over the marker like a derelict's hair. Plants and insects multiplied, though uncounted numbers of them were crushed. Only people did not thrive. When he left, there had been a town there. When he returned, with his captain's insignia new and fresh on his shoulders, the scars where the houses had been were already fading. There was nothing left of them but the names on the marker. His son's name drew his eye without his willing it: his own name among the dead, his wife's name beside it. By the time he could come back again, even the names would be effaced. He wished he had not worn his uniform. If he had come in a farmer's shirt and jeans, he could have thrown himself on the wet ground and grieved. But the pressed cloth held him stiffly upright; it would not let him fall.

Long years and thousands of miles had worn away the sharp edges of his grief, but now he felt it piercing him again as if he had just learned, for the first time, of his family's death.

"Stop it," he said inaudibly. If the pressure on his wrists had relaxed, he would have fallen to his knees. But Singer, having found a usable reference point, probed ruthlessly through his mind. Singer uncovered all his other dead—faces he had forgotten himself—as if turning over fallen stones from a ruined city. Old losses raged and burned in him again like a dying fire whipped to life again by a strong wind.

Singer's contempt was cold against him.

They killed your children, and you didn't make them pay?

It was a relief when Singer found what he was looking for. He saw all the offices Kruger had ever visited, and the faces of the men he had pled with, argued with, raged at. He saw the place where Kruger had stolen the maps. From some detached level, Kruger watched himself remembering things he had been unaware he knew. He found that he had underestimated Singer. The mind that seized on names, faces, and architectural details almost faster than he could recall them was strange but frighteningly intelligent.

The plundering of his memories slowed and stopped, but Singer did not let him go. The grip on his wrists became a ring of fire that spread down through his fingers and then up his arms. His whole body burned and tingled. The heat grew inexorably, a terrifying sensation as if he might explode into flames. It hurt, first in his joints, then burning in his chest and belly till it seemed that his blood was on fire. It reached a pitch that seemed unbearable; then slowly, it ebbed away.

Singer loosed his hands. Kruger slumped forward onto the table. He felt weak as water, but he did not seem to be hurt, at least not outwardly.

"What did you do to me?" he asked hoarsely.

"Nothing bad. I think. To your body. About the other, I am sorry. I had to know. Only the men in the tower matter. The rest, your business." The crazy look was gone. Nothing showed in his face but exhaustion and deep sadness.

"What are you going to do tomorrow?"

"I will talk to them in a way they can understand," Singer said grimly. "I will sleep in your house tonight, because I am very tired. Don't move against me while I sleep. You don't have the speed."

He started to get up but turned back again.

"I am sorry your son died. All your sons. I have no sons; I had brothers."

He touched Kruger's wrist again, but lightly. "Let me do what I must do. You cannot stop me. Don't try. Please, Makho. If you owe me something, pay me this way: Don't make me hurt you."

He stumbled toward the bed, fell on it, and was asleep as he fell. Kruger pulled the blanket over him. Cautiously, he sat down on the other side of the bed. Singer stirred uneasily; Kruger watched, wondering if Singer was going to leap up again and break his neck. Instead the sleeping man flung out one hand to touch Kruger and then became still, as if he recognized him even in his sleep.

Kruger tried to sort out his thoughts, like a man picking up the files after his office had been ransacked. Asleep, with his damp, too-long hair falling over his face, Singer looked pathetically young to be so scarred and worn out. He looked helpless. But Kruger had no doubt that if he moved to the door or the telephone, Singer would be on him like a wild animal. He had never encountered a will as sharp and indomitable as the one that had held him that night. He had thought of Singer as lonely, silent, illiterate, a bit simple, really, in spite of his natural talent for tracking and killing. Now he realized that those thoughts had been subtly arranged for him and that he had accepted them without asking any of the obvious questions. He had been set up.

He tried to remember the days when Singer had worked for him.

Funny. What I see is the top of his head, mostly. Always hunched over, working on something. Making himself inconspicuous. He hardly ever looked me right in the eyes, and when he did, I always believed him. I believed he was a homeboy from the mountains. That's ridiculous. There's training in everything he does, just not our kind of training.

Singer was unique. Kruger did not know if he was trying to protect Singer from his superiors or them from Singer. But he knew for sure that he was not going to leave him on his own again.

Eventually Kruger slept, but lightly. He kept waking up and checking to see that Singer was still there. He woke up one last time; light came in the uncurtained windows. Singer was not with him, but to his great relief he heard sounds of movement in the next room and knew that he had not left yet. He reached automatically for his crutches, but they were not by the bed where he always left them. He thought about calling for help, but his pride revolted. He had already been helpless once in front of Singer.

He pushed himself up on the edge of the bed, eyeing the distance to the door. He thought he could make it that far; the crutches had to be in the living room. He gritted his teeth as he put weight on his feet, but the expected pain never landed. He took three light steps to the door and seized hold of the frame; nothing hurt anywhere. Stepping through that doorway felt like stepping out the hatch on his first jump.

"Singer!" he shouted.

Singer came out of the bathroom. He had washed and had combed his hair till it shone like gold again. He had smoothed out his battered clothing as well as he could. He looked as if he were preparing for a party.

"What it is?"

"This!"

Kruger held out his hand, flexing the fingers to their full extension, then clenched his fist till it went white. The knuckles no longer stood out like knots in old wood.

"You quit, Makho," Singer said. "Now I take that away from you. Not going to let you crawl off and die. Now you have to choose."

Kruger looked down at himself. He had the old familiar body back, but it had become as strange to him as a new planet. Something had happened, and the wonder of it was greater than the fear.

"I'm coming with you, son," he said.

Singer's eyes darkened. "No."

"You're getting above yourself, boy," Kruger roared. The force of his voice amazed him. He had not been able to shout like that in years. "Who put you in charge of me? Do I look like I need a nursemaid? You aren't thinking straight. You wouldn't get through the door without me.

"I'll cut you a deal: I take you as far as Gero's office. After that, you're on your own, I'm on my own. Deal?"

Singer stared at him. Finally the ghost of a smile crossed his face.

"Deal," he said. He held up his fist, and Kruger rapped knuckles with him.

"Let's go."

"You want me to drive?" Singer offered.

"I didn't want to hurt your feelings before," Kruger said, "but you are the worst driver I've ever seen. I haven't been able to drive in over a year, but I can do better than that."

He did not call ahead; he figured the less time they had to prepare for him, the better. His ID got him through the gate; the guards there did not care who he was, only that he had clearance.

He stopped at the front desk.

"General Kruger to see Mr. Gero," he said.

"One moment, please; I'll buzz Mr. Gero's office," the receptionist replied automatically. When the response came back through her earplug, she gave them a sharper look.

"Mr. Gero is not expecting you," she said. Recognition appeared in her eyes. She was too well trained to say it, but Kruger could almost hear her thinking: Aren't you the one who's supposed to be dying?

"I'm sure there's a mix-up. He does want to see me. Tell him we're here to discuss the Clausewitz file."

He spoke quite loudly and saw with peripheral vision how several heads turned toward his voice. The Net was still leaky, then.

"Please step inside," she said hastily. She ushered them into the inner office, where a heavy soundproof door closed behind them. Shortly she came back. "Mr. Gero will see you now."

A husky, well-pressed sergeant appeared and escorted them through an exit that led to elevators, not back to the lobby. He took them to the fifth floor and walked them down the hall, staying half a step behind them and to their left. Kruger thought hard as they neared their destination. Singer did not appear to be armed, but he never went anywhere without his knives. Kruger could not imagine why he would be there if not to take Gero out. Gero, and possibly other people, too. But why? Because he held them responsible for the destruction of Kruger's command? That makes sense for me but not for him. I'm missing something here, he thought frantically.

He knew that the sergeant was armed. Possibly there was more protection around Gero that he did not know about. If Singer made a move, he would be annihilated.

Maybe I can talk fast enough, work on Gero with what I know, get them to sit down and talk it over. I have to stop them from trying to take Singer into custody; he'd go berserk.

They entered another outer office. The door closed behind them; the sergeant stood at ease beside it. A man came through the inner door.

"Donohue, would you step out?" he said to the secretary. She vanished unobtrusively.

"Marcus, wonderful to see you looking so well," he continued. Kruger heard him, but at the same time he felt, like heat from molten steel, the intense rage rising in Singer.

"And this is—?"

Simultaneously, Kruger saw Gero freeze as he got a good look at Singer's face and felt Singer gathering himself to move.

"Singer. My name is Singer."

Kruger realized too late what was about to happen.

"Don't—" he shouted, just in time to spoil Singer's move. Gero hit the deck behind his desk as Singer loosed his knife and came flying after it. Kruger turned around and saw the guard at the door sinking into a crouch, the barrel of his gun wavering as he tried to decide where he should aim. Without thinking about it, Kruger flung himself between Singer and the gun. The guard did not expect to be jumped by an old man with stars on his shoulders, and Kruger reached him before he could bring himself to fire.

They went down together in a confused tangle; the gun went off several times before the guard lost his hold on it. Kruger felt a brief surge of triumph that suddenly vanished. His throat spasmed shut. Heart attack? Blinded by tears, he wheezed for breath and vomited violently. They were pumping gas into the room.

God in heaven, what a fucking mess! was his last conscious thought.

28

Singer was hurt by the fall and enraged by Kruger's stupidity. But he was not too preoccupied to notice that the man he called Cold Eyes had glanced sharply toward the top edge of the wall, lined with small, unobtrusive grilles. He caught the first bitter hint of something in the air that was not right and did as his quarry: held his breath and scrambled for the inner office. He scooped up his knife as he went.

Gero fled through a connecting door into the next room. The gas attacked through eyes and skin even if he did not breathe, Singer found. Gero was doubled over and choking as he went through the door, and Singer's eyes and nose were streaming so that he was half-blind. He reached the door but could not see his enemy when he got there. Vaguely he glimpsed the shape of another man rising from behind another desk. He did not trust himself to aim; he jumped the desk and kicked the man in the face as he went by.

He tore off his shirt as he lunged after Gero. It burned his skin; he thought the gas must have soaked into it. When he looked out into the hall, he saw two armed men racing toward him and concluded that Gero must have gone in that direction.

When they burst into the room, he was crouched on top of a set of shelves. The gas was not like smoke; it was heavy and sank toward the ground, so it was easier to control his breathing up there. The men looked around at eye level; neither seeing nor hearing him, they hurried toward the far door. He felled one of them with his knife, then landed on the other and broke his neck. Once he had their fire weapons, he, too, could kill at arm's length.

He was in the quicksilver calm of harrarne again. The familiarity of it comforted him. Perhaps he could stay in it to the very end. There would be no need to come back to the slow pain of ordinary time, to the ache of damaged flesh, the sullen cold of nightfall, or the counting of the dead. He was living in the swiftness of light, in a world where a flick of shadow spoke a name and death's smile could be heard in the whisper of a folded sleeve, where his breath sucked the life-giving sweetness from the air the way fire sucked at dry wood. There was nothing to stop him from burning out like a falling star. He had erased the tracks behind him that could have drawn him back to earth.

He could see clearly the map he had drawn from Makho. There were seven offices in that corridor. Each of them held a man who had known and consented to the destruction of the People. Harlan was dead. The other dead man, in this room, had to be one of them. He and the one in the next office wore the soldiers' clothing and belonged to Nymann, who was called *jenh-ralh* and was the master of this city. But it was the others who were truly dangerous: Cold Eyes and his two captains, who had no special marks to show what they were but who moved faster and saw farther than the soldiers. All of those must die. He gave a fleeting thought to Makho, left in their poison air. But Makho had made his choice.

There were others: the man called Simonds who had gone with Cold Eyes and the others who had flown the death birds that brought the fire. But they had only followed, unknowing. Time for them later—he would cut off the snake's head and let the tail move while it could. A part of him knew there was no later and felt cheated, but he returned himself quickly to concentration on the present.

Those halls were a trap: straight walls, no place to hide. They expected him there; they had not expected him up above. Remembering Mooney and the hospital, he went up the shelves again and moved aside one panel in the ceiling grid. Cautiously he took hold of the metal supports and pulled. They gave a little under his weight, but they held. He lay spread-eagled in the space above and inched himself along.

The map in his head told him that he was beyond the room wall; he heard voices and sensed a large group of people below him. He worked the panel loose in time to see another set of guards herding them into one of the offices. He grinned; that would make his job easier. He moved sideways, inch by inch, till he could look down into the room.

The women were huddled together in one corner, and that made things easier, too. Killing slaves was wrong and pointless, but he had already decided that he could not afford to make distinctions. If they got in his way, they were dead; if they stayed apart, he would let them live. The men had gathered near the door, trying to take control of the situation. There were half a dozen, but not all those on his list were there. One, a man with dark skin like Bates, he recognized from Makho's memory; there was another at the desk, whose room it was. He knew that Nymann was absent, because Nymann would have stars like Makho's. There were leaves and birds of prey—no stars. But it would do for a start.

He braced his arms securely and unleashed his weapon. Death from above: There was an ugly humor to it. He could feel them dying, a dark song cut short, while the high harmony of the women's terror continued. He cut down the guards as they came back through the door. One of them thought fast enough to aim upward as he fell, and Singer rolled sideways to avoid the line of bullets.

The shots warned him that he was not permanently safe up there; soon he would have to move down and try to get something more solid between himself and their weapons than the thin white ceiling panels. As he rolled, he glanced around for anything more he could gain while he was still up there.

The dusty space above the ceiling extended a long way. In one direction he saw something like a metal shaft—possibly another passage to an unexpected reappearance. He scrambled that way and found a door in the side of the shaft. It was small and opened into darkness. A cable ran downward, and below him something was moving. He sprayed it with fire. The cable held, but bursts of sparks flashed briefly, and something parted. When the sparks faded, the thing had stopped moving. He decided that he was better off not trusting to an unknown darkness.

But he knew he had to get down from there quickly. He had been making enough noise that they would find him soon. He would have to go down and try to find Gero in his own house—a game of fox and hare but played out in a maze of walls, not on friendly earth where he would have been at home. Where would Cold Eyes go? Certainly he would not freeze like a frightened rabbit. The others were animals, but he was a beast that thought. He would find the maximum advantage for himself. Suddenly he knew what Gero would do: He would go back for Makho. Then he would make himself safe, somewhere, with that source of information and wait for his enemy to come to him. Singer listened, listened, and finally found what he thought was Makho—the half-formed dream mutterings of a deeply unconscious man. Slowly he moved toward that trace.

Behind him, in the elevator he had fired on, he left fifteen men, armed with riot control weapons and explosives, jammed together in the dark. An armored security elevator, it would take some time to open from the outside.

Ahead of him, Gero crouched in Nymann's office with the general, three guards, and a medic. Kruger's body was laid out on the desk. He was still unconscious, though Gero had ordered oxygen and stimulants administered. They were the last living men left on the floor; they had heard the screaming women run down the hall toward the stairs. Gero peered intently into the screens that showed the view from the hidden cameras that constantly scanned each room. He switched rapidly from one camera to another, looking for something he could not find.

"Damn it, he's got to be here," he muttered. "Where is that security team I called for?

"Get him conscious," he snapped at the medic. "I have to talk to him right away!"

His fingers paused on the keys.

"The ceiling," he breathed. "There are no cameras up there. All right, you snake, we've got you. You'll come to us."

He positioned two guards at cross corners of the room, one just beyond the connecting door in the next room, and himself behind the desk where Kruger lay. He was ignoring Nymann as if the general really did not matter. Then he signed for absolute silence, and they waited.

Singer did not have to hear them to find them. He could not tell exactly where the others were, but he could feel the dull flicker that was Kruger, surrounded by enemies. His intuition told him that Cold Eyes would have set a trap for him, with Kruger as the bait. Gero did not yet understand that he himself was the bait. All the subtlety of movement that Singer had lost among the soldiers had come back to him in his days on the hills with Saldivar. He used it to move noiselessly toward the listening men. When he knew he was close, when he knew that Kruger was no farther away then the next wall, he stopped. He had to find out where they were without showing himself; he was not in a hurry to spring their trap.

Taking a chance, he stretched out the rifle barrel as far from himself as possible and tapped once. He heard the faint, startled intake of breath from the man below. He fired through the panels at the sound and smashed feet first through the ceiling, still firing. He rolled as he hit and came up in a low crouch. He was looking through the doorway into the room where Kruger was. The soldier who had guarded that doorway was dying in the corner. Ahead of him he could see Kruger, gulping raggedly for air and trying to sit up. Cold Eyes had a tight lock on him from behind and was grinning over his shoulder at Singer. It would not be hard to hit him if he did not mind killing Kruger.

Time stopped then for Singer. He knew that he was blowing his last chance. He was going to die with the blood of a thousand brothers still on his mouth. But he could not pull the trigger. He kept moving, but he knew with every move he made that he was done for. The dark shadow of the Soul-eater was on him, riding him down.

Still he turned and cut the legs from under the soldier he could see; he knew there was another one just beyond the wall, out of sight. Gero moved slightly in alarm as the soldier fell, leaving the ribs under his left arm exposed for a few seconds. It was not a conscious decision; Singer simply knew that he did not have the accuracy he needed with the strangers' weapon and pulled his last knife instead. It was a perfect throw; the point should have sunk deep between the ribs, but instead it fell and spun away across the floor. Cold Eyes was wearing something under his coat that turned edges.

Singer threw away thought with the alien rifle. The scream of rage that ripped from his throat as he hurled himself across the room was Deronh's old battle yell. He slammed to the ground, tearing his enemy loose from Makho in the fall, oblivious to the third man still armed to kill him. He was ready to tear Gero's throat out with his bare teeth. Cold Eyes fought him off frantically; Singer could feel the heavy layer of protection under his clothes, and the man had a warrior's strength. Even as he struggled, he gasped aloud, "Don't shoot! Don't shoot!"

The meaning of those words penetrated Singer's mind a single moment too late. He thrashed and rolled, gathering his feet under him for a mighty leap, but not quite soon enough. The last guard had loaded with antipersonnel rounds for close quarters. The blast, at two-meter range, missed its intended impact against Singer's chest, but it hit him across both legs.

Singer knew that something had happened to him, but he was too shocked and dazed to know what it was. He got up on his elbows, but his legs would not move. There was still a lot of noise around him, people yelling at each other.

"I told you to hold your fire! If he dies, I'll have you skinned alive."

Makho was cursing them, though he sounded like someone else because he was crying, too.

Singer could feel his legs again; someone was manhandling him.

"Dammit, hold still," they said to him. He was trying to crawl away from them. Part of the noise was himself, moaning. Gero's para seemed to be trying to stop him from bleeding; he could feel the floor around him wet and slick already.

"Get him upstairs, to security. General, you too. All of you," the cold voice said. "We have to assume he's not alone."

The para's face loomed over him. It seemed very large and pale, and the mouth hung open.

"I need a stretcher, I need a medical team," the mouth said stupidly. "I can't move him. Look at him—he's shredded."

"Do it!"

They grasped him by the shoulders and thighs. As they lifted, he got a brief glimpse of the sodden, dangling mess that was his legs, and he felt a tearing pain as if giant claws were ripping him apart. He fought against their grip, but they kept dragging him.

They paused briefly somewhere out in the hall.

"The elevator's out. More sabotage. Get to the stairs—quickly."

They carried him up and up, the pain intensifying with every step.

He was briefly relieved when at last they set him down on a hard bed like a table, but then they tied him down with straps across his arms and chest. The agony in his legs could not get any worse, but he was sick with fear as well. All he could do was rock his head and bite his lips ragged, but he could not even feel that.

He wanted to call on his memories, on all the disciplines that should have come to his assistance, but his mind stayed empty and his body would not comply.

I wouldn't remember and now I can't, he thought. I failed them, and they have left me.

Gero took Kruger into the next room.

"You didn't have to shoot him," Kruger said. "It didn't have to come to this. I brought him here because he wanted to talk to you. For God's sake, get him a real doctor! He has proof, proof that the camps really exist."

"Shut up," Gero shouted. "You think your amateur snooping is so important. You don't have a clue about what's really at stake. You've been violating classified treaty provisions since that fuckup last year. You've been warned to back off time and again; you've had direct orders! So now you're up to your neck in shit, and so are the rest of us, thanks to you.

"We already know this character you've been harboring is an assassin and a terrorist. It's absolutely essential to find out who he's working with and exactly what his objectives are. That's all that matters. Your imaginary POWs are irrelevant. One man's life is irrelevant. Do you understand?"

"What treaty?" Kruger asked. He could still hear Singer's cries of pain; he could not think.

Gero glared at him, breathing heavily. "I'm going to tell you, Kruger, just so you'll be under no illusions about your future. You'll be spending the rest of your short life on a closed ward. How pleasant that will be for you depends entirely on how much cooperation you can give me in the next couple of hours.

"The treaty in question regulates relations with the autochthonous peoples of this planet. Does that surprise you? The major clause of this treaty calls for complete secrecy on their existence until the problem is dealt with. Try to imagine what would happen back on the world if their existence became known. There would be agitation for us to roll back our colonization effort, give up the base. This planet is absolutely essential to our expansion; we can't let that happen. Furthermore, if fools like you do succeed in blowing the treaty open, all you'll accomplish is to hand the place to the Union on a platter. I'm prepared—and authorized—to go any length necessary to prevent that.

"But we have an immediate problem, right now. Do you know what that madman next door has done? He has wiped out the entire top end of my staff and two of General Nymann's key aides. God knows what his friends have been up to while we stand around chatting. He has to talk now, before it's too late to put a stop to this carnage."

Singer screamed again, and Kruger shuddered.

"What you're doing is wrong," he said desperately. "It's inhuman."

Gero laughed nastily. "Inhuman? Do you call that thing in there human?

"If you've lost all sense of duty to your own government, at least maintain some loyalty for your own race."

"What about the men in my command? The ones you set up to be killed? Were they human?"

"They were members of the Consorso, here to serve their nations and their federation. Too bad you saw fit to waste their lives on your private curiosity.

"I'll tell you what to worry about, if you're concerned about lives. Worry that the Union has already broken the treaty, that they're recruiting and arming the natives against us. If that's what's happening, he's going to tell us. I don't care what I do to him to get that information.

"Now, are you going to help me or not?"

"What do you want me to do?" Kruger asked stupidly.

"You have his confidence. Talk to him. Tell him we'd like to help him, but we can't till he gives us the information we need. Tell him not to jerk us around. He's going to lose his legs if he stalls."

Singer searched wildly for a way out of his agony, or if not for a way out, for some way to strike back. He could not break through the straps. Weapons—there was nothing within reach. The pain in his legs—the pain was like a pattern of fire, a separate searing spark for each tear, each shattered fragment. There was something familiar in that thought, and he ground his teeth and tried to block out the feel of the doctors' knives digging into his flesh.

The weapon he had used on Harlan had had a pattern in it, something he could touch without hands. It had frightened him then. He hungered for that bitter, scorching flavor. He found it, somewhere below him, in an iron box. To his amazement, the box was still full of men. They were carrying the weapons with them. He felt along the lines of force; the fire wanted to rejoin itself. The changes needed were small. At first nothing happened. He tried again. It almost seemed as if the little sparks were grateful to him for setting them free. They rushed together and blossomed out into a ball of blinding energy. It took only one to catch hold of the others; they were packed tightly.

It was not so good for the men. Those who were closest to the door finished prying it open and got out, leaving the scorched bodies of the others behind. Fire glowed and flared against the metal, and secretly the walls on the other side began to darken and smoke.

The results came to his dulled exterior senses a little later. The floor shook and rumbled with the muffled explosions. The others in the room uttered startled exclamations; Singer laughed, and they stared at him. He knew they were frightened.

It was a scrap of victory for him to take with him. The effort had taken what remained of his strength. A buzzing numbness crept over him, and his surroundings faded away from him.

"Do you still want to maintain he's harmless?" Gero shouted, dragging Kruger along with him. "There's someone in here with him."

"There can't be," Kruger insisted. "I *know* he's alone. You're wrong."

Singer was no longer struggling. His eyes bobbed erratically.

"What's going on?" Gero snarled. "I don't want him passing out."

"We're going to have to give him a rest," the doctor said apologetically. "I don't think he can take much more of this. Give him some recovery time and you could interrogate him indefinitely. But we're going to lose him if you keep the pressure on."

"No rest," Gero ordered. "Not for a minute. He gets a rest when he tells me what I want to hear. Bring him back up—now."

Singer felt their poison spreading through him as he was jerked back to consciousness. His hands burned, and his heart squeezed violently, pumping the drugs through his depleted body. They did not want him to die yet, but they would not be able to stop him for long.

Another face bent over him; it was Kruger again.

"Get away from me," Singer said weakly.

"I know you don't trust me," Kruger said. "But you have to tell these people something. They'll kill you. It isn't worth it. Give them something—it doesn't matter what. Is there someone else out there?"

"Dead men and demons," Singer said. But he was speaking Thanha.

"Shit," Gero said. "Not this routine again. Get on with it. I want him to remember his Delteix."

As he was dragged out, Kruger saw them start placing electrodes.

A very small part of Singer's mind remembered his name. The rest of him was being consumed. His body convulsed. His legs would no longer obey him, but they cramped and jerked under the power of the invisible fire, tearing themselves apart. The pain was one torment; the subtler torture was the panic of his body, screaming to him from a hundred places that it was being destroyed. This was no wound that would heal if he endured; it was death eating him alive. His strength, which had carried him so long, could not help him; he could only turn against himself to go as quickly as possible into the darkness at the edge of the fire.

The darkness was not the clear starlit night of the Heroes' Road; it was thick and smoky. It smelled like ashes; it moved with uneasy shadows. In a space between convulsions, one of them reached out and touched him.

"Dona?" he gasped as pain seized him again.

"Did he say something?"

"More monkey talk."

29

Saldivar was very still; even his breathing slowed and softened. Jan moved to offer him support but thought better of it; she was afraid to break his concentration.

His eyes snapped wide open.

"Oh," he said. "Oh. Oh, my God."

The color drained from his face like bourbon sucked from a glass of ice. He crumpled to his knees and then all the way to the floor.

"What's happening? What's the matter?" Jan said.

"My kamarh," he whispered in an ashy, distant voice that did not sound like his own. "If they hurt me enough, you'd come." He stopped responding at all.

Janet pulled his head onto her lap and tried to straighten him out, but he was curled inflexibly into a fetal position. Lyn grabbed his hands.

"Hold on to him, Janney!" she said. "I can't reach him at all. What's going on?"

"He's found Singer," she said in a voice hardly louder than Saldivar's had been. "He's hanging on; he doesn't have the attention for anything else. Singer's trying to throw him out; he doesn't want us to be there."

"How bad is it?"

"How bad do you think, if just tuning in does this to Paul? They're killing him. Madre'dio, what have I done to him! I didn't think it would be so bad. I thought he'd find him, but I didn't think he'd get hurt."

Lyn gasped as she finally made contact with them.

Where . . . Inside. He's inside. A hospital? No, soldiers!

Up. He thought they took him up a long way.

PCOM, Jan asserted with finality. *Tallest building around. I was in the flash room with Jon once. Computer system on fourth floor; controlled climate, protection. Holding cells on top floor. Soundproof floor. Security-lock elevators.*

PCOM. Lyn groaned. *The tower.*

She cried out involuntarily as they caught another flash of agony from Singer.

"Stop it," Jan said carefully, aloud. "This won't do us any good. Paul's so tight with him, I don't think I can bring him out of it. That's good in a way. Singer's laying some of the pain off onto him. It'll help. Anyway, Paul has to stay with him so we can keep a fix on him. But you and I have to be able to think. Try to disengage. Some, anyway."

"How can we get to him? We can't walk! They wouldn't let us in, anyway."

Jan laid Saldivar carefully on the floor in front of the seats. She got a blanket out of Lyn's bag and covered him with it. "Round up your crew. Our only hope is to find Singer fast."

"How the hell are we going to do that? Didn't you tell me the place was a fortress?"

"Get the panel off your board," Janet ordered. "I want to look at your ignition switch."

Lyn stared at her in shock. "You can't fuck with my controls!"

"Watch me. I need to reprogram your autopilot. But that doesn't do me any good if I can't turn the engines on."

"Oh, no. I know what you're thinking, but it won't work. That autopilot is strictly to stabilize and keep us on course in clear air. You can't use it to take off."

"I don't want it to take off. I only want it to taxi. Let me see the airfield again."

She touched Lyn's arm and caught a picture of the hangars.

"There we go. Taxi, turn left, and accelerate. That should do it. Well, you asked how we were going to get in, didn't you? Create a diversion, that's how. A big one. Now, get that panel off!"

Lyn complied, fumbling. Janet reached into the side pocket of her backpack and pulled out a flat red piece of plastic.

"Jacks charged me an extravagant price for this. I can bypass a mechanical switch and run a pulse directly through the circuits by transmission. I told him I wanted it to turn on my desk at work. I used it that way a couple of times, too. It works fine."

She attached the bypass as she spoke, then motioned to Lyn to replace the panel.

"Get the crew. You can tell them I'm a programmer checking out some kinks in the system. Make up some story about Pablo. When I get through here, I'll do what I can for him."

Lyn was gone into the half dark of the cargo deck.

The flight seemed to stretch on forever, like those roads in hell that turned and twisted on themselves but never led out. No, that was Singer's hell. Grim minds those people had, Lyn thought. Dawn came over their shoulders as they flew. It gave her a strange, unattached feeling to fly so high after such a long time on the ground; below them, only gilded crests and purplish shadows marked the dunes and ravines they had crawled through for so many weary days. She felt as if they had already left the only life they knew, as if they were already dead. No! Those were Saldivar's memories, his thoughts. Fiercely she shoved them aside. To live, she had to think about flying, and to do that, she had to cut herself off from the shared agony she felt in Saldivar and from Janet's fear and remorse. It was like being under anesthesia but still conscious, knowing that an irreplaceable part of herself was being brutally damaged but unable to feel it or do anything about it. She wondered if that was Janet's memory or Pablo's.

The landing was bumpy. Her backup pilot peered at her anxiously as he unstrapped.

"You all right?"

"Nothing that another round of the same won't cure," she snapped. "Listen, I want you all to get well clear of the aircraft when you get out. The ticktack over there is running tests on the autopilot. If she screws up, I don't want anyone hurt. I don't like blood on my bird."

"Are you checked out on vitos?" Janet asked quietly when the crew had left.

"This is a hell of a time to ask me that. That was years ago."

"The alternative is driving a moto through the gate at PCOM. Ninety-nine percent certainty of instant death. Do you think our chances in the air are better than that?"

Lyn's eyes widened as she realized what Jan had in mind. "You're fucking nuts, girl," she protested. "We're gonna get killed."

"Quite possibly," Jan agreed.

"Jesus Christ. And I thought you were too soft."

"If we do it right, we won't hurt too many people. I hope. Help me with Pablo."

They rigged a makeshift stretcher and rolled him onto it, piling Lyn's duffel bag at his feet.

"This isn't going to fool anybody," Lyn grumbled. "With these packs on, we don't look like ducks, we look like a couple of poor dumb humpers."

Janet flagged down the nearest cargo scooter. "Get us to the vito pad. This man has to be transported to the hospital, fast."

The driver looked surprised but moved to help them with the stretcher.

"Don't touch him," Janet snapped. "We don't know what he's got. You will report to the nearest medical officer and consider yourself in restricted access. Tell the officer to call the hospital for a briefing."

The tires squealed as the scooter leapt forward.

As they approached the vito pad, Janet pulled the transmitter out of her backpack. "Brace yourself," she said to Lyn.

Lyn heard the familiar rumble as the engines came to life.

Then she was back in the familiar seat, settling her shoulders against the straps, smelling the unique mixture of age and freshness as the ghosts of a thousand smelly feet, of body bags, food crates, and old grime mingled with the always sharp, clean odors of fuel and lubricant. Slowly the aircraft lumbered left and out the hangar door. The pitch rose as the engines gained full power. They were gaining speed much faster than ever before; she felt the wheels skip once, twice, but the plane held the ground. She was screaming at the top of her lungs to match the scream of the engines as they plowed through the hangar wall and smashed into the sleek jets inside in a ball of fire and a roar of unbelievable noise.

Janet was shaking her, she realized in midscream. Her mouth was still open, but she was in the scooter, not in the demolished cockpit. She could still hear the thunderous multiple roar and feel the heat that enveloped the field, but it was a bearable distance from her skin.

"Come *on*," Janet muttered. "Am I going to have two gorks on my hands?"

Lyn fended her off weakly. "I'm okay," she panted.

"Then why are you crying?"

"I feel like I just shot my own dog. I loved that old bird."

"If there were people in there," Jan said grimly, "they're dead now. I made a vow to harm no one when I became a doctor, and now in one day I've blown out a guy's brains, misused powerful narcotics, and welded a hangarful of mechanics to their wrenches. So forget your airplane. It went down in a blaze of glory, which is about the best any of us can expect. Let's go."

"What's going down?" the driver was shouting. They ignored him, slid the stretcher off the back, and staggered toward the vito pad. The driver tore off toward shelter.

The regular standby pilot for the medical flight stood on the edge of the pad gaping at the fire cloud. They manhandled Saldivar and the duffel bag full of weapons on board, and Lyn took off. The pilot turned around and stared up at them as he finally realized what was happening, but he was too confused to do anything.

As they rose, they could hear alarms going off, and they could see shapes scurrying across the concrete as pilots scrambled to get their planes in the air and away from possible sabotage.

"Circle over to your right, Lyn; I want to give them something else to think about."

Jan rummaged in the bag for her pickle jars and the incendiaries they had taken from the dead man.

"Put them in jars and they won't bounce when they hit," she explained to Lyn. "Pablo, will you for God's sake tell me if I'm doing this wrong?" she added.

But Saldivar's eyes were wild.

"Burning, burning," he muttered.

"You got that right," Janet said. She armed the incendiaries, dropped them into the jars, and shoved the jars out onto the fuel tanks below. It seemed childishly simple. There was a small explosion as the first to hit breached the tank. Lyn saw what she was doing in time to bank sharply away from the fireball that followed; the vito rocked in the updraft. Lyn switched her tongue to full automatic and loosed a blast of hot words.

"Next time you do something like that, tell me!" she finished up.

"Sorry," Jan said meekly.

Thick plumes of black smoke had risen to wind level and started to smear across the sky as they turned away from the airfield. Their flight to the tower was unnoticed; they were a gnat escaping from a forest fire. Lyn swung wide to get a good look at the roof before landing; no defenses were visible, though she was sure they were there. As the vito settled slowly downward, she saw smoke rising from the lower floors of the building as well.

"That's good!" Lyn shouted. "It'll take their minds off us. Did you arrange that, too?"

Singer must have done that, Janet thought. God knows what he was up to before they caught him. Damn, I wish Pablo were functional. It's no use putting me up against armed guards. I'll just get us killed.

30

O*migod, omigod,* the shadow said, fading under the breath of death; but it came back stronger than before. Time folded on itself, and Singer recalled his hands on Dona's face, on Palha's, and felt the shadow touch him. He tried to break off the contact.

Leave me alone. Don't die this death with me.

My kamarh, the shadow said. *You ran off and left me. Said you made some promises. Well, you promised me, too. You said,* 'Hennaon-de.' *You've walked around in my head enough that I know what that means. That means 'I will be there.' We're coming to get you, Singer. You'd better be there.*

As he spoke, Singer felt him calmly taking possession of the things he needed to make the link unbreakable.

So this is how it felt, what I did, he thought. Then thought was crushed in another convulsion. He screamed.

Get out, he begged as it ebbed a little. *You shame me.*

Palha ignored him.

That's your body talking, he said calmly. *Pull away from it. You know how, you just have to remember.*

Can't. I can't think.

Run with me, Singer.

Never again. No more running—look at my legs. Don't want to live your way, in a cage. Let me go.

Use mine, then, they work fine. Who told me this was our world? Run with me, Singer.

The strength in Palha amazed Singer. Somewhere behind him he could feel Lin and Zhanne, backing him up.

Yeah, they're here, but they're busy right now. Come on, get moving.

Palha lifted him, half carrying him at first, and they were running. The land was bare and hard and smelled of ashes. At first he could only feel Palha's feet; he rode his back, weightless as a ghost. The drumming of footsteps started to weave itself into music, not his music but something Palha remembered from that box. He started to listen, and as he listened he changed it. The sound of ghost feet changed to a music of two drums beating in rhythm around each other. He got a breath of the heart-rejoicing green scent of new grass; he could feel grass under his feet. And they were running, hard uphill through the dark, leaning on someone or carrying someone—which was it? His heart was bursting, and his breath cut him like a knife, but he did not let go of him, and they were running, one step ahead of the dark.

"What's going on?" Gero demanded. "I told you I don't want him to pass out."

The doctor checked him anxiously and shook his head. "I don't know what it is, but he's not dying. He's lost so much blood, his heart should be weakening, but it's stronger than ever."

"Get the old man back in here."

Singer could see every crack in Kruger's face as the old man bent over him. The faded eyes were red-rimmed with grief.

"I know what's happening now," Kruger said brokenly. "I didn't understand before. I'm sorry, I'm sorry. Please, for Christ's sake tell them what they want to know. Don't let them do this to you."

Singer's eyes burned as blue as lakes in hell. "Humans," he whispered. "Your people!"

"No," Kruger said. "Not anymore."

He grasped Singer's hand and felt again that strange soundless shock of communication. He tried to make Singer see what he wanted to do.

Before they can hustle me out of here again, I'm going to try to take Nymann. He has a pistol; I'll put it to his head and tell them to turn you loose.

He could not tell if Singer understood.

Singer ignored the old man's babbling. Whatever he might try was not going to work.

He shifted to bring himself an inch or two closer, and an arrow of pain tore through him. He could only lie and gasp until it passed, too weak to struggle against it. He felt that he was burning from the bones outward. He remembered how Nikei's heart had stopped beating under his hand. He felt pain run like a current through him and the sweat spring out on the old man's face, and he realized that Makho had just handed him his last weapon. It was possible that he had not yet failed. There was one move left.

His torn lips barely moved; Kruger could not have heard him if the words had not come to him on some force that was not breath.

"Their Asharya must come. The jenh-ralh. And Cold Eyes. You tell them, come here and I answer. Everything." His head rolled back, and he let Kruger go.

Janet smelled smoke as she went down the stairs at three leaps per flight. Her left ankle hurt slightly each time she landed; she had twisted it in the tussle with the roof guard. He had been staring at the smoke from the airfield when they landed, and as he turned around, she had fallen on him as if she were desperately wounded. He had not done any too good a job of catching her, but he had tried. Then she had stuck Lyn's pistol into him and told him not to move or she would blow his balls off. Beginner's luck, she supposed.

By the time she got down to the fourth floor, where the transmission-to-orbital center was, she could hear the fire alarms going off. The air was ominously hot and thick with an all too familiar charred smell, but she did not stop to investigate. Lyn and Pablo were alone somewhere on the top floor. She had to get back to them. Lyn had told her that it was stupid to run more risks to tell the Deltans what was happening. "That's not our world anymore," she had argued. But Jan insisted that it had to be done. "It's for my father—they killed him, too. Call it a deathgift!"

She ran through a spray of water and chemicals in the last corridor; the fire was close enough to set off the sprinkler system. But the center was dry and deserted.

It's a good thing I know more about their operations than they do, she thought. Looks as if the stupid bastards just bolted when they heard the fire alarms.

It was easy to do what she had watched the clerk do when Jon had given her the tour: slip the tab into the correct slot and code it for orbital and then for priority transmission to Delta, category vid/gen, for broadcast on commercial channels. The screen told her TRANSMISSION COMPLETE. If she could believe that, her message would be appearing on public newscasts all over Delta—in a few years.

Doesn't really make any difference to us now. We'll be long gone before they can respond. There are people in the here and now who'd like to read this, though.

She moved the tab to local transmission and coded it for Jackson's screen. The message would be waiting for him. Owe you one, Jacks, she thought. Good luck!

She thought regretfully of the fine hash she could make of their databases with the access available from this room. But she did not have time. Then she realized that brute force would be more effective. They had backups for their information; they did not have backups for the equipment. She swallowed; scrambling was one thing but actually destroying all those innocent, helpful machines looked like an act of desecration.

Where are you? Lyn called faintly. *Will you kindly blow the fucker to hell and get your ass back up here? I need you!*

Jan armed the last of her incendiaries and closed the door neatly and quickly behind her. She felt the walls tremble as she ran.

"He says he'll talk to you."

"Are we set to record?" Gero asked. He strode to the table and sat down. "You can start with your name and where you come from," he said.

"My name is Khalle, Khalle who was Singer once; I come from the north." The Thanha words were sweet as honey in his mouth.

"I can't hear him," Cold Eyes said impatiently. "Give him another shot."

"It could kill him," the doctor said.

"Do it."

Singer felt as if his heart would come apart in the poisonous heat of their medicine. He welcomed the pain. He could feel Lin and Zhanne and Palha; they were too close, but he could not spare them. Palha was ready to collapse, but Singer leaned on him ruthlessly. Without that extra strength, his body would stop.

"You said you wanted to talk," Gero said to him. "Don't play games with us."

"Closer," he gasped.

Gero stood and came closer, putting a hand on the table as he leaned nearer.

Singer's tethered fingers closed around Cold Eyes's wrist. The fearful smile that Kruger had almost seen leapt out of hiding like a winter wolf.

"I will tell you," he said. "I will tell you everything I know."

Gero did not like to be touched, but his attention was on the prisoner and what he could tell them. Winning felt good after so many months of hard work. Intelligence was the bottom line; a lard can like Nymann would never understand that. Know your enemy.

But the feeble touch distracted him; suddenly it hurt. It felt as if reinforced canvas straps had sawed through his skin. Angrily he moved to shake it off. Why could he not move? Bile rose in his throat as the pain soared from inconvenience into agony. His legs—his legs—

He started to scream.

Pain flowed through Singer like the tiny sparks that ran through hair-thin metal as fast as thought, to join together in a burst of light. It flowed through him and through the one he touched, the cold one whose heart lay open to the white-hot edge of an invisible sword. Gero had watched his subjects racked between two wires and wondered what they actually felt; now he knew. He knew the scalpel scraping on bone, and the needle probing flayed flesh. There was no corner of his mind, no memory he could escape to. Singer's memories seized and overcame his resistance. He was Nikei cut open from throat to groin; he was each man still in his seat as the wall of fire swept through the transport.

He heard a voice that sang in his head: *This is what you did to us. This is all I know.*

Singer's breath caught in his throat as the memories gathered and ripped loose from his control like the weight of an avalanche that finally looses its grip and falls. He let go of everything, and one by one he called on the names of his people. He called them down like curses, like falling stones, like fire from the sky. He lived each death again. Cold Eyes was dragged down with him into a thousand deaths. He was crushed, he was blasted, he was burning. He screamed until his breath was gone, and he could not stop screaming long enough to gasp in air again. They fell together through endless darkness; Singer drove the life in his enemy farther and farther down and followed it till it diminished and was gone.

It was quiet then. It was dark. He felt nothing, only a little cold. He seemed to be rocking, as if on that sea he had seen once. But there should have been starlight; a star had crossed the sky, reflected in the dark water, and someone had told him that all the stars were travelers. But there were no stars. He was here, finally. He was finished. But no one came to meet him. His heart trembled and became still.

Kruger saw Gero fall. The doctor turned toward him, white-faced; Nymann gasped and put a hand to his chest. The guards raised their weapons to ready but stood uncertainly, finding no enemy to fire on.

Even across the room, Kruger heard Singer's final message. In grief and rage, he turned on Nymann and struck him across the face as hard as he could. It was a weak blow, but Nymann went heavily to his knees, clutching at Kruger till they both fell. While loss and destruction raged through his heart, Kruger's tired old body struggled on the dirty floor for possession of a deadly toy. He had no thought of living any longer, but if he could get Nymann's pistol and kill him, his life would not have been completely in vain.

He expected to be shot, and when he heard two ringing explosions in rapid succession, he thought that maybe he had been. Then came the unmistakable din of automatic weapons in a small room. He let go of Nymann and fell flat on his face.

The door was locked, so Lyn blew it off its hinges. She gave each of the startled guards an economical burst and cut the doctor in half where he stood.

Janet had already reached Singer. She did not waste any time looking for a pulse; she started immediately clearing his throat to get him breathing again.

Kruger sat up wearily. He felt as if he were a thousand years old. He knew by the stillness and the emptiness in his mind that Singer was gone.

"He's had enough," he whispered. "Let him go."

"Shut up, you stupid fucking idiot," Lyn snarled at him.

Dropping her weapon, she climbed up on the table and held Singer's head in her lap while Janet worked on him.

"Give me some help here," Janet ordered. "Every system in

his body is shut down, and I have to stick with CP. Pablo, don't let go of him. Don't let go!"

Saldivar had dropped to the floor as soon as they had entered the room. He looked as if he were dead himself and gave no visible sign that he had heard.

Kruger looked at Nymann. He had never pulled the pistol. The general had not stopped any stray shots. But he was stone dead. He had a horrified expression on his face.

Kruger dragged himself across the room and knelt by Saldivar. Singer had not really lied to him, he recalled. He had just given the impression that Saldivar was dead, too. And he certainly looked as if he were dying. He was in deep shock, pale and breathing shallowly. Kruger tried to ease him into a more comfortable position. There was nothing else he could do.

Singer.

He did not answer. That name had burned away. He had been something else, something bright and deadly that was gone.

Singer.

They disturbed him. He had to make them go away.

Vaharonnai-de, he told them. *He died. A long time ago.*

He doesn't have to die. Not unless you want him to. People have a hard time staying dead around you. Some people.

The voice was urgent, but there was a hint of laughter in it, too, that treacherously reminded him of things he had once desired. Outside the darkness there was nothing but pain. He resisted them.

I will not sing again. Khalle they named me, and Khalle I was. The edge that is farthest front and sharpest, the edge that kills. They made me a weapon, and they cast me away from them as a weapon is cast. I did my work. Now I am finished. Leave me alone!

But they would not leave him alone. There was more than one voice. Something about them was familiar. There was the one like fire and the one like moonlight, the dark one like good ground and the one like a tarnished knife.

You are not finished, they said. *'In you there is a power against which there is no defense.' Isn't that what she told you?*

The power of death! I gave myself to that power. Now leave me alone.

You haven't understood! they said impatiently. *And there's not much time.*

We know the names of all your dead. They pressed him without mercy. *To kill for them is not enough. They ask another gift from you.*

No, please, he begged them in anguish. *Not again. I can't bear it.*

One of them touched him; he could feel it, and he had no farther place to run.

One by one, they named the names. But that time he could see them: not their deaths but the lives he thought were lost. He heard Lindhal laugh, and he saw Taurekke dancing. He saw Deronh swinging by Shiya's mane like a boy; he had forgotten that Deronh had ever been so young. He remembered spring green and winter snow, the hearth and the practice field, all that had been and would now live only in him, only if he would have it so. Only one person was missing: Hilurin, who would have understood and told him what to do. He could not see him, but he heard his music everywhere. They were dancing; each of them met him in the dance, spoke his name, and passed on. His hands were still empty. Where was the deathgift? The dancers parted, and the two of them stepped toward him, Risse with her white skin unmarred, Dona healed of his terrible wounds. They held something out to him, something that shone. As they put it in his hands, he felt their touch for a single moment.

Stay, he begged them. But his eyes were dazzled, and he did not see them go. They left the white horse in his hands.

There was a sound like wind roaring in his ears. He took a long breath that shook him from head to foot and seemed to tear the darkness apart as the light expanded to fill the world.

The light was coming in through his eyelids. He forced them open. He was back in his body.

Kruger heard that first long, rasping breath. He could not believe it, but he heard another one, and another. Then Singer tried to sit up.

"Easy, easy!" Janet said in alarm. Lyn supported him, her arms still locked around him as if she were afraid to let go.

Janet's hand rested over his heart, where she had bruised him in hammering life back into him.

"The power of death is not the ultimate power," she said.

His legs were a patchwork of swollen purple scars, but the bones were straight and the skin was whole.

"How did you do that?" he asked.

"I didn't think I could," Lyn whispered. "Then it seemed

like they were really there—those old people. The healers. I guess I could have made it look nicer, but I'm scared to mess with it any more."

"The scars will heal up by themselves," Jan said. "That's not important. And the surgical repairs that bastard did were adequate, such as they were. He saved us some trouble." She looked at Singer. "You'll have to take it easy for a while. Red blood cells take time to replace, they don't just come from nowhere, you know."

He stared at her; she was blood-smeared to her elbows and lecturing him as if nothing had happened. His face threatened to betray him. His hand went up in the old protective gesture, but there was no scar under his fingers.

"Oh, that," she said, looking embarrassed. "You can wear the others, if you like—I know you think scars are honorable. But you carried that one long enough. I erased it. Hope you don't mind."

He wrapped his arms around both of them.

"Thanks," he said. The Thanha words only meant "you make yourself tall." Sometimes Delteix was better.

They helped him to his feet. His legs felt unsteady as a newborn colt's, but he made it as far as Saldivar's embrace.

"Forgive me, brother," he said; no words were really necessary.

Kruger stood alone, feeling dazed. What he had been was gone, like smoke. He watched them embrace, wondering what they had become. As their tears mingled, he tasted warm, salty sweetness like the water of life. He touched his face and found that the tears were his own.

Singer looked at him over Saldivar's shoulder. *Come here, Makho.*

He took a step toward them, and Lyn and Saldivar reached out to pull him in.

No one can give you back what was. Can't be done. But you can pick up the gift that's offered—what is, what is to come. Your life.

After some timeless interval, Lyn cleared her throat.

"I hate to interrupt this tender moment, guys, but has it occurred to you all that this building is burning down? It might be tactful of us to leave now."

Kruger looked around him like someone awakened from a dream. "How?"

"I don't think we can go down the stairs," Janet said. "They were about to go when I came up. We'd be smoked out of here already if they didn't have it sealed off so well for security."

"No problem if our vito's still on the roof," Lyn said.

The heat was worse outside the room. When they reached the roof, smoke poured up from the floors below, drifting across the rooftop and dropping a rain of stinging ash. A cordon of fire trucks and armed troops surrounded the building. The plume of smoke from the airfield towered up like a black thundercloud.

"You know, if they see a medical flight taking off from here, they're going to want very badly to know who's on board," Jan said.

"All the better. They won't try to shoot us down till they know," Lyn replied. "Anyway, what's the alternative?"

They climbed in, and Lyn took off. By unspoken agreement, she headed north.

"What's the plan?" she shouted over the noise of the engines.

Before anyone could answer, the vito banked to the right, and the engine sound changed to a straining snarl.

"What is it?" Jan called.

"I don't know. I'm losing oil and hydraulic pressure. Something must have clipped a line or—oh, shit!"

The wing came up a little and then dropped as the vito headed for the ground.

Singer understood immediately from Lyn that she could not keep them from hitting the ground. Once again he was trapped in a steel spearhead, and the familiar terror rose in him, with the smell of fire. He took a deep breath. This time there was no wall in his mind, forbidding him to think about what he had done. He could remember. He could get out.

And leave them behind? Never again.

Hold together, he ordered them. Three of them were huddled close together already; Janet leaned forward and wrapped an arm around Lyn's leg.

"What the fuck are you doing?" Lyn screamed.

Remember that picture? The Wind Horse, those children riding. If you trust me—

The horizon tilted at a crazy angle, but he searched the hills till he found a spot that seemed to call to him and fixed it safely in the darkness behind his eyes. He had time. There were many instants left before the falling machine would strike the earth.

You are my true brothers, and I will live or die with you. Do not fail me now. Then he gathered them to him and stepped out into the abyss. And fell.

But not far. A foot or two—enough to tumble them breathless on the sun-warmed grass. Far behind them, the smoke of the burning tower shadowed the sky. There was still time to watch as the abandoned metal thing fell from the sky like a spent arrow.

"How did you do that?" Saldivar whispered. "Forget it. Stupid question."

"Do you think maybe you could bring us along some clothes next time?" Lyn said.

Singer was embarrassed. "Sorry. I didn't learn how yet. I think I was in that plane that burned. I was in the fire. Then I was outside—like this. That's what they wanted to know—how I can be alive."

Janet looked down at herself in dismay.

"Oh, no, my portable," she said desolately. She looked back to the spot where a small pile of rubble marked the resting place of their vito. "It'll be totally smashed."

"It's on your back," Lyn pointed out.

"How can it be? I'm—" She felt for the shoulder straps. "How did you do that?"

Singer looked embarrassed again. "It has thoughts in it. Feels more alive than clothes." He shrugged. "Hard to explain."

Lyn grinned widely. "Well, unless we want to hump it buck naked through the snow, we better go see if there's anything left in the wreckage. It's winter, folks. It'll be fucking cold in those mountains."

The vito had broken apart when it hit, scattering fragments across the grass. They recovered their packs. One had split open, but they found most of the contents. They dressed quickly, watching the sky for a search team.

"We'd better be moving on," Kruger said. "Singer, give us a bearing."

"Not for me to give orders, Con-el," Singer teased him. "But this is my thought, brothers. Zhanne has sent a word to her people. Now we will go to mine. The Rock lives only in us. But there are River People, Drygrass People, People of the North Hills. Not brothers, but what do you call them? My cousins. They will know me.

"We will show them what my brothers have shown me: This world is for those who want to live here. It will not be bound with wire or taken with steel. We'll show them there are many kinds of people—all of us *Thanha*—humans. Those we leave behind us would not listen to that, so we must learn to make them listen. We'll gather the others, teach them how to stay alive, how to fight the fire from the sky. When we come back, they'll listen."

"That's a large plan," Lyn said. "Do you think it will work?"

"How can I tell?" Singer said with a shrug. "I am no one's Asharya. But I tell you this: I am still Singer, and my barhedonh is small but very great in heart. They will listen."

"Do we take these?" Janet asked, reluctantly picking up the rifle she had dropped.

Singer nodded. "We'll need each other's songs, and weapons, too, for a long time yet. Good teachers showed me yours, and I'll pay you back on the road; I'll show you mine. There's time. The world is wide enough, the road is long enough. The Road to the North."

With a smile of pure happiness, he led them deeper into the grass.

He started to sing when they were safely hidden among the gentle hills. He sang the "Elassyon" first, the song for after the fires, the morning song, and made them cry once more. Then it was time for the heart-loosening songs, the ones that made the living laugh and forget the long night in the pleasure of life. But the songs of the People were all strange to them, so he found what seemed a good one in Kruger's mind. They sang it in five-part harmony so clear and true that it would have sliced glass like a laser. They took turns making up the words that were missing, for the song was very old. They laughed very much, and Singer was not sure why. All their words sounded right and good to him. The song had once been called "Why Don't We Get Drunk and Screw." Singer made it sound like a hymn.

About the Author

Ann Tonsor Zeddies spent the first three summers of her life on a mountaintop in Idaho. She wanted to be a cowboy, but decided to be a writer instead when she found that the frontier had moved off the surface of the planet. She grew up in Michigan and graduated from the honors English program at the University of Michigan. She has written book reviews and newspaper articles and served a term as an editor of scholarly books. She now lives in Kansas with her husband and four children ranging from toddler to teenager. Their household includes cats, computers, a gimpy old horse, and several tons of books. When she has time, she gardens, swims, rides, and reads everything in sight. She likes deep woods, high hills, cold water, strong coffee, old friends, and good talk.